Phoebe
& the Ghost of Chagall

a novel by Jill Koenigsdorf

Phoebe
& the Ghost of Chagall

a novel by Jill Koenigsdorf

MACADAM CAGE

MacAdam/Cage
155 Sansome Street, Suite 550
San Francisco, CA 94104
www.MacAdamCage.com

Library of Congress Cataloging-in-Publication Data

Koenigsdorf, Jill.
 Phoebe and the ghost of Chagall / Jill Koenigsdorf.
   p. cm.
 ISBN 978-1-59692-383-6 (hardcover)
 1. Women artists—Fiction. 2. Ghost stories. 3. Humorous fiction. I. Title.
 PS3611.O3643P48 2012
 813'.6—dc23

                         2012035659

Manufactured in the United States of America

10 9 8 7 6 5 4 3 2 1

Book and jacket design by Dorothy Carico Smith

For B., who opened the door at midnight in Paris for a drenched American stranger with a backpack and said: Come inside.

And for J., sage and bon vivant, who persistently helps me to navigate even the roughest seas.

PROLOGUE

The Thief had never really thought of himself as a thief until the instant he became one. He considered himself an Artist, and, while seemingly destined for the outskirts of the circle of Paris's driven and talented before the first Great War, he could at least warm himself in the white heat of their passion. These Artists, "his" Artists, lived and worked in the buzzing, beggared worlds of studios like Bateau-Lavoir in Montmartre or La Ruche in Montparnasse. They would not have known The Thief by name, would have dismissed his paintings as "derivative," had they ever made the trip to his studio. A few of them might have registered him on their periphery at the cafés they haunted, or skulking along the walls at a gallery opening. Thus, in his anonymity, The Thief was both privy to the their world and fated never to enter it.

The Artists did not make their exodus from Paris all at once, though it hit The Thief that way. In the years before 1914, the cafés were electric with debates about the new art movements. Artists who had immigrated to Paris from Italy, Spain, Russia—from all over the world, just to work amongst one another, to share in the fertility—shouted and drank, defending or deriding Cubo-Expressionism or Futurism or Neo-Primitivism with a fervor that often escalated into brawls. Then overnight, the discussions were all of war. The Thief decided that he might as well just wait out this war, right there in Paris, as he believed the talk that it would not last long. Soon, there was a barrenness in all the once-throbbing places, as though an evacuation had taken place and The Thief had somehow been left behind. The Bateau-Lavoir and La Ruche resonated a dark quietude, as if all the artists were hiding from him, holding their breath. It was in these abandoned studios that The Thief became The Thief.

He noticed that one of the studio doors was ajar and, after looking about to make sure no one would see him, he stepped inside. A half-finished painting depicting some sort of splintered jester leaned on its easel. As if in the landscape of someone else's dream, The Thief took up the artist's palette and a paintbrush, and brazenly added a few of his own marks to the piece, and experienced a thrill he had never known. He looked around then, making sure the studio was indeed abandoned. Surely this person had left in a hurry. Why would they leave the door unlocked and so much of their work vulnerable? The Thief rifled through some of the paintings there, feeling a bitter blend of astonishment and envy at their beauty. He recognized in that one instant that he would never be a peer in this group of painters, as he had once believed, and with this dark dawning, he stepped into another role.

The Thief heard muffled voices and rumblings in the adjacent studios, but was imbued with a certain calm, a righteousness that made him feel invincible. Emboldened, he explored the room, opening drawers and drinking a glass of water from the artist's own chipped cup. Then he spotted, wadded up in the corner, a filthy bag made of some sort of heavy cloth. He could tell it would be large enough for his purpose. In no hurry, he traversed the small space, opened the bag, then gathered up a dozen of the more portable paintings, as if he was picking wildflowers, and shoved them inside.

Over the next week, The Thief repeated this process at several of the rooms he found deserted in both establishments. He was astonished that on no occasion did he ever encounter resistance. Then once, well after midnight, a drunken artist he recognized only slightly, a man with thick lips and a strong, protruding forehead, suddenly appeared, blocking his path in the hall of La Ruche. Impaling The Thief with a nasty leer, he leaned in close and slurred: "Hello, jackal. Hello, little vulture. Come to pick the bones clean? Eh?"

The Thief tried to make light of this with a short laugh, but as he attempted to push past, the man stood fast, arms outstretched, Christ-like, one of his large palms against each wall. The Thief squirmed like a bug pinned to a specimen board, utterly exposed. Then, just as suddenly, the man gave a sharp grunt, dropped his arms, and lurched into his own room, as if the little man wasn't worth the bother. Shaken, The Thief hurried on his way weighted by more than his heavy bag, filled this time with five slightly larger paintings, of seascapes and the sharp-edged fronds of distant palms.

Once in his own dingy room, The Thief locked the door behind him and spilled out his new plunder, lining all of the week's takings, ten in all, along his mattress and the floor in front of it. What would he *do* with it all? No one had any money these days. None of these artists were in high demand or even known beyond certain Left Bank establishments. Besides, how could he profit from the stolen art? Surely the artists would return any day now and word would spread and he would be found out. The Thief did not sleep at all that night. For the first time, doubt made him squirm. Then war broke out in earnest and he no longer had to worry. He only had to believe in the value of what his own eyes saw and what his own hands could never create. All that was required of him now was patience.

CHAPTER ONE

Marc Chagall appeared exactly twenty-five years after his death, in the twenty-first century, in the brightly tiled wonderment of Phoebe's kitchen in Sonoma, California. Once he got his bearings, he stood in the center of the kaleidoscopic room, appreciating all the color and watching Phoebe's daughter Audrey prepare for a surprise birthday party that would begin in less than two hours. Chagall did know certain things before his arrival: that Phoebe was currently at work, something to do with wine or wine labels, that she was in danger of losing her home, that a small painting he had painted before the first World War that rightfully belonged to Phoebe had ended up in the hands of another. But Chagall did *not* quite understand why or how he had come to know these facts.

He was relieved that Audrey could not see him there, as every aspect of this return was so new and strange to him, and being invisible gave him more time to adjust. He was able to simply enjoy being affiliated with her busyness as she went over lists aloud, checked the oven, and tossed little scraps of cheese to the two black-and-white dogs that wagged their tails at her feet.

Upon first arriving, however, Chagall had quickly ascertained that the dogs *could* see him, for they rushed toward him, hackles raised and teeth bared. Instinctively, he shrieked and backed into a wall, even though he was well past any danger of feeling physical pain. Audrey shouted, "Mechant! Gamut! No barking. That's enough. There's nothing there! *Quiet!*" At this, the dogs sat down heavily, suppressing their low growls when they glanced his way. And he, who loved dogs, could do nothing but make little clucking noises at them, calling them dear and darling in Russian, *Dorogoi, Milyi,* wondering whether, if he stroked their heads, they would be able to feel his touch.

While she was absent, Chagall decided to explore Phoebe's studio, a smaller detached building surrounded by thriving lilac bushes and an old fence that sagged under the weight of wild grapes. He felt unduly pleased when he noted that she had several reproductions of his own work, albeit in poster form, framed on her walls. He leaned in to examine his "Bride and Groom with Eiffel Tower," and was instantly transported back to 1928, the pleasure of learning to drive the rusty Overland, that first war over, at last able to return to France. With his wife and daughter by his side, he had explored the bounty that was Provence, onward to Auverge and on farther, to the Pyrenean coast, the first time he had felt free in so many years.

"Soon," he said aloud to the empty chair at Phoebe's desk, "you will have a *real* Chagall, the one that is meant for you. A painting you should have had years ago. Then, we'll see about all your other troubles…and maybe a few of my own as well."

For Chagall secretly had hopes of solving some of his own mysteries while he was here. Over one hundred of those first paintings he had done in Paris had gone missing during the First War. Poof. Vanished. And despite his efforts while alive, he could never find out what became of many of them. Even when he had achieved fame and fortune beyond his wildest dreams, he had never been able to let that go. Once he passed on and saw that a vast number of things might be revealed to him after his death, he eagerly anticipated learning the whereabouts of these paintings at last. But whatever information was to come to him came only in bits and pieces, esoteric fragments. So the places his art had come to rest remained unreadable, a tease, in that he could see only snippets. The living, those who believed in ghosts, always said that ghosts returned when they had some unfinished business. Maybe there was something to that.

He saw that Phoebe kept her paints in an old cigar box with a white owl on the lid, and he poked around, curious to see which oil colors she was drawn to. Naples Yellow. Amethyst Genuine. Chinese Cinnabar. Mountain Green. He leaned closer to the paints, longing for their scent, but he had been dead long enough to know that taste, smell, and touch were no longer available to him. He put his own thumb in the indentation her thumb had made in the soft metal of the tubes. *Eh*, he thought, wistfully closing the lid on the cigar box, *be grateful for hearing and seeing*. And time was so different, too, after he left this place. The blink of an eye and an eternity all seemed to happen on the same plane. He had quite forgotten things like anticipation, urgency, one day ending and another beginning. In that other place, there was only...ongoingness. But here, he was already reacquainting himself with that feeling of excitement. He was looking forward to meeting her, to being seen.

The guests were starting to arrive, driving past the small blue house, looking for parking at least a block away so as not to cause suspicion when Phoebe arrived home from work and pulled into her driveway. Chagall still found the act of motion here, getting from one spot to the next, an interesting proposition. He would place one foot in front of the other and while the impetus felt like walking, it was more akin to floating just above the ground. Air strolling was the best way to describe it. Of course he could actually fly, but not in the physical way of a bird. No exertion of wings, just a focus on a certain destination, then a rush of air and there he was—in a treetop, on top of a car, who could say? He liked to try and slow this action down, so he could appreciate the airborne journey, but he was still fine-tuning arrival at the farther distances.

Chagall sat on top of the refrigerator and observed the arriving guests. She had quite a few friends, this Phoebe. The daughter hugged them all, then started giving out orders about food or drink, instructing them where to hide.

When they heard Phoebe's car over the din, all chatter stopped and the guests scattered like wild chickens to crouch in bathroom and closet. Since no one but Phoebe would be able to see him, Chagall could stay on his perch, accessing this woman who needed his help, gauging her reaction to the "SURPRISE!" When it came, she jumped, letting out a short scream, and for a split second, before she broke into a suspended smile, she looked absolutely bewildered.

He continued to study her, now from an obscured corner of the living room, noting that she was an animated woman, a gesticulator even, with a gymnast's compact build and hair as curly as his own, but that pre-Raphaelite, Titian red, whereas his was grey as a storm. She wore a sheath dress the color of a stalk of celery, and he imagined that many of her clothes were in that lettuce palate favored by redheads. On one of her feet, the toenails were painted this same bright green, yet on the other, orange, which told him both that she was eccentric and that she had not reconciled herself to the more staid demands of maturity. That did not bother him one whit, as he was aware that he too had a reputation for impishness. She had the sort of heavily freckled, Celtic complexion that bruised and sunburned so easily. And, while he himself was not such a fan of Realism, had he wanted to paint her—and being back here certainly did rouse that yearning to paint—he knew it would have been a challenge to match the exact green of her eyes. Jade? No, a less milky green. Myrtle, perhaps.

After Phoebe's startled state subsided and the rhythm of the party got underway, she finally noticed Chagall. She looked at him curiously, then quickly turned away. Of course she would be baffled by his presence, here at her birthday party. He saw her trying to place this old man, wearing a paint-spattered smock and some sort of clogs from another era. Chagall looked down at his feet. How he loved those sentimental wooden shoes, the ones the French called *sabot.* He had never been able to bring himself to part with them. He could stand in them painting for hours without any pain in his feet. Chagall was reassured by those shoes, here in this place that was at once familiar and so foreign. He wondered if he had actually been buried in them, which would have been fine by him, or if this current costume was just that, his earthly disguise, The Painter. And if it was the latter, how *had* he come to be wearing them? He still had so many unanswered questions about how things worked in the afterlife, even though he had been experiencing it firsthand since 1985.

He gathered from the conversations taking place around him that this birthday, Phoebe's fortieth, was a landmark for her, as she seemed flustered and overwrought, even though the smile never left the face. He knew a little bit about her big worries, but needed to hear more. Had he been able to impress upon her how precious every single year was, even in the midst of her current troubles, he would have gladly done so. But he knew full well that the human animal typically did not give much thought to its own mortality.

Chagall saw that Phoebe was still stealing quizzical glances at him, longer ones now. She stopped speaking mid-sentence, her wine glass poised in the air, and he suspected her mind was racing through some mental photo album of her acquaintances. Although Chagall's face was certainly well known by the time he died, and probably would be recognizable to Phoebe, since she too was an artist, she most likely would not initially identify him as "Chagall the Artist," because that would mean she was seeing a dead man at her party, and naturally that would be hard to reconcile. Now she was craning her neck outright to get a better look at him, so intently that the person she was talking with also began looking around the room to see what had distracted her.

He sighed. There was no putting it off any longer. He needed to make his presence clearer to her. He made sure she saw him walk purposefully right through a group of her friends, literally *through* one or two of them. None of them acknowledged him in any way. There, now she would know that he was visible only to her. Ah, he saw that he had frightened her, and automatically held his hands out to her in what he hoped was a reassuring gesture. Phoebe's eyes opened wide, then she refocused her attention with an almost hysterical enthusiasm on the woman with whom she had been speaking, a friend who now regarded Phoebe with wary puzzlement.

Chagall wished he had been given more guidelines, or at least some sort of earthly behavioral compass. In fact, since his death, he had not once been called back to help anyone. He had heard that this did occur on rare occasions, and had been secretly longing for his own turn at contact. To interact with a living human being, after so much time…it seemed too remarkable to even imagine. He'd had so many questions, mainly about the solidity of this world versus his new…etherealness? Was that the best word for his current, misty state? Was he akin to a hologram? A vapor? Some sort of smoky genie emerging from a lamp? How would it work exactly? Would he walk, fly, or some intersection of the two, just like the creatures that he had created in his paintings? While he was gradually gleaning how things worked back here, he had arrived in this room with neither practice nor a chance to experiment. There had been no preparation on his end because the time had come when Phoebe summoned him—or rather, she had specific quandaries that he alone was best qualified to mend. He would, he decided, loving the aptness of the modern verb, wing it. In the meantime, he retreated back to the corner of the room. She had seen enough of him for one day.

CHAPTER TWO

Phoebe wasn't completely sure the older fellow was really there. She had glimpsed him, off in the corner, shortly after "SURPRISE!" had been shouted and the lights had come on, and she, flabbergasted, had brought one hand to her heart and the back of the other to her open mouth, like the heroine in an old horror film. And certainly by now, a good hour into the festivities, she had had some wine, and yes, also some champagne, so maybe that was a factor. She wouldn't look that direction again unless she had to. Wasn't there going to be cake? Cake might act like a restorative sponge, absorb some of the alcohol presently sloshing against the pilings in her empty stomach and causing such hallucinations.

Unlike Phoebe, her daughter Audrey always cut corners when it came to nibbles. Well, it was a surprise party, after all, so in all fairness, she had been forced to shop on the sly. Phoebe popped the last chalky carrot stick into her mouth. Forty. How had that *happened?*

Oops, she'd looked at him again. No, she definitely did not recognize the man moving about amongst her friends. Or rather, she recognized bits of herself in that face, especially in the downturned eyes that were both sad and hopeful. And she vaguely placed the tumult of his features, the fine lips and bones bumping up against the peasant ears and nose. And what was that relic of a smock? It could have belonged to a person from one of her art history books, or perhaps from the E volume of her cherished *World Book Encyclopedia*, under Expressionism. Or, come to think of it, the C volume. Yes, C for Cubism, or for…? She decided he resided in C. But each time she tried to discern whether or not he was visible to others at the party, she would look up and he would be gone.

"Were you really surprised?" asked Audrey, sidling up beside her and throwing her arms around Phoebe's neck. After nineteen years, Audrey still took Phoebe's breath away. Audrey was only three years younger than Phoebe had been when she had given birth, but so much more confident and lovely, the veil of dark hair, that permanent dewiness to her skin.

"I mean, you must have suspected something. I've been acting so weird since I came home from school, right? Every time you came into the room when I was on the phone I just stopped talking. And I was being all mysterious about where I was going and all. You knew, didn't you, Mom?"

"None of that is unusual behavior for you—no weirder than usual," Phoebe joked. Then she hugged her and said, "Honestly, sugar, I really, really didn't suspect anything. I was thoroughly and profoundly astonished."

"Well, forty *is* one of the biggies," her ex, Phillip, said gravely, placing his hand presumptively in the small of her back. He was Audrey's father, so she resisted the urge to swat his hand away. "Not that *I* would know." He grinned broadly at Audrey and she gave her mother a wary look, then backed away.

Phillip was four years younger than Phoebe, and for the entire decade that they were married, he never let up about their age difference, as if it were some giant chasm between them. This was especially true in regards to music, as in: "Oh well, Prince, I guess he was more *my* generation."

"Forty is the new twenty," Phoebe exclaimed gamely, an odd clown's smile frozen on her face. She didn't believe herself for a second. She stole a glance back toward that corner of the room where the old man had been and found he was staring directly at her. He ventured a nod. She started and looked away. It wasn't the first time lately she had seen something that she wasn't *entirely* sure was actually there. Last week, while walking her dogs on a deserted trail, a cowboy on horseback with a copious mustache, glossy as an otter's belly, had suddenly appeared, wearing an Australian sheepman's coat and leading a pregnant pygmy goat by a long rope.

"That's Lily," he called down to Phoebe in a deep voice, slowing a bit. The goat looked up at her with what Phoebe clearly recognized as pity in her limpid eyes, a half-chewed strand of ivy hanging from the corner of her nimble lips. "'Sarrite…" the cowboy coaxed her. "Lily won't bite."

Then he tipped his hat and was gone. That time Phoebe had stood on the hot trail blinking, questioning whether he had been a mirage. Compounding her suspicions, the dogs had not reacted in their normal frenzied way. Her life was presently so off-kilter, her situation so incompatible with the person she once believed she was, that she barely recognized herself. Hence, she didn't get so ruffled by strange sightings as she might have a year ago.

She thought now of the rhyme her mother had often recited to her as a little girl, the one so mysterious and delightful:

> "*I saw a man upon the stair—*
> *I looked again,*
> *he was not there.*
> *He was not there again today.*
> *Oh my, I wish he'd go away!*"

Phoebe looked at the artist again. At least he hadn't transmogrified into a seahorse wearing a party hat. There was still a small chance, she reasoned, that he was indeed there. She studied him. Of course, she realized, actually snapping her fingers. It was Marc Chagall. The tumult of grey curls. The aquiline nose. The impish eyes, and that outfit—all of these should have been a dead giveaway, *dead* being the operative word. Phoebe felt a rising panic then and made a beeline for the wine table.

She was under a lot of stress, she told herself. Unbeknownst to any of these people, her friends and neighbors, Phoebe was about to lose her home, this beloved Blue House that they had all come to enjoy as much as she had over the years, gathering so often around the long table out in the back field, laden with figs and olives from her own trees, and everything, in the summer, from the pesto to the tomatoes to the melons, grown in her own raised bins. The Blue House was the first house she had ever owned, and she had been so proud not to be a renter anymore, even if buying it had been quite a stretch for her six years ago. Obviously, more of a stretch than she could handle. She wouldn't think about that poisonous word, "foreclosure." *She* was not the type of person who got her home taken away from her. At least…she never had been before.

Phoebe stopped fighting it and raised her glass to the man whom clearly no one but she was seeing. She went ahead and toasted Marc Chagall, the magnificent, deceased painter. She didn't care anymore. He smiled at her, a bit ruefully, she thought, mirroring her toast back to her from across the room, his strong hands around an imaginary glass.

In truth, Phoebe had hoped to just come home from work that day, walk her dogs, put on a baggy green dress, open a nice, jammy bottle of Zin, make some pasta, and watch anything HBO had to offer. It had been a long day (week, year…) and Phoebe was trying to keep that pesky morose feeling at bay. She needed to…decant. But Phoebe could rally. Sure she could. So what if she was seeing ghosts. No little nervous breakdown was going to spoil this party. A lot of effort had been put into this celebration and it was her duty to appreciate it. She looked around the room and smiled warmly, if a little woozily, at anyone who caught her eye. Yet she was forced to admit that she was not aging gracefully. At the same moment as her concession, her friend Joyce, who had quaffed even more wine that she had, approached, slapped her on the back, and said in a husky voice, "You made it, kiddo. It's all downhill from here." With that, she lifted her glass and drifted away.

"Ignore her," her neighbor Katie said, arriving at her other side. "You look great. I think we all do. To forty and fabulous!" she cried, also raising her glass in a toast. What was with the compulsion to toast after every utterance?

Fabulous. Or at least forty. And here she was, stunned and blinking at the veritable pyrotechnic display that was coming her way, Audrey's arms wobbling a bit under the weight of the thing. Her birthday cake, arriving at last. Could she possibly inhale mightily enough to blow out that forest of flame? Phoebe was very superstitious. Each morning, she fished out a Chinese fortune from the decade's worth of them saved in a shoebox under her bed, and allowed that to forecast and instruct for the coming day. She squinted at the candles coming toward her. Yes, she *wanted* all her wishes to come true. She badly wanted the "one to grow on."

"How's a gal supposed to blow out forty candles in one breath?" she mugged to her audience.

"Forty-*one*," Phillip corrected, and the crowd yuck-yucked.

But just as she was gearing up to blow out every last one of those damn candles, visualizing, as she warmed up, the illustrations she recalled from her childhood fairytale books of the North Wind, eyebrows fierce and determined, cheeks puffed out and rosy as apples—just in that instant she had to take one more peek into the corner, just to see if the painter was still there. And there he was, taking it all in, his smock dappled with every color that came in a tube. He was looking at her intently, with compassion, as if he knew her. In spite of it all, she found the apparition extremely comforting, and, had she not been surrounded by dozens of others who could not see him and might have thought her mad, she would have enjoyed sitting in a quiet corner with the man, talking about art, Paris, Russia, and maybe even the afterlife.

She tore her eyes from him, refocused on the candles, inhaled with all her might, and blew. Incredibly, she got about thirty of the candles with that breath, knowing that straining to get those final ten would surely kill her. She attended to each remaining one as fast as she could, little bits of spit flying from her mouth in her urgency to extinguish them all. And just as she had gotten the very last one that would surely bring her good luck, calling upon the ultimate gasp of air left in her burning lungs, the little candle sputtered, then reignited. Phoebe thought she might cry.

"That was my idea, Mom!" Audrey shouted proudly, jumping up and down like she used to on the playground in her "Notice me! Notice me!" urgency. "The trick candle. It's so you'll always have one to grow on!"

Phoebe rolled her eyes to the heavens, then kissed her daughter's warm cheek. And when the guests clapped and cried: "Speech!" Phoebe paused for a moment, then cleared her throat, looked around the room, and said thoughtfully: "I have much to be grateful for, so much. My friends, my dogs, Gamut and Mechant," and here she raised a glass toward the bedroom where they had been banished so as not to shove their noses into her friends' crotches or pilfer food from unguarded plates. Then she faltered for a split second, and to cover this began to ramp it up, ticking off some sort of life list. "And I am so *lucky*, for…for poetry! For wine! For being able to, well, *sort of*, make a living from my art! For all my travels, and…" Here she looked around the room, trying to take in all the expectant faces, many of them friends she had known for most of her life, a few who had flown great distances to mark this passage with her. Then for some baffling lapse of reason, she added, "And for all the men I have been blessed to love!"

The men I have been blessed to love? Had she really said that? Ugh, but the crowd laughed and hooted, unfazed. Phoebe finished, in a voice hoarse with emotion, as triumphantly as a politician on a stump, "I think I have packed more living into these forty years than many do in a lifetime. I am grateful. Grateful for it all!"

"You sound like it's over!" her friend Helen hollered from the sidelines. "We're just beginning!" Everyone cheered and, apparently incapable of breaking this stream of quirky behavior, Phoebe actually curtsied.

Then she backed away from the cake and let her daughter do the serving. She saw Chagall clapping as sincerely as the rest of them, and she shook her head in hopes of clearing it. She glided over to the multi-colored stack of plates, took one off the top, and held it humbly out to her daughter, asking, in that moment, for nothing more than her piece of cake.

Moshe Shagal was an active sleeper. In his narrow bed in the water-blessed town of Vitebsk, Russia, he twitched, his fingers fluttered as if playing an unseen instrument, and short owl-like yawps escaped from his lips. His father felt such tenderness as he watched his son in the thrall of his dream that he was reluctant to disturb him. But Moshe could always smell his father before he heard him. The odor touched him even before he felt the man's hand gently shaking his shoulder. No amount of washing could completely banish that briny scent. Day in, day out, his father hoisted massive barrels of herring, readying them for sale, and his body was shellacked with their slime and scales, their fishy essence living on in his very pores. Moshe imagined that if a person was so perpetually immersed in such a strong smell, his own senses would soon enough cease to register it.

"Moshe," his father said, giving his shoulder a shake. The boy barely opened his eyes before shutting them again. He grumbled and turned his back to his father, for it was winter and still dark and he was so nice and warm. Plus, he knew that as the eldest son, something would be demanded of him.

"I'm going now to shul before work. Your mother needs your help at the store. Get up now and help her feed and dress your brothers and sisters. I'll bring home some fish tonight."

He paused and looked down at his son, love turning his broad face into a soft dough. He wanted to say something important, but squeezing the boy's shoulder once more settled upon: "Help your mother." With that he headed out to shul before starting his workday with the fish.

When the herring were alive, Moshe thought the fish were beautiful, like lightning, sleek and shimmering like liquid silver. But moments after they died, their eyes grew flat and their skins dull, no longer alight with flecks of opal. That transition, so fast and so final, in equal measure frightened and fascinated young Moshe. It seemed to reflect how he himself felt in his village, how one minute you were swimming along, safe with your own kind, then the next, you rounded a corner found yourself in dangerous seas, out of your element, vulnerable to attack. Even though his neighborhood was comprised largely of Jews, people he had grown up with who were like an extended family, whom he saw at temple or the bakers or weddings or funerals, he did not have to be told that there were many outside of his small world who did not like Jews, even those Jews whom they did not know personally. They did not like them simply because they were Jewish.

And so Moshe felt badly for the herring, even though it was his father's selling of the fish that put butter on the family table, and made it so his mother could bribe the headmaster of the town school so that a Jewish boy such as himself would be allowed to attend classes. Yes, despite the money the herring brought in, Moshe felt badly for the fish. For didn't their very presence on the family table and in the market stall show that maybe there was *not,* as went the old adage, safety in numbers? Was not each barrel that his father lifted onto his shoulders proof that even in their great, swift, graceful schools, the herring were not so safe, that they could indeed be captured and harmed?

Moshe turned things around in his head too much and didn't like how that made him feel. So he rose and shuffled over to his younger siblings' beds, waking them and telling them to wash the sleep out of their eyes and get dressed. He helped the youngest ones accomplish this and loved the way they looked up at him, so trusting and respectful, as he helped. And when he came into the kitchen and his mother handed him some warm tea and a fat slice of challah bread with butter, he smiled at her, and taking that first bite as she watched, willed himself not to also taste the faint but unmistakable flavor of herring.

CHAPTER THREE

It was perhaps the most surreal experience Phoebe had ever gone through. She was sitting in her own home, surrounded by things that, were she to need to buy them today, she would not be able to afford.

"Things don't matter," her family often reminded her. "*People*, friends are what matter." And of course Phoebe knew that to be true. Still, she had created a beautiful home, a haven, with art on the vibrant walls that she had painted blue and pink and grassy green. The shelves were lined with carefully chosen curio, a Mexican clay turkey here, a handbag festooned with glittering sea creatures there. There was nothing extravagant or pompous in her choices of furniture or dishes or possessions, but each one was special, one of a kind, and Phoebe was hopeless when it came to "downsizing."

What made a house a home? Phoebe had asked herself this countless times. When she awoke in the middle of the night, troubled by visions of jack-booted thugs kicking her door down and stuffing everything they could get their hands on into large bags while she mutely watched, she told herself not to fret, that she could make herself a beautiful dwelling anywhere. She should just give up on this place, sell off most of her old treasures, even though they had been handed down from other eras, had belonged to people who were dear to her. She found a great visual comfort and joy in old things. Old things had stories to tell and imparted a certain loveliness to her walls (and in truth, any flat surface) that freshly minted objects just could not compete with.

Phoebe was not a minimalist by any stretch. The teapots and salt and pepper shakers, the Eiffel Tower snow globes and bird wallpockets, these were a part of history, of her own history, for four decades. But it was coming to the point where she could no longer avoid thinking about what she would do if—when—she lost her home.

But a home was not merely things. She knew that. It was the people inside, the gatherings, the birds that visited, the plants and trees that grew there, the memories one made inside the building's walls. The memories. Phoebe had created many fond ones under that mossy roof. And her studio! So perfect for painting and thinking, the roan mare off in the distance at the base of Sonoma Mountain, something to count on in every season.

In the symbolism of dreams, the house represented the self, each room a facet of one's own personality. She had been having anxiety dreams about her house: beams that collapsed just as she was passing under them, almost knocking her unconscious, garages and attics in great disrepair, full of rats and spiders and mess. It didn't take Sigmund Freud to tell her what all this meant.

Phoebe truly, deeply, desperately did not want to lose her house. It made her dizzy to consider how quickly, once the economy began to falter, she had less and less earning power and how glaringly unaffordable her giant mortgage payments became. She had worked at the winery for almost ten years, was close with her coworkers, and one day her boss simply asked her if she'd like to take some "furloughs." But she knew he wasn't really asking. It was more a question of: how would you like to work less so you lose your benefits but at least know that you will still have a job? She had applied for every program her lending bank offered. "We're here to help homeowners like you!" unctuous voices assured her. "The *last* thing we want is for you to lose your home." But she had discovered, after jumping through every hoop they put before her, that this was simply not true. They kept just the right degree of hope alive, but only qualified less than three percent of homeowners for any help at all.

The phone rang and she responded with Pavlovian heart thrumming, the sweat glands under her arms shifting involuntarily into overdrive. She did not answer, knowing that it was the bullying creditors from overseas. Was it really *that* much cheaper to hire a very young person from India to perform this delicate task? How could they possibly empathize, there, in their foreign country, safe from the boundless greed of American banks? And they always managed to sound both polite and threatening at the same time.

At other times, they were grave, like a doctor delivering a diagnosis of cancer. But always, consistently, they sounded ridiculously young, a smug triumph creeping into their tone as they pronounced foreclosure to be inevitable. She alternated, when dealing with them, between hostility and hysteria: "Yeah? And what are *you* going to do about it? Come to my house and *arrest* me? All the way from whatever country you're calling from?" To maternal compassion: "What a terrible job. You poor thing. I understand that you have to act this way, but I honestly can't pay the whole thing anymore or I truly would. I'm applying for help, but I fear it may not come in time. And," she always made sure to add, "I know it's not your fault."

But mostly of late, she chose avoidance. After so many months of this messy saga, Phoebe had a sixth sense about incoming calls. She could tell when the ring of the phone was a collection agency and would just let it ring until the answering machine picked up the stern, "Hello? Ms. Rosen? Missus?" Then there would be the relief, probably on both ends, that came with the click. Her answering machine always recorded an annoying two minutes of dial tone, then the beep-beep-beep of the receiver off the hook, then the electronic female saying, sweetly, as if speaking to a rather slow individual: "If you'd like to make a call, please hang up…" Sometimes Phoebe would press play on her answering machine just to listen to the assertiveness in that first hello. It never failed to register in her a pathetic triumph at the tone of defeat that soon accompanied the uttering of her name.

How the hell had this happened to her? She had gone to private school for sixteen years, had contributed to her IRA every year, and had worked since the age of fifteen. Phoebe recalled that first job, scooping ice cream at Baskin Robbins in Kansas City, her brown poofy cap strangely Soul Train, and her pink synthetic mini dress uniform stained and pilling almost within her first hour there. The manager, a skinny fellow, only a bit older than she, with the largest teeth Phoebe had ever seen, took Phoebe's training very seriously, and as they stood inside the freezer, their breath coming out in white clouds that lingered between them like thought balloons in comic books, he said solemnly, "These babies have a shelf life of five years," and he caressed the beige cardboard lid of a tub of Mandarin Chocolate Ice reverently, the warmth of his fingertips melting the surface frost and leaving little trails.

"Five years?" Phoebe had asked in alarm. "What's in this stuff, formaldehyde?"

His mouth pursed into a thin line of disdain, and after that, he kept conversation to a minimum and assigned her the undesirable five-to-eleven p.m. shift, all summer long.

A week after the surprise party, two of Phoebe's childhood friends, who seemed astonishingly unscathed by the recession, had generously treated her to a birthday dinner at the type of fun, upscale San Francisco restaurants she used to frequent before everything went south.

"Phoebe, I'm going to be straight with you," Gwen had said, bringing out her modulated, headmistress voice. She paused to pour herself a third glass of Viognier before going on. "Your problem is that you have a strong sense of entitlement."

They were sitting in a plush booth that made Phoebe feel like she was on a train. Gwen reached across Phoebe to spear a fried artichoke heart. "You're a princess, Phoeb. Admit it. Buck up. Times are tough. We can no longer assume we will have a nest egg or that our children will have the cushion that we all enjoyed at their age."

"Excuse me?" Phoebe asked incredulously. "*I* have a sense of entitlement? You two have husbands that make, I'm guessing, several mil a year. How are things tough for you?"

"Don't belittle our contributions as full-time moms," Sally said hotly. "You should know better! Ours is the most underpaid job in the universe."

"I know, but I worked even when I had Audrey," Phoebe said. "And besides, your kids are almost in college now. What do you do all day?"

"Here we go," Sally said, shooting Gwen a look that made it instantly apparent to Phoebe that they had discussed her behind her back.

"Just what does *that* mean?" Phoebe asked Gwen sharply.

"Listen, this isn't a competition," Gwen sighed. "We appreciate what we have and know that not everyone is so lucky, though in fairness, our husbands work many, many fourteen-hour days. It's just…well, don't go assuming *our* lives are all roses either."

"I don't," Phoebe said, relenting, but still twisting the napkin in her lap into a tight tornado. "But at least when your lives aren't going well you can rent a night at The Claremont Spa and that eases the pain a bit."

"Come on, Phee-Bo," Sally said jocularly, hugging her and giving her shoulders a little jiggle. "Maybe it's time for a change. Shake things up a bit. You're forty now, straddling youth and middle age, and that is exactly when the universe seems to throw everyone curveballs."

Gwen nodded gravely.

"Oh yeah, curveballs," Phoebe said. "Like divorce, my daughter leaving the nest, my hours being cut back at the winery—like these aren't enough change?"

Phoebe was warming up to the injustices, feeling sorry for herself and about to launch into a good long rant. Luckily, she managed to restrain herself, opting not to mention that she had lately been dipping her toes into the waters of online dating. She would not confess that her medicine cabinet was lined with little bottles of herbal sleep inducers containing at their base Valerian root, which smelled like old socks but was, as was mentioned even in Shakespeare's plays, said to invite good dreams. And finally, in the growing list of things Phoebe would keep to herself, she would certainly not disclose, as much as she loved these

women, *anything* about the apparition in the painter's smock she was
certain she had seen at her birthday party.

She softened and refilled their wine glasses, saying, "Money, feh!
Let's not go there tonight, please? Sorry. It's just that I feel like a piece
of chum in a sea of sharks. If I lived in Arkansas or Michigan or somewhere, they could threaten to foreclose all they wanted, but knowing
how long the house would sit empty and not sell, it would be worth
their while to help me. They would think twice. In Sonoma, I feel like
they can't wait to give me the boot and put my wonderful house on the
market, because they know someone will jump right in and take it."

Gwen and Sally fidgeted and Phoebe knew they were ready to move
on to brighter topics, like where their kids were applying to college or
where they were spending their summer. Phoebe used to be in synch
with such conversations but these days she felt a bit out of the loop
when they traded such tales. In the background, rising above even the
restaurant din, she overheard some blowhard pontificating about "economic Darwinism."

"It all just boils down to economic Darwinism, Fitch," the Blowhard said. Then he took a more patronizing tone and used his friend's
surname. "It's like this, Ray: survival of the fittest. Or the savviest. Let's
face it: the ones who have the best financial cushion to get them through
these lean times are the ones meant to survive. The rest, as it is in nature—the idealists and dreamers and those who want a free ride—well,
that's what recessions are good for. They weed out the weak, the ones
who are a burden on society."

"Oh I see…like Mom and Pop businesses? Like artists, musicians,
actors, writers and the like? The small gallery owners such as myself?
Are those the freeloaders you're referring to? Like anything that may
not be a big box store or a giant chain conglomerate should just bite the
dust, right? And that is a good thing…how?"

Phoebe whipped her head around to see who he was, this man Ray
or Fitch, who responded to the cretin exactly in the way she wanted to.
Ray looked like paintings she had seen of Pan, with dense black curls,

mischievous eyes, open features. All he needed was that little flute. His friend, by contrast, had the smooth face of overbred pedigree, nose as diminutive and unobtrusive as the head of an old nail. Phoebe didn't realize she was staring until Ray met her eyes and rolled his own in exasperation.

"Phoebe, are you even listening to us?" asked Sally, waving a hand in front of Phoebe's face. "Gwen just asked you how things were going with, you know, your house."

"I thought we weren't going to talk about it?" Phoebe said, confused.

"No, we're concerned. We love you. We just don't want your nice night out to turn into a pity party," Sally said, ever the blunt one.

Phoebe took a deep breath, wondering how to summarize the past year of misinformation and helplessness, of waking up in the middle of each night in a cold sweat about losing her home. And yes, of shame.

"I'm still working on it." Phoebe admitted. "Applying for this program, the Keep Your Home Plan, or maybe now it's called the Making Mortgages Affordable Plan, or the You Can Apply but We'll Lose Your Application Because WE Get a Kickback from the Government for Every Application We Process Plan, or perhaps this week it's called the We Make More on the Insurance than We Do by Helping You Plan. Or maybe the Endless Maze of Paperwork with No Rewards Plan." Phoebe's voice was rising and she saw the waiter start to approach their table, but think better of it and do an about-face. She tried to calm down and continued: "They change the names so many times, I can't keep up. I have about twenty different 800 numbers to call. But you know I really believe, with all the myriad toll-free numbers and department titles, that it's actually just one big phone bank somewhere in India, with only about a dozen operators, because you're always on hold for at least forty minutes and no matter who answers the phone they always tell you they are sorry ma'am but they need to transfer you to a different department. The left hand does not know what the right hand is doing!"

In spite of her best intentions, Phoebe was quite agitated now and her friends traded another look. Phoebe saw it and let the hand she was gesticulating with fall with a thud into her lap. "God, I'm sorry I'm so boring right now. I guess…there's just a lot going on."

The women allowed the conversation to flow to easier stuff, gossip about others from their hometown and shared viewings of photos on cell phones, until they looked around the restaurant and saw that they were the only ones still there.

"Yikes! We should let these poor people go home. Sir?" Sally called out to the patient waiter, making that universal midair scribble, the mime of someone signing a check. Then she turned back to Gwen and Phoebe and said with a touch of pride, "We still always close the joints down."

Some of the staff had already changed back into their civilian clothes and were having a post-shift drink at the bar. Phoebe had parked blocks away wanting to avoid the cost of a valet, so when the valet brought Gwen's car, she hitched a ride.

"Goodnight, sweetie," Gwen said, as Phoebe beeped her car's locks open and stepped out of Gwen's car. "It'll all work out."

"Yeah," Phoebe said, leaning into the passenger side again. "It sure better. Thanks so much, Gwen. I mean it. This was a real treat."

"Anytime, you know that. This too shall pass, as they say, but we all know: friends, that's what really matters."

On the long drive back up to the North Bay, Phoebe considered her situation. The honest truth was, she *loved* her house. It was nine hundred square feet—compact, she called it—and each room was painted a different color. Gloriously, there was even a swimming pool which, while small, the original owner had nonetheless taken the time and expense to tile on the bottom with a mosaic rendition of Michelangelo's "Creation of Man." Behind the high, jasmine-cloaked walls, Phoebe swam naked whenever possible, hovering over the tiled portrait, letting the ripples still until the old man that was God and the spectacular fleshy man that was Adam came clearly into view. Sometimes she would play as she floated there, extending her own pointed finger down toward Adam's other hand from above, joining in the circle of creation.

There was a separate guest cottage where she painted for at least two hours every day, all year. During the first hour, she painted the wine labels that provided her some income, but that was just a warm-up for the second hour, when she devoted herself to her own work: currently, a series of brightly colored whimsies inspired by fairy tales and myths. She made sure the little wood-burning stove was stoked in the winter so her hands didn't get stiff, and when there was a lull in the flow of expression, she would turn her gaze to the familiar titles of the art books stacked on the floor-to-ceiling bookshelves, the names on their spines inspiration to plunge ahead.

But the best part was, Phoebe could grow anything on her property, as if the soil had not been amended with her old tea bags and melon rinds but with some sort of high-octane fairy mulch. Cherry pits spit out in summery abandon would be foot-tall saplings growing by the same hammock come the following spring. Wild grapes from seeds that a bird had probably delivered, after a snack at one of the many nearby vineyards, now cloaked her back fence with glossy leaves and deep juicy clusters. Her fig tree produced great bushels of perfect Mission figs not once but twice a year, and she arranged them on the lovely pottery made by her French neighbor, where they sat like fat sultans, almost too beautiful to eat. Even the exotic stuff she had planted as an experiment, like sorrel or rainbow chard, would take hold in one of her raised bins, spread and endure, impervious to the occasional freeze, even surviving the trespasses of the mice who lived beneath their green canopy in the cooler months, the juicy leaves both shelter and supper.

Every rose bush, every lilac, every paper white and tulip, or the permanent crops like asparagus and strawberry—these she had planted over a decade ago, tended them, breathed in their fragrance, then ate them still warm from the garden.

Phoebe had aligned herself with the seasons by the things she observed on her small half acre, and came to anticipate such markers as the arrival of the Cedar Waxwings concurrent with the ripening of the persimmons, the tree belonging to her deaf next-door neighbor the branches ignoring all fences. He had shouted at her every autumn, as he no doubt continued to hope others would shout back at him so he could hear them, that she should help herself, that he "didn't like how the damned things came off in his mouth." So she watched the birds' lovely masked faces from the back porch as they greedily stuffed great globs of orange persimmon pulp into their beaks. It was these living things she could not bear to give up—far more than the buildings or the possessions inside them. They gave her such a sense of bounty and connection.

This was the house she had bought when Audrey was in middle school, right after the divorce. Somehow $2,500 a month, plus all the expenses of just living, or living well, in her case, seemed feasible back then. These past two years, Phoebe suddenly found herself treading water and carving away at her savings. At least she *had* savings, but not for long. Maybe Gwen and Sally were right. Maybe she had gotten too used to the good life…or at least the pretty good life. Phoebe was not avoiding work. She liked to work. If only she could figure out something, *something* better than the odd jobs she took for fifteen dollars an hour, or her twenty hours a week at the winery. She needed a job that paid enough to enable her to save her house, even leave her with some leftover to provide for her daughter. That was a lot of money, she knew. So what could she possibly do to come up with that?

Just as she was unlocking her front door, the phone rang. It was almost midnight and Phoebe's heart beat staccato as she started across the room to answer, imagining some accident, an emergency. But then she hesitated, her hand hovering uncertainly over the receiver, as the machine picked up and a young voice with a foreign accent called out her name, beseechingly, needy as a baby bird, over and over, into the empty room.

CHAPTER FOUR

When Ben Rosen got his shipping-out orders in 1944 from a boot camp in Ft. Sills, Oklahoma, he was more than ready. He was a lanky nineteen-year-old with a large Adam's apple that bobbed up and down when he was nervous, and knees and elbows that seemed to be consistently bruised. He had never been outside of the Midwest and was eager for any scenery that did not involve cows or corn.

"How you gonna keep 'em down on the farm, after they've see Paree, eh Rosen?" joked fellow buck private Cliff, quoting the popular song from that other big war. Ben was preparing to leave the next day at dawn, and there was the definite possibility that he would indeed end up in France. Cliff had been hovering for the past hour, persistent as a mosquito, watching Ben pack and hopping from foot to foot as if he had to pee. Ben stopped packing and frowned at him.

"Naw, don't mind me, ole Bud-bud. I'm jealous is all. I'd give anything to see some action, get out of this backwater hellhole."

"Don't worry, bucko, you'll be shipped out next. I heard General Eisenhower's got something planned for every able-bodied base rat, and what's needed for this war *ain't* gonna happen in Oklahoma!"

Even though he had heard gruesome tales from other men who had returned home shaken and jumpy, Ben still viewed his deployment more as a chance to "see the world," a cultural or educational opportunity, than a dangerous endeavor that could potentially end his life. Sure, he knew there was that possibility, he wasn't stupid, but the thought of getting out of the Midwest and seeing Europe seemed more than worth the risk. Plus, he had endured six months of grueling training and was itching to test everything he had learned.

"Kiss a can-can dancer for me, Bennie-boy!" Cliff said, flicking what was left of his cigarette out the front door. Then he turned around and added with a leer: "Oh, I forgot, you're married." With this, he gave Ben a big grin and headed for the washroom.

Yes, Ben was married—to Ruthie, poor kid. He dreaded giving her the news that he was going halfway across the world and no, he couldn't tell her for how long. He'd joined the army so soon after they got married that it seemed like he was yanked out of the honeymoon and dropped into the thick of basic training before he'd known what hit him. But she'd be okay. And he was glad she hadn't gotten pregnant yet. He knew a lot of guys in that situation, and the guilt they felt was awful, their wives having to go it alone.

Ben called Ruthie from the train station and broke it to her. She was quiet for a full minute, then composed herself and said sternly: "You just better come home in one piece, Mister, or you'll have to answer to me in the sweet hereafter." Ben swallowed hard, told her he loved her, and replaced the receiver.

By the third week in August, after he had been in France only two weeks, Ben was involved in what his captain had assured his division was only a "mopping-up operation" in a rural area about sixty miles outside of Paris. It was a warm day, and they were setting up camp in a field of sunflowers outside a fine old farm house. Many Parisians who had fled to the country had heard that it was only a matter of time before the Germans would evacuate Paris, so they were returning to the city in droves. Ben was eager to get to Paris also, and felt that they were just biding their time out here.

"Only problem is," one of his fellow soldiers grumbled as he hammered in a stake on one corner of the tent, "the Krauts don't take kindly to being mopped up."

No sooner had these words left his lips than a lone German appeared out of nowhere with a Steyr submachine gun. His movements were unsteady, as if in a trance. Even though he was still a fair distance away from the camp, the young soldier just pointed the weapon in their direction and opened fire, spraying bullet in a sweeping motion, as if he was watering a lawn. All the men threw themselves onto the ground, shouting and scrambling for their weapons, but it was Ben who managed to get off a fatal shot before diving into the dirt. He had never killed anyone before—or if he had, with a grenade or with tank fire, it had happened from a safe distance, so that he had not been forced to witness the aftermath of his actions. This time, he actually saw the expression in the German soldier's eyes, up close and personal, looking right at him as if asking: *Why'd you have to do that? I'm just some guy like you, doing my job.*

Ben flung his pistol onto the ground as if it scalded his hand, and began to run, just run, away from that man, his own age and build, away from that look, not knowing or caring where he was headed. Ben's lungs were burning as he passed the farmhouse and raced out into unprotected territory. He ran so hard he tripped over rocks and roots, but picked himself right back up and tore off again with no plan other than to run. Finally, dizzy and unable to keep going, Ben bent over at the waist, his palms on his knees, and willed the panic and nausea to subside, sweating and gasping for breath. He wasn't sure how much time had passed, but eventually, he was ready to walk back to his unit. When he made it back to the farmhouse, the others didn't grill him. They just looked him over, nodded, and made a place for him in their circle.

The men sat quietly for a long while, their backs to the dead soldier. No one had moved him and Ben wondered if that too would be left up to him. He hoped not. Soon, the family in the farmhouse ventured outside, lingering in the doorway, but the father walked directly up to the corpse and kicked it with all his might. The men were stunned. Then the farmer turned to Ben and clapped him on the back, saying without any remorse: "*Felicitations.*" He called out something in French to his wife, and she nodded then turned back to the house, returning a few minutes later with some sort of—could it be?—cake.

The men couldn't guess how the woman had gotten the butter or flour, but she calmly knelt on the ground within their circle and placed a perfect slice of cake into each man's open hand. They all chewed silently, some of them half shutting their eyes with the pleasure of it. They tried to act as if it was the most natural thing in the world to be eating this special, sweet creation with a dead body only a few feet away. The farmer had at least flipped the soldier over so his back was to the sky and none of them had to worry about encountering his face. The men eventually dusted off their hands, licking any trace of icing from their fingertips, and it was Ben who broke the silence, telling the woman in his broken French that hers was the most delicious cake he had ever eaten. She gave him a big smile, a missing front tooth only adding to its charm.

This is what struck Ben in his short time there. France was full of tanks, explosions, death, German occupation, and continual fear. But then along with all that, there were people like the head of this farm and others, the regular folks of the country, just trying to live their lives. Plowing the fields, kids still doing what kids did, women making cakes, everyone carrying on…at least as best they could. Ben was very moved by it, and wanted so badly to make a difference for these people. He thought of Ruthie back home and about the children they might have someday, kids who would, God willing, never know what it was like to have foreign soldiers on their own land.

One evening, a few days after the surprise attack, the men went into the nearby village and they saw three women with their heads shaved, the tops of their dresses pulled brutally down to their waists so their breasts were exposed, their wrists tied in front of them with rope. They were being led down the main street, plodding behind an old ox cart, the ribs on the oxen distinct as prongs on a rake. Two of the women looked down fearfully, but the third had a sort of defiant radiance about her, chin held high.

"*Collaborateurs,*" a man standing near Ben hissed, then stepped forward to join the jeering mob. The women looked amazingly dignified, despite their raw-looking scalps and uncovered breasts. Ben shuddered to think what dire circumstances would have forced them to collude with the enemy. He refused to believe it was anything as simple as easing their own lives, the consequence of greed.

"Maybe they had no other way to get food for their children," Ben said aloud after the procession had rounded the corner and disappeared.

"Geez, Rosen, you're such a romantic," a soldier named Saul said, snapping his cap in the air in front of him before positioning it rakishly back on his head. He gave Ben a little push, moving them along in their pursuit of a beer.

"They're getting the treatment they deserve. You and I, most of the Americans, except those poor sons of guns at Normandy—geez, Rosen, we were so goddamn lucky not to have been sent to that beach—well, we *are* lucky, is what I'm sayin'. These Frenchies, they've been living with the enemy waltzing all over their country and treating them like dirt for a long time. We're just joining in the last act. And we get to be the heroes. Us! Heroes! And all by goddamn chance."

"You're probably right," Ben said, looking over his shoulder in the direction the cart had taken. "I just feel like everybody, all of us, are just doing what we need to do to survive." Saul could tell his friend was warming to the subject. "It's one more thing we all have in common, no matter whose side we're on. Extreme situations make you do things you never thought you were capable of."

The men walking with him knew he was also speaking about himself, about having killed a man close to his own age, from a distance that gave death an undeniably human face. The men knew he wasn't sleeping right, because they too had once or twice experienced this close-range glimpse of death and it was something none of them would ever completely forget.

"Let's buy this man a beer," Saul called out to the rest. "He's sure earned it."

Shortly after that night in the village, where they were sent to "sweep up," General Eisenhower ordered all American troops into Paris, to take part in the liberation. The true liberation had already happened on the 26th of August, 1944, before Ben's division arrived, but he quickly saw what Saul had meant about them being instant heroes. The celebration was still in full swing even though two days had passed, and Ben found himself swept up in the abandon of the fevered streets. He barely had to move his feet but was pushed forward in a swaying mass of ebullient French people. He saw sailors ricocheting between women like happy pinballs, kissing whichever one they happened to land against. Parisians had climbed up high onto street lamps and Metro entrances and were singing the Marseilles in voices hoarse with emotion and spirits, out-siders joining in loudly, humming along when they did not know the words. Ben wondered what those first hours of liberation had been like, if the people were still going this strong two days later.

"A beer, *mon ami!*" Saul called out to him, and Ben craned his neck above a logjam of revelers to see his buddy, each of his arms around slightly swaying twins who hugged him close like bookends. "Follow us!"

Ben smiled and said, "*Excuzez-moi! Excuzez-moi!*" as he pushed his way through a stream of happy Parisians toward Saul. One of the twins pulled away from Saul and took Ben's hand, smiling and repeating, as if soothing a young child, "Okay. Okay. Mister! *Vive la France!* Okay! Sank-you-verrry-much. Okay-dokay!" as they made their way toward a café, overflowing people already spilling from the entryway.

Just then, as movement stalled for an instant, Ben noticed a flash of color—orange and blue—lying on top of a pile of broken chairs, glass, and soiled clothing heaped at the mouth of an alley. It was a small painting, and though Ben saw only enough of it to appreciate that it was lovely, and certainly not a thing to be tossed onto a pile of garbage. He managed to swoop down and grab the little framed canvas a split second before being propelled forward in the surge of the crowd, and despite the crush, he was just able to slip it under his jacket, where it would be relatively safe. He knew this was just the start of a night that was destined to grow more and more raucous, and he wanted to protect his find.

People were packed so tightly in the streets and cafés that dancing with one of the numerous and willing local women became less like a duet and more like marching in place. On the dance floor, which was pretty much any flat surface, Ben repeatedly bumped up against five or six strangers aflame with hilarity, unable to stop dancing. Even through his increasing inebriation, Ben was able to keep track of his treasure, refusing to remove his jacket even though it was so stifling in the room he thought he might pass out. "His" twin teased him about this, stroking his forehead and saying, "You are a shy boy?" He responded to this by dancing with her until dawn, twirling her and buying her all the champagne she wanted. He even kissed her, because, well, marriage was in another world and what happened on this monumental day didn't count.

It wasn't until he returned to his bed at the hotel, stepping over the various snoring soldiers who shared the room, that he finally had a chance to examine the small painting he had found. Ben stared at it in wonder. He knew little about art, yet he sensed that this was something special. It was beautiful, a perfect thing. A rectangle no bigger than a phone book, yet it contained a whole universe. Was it a circus? It was surely some fantastical world, alive with wondrous horses with large eyes that looked so merry one second and so sad the next. There were acrobats walking on air, and a contortionist with her head set upside down upon her neck, smiling right at him, her feet arched way over her head as if she was forming a rainbow with her own body. Everything in the painting was topsy-turvy, and so vivid. And…what was that? A fish? With wings? Well, why not! Fish could fly. Some could walk, too, he'd heard. It was a great big world and swimming wasn't the only option. He felt giddy just holding the painting in his hands, and squinted to look closer at the fin of the flying fish. He saw that the artist had hidden his signature there, but all Ben could make out was an H and an L. Probably no famous masterpiece, but that didn't matter. The painting would always remind him of this one wild and free day, of his first time in Paris.

As if the jubilation contained in the painting was contagious, Ben felt, for the first time in ages, such promise for the world. Paris was not burning. And maybe he'd even had something to do with that glad outcome. Ben found a pencil in his jacket pocket and flipped the painting over, and, carried away by the emotion of the past few weeks, wrote on the back of the canvas with a thick flourish, using the broad stub of flint: "For my dear wife Ruthie Rosen. Paris, Liberation, August 28th, 1944. May our world together always have such magic. Yours forever, Ben Rosen."

As the red dawn light outlined the gargoyles, devils, and spirits on the ancient and impervious Notre Dame cathedral, Ben lay down on a bare cot, wadding his t-shirt up to make a pillow. He drifted off to sleep with the treasure on his chest, hidden by a sheet, and dreamt of different women on either side of him, there in Paris, on this strange bed—his wife Ruthie to his right, and on the left, the giggling French girl whose name he could not say. The women made a ring with their arms and slept that way, with Ben safely in the center.

CHAPTER FIVE

Every morning, Bernadette awoke at six, never needing an alarm, even if sleep had been slow in coming. Bernadette opened her eyes, rotated her feet until they made a satisfying cracking sound, then flung aside the light *couverture* that she had made years ago from pieces of lace and fabric that had belonged to her mother. At the bathroom sink, she tapped some baking soda into her palm, rolled the toothbrush around in it, and brushed vigorously. Bernadette was extremely proud of the fact that even at the age of seventy-eight, she still had all her own teeth.

For forty years, she had been known as one of the finest makers of porcelain dentures in Paris, and she had long suspected that everyone from presidents to royalty probably had one or more of her cuspid creations in their mouth. Bernadette had enjoyed her work, and had it been up to her, she would never have retired. But in France, as everywhere else in the twenty-first century, machines could come close to—although, she believed, never quite duplicate—the skills of those who made things by hand. Still, the machines could do it faster and cheaper.

So now she was in the south of France, away from that dynamic city where she and all her people had been born and died. Provence offered her a slower pace, even if she was not the sort of woman to accept the offer. Instead, on her sixty-fifth birthday, she had officially registered her lavender farm as a gîte, a bed and breakfast. She loved that word, from the old French *jit*, meaning "little corner to cuddle." Hence, with her gîte to run, and especially now that her husband was gone, Bernadette found few opportunities to linger in bed.

Bernadette brushed her thick grey bob with the boar-bristle brush with the ivory handle, which had belonged to her great grandmother and was still in good repair. She had lived through a war and scarcity, those experiences remaining in her very core, so she deplored the throwaway culture of today. Each time she used a utensil or machine or, yes, a hairbrush that still functioned, perhaps even better than its current counterpart, it was deeply gratifying.

She brushed her hair twenty, forty, fifty strokes, until it crackled. Then she regarded herself in the fine old beveled mirror. A woman with eyes the color of grey seas and a very direct gaze, with a peach fuzz of blond down outlining her ruddy cheeks looked back her. Winter, spring, summer, and fall, Bernadette's complexion was that of a woman who had just stepped away from a hot stove, as was often the case.

Satisfied, she turned away from the constancy of her own reflection and marched through the living room to her kitchen. She struck a match to ignite the stovetop to boil the water that she would pour over the coffee grinds waiting in the French press. She watched the wisps of smoke from the match coil around shafts of sunlight, like snakes or their ghosts.

"*Merde*," Bernadette swore under her breath when she heard the pigeons cooing. Didn't these messy, nuisance birds know that there was a season to propagate? They seemed to lay eggs year round, and they simply would not get the message. She climbed up a small stepladder and opened the door that led out onto the rooftop, then felt around in the pigeons' nests for eggs. She found two and hurled them with all her might off the roof far into the garden below, the adult pigeons pacing and scolding her with their muffled protests.

She didn't know why she hated these birds so much. Indeed, during the rationing, during the occupation, her mother had served them all pigeon for dinner on numerous occasions. And guinea pig. And odd root vegetables that tasted like dirt and rocks. This had kept them from going hungry. Still, even though Bernadette destroyed their eggs, the pigeons never nested elsewhere. She returned to her kitchen, washed her hands, and slowly pushed the coffee press down through the water, smelling the dense perfume of the grinds.

She had an inn to run, and while she often missed the bustle of having her husband and sons in the kitchen, she reminded herself to fully appreciate these early morning moments of solitude. She knew that by ten o'clock each evening, she would be desperate for this alone time. She warmed and frothed the milk in a chipped yellow pot on the stove, pinching off the skin that always formed on the surface as the milk cooled. Since childhood, this had been a favorite ritual, though it used to repulse the others in her family when she lifted it right off and dropped the fine membrane into her mouth. By this point in her morning routine, it would be 6:20, and she would slather a warm piece of baguette with fresh butter, sometimes goat butter from her own goats, topping that with various jams that she had made herself from the fruits and berries that had been on the property for more than a century. Each morning, she savored this *tartine* and café au lait, letting the sugar she had sprinkled on top of the foam stay a moment on her upper lip before she allowed herself to lick it off.

But throughout her customary breakfast, in fact from the moment she first opened her eyes each day, Bernadette was restless. She knew she would go out to her pottery studio, take the small painting out of its hiding place and just look at it for a long time, ever amazed that even after sixty years it still transported her. It was her secret, the beautiful painting, but also, because it had to be hidden, because it was not rightfully hers, because keeping it had required that she lie to several people, including her brother, it was the very definition of a guilty pleasure. And it drew Bernadette back, every time.

After her husband had died, Bernadette thought of finally bringing the painting out of hiding and hanging it opposite her bed so she could stare at it in the mornings and take comfort in entering the cherished worlds of the fish that flew, of girls in tutus, as flexible and open as new saplings. If any of her friends or the guests at the inn should somehow discover it or ask questions, she practiced saying, "Oh, this is an old reproduction—a good one though, no? It's from that big Clignancourt Marchee des Puce, years ago now. We'd better not touch it, though, as I'm always afraid the thing will disintegrate someday. I think someone once stored it in a wet basement, if you can imagine."

While Bernadette was a scrupulously honest person in all other areas of her life, this was, of course, a lie. She did not want anyone to touch the painting because they might see, as she had, even as that young girl who accepted it from her brother, that it was probably *not* a copy at all, but truly painted by the hands of the great Marc Chagall. And Bernadette certainly did not want some nosy friend to turn the painting over and see the inscription there: "For my dear wife Ruthie Rosen, etc.," for then they would ask her why, if she knew it was an actual Chagall, she had never tried, in all these years, to contact this Rosen woman, or her children? And of course she could shrug and say, "Oh now, a real Chagall? I don't know about that. I picked this up at a flea market for a song. I do not think the clever man selling it would part with a real Chagall."

But while she anticipated accusations and practiced making her responses nonchalant and convincing, she could never quite imagine herself ever coming clean about this enormous misconduct. She justified her transgression by telling herself she was protecting the painting. *No, better to keep it safe in its lair, where I can watch over its beauty. Where no one can take it from me.* For Bernadette knew that she absolutely had to possess this painting from the very instant she had reached out for it. She had only been thirteen years old, a child, really, in 1944, but had solemnly promised her brother that she would mail it to the address he had written on the package he gave her, a place called Oklahoma, in America.

"This man is my friend," her brother had said solemnly, so handsome in his uniform as he knelt before her to look her in the eye. Her brother was six years older than she, just the right age for fighting in this war, so he had missed out on knowing his sister, and the girl she had become.

"He wants to offer it to his wife and I told him I would make sure, after things calm down a bit, that we would mail it to him. Can you make sure of that, Beebee? I have orders to leave Paris today. Give the post offices at least a week to get back to normal, and here is some money to cover the stamps. *Je conte sur toi, ma peche.*"

I am counting on you. His last words to her. He kissed her on both cheeks then and handed her a small package wrapped in brown paper, ready to be mailed. Bernadette felt heavy with the responsibility, but also proud to be seen as so capable and trustworthy. Yet being a young girl, she was also curious.

Under normal circumstances, her brother could have counted on Bernadette. But the girl had been without for so many years, had eaten thin soups made from weeds, onion skins, even grass. She was so hungry that she had eaten boiled snails and their shells as well—oh God, what she had *not* eaten? Hard breads made with scant oil and no eggs and bearded with mold, rancid meats of unknown origin, even acorns. She had endured the lewd remarks of the soldiers that entered her father's store and simply took whatever they wanted without paying, and had looked the other way and felt ashamed for her cowardice when they taunted or brutalized someone right in the street. She just kept walking, as did many, but it gnawed at her. To maintain her dignity, she had tried to make outfits for herself and her sisters from her father's old suits, copied from styles she had seen in magazines. And it felt wrong to her that the Jews, in her beloved Paris, had to ride in the last train of the Metro cars and wear that yellow star like a brand of shame. Paris was a modern city, a beautiful city. And as she told her own children so many years later, "You have not lived through war, really, until it is fought on your own soil. You cannot say you know war until you have known hunger and smelled death."

So maybe she had been bitter about all the deprivation she'd experienced as a young girl. Or maybe she had been starved for beauty, wanting so badly to possess something of real value. But once she had ridden her bicycle home that day, to their apartment above her father's shop, shut the door to her room and carefully opened the paper at the top of the small rectangle, fully planning to slide the painting back in, once she had seen its color and life and mastery, its absolute specialness, Bernadette knew that she could never part with it.

Right then, she began making up her story, about the package having fallen out of her satchel on the ride home, and though she had retraced her route and asked people in the streets and searched until dark, she never found it again. Her tears came easily, even when practicing the telling of this lie, for what a loss that *would* have been, something that made her weep just to imagine. Her brother, as she knew he would, wound up comforting her after he heard the tale, and while disappointed, sighed, "Oh well, he is in America. He will find other pictures there surely for his wife. This was just a pretty little nothing." But Bernadette knew, even back then, that this man, this Ben Rosen, would never find a picture even remotely like this one.

But she did not want to think about all this today. She had replayed this moment of deception so many times over the years that the scene would sometimes pop into her head unbidden, like some annoying jingle or a song's refrain. She gulped the last of her coffee down, the best part, the moist crumbs and melted morsels of butter and strawberry jam all at the bottom of the morning bowl from having dunked her tartine before each bite. She rose from the table and headed outside into the warmth of a midsummer morning. Her bees were already hard at work burrowing their heads deep into the fragrant layers of the fat, peach-colored roses and the dense spikes of lavender, golden balls of pollen thick on their legs and abdomen.

"That's it, my fellows," Bernadette said, pleased and soothed by their buzzing industry, standing in the midst of them. "This will be a good year for honey. *Allez*, keep it up."

With that, she entered the cool, earthy sanctuary of her atelier, where even she, a petite woman, was obliged to duck a little, as it was an old stone building, shaped, curiously, like a beehive, and it had a low door. She headed straight for the back wall, where she kept the trays filled with honeycombs. Her husband had devised a wonderful system where he cut squares in the wall of the studio, constructing sliding wooden panels with handles that when lifted, revealed glass panes that sandwiched the hives. There was a removable panel on the outside, so the bees could come and go to their combs in finer weather, and another that could slide open on the inside, should Bernadette want to watch the bees crawling around and adding wax to their comb while she sat at her pottery wheel.

But now she walked over to one of the sliding wooden panels, the one she never raised unless she was alone, and opened it, her heart pounding in anticipation as it had every day since she first saw the painting. Through all of the numerous and ingenious hiding places Bernadette had devised, this one was the best. People were afraid of bees, so even though this particular door revealed not a tray full of bees adding to their comb but instead a rather small and magnificent painting, no one would ever get close enough to notice. Today, as always, Bernadette's hands trembled as she reached for it, as if she too were afraid of being stung.

CHAPTER SIX

"**M**ore wine?" Ray Fitch asked, lifting the seventy-dollar bottle of Oregon Pinot toward his date in a tone at once gracious and resigned. In his mind he added, *More expensive wine, Date Number Fifty-eight? Even though you clearly do not find me to be your soul mate? And even though I will be paying for this extravagant meal meant to woo you and sweep you off your feet?* But, no, he would not say this out loud. Instead, he smiled warmly at Date Number Fifty-eight, and held his own glass up, admiring the liquid velvet of the Pinot catching the candlelight in its glass. Pinot Noir, also known as the "heartbreak grape" because it was so fussy, so hot and volatile when fermenting. Ray smiled at how appropriate this was, given the current state of his dashed hopes in the dating marathon he had stupidly agreed to "at least give a fair try."

"This is good," said Date Number Fifty-eight, almost guzzling the stuff, and smiling gamely. She, at least, was one of the friendlier errors. Her name was…April? No, June! That's right. Like the month.

June licked her thin upper lip and queried: "How did you describe it again? Moldy?"

"No, um, I think I said mushroomy. It just has an earthy cherry flavor. But honestly? These wine terms are bit esoteric," Ray said, chuckling, trying to be more congenial, to help her out.

"Well, all I know is that it tastes good!" she said emphatically.

"I agree," he said, clinking his glass to hers. June gazed at him woozily. It was sad. Either he wasn't right for them, which was the case about eighty percent of the time, and they looked disappointed the minute they laid eyes on him, or if not that instantaneously, then the minute he said his first sentence. Or, as was apparently the case this evening, they were smitten and he, despite his best intentions, simply was not. Yet each time, being human, and maybe even being an optimist, he never failed to get his hopes up.

Only two more hours to go, Ray consoled himself. Then either or both of them would trot out the phrases: "I've got an early day tomorrow." Or: "I'll call you soon." Or: "That was fun!" "Yes, that *was* fun." Each one probably collapsing in relief once behind their own closed doors. *God*, Ray thought, *one shouldn't have to date in one's forties*. There was something very wrong with this. One should be enjoying the empty nest, traveling to exotic places with the love of one's life, the spouse of the silver anniversary, or even the crystal anniversary. One should be able to relax a little with the comfort of having a partner in crime, a friend to grow old with. He always found these women so hard to please, as if they'd been hurt so badly that there was no way in hell they were going to make it easy for anybody. Or else they'd been alone so long there was no chance of softening or compromise or even branching out of their sad, lonely, single rituals. But who was he to talk? He'd been single since Rachel said she couldn't handle his "rage issues" one more second.

"It's called *passion!*" he had screamed at her back as she got into her car, just like in the movies, and simply drove away from twenty years of marriage.

"At least I'm not a zombie!" he'd added at the top of his lungs, even though she was now just a cloud of dust, way out of earshot. And on that note, they began divorce proceedings. Of course they had Martin, who had turned out blessedly well, so they would always have to have some contact. Now, two years after their split, Rachel had found "her dream man" and seemed genuinely happy, so it was easier to be her friend. But clearly Ray had not found his own "dream woman," or even one he could imagine going on a hike with, or preparing a meal for. And this online dating thing was a last resort, forced upon him by well-meaning friends.

"So," said June, straightening in her seat and pushing her wine glass away as if it might bite her. "Where are you from?"

"Originally?" Ray asked. "Well, I was born in Chicago but I've lived the past two decades or so in Northern California. Came here for college and never looked back." He had said these words so many times they felt hollow, and he had a moment of disorientation, where he wasn't sure where or whom he was, unsure that he *was* actually born in Chicago or even *had* gone to college in California. "And you?"

"My God, Ray," June said, smacking the table soundly with her fist. "I cannot tell you how refreshing it is to have a man ask me about myself for a change! Full disclosure here: I have been on at least a dozen of these Cupid-dot-com dates and the men, my God, they go on and on about themselves and like a good little girl, I just sit there and pump them with questions. And do they ever once think to be even a teensy weensy bit curious about yours truly?" She was flushed now and her volume was rising so that the couple at the table next to theirs turned around to look at her, shooting Ray a split-second look of what was unmistakably pity, before going back to their own little world.

"I'm guessing no?" Ray accommodated.

"No!" she cried. "Ya got that right, Pardner! Never!"

June was transforming before Ray's very eyes into…what? Cowgirl? Wronged diner waitress? Bitter truck driver? He was intrigued, if only for the entertainment value.

Just then a waiter was standing near her holding two plates with folded kitchen towels and asking, "Duck in wild plum reduction with hand-torn baby lettuces?"

June blinked as if regaining consciousness.

"That would be the lady's," Ray said. He had never in his whole life been one of those men who referred to females as ladies. But the evening was suddenly off kilter and he didn't give a hoot anymore about anything.

"So *you* must be," the waiter said, flirting shamelessly, "the line-caught opah with Buddha hand citron sauce and Lion's Mane mushroom and sorrel risotto!" Was the waiter batting his eyelashes as he lowered the plate? Well, at least someone found him attractive.

"I've been called worse," Ray responded jovially. But when he turned back to June, all the color had drained from her cheeks and she looked mortified and bewildered at the same time. Ray was poised to apologize for something, anything, when June pushed back from the table and whispered:

"Can you excuse me a moment?"

"Is everything okay?" Ray asked, concerned.

"I just…I just need to go to the powder room." And with that, she virtually bolted from the table, her napkin fluttering from her lap to the floor. Their waiter swooped to retrieve it, handing it back to Ray with a flourish, like a suitor returning a woman's purposefully dropped hankie.

Ray pondered her departure as the quiet of the small table engulfed him. Too much wine? Didn't like the "lady" handle? Was afraid she'd spoken too frankly? Ray smiled broadly over at the neighboring couple and gave an exaggerated shrug, like a big lunk in a romantic 1940s movie, as if to say: dames! Who can figure 'em? The couple smiled back in a polite, if fleeting, fashion.

Good God, this dating thing was living hell! Why was it so hard for a man and a woman, of any age, just to connect? Go out, eat, laugh, and converse? And maybe a little sex now and then—would that be too much to ask? Ray looked at his plate of gorgeous, artistically arranged food, and his mouth began to water. He was dying to taste it while it was hot. The charge for this meal was going to be at least two Benjamins, and if he were paying, which he was pretty certain he was, would it be too much to ask to have the pleasure of experiencing it as the chef intended it to be consumed? Ray loosened a delicate morsel of opah with the tip of his fork and a fine mist of fragrant, citrusy steam rose from the fish. He shut his eyes and let the flavors play on his tongue. No, he should wait. It wasn't nice to start without her. But what was she doing in there?

He arranged the garnish of a kumquat rind intertwined infinity-style with a glistening lychee so that it covered his indiscretion. And he waited some more, sipping his wine and trying to act fine about every little thing. A good fifteen minutes went by, during which he pecked surreptitiously at his food, then tried to cover the bare spots on his plate by repositioning the diminishing remains of his meal. Suddenly, there was June, and he started. Her eyes were red-rimmed and she stood tableside with a ghoul-like silence and severity.

"Oh, June," Ray said, clutching his chest to let her know she'd startled him. "I was starting to worry."

"Ray," she said in a monotone, looking down at him, definitely not intending to sit back down, and Ray felt as though he were about to be scolded, so he too grew serious. "I'll be honest with you, Ray. I have upchucked. Not romantic, but true. There you have it. I am deeply sorry. I think I was nervous and consumed the wine too swiftly. And now I must depart."

Upchucked? Depart? Who was this woman?

"Oh, June, what a shame. I'm so sorry. Let me at least take you home," Ray offered, civilly.

"No, Ray," she said urgently. "I want you to stay. This wasn't…right, for me. I want to be alone now. I am sorry." With that, she was gone.

By now Ray had given up caring what the couple at that next table thought of him. He wished he could invite the young waiter to have a seat, have a glass of this *deelish* chock-full-o'-cherry Pinot Noir. At least some levity could maybe be interjected into the fiasco of the evening. But instead, Ray tucked June's fallen napkin into the collar of his shirt, held the knife upright in his left hand and the fork upright in his right, as if he were getting ready for a plate of barbeque. He slid June's plate over and placed it alongside his own, the edges overlapping. Ray Fitch poured himself the last of the wine and then, calm as you please, began to eat from both plates, first one, then the other, not wanting to rush, yet already wishing he too were back home, because if there was one thing he hated, it was eating out alone.

CHAPTER SEVEN

"Hi, Kate," Phoebe said, pushing through the doors of the long chicken coop that had been converted into an architectural marvel and was now the Ravenswing Winery's business office. It was quite commodious for a former chicken coop. State-of-the-art paint job inside, too, warm ochres and soothing pistachios. "What's on the lineup for today?"

"A young writer from the *Chronicle* wants to watch you paint at some point and to ask you about wine labels. You know, how you come up with the ideas, how they evolve, and the like. I think it's going to run in the Food section next Sunday."

"Well, she won't believe me when I tell her where I get my ideas," Phoebe said breezily, and it made her giddy to confess her secret in such a way, safe in the knowledge that everyone would assume she was kidding. "I channel the ghost of Chagall."

"Oh, of course. And why would she *not* believe that?" Kate answered, rolling her eyes.

"Well, don't say I didn't warn you. No, I'm happy to talk with her, but right now I've got the completed paintings for the '08 Cabs and Zins. Take a look."

Phoebe's hands trembled with excitement as she took her paintings out of the fine old leather postman's satchel she had gotten years ago at a Paris flea market, back in the days when she could afford to travel. She spread out all the watercolors she had done that past week on top of Kate's desk and stepped back, biting her thumbnail and waiting for a reaction.

"Wow, missy! You *did* channel Chagall's ghost. A red raven? A green one? We've never done stuff like this before. I love it…but do you think James will?" Kate asked hesitantly.

"Yes, actually, I know he will," Phoebe said, gathering up the bright paintings. "I even think people will buy this year's vintage specifically for the labels. I know I choose wine that way sometimes."

"Well, you sound very confident," Kate said. "Good for you…and they really are pretty amazing. And watercolors, that's a slight detour for you, too. But they're not that much like Chagall—still very Phoebe, except way more colorful."

"It's the new me," Phoebe said, tilting her chin up and batting her eyelashes. No one at work could have possibly known just how much she meant that.

The weather had been so glorious the past week, all the spring mustard blinding yellow in between the rows of dark, gnarled vines. She thought fondly of the old Herb Caen columns in the *Chronicle*, one in particular where he wrote, "I imagine heaven to be a lot like Sonoma in the spring." Phoebe always gave a silent thanks to all the Italians and other dreamers who had settled in the region, for they made sure, hundreds of years ago, when they first started planting the old vines, to sow mustard alongside their grapes for the nitrogen the plants contained. Today, those miles of dazzling yellow flowers all over both valleys were the first harbinger of spring in Sonoma and Napa.

In fact it was the mustard that had gotten Phoebe outdoors to paint on that extraordinary day last week. With so much on her mind and the deadline approaching for the new labels, Phoebe had taken her easel outside of her beloved, and now threatened, little studio. She had seen Chagall's ghost three times since her surprise party, and each time, though he seemed kind and unthreatening, it had completely discombobulated her. She knew that nothing would ground her like painting, and she was in good spirits as she looked up at the green slopes of Sonoma Mountain, with those wonderful old Clydesdales that someone had turned out to pasture grazing at the base. They were reassuring fixtures off in the distance, a perfect fusion of sturdiness and grace. She decided, for the Zinfandel label, to paint a raven sitting on the back of one of these horses, looking directly at the viewer, a sprig of mustard in its beak. There always had to be a raven somewhere in the painting, and this was fine, as Phoebe loved ravens, their cunning and loyalty to their mates.

Just as she was trying to come up with an idea for the Cabernet label, she saw the ghost again, sitting in the damp grass and leaning his back against her olive tree.

"Why not one bird feeding another bird a whole cluster of grapes— you know, some interaction?" he asked her. Again, Phoebe looked around her yard, checking to see if any neighbors could hear or see the ghost in the smock.

"And why always a black raven?" he went on, an orange feather falling in slow motion from the branch above him and snagging in his tumult of grey curls. "Why not a green raven or a magenta raven or a red raven? You are too hampered by realism, my dear."

"Apparently, judging from my continued sightings of *you*, that is not entirely true."

Something had shifted. Phoebe said these words aloud, no longer pretending that the ghost was not there. She was resigned to his entrances and exits now and had decided to just run with it all. Her dog Mechant cocked his head at his mistress, but Gamut, the more social of her two beasts, was already resting her head on Chagall's thigh. Phoebe looked around nervously to make absolutely certain that there was no sign of her neighbor Teddy, who was fond of his midday "Brewskies" and who, even after so many years of being neighbors, still called her Mimi each time he saw her.

Satisfied that she was alone with her ghost, she stepped away from her easel and asked seriously: "Are you Marc Chagall?"

"Yes, that is who I am," he said, easing the dog off his lap. He stood and gave her a quick bow. He started to walk toward her and went on, as if musing to himself: "Or rather, that is who I *was*. Now I am still him, but not many can see me."

"Am I having some sort of nervous breakdown?" Phoebe asked him in a faltering voice, although this was silly of her, for if he were a delusion then no matter what he answered, she would still remain dubious. "I mean from the stress of all the money stuff? You know, losing my home, the recession…foreclosure…" Her stomach clenched just saying these words.

"Hah!" Chagall said, brushing off the seat of his work pants. There were two sizable wet spots there from the damp ground, but they vanished seconds after he stood. "You Americans call it hardship if you can't afford six vacations a year and fois gras each night! I lived through two wars, and granted, I was in Europe and not America during what you called your Great Depression, but I am certainly no stranger to poverty. Nor to persecution."

It was the first time the two had exchanged words. Phoebe had been hoping for something a little more revelatory, not a lecture.

"Listen," Phoebe sighed. "I have a deadline coming right up and I admonish myself plenty, usually all night long when I should be sleeping, so I really don't need some *phantom*, an artist who, by the way, actually got to experience that rare phenomenon of being appreciated in his own lifetime, telling me to stop sniveling. I cannot even believe I am seeing you, really, and I certainly shouldn't be talking to you aloud. So no offense, but please don't visit me anymore."

"Phoebe, my daughter, this wounds me," Chagall said, hanging his head and bringing his hand up to his heart. Gamut whimpered and sat at the painter's heels, choosing sides. "We, none of us, knows the depth and breadth of the mysteries of the world. I have seen many wonders since I departed this Earth and I am seeking answers still. But all I can tell you is this: *You* chose *me*. I do not have the power to return randomly to visit the living. You called out to me and I responded. I cannot leave until we solve your problem. I am sorry, but that's how this works."

"I did *not* call out to you! I do not even call out to the living for help very often, let alone the dead. What are you talking about? Whose rules are these? Who is in charge? Is there a God? Heaven? Hell? Nothingness? What happens after you die? Where are you returning *from?*"

Chagall walked across her yard, his brows knit with concern, and stood near her.

"Too many questions when we hardly know one another. May I?" he asked, pointing to her paintbrush.

"Paint? You want to paint?" Phoebe sputtered.

"Well, being back here for such a short while, I am still not sure about the rules. I have discovered that I have so little physical strength, to move solid objects and the like, that I doubt I could actually paint unassisted. But I suppose that if I have a conduit, a medium—like you, for example—I can somehow activate things, work through the person. If you don't mind...?"

Phoebe held the paintbrush up in the air as if she were about to start painting herself. "I'm game," she said. "Channel away."

"Thank you," Chagall said. "I appreciate it, since I know artists are reluctant to share their tools."

At that moment, she felt Chagall set to work, *through* her. It was her arm, dipping the brush into the water then rolling it in the brightest of her watercolors, letting the brush sit on the paper for a moment before moving on so that the colors bled outside of their borders, so that each creature and structure was saturated with color and life. But everything felt sped up. Her fingertips felt tingly, but other than that there was no sense that the ghost was inhabiting her. It was more like he was a conductor and she playing an instrument under his direction. Even though Phoebe was holding the paintbrush, she was watching the act happen outside of herself. She witnessed the creation taking place on her canvas as if it was animation: everything in flight, the red raven, the green raven, the clusters of purple grapes they were offering one another.

The atmosphere of the canvas was filled with floating wine bottles and anthropomorphic olive trees and even what looked like a small Ferris wheel that had come off its base and was being chased down a shady lane by a child with her smiling head upside down on her neck. Phoebe felt like she was on some sort of wild ride, no longer in control, just swept along within something larger than herself, and her breath came in shallow, rapid puffs. She began to giggle and couldn't stop.

"*Voila!*" Chagall said, spinning around and relinquishing her brush, then stepping aside so she could see what he—with her help—had done. She felt a loss when he was no longer at the helm, for what artist wouldn't leap at the chance to paint like Chagall, to actually channel his creative process, if only for an hour?

"I am not typically a watercolorist," Chagall said, looking at the canvas they had painted in tandem. "But here is a wine label that I myself would like to see on a bottle of Cabernet Sauvignon. Though we all know that it's what is inside the bottle that matters more."

The painting was exquisite. It was too wondrous and full of life to shrink onto a mere wine label, and Phoebe knew even now that she would save it, frame it, maybe even show it as proof to any disbelieving friends when she told them how she had been visited by the ghost of none other than the maestro himself, Marc Chagall. She wondered too if she would retain some sort of bodily memory of how it was done, if she could replicate such painting after he had left her. God she hoped so.

"It is beautiful," Phoebe said raptly. "Thank you. I still can't believe you have chosen me for some reason. I can't understand why, and I just can't believe…"

"The painting is just a suggestion, my dear, an example of another way to see. And again I must remind you, *you* asked for me and I came. Not me specifically, I will clarify, but with problems that, it was believed, I in particular could assist you in solving. So in other words, I am on assignment and have been matched with you to work on that."

"Hiya, Mimi!" Teddy slurred from over the fence. "Talkin' to your picture?" His greetings were always laced with some sarcasm that she, especially at this amazing moment, could not stand.

"Guess I am, Teddy," she yelled back, gritting her teeth in irritation and looking away from the canvas for a minute to wave at him perfunctorily. When she turned back, the canvas was once again blank and Chagall nowhere to be seen.

Of course, Phoebe thought, stamping her foot involuntarily in frustration. *I imagined that entire thing. God, this is getting too weird. Maybe I should talk with someone, a therapist. But I can't afford it right now. Maybe I'll just Google "hallucinations while under stress."*

Though Phoebe was deeply disappointed that the painting was gone, she threw some toys for the dogs for a few minutes to clear her head, then set back to work. She had no sense of how much time had gone by since Marc Chagall had painted *through* her, but she noted incredulously that when she took up her brush to start fresh, it was indeed still stained with the remnants of some bright fuchsia paint, a color that, under normal circumstances, Phoebe herself never would have used.

CHAPTER EIGHT

Moshe knew that it was his mother, more than his father, who was behind his studying art. He knew it was she who had encouraged his drawings and paintings, even when he was just a young boy, to the point of enlisting their neighbor Peter, already renowned for his artistic prowess, to tutor him in the man's studio. But though his mother wanted to expose her firstborn to as many opportunities as she could, she may have been less supportive if she could have predicted that it would take Moshe away from his family.

Peter looked down at his work that first day and said, "How did you learn to draw?"

"I copy pictures from books," the boy replied. He could not tell from Peter's expression if he found promise in his drawings or not, but he must have seen something there, since he did agree to take the boy under his wing, and free of charge.

"That mama of yours is quite the saleswoman," Peter said, handing the boy's drawing back.

"Yes," Moshe said. "She is well suited for running the grocery store. I hope I am worth the investment."

Peter began tutoring his new pupil using traditional figure studies, classical Greek busts and bowls of fruit and the like. For weeks, Moshe kept waiting for some more experimental exercises while really trying to hone his practical skills. But he was forced to admit that he was restless, that replication had never been where his heart lay. Moshe did not want to seem unappreciative, but he already had some of his own ideas about how to paint and draw.

"You're not giving this much effort," Peter said to him one day after class. "Does art no longer appeal to you?"

"Very much," Moshe said, putting down his pencils and shutting his tablet. "But not so much just still lifes and realism. I...how to explain this? I want the skill to draw and paint what is in front of me, yes. But more than that, I want to show what is *inside* of me."

It was true that often what poured forth from his student didn't necessarily resemble the subjects as literally as Peter might have liked. But he had seen promise in the boy, even though he felt he was making poor artistic choices. He looked at Moshe for a moment as if trying to make a decision, then said, "Then I can't teach you anything more, because it is my belief that art is fundamentally about the classical work, the exercises and the learning how to look at objects and really see them in their entirety. That is what I believe makes for a serious artist. These other more modern interpretations...I am sorry. I cannot offer you that."

Moshe was torn. He was worried that he was being arrogant, ungrateful. But Peter was having none of that. and even helped convince his parents, no small feat, that their son showed promise and should attend the Imperial School of Fine Arts in St. Petersburg, even though that meant leaving Vitebsk. After all, Peter reasoned with them, there had been higher expectations of this boy. He was the eldest son, with eight younger siblings and by rights should have just stepped into his father's line of work. Yet, in fairness, if his mother had seen something special in him, had fought so hard all his life to expose him to culture, to violin and art and piano, why should either she or her husband be so surprised that now he wanted to really reach for that goal of making art, and to dedicate himself ? What did they expect?

"What will you do for money in St. Petersburg?" his father had shouted when he confessed that yes, it was true, he wanted to continue with his art studies. "Making drawings does not put food in the belly. You're a Jew and there are quotas for all the state schools. Your mother won't be there to pull strings. Here, you can come with me to the warehouse. You have family. You have work. Here, you have a future."

"I will do whatever I have to do to study there," he had told them in a voice more forceful and defiant than he had ever used before. "I cannot stay here. I want more."

His parents could do nothing to convince their son otherwise, so they sent him off with enough money to get settled, hoping that he would see how idealistic he was being and soon return. This money quickly vanished but, true to his vow, Moshe cleaned houses, retouched photos, made signs—anything that would keep him in school and art supplies. It was all worth it. Even in his wildest dreams, Moshe couldn't have predicted that by the age of twenty, he would actually be in St. Petersburg, at the Imperial School of Fine Arts, living and breathing art, art history, model drawing, oil classes, sculpture, pastels. It had taken so much effort to get there, was so contrary to everything that his life was supposed to be, that as he explored the bustling streets those first weeks, he could scarcely believe that he was actually a resident of this beautiful, enormous city.

His family never let him forget how lucky he was, to be a Jew at this magnificent art school, this "window onto Paris." Each morning, tired from working so many jobs and being in this strange and giant city, he spoke words of encouragement aloud to himself, as if he was both the runner in a race and the onlooker cheering him. He *had* to keep believing in his own potential, and prove it to those in a position to help him. Talent was never enough.

Luckily, he befriended one such man, a lawyer named Max Vaclar, who was so taken with his work, that he gave him a monthly stipend to ease his life somewhat in the new city, eventually even offering to send him to Rome or Paris—anywhere he wanted to further his studies. In time, Moshe began to shared his patron's confidence in himself. He no longer felt like the simple village boy Moshe Shagal. He was now a twenty-year-old man, an artist, who called himself Marc Chagall.

When he finally made it to Paris, Marc roamed the streets in a constant state of gratitude, and more, of excitement. *This* was where art was being created, where fresh ideas were being born. How he wished he spoke the language! *Just be patient,* he told himself. *There are enough of us refugees here that we will find one another.* And so they did.

It was four o'clock in the afternoon and Chagall was waiting at a table in local hub, Café Verre Volant, the aptly named Flying Glass. Yes, he actually had someone to wait for: his new friend, the astonishing poet Guillaume Apollinaire. Guillaume was an inspiration, as ease everywhere, larger than life and he spoke Polish, French, Italian, and, blessed fellow, Russian. Chagall wanted to buy his friend a drink, but felt around in his pocket for some change and came up with only a few sad centimes, light and puny, insubstantial coins, probably not enough for a cup of coffee, and certainly too few for the *Saucisse de Toulouse,* sausage and mashed potatoes, that was the special of the day. A shame too, because its fragrance was filling his nostrils and making him salivate.

"*S'il vous plait,*" Chagall called out to the waiter, the French new and daring on his tongue. "*Un café.*" The waiter nodded and, out of the goodness of his heart, also placed a small basket of baguette on the table next to the coffee. He knew hunger when it looked up at him, though so many of these young artists were too proud to admit it.

Even though Chagall was surprisingly homesick for his village, for Russia, his language, things familiar, he knew he was in the best part of Paris for an artist. Montparnasse. He had immediately found a very cheap room in an odd twelve-sided building called La Ruche, or the Beehive. The rooms were shaped like wedges of cheese and utterly lacking in amenities, but God, the company! Georges Braque, Jean Cocteau, Diego Rivera, Maxim Gorki, Chaim Soutine, Max Jacob, Amedeo Modigliani, and yes, his friend now, Guillaume Apollinaire. These were his *neighbors!* Chagall put three lumps of sugar in his coffee and, stirring dreamily, smiled at the very thought of it. Jews, immigrants, poets and artists, he was in the thick of things, a moment in history that he was sure had never existed before and would never again.

No one slept. His floor was littered with old soup cans and spattered with drops of paint. At any hour, he could hear singing or fighting in Italian, the wailing of a disgruntled model, political arguments in Spanish or Russian, the squawks of escaped chickens that Modigliani had brought back from Les Halles to sketch, and of course the endless debates about Picasso and Braque and this new Cubism. Why shatter images when whole they contained so much? Chagall always asked them this during their great, marathon discussions of art. But even in his own work here, in this City of Light, he could not help but be influenced by the movement, by the experimentation of his peers, and he found prismatic versions of pitchers and soldiers and plates of fruit inserting themselves unbidden into his paintings. He was living in a great goulash of ideas and passion, and felt compelled to be worthy of such company.

"What, you are not hungry?" Apollinaire asked, arriving flushed with pearls of rain in his dark hair, bending down to kiss him on each cheek.

"You torture me, my friend," Chagall said, slapping the contents of his pockets onto the table. "No allowance for another week and I have to buy paint, not food. I wish I could treat you to...."

"Ask the owner if you can trade a drawing for a plate of sausage," Apollinaire interrupted. "He's very accommodating." Apollinaire reached across the table and to take a gulp of Chagall's very sweet coffee, then, making a face, he pushed it back towards him. "And just look at these walls: you'll be in good company!"

Chagall recognized now that all the framed and unframed, large and small, quick sketches and paintings that wrapped around the café's walls were the creations of his peers. He was still fairly new in town, but had already come to know their various styles. He stood, swallowing his pride, stood, and approached the owner with the proposition of a trade, *Saucisse de Toulouse* for a drawing?

"Are you going to be famous?" the owner asked him, brusquely, barely looking up from his skilled espresso-making. "Because I only do trades with artists who are going to be famous."

"Yes, then!" Chagall said enthusiastically, hunger giving him the necessary confidence. "That would be me. I am going to be very, very celebrated."

He set two cups down on the counter then shouted "*Deux espress!*" so loudly that Chagall jumped back. Then he looked him up and down and asked: "Do you have paper with you?" he asked.

"Can I use this?" He showed the owner his sketchbook tablet, the papers rippled from dampness.

The owner sighed and, with a sweep of his hand, directed Chagall's attention to the vast array of African masks and Minotaurs and nudes and slices of fruit, all depicted on every manner of canvas and tacked to the wall.

"Okay. If you think so. Why not?" he said, jutting his chin out, motioning him to sit.

"Who makes less money," Apollinaire asked genially once the waiter set the delicious plate of sausage down in front of Chagall, "poets or artists?"

The waiter thought a moment, then answered, "Artists. It is a close contest, but I say this only because an artist has to buy paint, and *usually,*" and here he shot a glance at Chagall's sketchbook, "supplies. Whereas the poet just needs a pen and something to write on. But then, I have a soft spot for painters. But don't worry, the boss does not discriminate. Sometimes he feeds the poets, too. *Bon appetit.*" And with this he placed a savory, steaming dish down on the table.

"Help yourself," Chagall told his friend, barely controlling his impulse to just bend his head to the food and consume, like a wild animal on a fresh kill. "But let me eat a little first before I faint."

"No, I have eaten. You enjoy. I will have a coffee."

Chagall wondered if his friend was lying just to allow him his fill, but he was too hungry to insist. Chagall almost wept with the pleasure of the savory dish, the meat, the way the sauce with its perfect spices coated every vegetable. When he had finished, Apollinaire asked, "You said you had a new painting to show me?"

Chagall was drawing now, the pay for his meal, and though it was tricky not to tear through the wavy paper with his sharp pen, Chagall had managed to draw a carousel figure, this time a billy goat, wearing a beret and smoking a cigarette, a mermaid swimming in the space above him. He signed it boldly in the right lower corner, and presented it to the owner, who studied it a moment, nodded once, then took a small hammer out from under the cash box and added it to the wall of sundry offerings.

When Chagall sat back down, he picked the conversation up again, answering Apollinaire's query.

"The new painting is an oil. A tribute to the girl I am going to marry," Chagall said excitedly. "Her name is Bella. I met her, strangely enough, while I was in school in in St. Petersburg, even though she lives in my own village. I was on a visit home and there she was. What do the French say? *Le coup do foudre?* A bolt of lightening. Funny how you leave a place, then something happens that makes you return again and again."

"Ah, Bella! Means beautiful!" Apollinaire said. "And is she also beautiful? And Italian?"

"Yes, very beautiful. And no, not Italian, only her name. Absolutely Russian. She is my Russia. She knows me completely already, without any history between us. We both were alone on the street of my village one day and we just looked at one another and the rest of our lives were set in that second. Even her silence is my own."

"Ah, my friend," Apollinaire said, shaking his head and taking a swig of the wine he had ordered, "you are such a romantic. No wonder you will not join in with these Cubists. Too much head and too little heart. And where is this bride-to-be?"

"She is still too young, and she is still in Russia."

"How young?" he asked, cocking an eyebrow with interest.

"She is fifteen. But when it is time, when my art is showing in galleries, when I go back to Russia, I will marry her. I know it. Her parents are jewelers, and they, of course, think I am beneath her, but what we feel… well, we will prove that ours is not some fleeting infatuation. Look, it is all here in the painting. It is called *Dedicated to My Fiancée.*" With this, Chagall reached into his satchel and produced a rather shocking painting, which he laid on the table. It depicted a man with a bull's head, a lusty, confident look in his large eyes, wearing a red robe. A woman was curved around his shoulders, a thread of saliva between their mouths, a wine carafe and a hookah at the bull's feet.

Apollinaire slapped his forehead. "No, this is too good! *Mio dio!* But it should be called, *Golden Ass Smoking Opium.* It is more bawdy than your usual."

"Bawdy?" Chagall asked earnestly, wanting to be clear on the sense of the word.

"Well, let's just say, it is not cherubic nudes and bearded villagers playing fiddles," Apollinaire said, holding the painting up in front of his face and cocking his head as if looking into a mirror.

"Will anyone want to show my work?" Chagall asked, sweeping his wild forelock off his face with great urgency. "I can't tell anymore if it's good or a waste of time."

"Yes…and soon." Apollinaire took a gulp of the wine he had ordered and licked his lips. "I have been speaking to some people who are quite captivated by your paintings. All this fresh color, seen through the optimistic eyes of the newcomer. Yes, I think you told the truth to the *patrone* tonight. You definitely *are* going to be famous."

"And you," Chagall said, clapping his friend on the back, encouraged. "And all of us here in this inspiring place in this stunning moment in these modern times! And oh! Can I ask you something?"

"Anything," Apollinaire answered.

They were both fervent and a little drunk and feeling every utterance as if it was the most important thing ever spoken. Perhaps too it was the of sleep, the wonderful fullness of his belly, or all the fast transitions demanded of him in this new city, but Chagall asked in absolute sincerity, "Is it allowed to spend the night in the Louvre? I want to live there, be amongst it all. A few hours here and there will not do."

Apollinaire thought a moment, rubbing his chin, then shook his head gravely, resisting his first impulse to laugh.

"I think, unless you could manage somehow to get locked in, the guards will throw you out at closing time. You must spend the night inside only in your dreams. Do you think you can you do that, my friend?"

"Yes," Chagall said, as if rising to a challenge. "Yes, I believe I can."

He got up and downed the last of the wine in his friend's glass. "Want to join me?"

CHAPTER NINE

"Voila," said Bernadette, smiling graciously and placing the breakfast tray down in front of the Germans. "*Oeuf a la Coq pour deux, miel de Lavandre, et pain aux noix, fait a la maison, et les café presse. Bon appetit!*"

On some level, Bernadette always half-expected a small spate of applause when she set down her breakfasts. Everything except the coffee—which meant the goat butter, the walnut bread, the lavender honey, the eggs, and the *chevre*—all of it was prepared from the animals she raised or the fruits and vegetables she grew right there on the farm. She even made the bowls, plates, and cups that the food was served from, when she had time to get into her pottery studio, usually in the off season. And all this done by a woman in her early eighties! Bernadette exulted in her ability to take the bounty of her own land and transform it into pleasure for her guests. Whether it took the form of lavender oil or beeswax candles or her own olives and cheeses cured in the lavender, they would have an experience to remember at *La Ruche de Lavande*.

It was a lovely August morning, promising a wonderfully warm afternoon, not the oppressive heat Provence had endured the past two summers. If she paused for a moment in the midst of her chores, Bernadette could hear the bees working over the lavender fields—thousands of them, so many that the air buzzed. Two more weeks till the lavender harvest and almost all her rooms were rented through October. She even had a big group of cyclists from the Byroads Company booked this month, and they were always easy guests. Last year had been another story, what with that heat and all the Americans in fear that they would be losing their homes and not spending anything for travel. It felt like something must have shifted in the U.S., and in Europe, too, though things were still not as busy as they had been only a decade ago, when the streets of France were bustling with happy tourists.

And now, this summer, she was almost too busy, so maybe with this wonderful new president—though the poor man had inherited such a colossal mess—just maybe things were looking up again. Her sons had agreed to come and give her a week's break in September so she could recharge and take her own vacation. One could only do so many petanque-and-pistou evenings before one began to crack.

Ah, her sons. Pasqual, off in Paris working in a skyscraper, his career something involving solar energy—always a do-gooder, that one; and Gerard, in Tahiti, married to that gorgeous women who had provided her with exceptional grandchildren, even though Bernadette suspected the woman hadn't more than a high school education. Bernadette adored her sons and respected their choices, and she certainly could never have fixed up this farm, all the stone buildings in such disrepair, without the masonry skills both boys possessed.

"*Merci*, Madame," said her German guest's wife, clearly admiring the plates set before her. Bernadette nodded, pleased. The Germans were regulars, booking their eight day stay the same week each time, years in advance, making certain they would never have to face a change of plans. Bernadette wondered what it must feel like to count on things so confidently, to feel that you had such control over life's vagaries. The wife was an affable woman, a bit mousy perhaps, but at least she made an effort, whereas the husband didn't even look up from his *Die Welt* when she put their food down. But he did keep booking, so at least she knew she had met the man's impossible standards. And where did he get a German newspaper? A German newspaper every day of his vacation in their little village in the south of France? Did he have it sent? Her lavender farm was a good hour from Avignon.

Bernadette had to laugh to herself. Of all the fates, given her history, it was such perfect irony that the majority of her guests every year were German, given that her childhood was so clouded by the occupation. And why not? Why would anyone want to stay in a cold, grey place when one could be in the Luberon, on a working lavender farm? With three-hundred-year-old walnut trees and a swimming pool perched on a hill that looked out upon miles and miles of lavender? Sometimes, in a rare quiet moment, Bernadette couldn't believe she had ever been able to afford this place. But her apartment in Paris sold at its peak price, and though this farm needed a lot of work, the staff who had worked on the farm for decades promised that if she bought the place and kept them on to work in the fields and orchards, they would happily help her mend roofs and plaster walls and turn the big farmhouse into a proper B & B.

"Bernadette, did you make this jam?" an English guest called out to her as she returned to the kitchen to get a breakfast tray for another table. "It's delicious! I taste something I can't quite place…" Here she trailed off, taking another little cat lick from her spoon.

"*Auxmondes*," Bernadette told her, looking to her left and right before whispering, "almonds. I put a few in my cherry *confiture* and also in my apricot. It gives it a nice texture, too."

"I was going to guess marzipan, but it's milder than that. Thanks for satisfying my curiosity," she said, adjusting her spectacles back on her face and returning her focus to the book she was reading. Ah, the Brits, so chatty and cordial. She liked the Brits for their good nature, though often felt they never really rolled up their sleeves and dove into the place. The Americans, that was their role. Up at dawn to help with the lavender harvest. Asking if they could learn to milk the goats. Climbing up on ladders to pick cherries or walnuts or whatever was in season and needed to be picked. They were game for everything, but seemed incapable of just sitting still by the pool with a book or lingering after dinner until midnight, talking. They were very energetic and up for new things, but lacked staying power. And the Italians…ah, the Italians. The humor, the *joie de vivre*, their appreciation of a good meal, a good wine. The way they were with their children. Bernadette wished she had more Italian guests, but it was usually Germans and Americans—and now, with the dollar ailing, principally only the Germans.

But this week, they had a nice mix. She overheard that Brad, a sunny, six-foot-three-inch architect from Chicago, was trying to organize a game of pétanque later in the afternoon when it cooled off somewhat.

"Whaddya say, people?" he called out, patting his firm body dry with his towel after swimming many laps in the pool. "It'll be us and the Aussies and the Brits, the English speakers, against the Germans and Italians and French. We'd be at a disadvantage, since we don't play pétanque in our native lands."

"We play it," the British woman chimed in. Then added less surely, not wanting to seem mutinous of her new unit, "On occasion."

"Yes," said the Italian, walking to the edge of the pool, "you will indeed be at a disadvantage. But you are all so used to being the big sporty first-place winners in everything that a little humility will be good for you."

He was clearly not mean-spirited in the least, so everyone eating breakfast around the pool joined in the playful rivalry. The wife of the Australian said, "Yes, but we catch onto things so quickly where I come from, being such a wild and young country, that we may end up beating you pros anyway."

"I can see this is going to be a rousing game of Booce," said the Italian, rubbing his hands together. He leaned down and said in a low voice to the English woman: "And Baci, similar to the name of our game, you know that means kiss?" With this he turned and did a cannonball into the pool, making a big splash that caused those closest to the water to groan and make a fuss. So much for the rule of waiting twenty minutes after eating to swim.

A French woman called out to Bernadette in French, saying, "I think things will go much better for our game this evening, Bernadette, if we are supplied with copious quantities of pastis. And ice! The Americans love their ice!"

At that, everyone who understood laughed and Bernadette replied, "I'll make a *pistou* for after the game, and we can all celebrate our wins or drown our woes in lots and lots of garlic."

The guests hoisted their coffee cups in a toast, then, as if choreographed, rose from their various tables and scattered, off to explore *La Belle Provence.*

CHAPTER TEN

"Well, that's a horse of another color," Phoebe's boss James said, looking at her sketches. "Wow, Phoebe, what happened to you, somebody press the overdrive button on your color palette?"

"Listen, do you like it or not?" Phoebe asked him, surprised by just how much she wanted his approval. "Because I think these are some of the best labels we've ever had and I think they're going to sell a lot of your wine. Look at Yellowtail from Australia. Before them, everyone thought, 'Oh, let's just have an understated wine label. It looks classier.' Then they came out with that yellow kangaroo and made a gazillion dollars on their Shiraz, and now everyone's getting playful and taking chances."

"Calm down, calm down, I hear you," James said, pausing to study a particular label that featured a trio of ravens in primary colors, standing on each other's shoulders balancing on a galloping green horse, acrobat-style. "I like these!" he pronounced. "I really do. I'm impressed. They're just…not your typical style."

"Oh?" Phoebe asked. "And how would you describe my typical style?"

"Great, but usually more…traditional. Less…vivid? You know, more like what a person might actually see around them. But hey, let's get at least a couple of these going and see how they're received. Let's

see, I'm thinking we should we just start out with fifty cases of the Zin
using…um…this one? The image of the hot pink ravens tossing grapes
back and forth to one another with the upside-down weeping willow
tree below. Phoebe? You think that one is better for the Zin or the Cab?"

"James, we need labels for both of these vintages," Phoebe said, laying some more of her paintings on his table. She had never been this
assertive before, and honestly, she was enjoying it. She felt reckless, as
if there were some other person inside her that did not care about losing this job—or rather, a person who never even considered that this
would be the outcome. This Phoebe was different from the one who
agonized about her current, dismal financial state and tread lightly
whenever possible around her boss. The Phoebe with all the confidence
continued, "Why not just take a chance, James? Use two of my paintings and get the Cabs and the Zins out there. We've never waited to see
the public's reaction to a wine label before. It's not like it's obscene or
something. What's the risk?"

"Oh, I don't know…" he said, lifting the corner of several of the
paintings gingerly. Then he visibly brightened and looked up at her.
"Sorry, Phoebe. I'm guess I'm just getting a bit stodgier in my old age.
Change always discombobulates me. And what with the economy and
all." He trailed off, as people often did after uttering those words, "the
economy," as if it was an omnipotent foe, or worse, as if it was Fate.
"What with the economy" encompassed all that was shaky and unknown.

"James, you're younger than I am. And discombobulation can be a
good thing, for Ravenswing and all of us, from time to time."

"Clearly you are a proponent," he said, holding up her drawings
again and cocking his head one way then the next, like a dog might
when it heard a noise it did not recognize. "What say you, young Kate?"
he asked in Medieval fashion, bringing Kate into the discussion. In that
playful question Phoebe distinctly heard something new…deference?

"I think they're the best stuff she's ever done," Kate said without
hesitation. She had been quiet until now—until she saw that James was

on board. "They're like a good dream. They're out of the ordinary. I wish the world *did* look like this. What a blast that would be!"

"A bit dizzying," James said. "Well, I guess we'll run them both as planned and keep our fingers crossed. Seems a bit of a foolhardy time to take chances, though, given how sales are down and everyone is still cutting back. My God, will they ever *stop* cutting back? If this 'downward turn' keeps up, entire generations will have to be re-educated. Our generation will be the last to have known abundance and a sense of security. We will have to hire tutors to show our youth how to spend their money on things like wine or travel or flowers. It will be bred out of upcoming generations like the pinkie toe, and they will have to be reconditioned."

Phoebe interrupted, as she saw that James was warming to the theme and would begin to run with it.

"Or," she said excitedly, "maybe a recession is the *best* time to do something foolhardy. After all, nothing left to lose!"

After the meeting, Phoebe walked across the property, past the wild roosters that strutted all over Sonoma like they owned the place. Purportedly, the fowl were the result of a long-ago spat between two locals, one angry man just setting them loose around town, knowing they would proliferate like mad, cause traffic snares and be a general nuisance. Many of the roosters seemed to like this particular spot at the vineyard, enjoying everything the mighty old Live Oak trees had to offer: the shade, their acorns, and even, nearby, an errant clump of grapes or two.

Phoebe stood in the courtyard for a few minutes before entering the tasting room. She had always loved that idea, that there were entire rooms all over the two Valleys designated for the sole purpose of tasting. She halted on the patio, mesmerized by a hummingbird sipping from blossom after blossom along a trumpet vine, his sparkling emerald body nearly disappearing into the throat of the flowers. It was always cooler in the tasting room, its long wooden counter and tall chairs polished to a high gloss. The walls were lined with large, stately portraits in heavy gilded frames of all the Italian ancestors who had started Ravenswing, all the way up to the portrait of James and his wife and two daughters, with their rescued, jittery greyhound, Crush, displaying perfect erect posture at the family's feet. In the hearth, Felipe had put an old white stoneware pitcher filled with multi-hued sunflowers he had picked from around the property and already there was a faint skirt of yellow pollen from their centers around the vase.

"Hi, Felipe," Phoebe said, walking behind the bar and giving him a hug. "How's the inebriation biz?"

"Hey, Phoebe," he said, holding an empty wine glass up to the light to check for water spots. "Not many people out yet. Give 'em another hour, then they can justify some sampling. What are you up to?"

"Painting, actually. Lots. I'm inspired. Maybe them cutting my hours way back here was a gift on one level, though pretty soon I won't be able to afford paint and will have to start making my own from grass or mashed blackberries. Still, something's gotten into me where I just want to paint. Oh, and plant seeds. Is August too late to plant Cosmos?"

"Nah, they start to reseed themselves pretty soon, so whatever the finches don't get, you can help along. I know, I hear ya about the money situation. Everyone says the economy is improving, but they've cut my hours back, too. Listen, I've got something here that is very special," he said, lowering his voice and bending down to bring up a bottle with no label from under the sink. "Want to try a Malbec from my own vines?" He gave Phoebe a proud smile, poured her some, then began swirling it furiously around in the glass to aerate it. "Take a whiff," he commanded, placing the precious sample in front of her.

When the liquid settled, Phoebe shut her eyes and held it up to her nose.

"Mmm. Plums."

"And?" he asked excitedly.

She took another sniff. "Cedar?"

"Yes, good job! I actually put strips of cedar near the roots to give it a little vanilla."

She took a sip, and shut her eyes and rolled it around on her tongue.

"Wow, Felipe! All I can say is watch out, Argentina! This is wonderful. You should give James a taste."

"Yeah, I'm just not so sure how he feels about me competing with him." Here they both burst into laughter, as Felipe had only a few plants in his front yard, about a third of an acre, and Ravenswing had ten thousand.

"It is moments like these that one rues the fact that one is no longer alive," Chagall sighed wistfully, sitting on the bar and lowering his head to sniff the bottle of Malbec. Chagall looked startled and jerked back from the bottle. Was he mistaken or was his sense of smell actually returning ever so slightly since he had first arrived? Phoebe stopped laughing, her eyes darting between Chagall and Felipe, who continued to chew on his wine with a look of deep concentration. Nope—nobody saw the ghost but her. Phoebe let out her breath, then downed the last gulp of her sample.

"Well, Felipe, thanks for that taste. I'm off."

"Good to see you," he said, and as Phoebe turned to go, she saw that Chagall had managed to lift the little stained Malbec cork from the countertop and place it in his pocket. He gave her an impish smile, then was gone.

Phoebe was meeting her actress friend Molly for a glass of champagne at Glorieta's Champagne Cellars at four. They hadn't seen each other in weeks and were eager to catch up. Given how overextended Molly perennially was, Phoebe knew she could take her time driving there, as her friend wouldn't arrive until at least forty minutes past, right about when the workers wanted to close and go home. But the folks who worked there knew the two friends and indulged them, allowing them to order right up until the last minute. For years, this had been their spot, where they had helped each other through divorces, illness, worries about their kids, and where they came to celebrate as well. Perched high on a hill, sitting on the outdoor patio, the women had talked through all types of weather, looking out at rows of vines laden with those diminutive, sweet champagne grapes. In fact it was on that very patio that Phoebe had made the vow that someday she would find a house in Sonoma and move here. Driving up Glorieta's long driveway now, Phoebe actually found herself wishing Chagall would show up again. She had so many questions about her future, about what advise he could give her to save her from the precipice, questions that Molly couldn't possibly answer.

Phoebe parked, grabbed her small black journal that was filled with sketches and poetry she had composed, and made her way up the steps to the tasting room and patio. Halfway up the steps, a man with curly dark hair was deeply engaged in conversation with another man. He was gesticulating insistently with his hands and Phoebe thought he looked very familiar but could not place him. As she stepped aside to let them pass she overheard his friend say to him, "I'm telling you, Ray, give this guy a show. Sure, he's edgy, but your gallery could use an infusion of young blood."

Ah, it was the man from the restaurant—Fitch, with the robust, Satyric, Mediterranean look that she was powerfully drawn to, the wild Neptune brows, the playful mouth, the imposing nose. And that fury of black curls. He glanced up at Phoebe as they passed one another and they shared a cordial smile, but did not stop. *Why would he,* Phobe asked, telling herself to stop being ridiculous. As she took her glass of champagne out to the terrace and found a table in the shade, she thought, *small world.* She took out her journal and started a poem, deciding to call it "Rough Patch:"

Does is show? Is it glaringly apparent?
I am like the lizard that has
dropped its beautiful blue tail,
& barely slipped out of their grasp—
Let the predators hunt that discarded thing instead.
But now, with its one life-saving trick
used up, lost

it slinks about,
Waiting, truncated and vulnerable,
For a new one to regenerate,
Knowing too that what grows in its place
could never be so colorful.

Ach, woe is me, Phoebe said, reading over what she'd written.

"Sorry I'm late," Molly said, out of breath. "Horrendous traffic from Berkeley. I want your job, by the way," she added, smiling over at the male component of a couple at the table next to their own. A shameless flirt, her friend Molly. He, of course, smiled back.

"Hmm," Phoebe said dubiously, deciding not to chastise her this time for being a half-hour late. She closed the book on her sad little poem. She appreciated her visits with Molly even more these days. It was nice to be around someone whose life was as much in shambles as her own.

"I took the liberty of ordering us some smoky almonds and two glasses of their 2005 Brut Rose. Yum yum. Just look at that color!" Molly said. "Like the tutus we used to wear in ballet class."

When Phoebe held the fluted glass up to her lips, the effervescence tickled the tip of her nose. Molly moved Phoebe's half-finished first glass out of the way, cleared her throat officiously, then took a taste of the Brut Rose, savoring it with her eyes closed. Pleased, she held her glass out and made a reverential toast: "To the cotton candy and straw-berries that gave their lives for this glass of champagne."

With this, the two friends clinked glasses. They sipped in silence, looking out at the olive groves off to the right and all the rolling green below. Two sparrows squabbled over a breadcrumb at the base of their table. A diminutive butterfly the color of moonstone fussed within the blossoms of the Butterfly Bush to their left. It was so quiet, the entire patio simultaneously caught up in contemplation, that Phoebe could hear the fizz in her glass. At last, she asked, "Mol, do you believe in ghosts?"

Phoebe had definitely not intended to bring this up with anyone, but after a glass of champagne, she was something of a blurter.

"Oh, most certainly," Molly said without hesitation. "When I had slumber parties as a teenager we would call back various dead celebrities using my Ouija board. Oh! Did you know that Ouija stands for yes-yes? As in *oui* and *ja*?"

"No, I didn't know that. So go on."

They could flit from topic to topic, interrupting themselves with sudden associations, for hours without ever losing their thread. Phoebe's ex had called it "Girlspeak."

"Anyway, I definitely saw the ghost of Marilyn Monroe. She had the fluttery white dress on like in *Seven Year Itch* and it swirled around her in the darkness. Everyone at the slumber party saw her, too, not just me. But I'm the only one who heard her speak."

"What did she say?" Phoebe asked, eating the last almond. She looked around, glad to see that there were still other people here; maybe they could order a second glass of the bubbly.

"'I have lost my pen.' And she said it in that breathy child's voice. It was very touching somehow and I wasn't afraid. And you know, I've always been a little psychic. Often I can sense who's on the other end of the phone before I pick it up. Or I'll wake up in the middle of the night and just *know* my son's in trouble at school. And sure enough, the next day, he'll phone and say: 'Mom, I got another ticket for tagging. Defacing public property. Man, don't they see that it's art?'"

They paused again to drink. Phoebe was relaxing, thinking about how nice it was to be around someone as quirky as she was. She said, "Molly, you don't really have to be psychic to see that coming. The kid never learns. Graffiti on canvas—good. Graffiti on wall of main library—bad."

"Yeah, I know," Molly sighed. "He's out from under my roof now so I can't lose sleep over it. But why'd you ask about ghosts? Visitations in the dark?"

"No, actually, in broad daylight. I wonder if I'm losing my mind."

"Ooh, that's a brave ghost!" Molly clapped her hands excitedly.

"He says that *I summoned him,* and only I can see him."

"Shucks! I would like to meet him. But wait, you *talk*?" Molly asked, some of her champagne foaming over the lip of her glass as she used it to gesticulate. "What does he look like?"

"Actually," Phoebe said, looking around to see if anyone was eavesdropping, "it's Marc Chagall. God, I shouldn't be talking about all this. I sound absolutely insane."

"Oh come on, it's Northern California. Nobody would even bat an eye if you said you were channeling the guy, let alone that you saw him one time."

"More than once. Plus…he painted. On my canvas. When I had a deadline at the winery."

"Oh my God! Show me!"

"The painting disappeared. But not before I saw it. And it was so beautiful, Mol. If only…it would have been some kind of proof." Phoebe stunned herself by bursting into tears.

"Phoebe, sweetie, what's going on?" Molly said, jumping up to console her.

"I feel old and all alone and I'm going to lose my house and those bastards won't qualify me for any of the programs they were supposed to qualify people like me for with all that bailout money. Plus, I'm seeing ghosts. I'm divorced. I can't get a job that pays much or gives me more work than twenty hours a week. My daughter doesn't need me anymore." Phoebe paused to inhale. It had all come rushing out of her. "I just feel…lost, Molly. And embarrassed. Useless."

"Is that all?" Molly said, hugging her. "Being forty and seeing ghosts, that's nothing. Feeling uninspired and afraid, that's what we should work on."

"I think I'm seeing Chagall because I'm stressed," Phoebe said, sniffing and blowing her nose on the napkin. "I thought I'd have a partner, some security, even advancements in my job by now. And my *home,*

Molly. If only I could count on that. I can't stand this feeling of helpless-ness, like every single thing is out of my hands."

"I know. Lots of folks are in the same boat, if that's any help. But let's talk Chagall," Molly said. "He said you called for him. I would im-mediately ask myself: What does Marc Chagall have to teach me?"

"Wow, Molly, you're so new-agey," Phoebe said, giving a short laugh and touching the corner of her eye with her fingertip.

"No, seriously, what has he *already* taught you? Of all the spirits, why him in particular?" Molly was clearly jazzed by all this. She leaned closer and took Phoebe's hands. "You have to look at these things. Stuff like this is a gift."

Phoebe appreciated her friend's openness to the supernatural, even her encouragement, but she knew most others would think she was losing it.

"Remember when we went to St. Remy in Provence all those years ago? Rented that tiny orange car, like a VW bug that had been cut in half…what was it?"

"A Thingo!" Molly cried. "God that was fun. I think getting lost in all those small villages and forking off all those roundabouts was the best! Remember when we swam naked in that lake and that snake started swimming toward you?"

"A deadly viper, no doubt. I remember the markets. Wow, so much sensual input. I was so happy there." Phoebe trailed off wistfully.

"Why are you thinking about all this now?" Molly asked. "Because Chagall lived there?"

"No, I just am trying to get back in touch with things that make me truly happy. I feel like…a husk. I'm really frightened by this appari-tion, Mol. It's not like me. And I know this is the *last* thing I *should* be moaning about, but I just wonder if I'll ever be able to afford to travel to France, or *anywhere* again. The thought that I may not go again before I die makes me feel absolutely defeated. Don't I sound spoiled?"

"Before you die? Oh, come on, my friend. People short on funds have been traveling since time immemorial. This may be something I can actually help you with, if you're flexible about the fashion in which you actually make it back there. You know you're not as bad off as many, right?"

Phoebe nodded, looking down. "Of course."

"I'll put my thinking cap on to see what I can come up with. Remember how my dental hygienist found that incredibly cheap spa in Mexico? She's really good at finding ways to travel for a pittance. I'll call her. But listen," Molly said sternly. "You swore to me you would try some of those online dating things. It's not healthy to be alone for too long. We start exuding some vibe, like don't-touch-me-I'm-just-fine. Besides, I know so many people who've met their soul mates that way. You've got to at least try."

"I know, I will. They're just so…frontal."

Now Phoebe noticed that the staff was staring at them from the bar, lined up with their arms crossed.

"Oh God, we're the last ones," Phoebe said, quaffing her champagne and standing. "Again."

"Sorry!" Molly called out to them. "Once we get started, you know…"

"No problem," their waitress said, but the minute the women stood and came inside the lights were shut off and everyone in the gift shop and the small kitchen began to leave. Walking down the many steps to their cars, Molly linked Phoebe's arm and said, "Leave it to me. We'll figure out a way for you to go back to France without spending money you don't have."

"No, I have to put that out of my mind. It should definitely not be a priority given the balance in my savings account. Sorry I brought it up. Sitting up there with you today made me miss Provence for some reason, that's all."

As Molly backed out of her parking space, she slowed down alongside Phoebe and rolled down her window, saying, "And promise me you'll think about this…visitation. Really, really ask yourself: What does this man have to teach me? What is he trying to tell me?"

"Alright. I'll give it some thought," Phoebe promised. "If I see him again, that is."

"Oh, you will," Molly said. "I don't doubt it for a second."

Phoebe sat in her car for a moment and watched her friend drive away. The dusk light was outlining all the flowers and leaves in a gilded pink, and as Phoebe looked up toward the tiered rows of vines, she did see him again, doing a little jig—a good dancer, she noted. He was making his way toward her car, walking down the hill like a tightrope walker, balancing a champagne flute on his head. Then there he was, in the passenger seat, ready to talk.

CHAPTER ELEVEN

"**L**ook at these paintings," Picasso said to Georges Braque as they barged into Chagall's studio. There was almost no space left on the floor and the visitors had to clear a path to his easel, carefully nudging months' worth of detritus out of the way with the toes of their shoes. The skins of tubes of paint that had been sliced open to get every last drop, stale heels of baguette, old cans, paint-stained rags, stubs of candles, eggshells—all of this and more littered the old wooden floor of the studio.

"Good God, man," Picasso said to him. "Being driven is one thing, but how can you create *anything* in this pig pen?"

"Well, here, none of the neighbors complain," Chagall said wryly. Picasso did not live in the Beehive, but would often visit—"slumming it," the other artists joked. Everyone who lived there felt lucky, knowing that they were in the thick of things, and they assumed that outsiders stood drooling at the gates.

"Georges," Picasso went on, tugging his friend by the arm and steering him toward this painting or that. He was not a tall man, but had the compact musculature of a gymnast. "See? What have I said? Our friend is not fully embracing Cubism, just dipping his toe in the water."

"Life is fractured enough," Chagall said, wiping his palms on his trousers and moving some newspapers off a chair so one of them could sit. "I do not see things splintered like that, like puzzle pieces."

"What did Monsieur Apollinaire call this new style of painting?" Braque asked, ignoring Chagall and leaning in for a closer look. "Supernatural?"

"Surreal," Picasso said. "But he does not really paint in that style, either. Marc!" Picasso suddenly cried, peering closer at one of Chagall's newest paintings. "Are you painting over used canvases?"

"Are you offering to buy me new ones?" Chagall answered.

Picasso grunted. He and some of the others had set up their studios in another oddly shaped Montmartre residence, named the *Bateau-Lavoir* or Laundry Boat because of the way the old structure creaked and swayed in the storms. Admittedly competitive with one another, the virtuosos loved nothing more than to get together and argue about art.

"But you can see the lines of the old paintings through your Gesso! At least apply it thicker!" Picasso continued. "Doesn't that earlier painting contaminate your visions for the canvas?"

"When I am through with the painting, every line visible to the eye will be a thread in a tapestry of my own weaving. Intentional," Chagall said. He had never had such a long conversation with the infamous Picasso and was enjoying the debate.

"And look at this, Georges," Picasso said. "The man has been in Paris for three years and what does he paint? Russia! Every painting some little scene from the *shtetl* he left behind. Fiddlers and rabbis and cows. Where is Paris in any of this?"

It was true that Chagall was homesick, especially since he was finally engaged to Bella. When he wasn't dreaming about sausage, or borsht, or even, God forbid, herring, each night when he finally stopped painting and allowed himself to sleep, he dreamed of Bella, waiting for him back in Russia. But what if she didn't wait? He had found his muse, his love, and if she met someone else while he was so far away, if she forgot about him and her promise, he would die. He played it over and over in his mind, how his mother had not liked the nude drawings of Bella that she had once found in his room. It had caused such a rift that he had taken a room in the home of a strong policeman with a fine, imposing moustache who said that he could paint whatever he liked there, and furthermore, that Bella could visit, too. He had looked at Chagall with a wink that the young artist had found distasteful and said: "I am what you would call a 'free thinker.'" Then there was the night he brought Bella there and they explored one another—with passion—yet only up to a point. He had not taken advantage of her, though no one, including their parents, would ever believe that. It had been heavenly, until Chagall tried to open the front door so he could walk his love back to her parents' house and found the door locked and them locked inside.

Desperate, he had no other solution but to lower her down to the street through an open window. How the neighbors had clicked their tongues, and the word spread, and afterward, Bella's parents liked him even less, if that were even possible. They only saw him as a penniless artist from a lowly background. What could he offer their Bella? And who would have believed him if he had told them, *We are both still as pure as the untrodden snow*, even though that would have been the truth, at least in terms of what the gossips were imagining.

Thinking about his fiancée made him grow anxious. It was fine for a young man to live with so little, but once he was married, he would have to have money. He urgently needed a one-man show, to get his career launched, to get his name and his work out into the public eye. If it weren't for the Louvre, the vitality of the art here in Paris, his beloved friends, and maybe the pastries, he would have returned home a week after he had arrived. And now, Bella beckoned him as well.

"Come, you've interrupted my concentration now. Take me out for lunch and I will let you tell me the secret to getting locked inside the Louvre," Chagall said to Picasso.

"Your work at the *Salon des Independents* was very well received, by the way," Braque told him once they were out on the street.

"Yet I sell very little. I need paint. I need food. I need a one-man show," Chagall said woefully.

"Ah, comrade," Picasso said, clamping his hand on Chagall's shoulder and shaking him, "you are far too obsessed with money. Just paint. Money has a way of arriving."

The waiter at Le Verre Volant, their home away from home, greeted the trio and showed them to their usual table by the window, then brought menus and a carafe of house wine. By 1914, the place had garnered a reputation for having a soft spot for artists, offering generous pours of wine and cheap food with large portions. Each time the trio arrived there were more works of art decorating the walls, which one artist or another had surely traded for food or drink.

"Easy for you to tell me," Chagall said, pouring himself a glass. "Since you already have some money and I do not."

"You have enough," Braque corrected. "Everyone, all of us, if we can paint and show and eat, we have enough. Paris is a good place for an artist with just enough. In fact," and here he raised his glass, "here is to having *just* enough! Better for the likes of us than having too much!"

Picasso hoisted his glass offhandedly, unimpressed by this toast, as he had already had some shows in galleries and his work was creating a stir. But the other men were in high spirits and it was good to be in Paris right then and there, in such great company, a part of a movement rippling through all the arts that felt so vital, so significant.

"Your poet friend," Picasso asked Chagall, "Apollinaire? He knows a lot of people who can help you. Ask him. He thinks the world of your paintings…even if they are old-fashioned."

"Not old-fashioned, my fractured friend," said Chagall. "But springing from a world where color is God and stories need to be told."

"Expressionism?" Braque asked. "The Germans are big on that."

"Maybe no 'ism' at all," said Chagall. "I just paint the world I love it as I see it. It is not 'realism,' but it is my reality."

Three days later Apollinaire entered Chagall's studio.

"Your dream is about to come true," he said, grabbing a broom and beginning to clean.

"Wait, Gui, there might be something important lying there!"

"No, because why would you put something important *on the*

floor?" he boomed. "And don't you even care that your dream is about to come true thanks to *moi*?"

"Which dream? I have so many…"

"Don't be such a sad sack, Marco. People always say we Jews have a persecution complex."

"We are persecuted! Look at how my paintings are always hung on the unlit back walls at salons and expos! Mine are as good as the others there."

"Marco, we are tough. With us Jews it always goes like that joke: People hate us, they try to kill us, they don't get everyone, let's eat. That sums up all the big holidays, don't you think?"

Apollinaire saw his friend getting worked up and wanted to steer the topic elsewhere, with a little humor. He himself had been raised in New York, and had often heard how hard it was for Jews in Russia. And now here, in Paris, so many Russian Jews were in his circle of friends that he heard their stories first hand.

"I know, I know, unfair," Apollinaire said. "But all that might be about to change. I know a very big cheese in Berlin, Herman Walkin, and he wants to show your work at *Der Sturm* gallery there. It's what you wanted—a one-man show!"

Apollinaire wanted Chagall to be as excited as he was about the great news, but he knew his friend would have to ask some questions first.

"Berlin!" Chagall cried. "But will my work be appreciated there? Aren't they keen on darker, more tragic work?"

"Not at all. Look, Marc, your work is full of emotion, theatrical, and so is Expressionism. I think they will appreciate you there because you are doing something new to their eyes. And they even have their own artist who paints blue horses whose last name is your first name, Franz Marc."

"Oh God, but do I have time? Which ones shall I offer him?" Chagall was now looking wildly around his studio. "When does he want them by?"

"You have a few weeks. I'm sorry the timing is so bad."

"Timing? Why?"

"Well, there is this small business about a *war*. Have you had your head in the sand? If it comes to that, and I am pretty certain it will, I plan to enlist."

"What? I have not heard much talk of this sort. And besides, why you? You are not even a French national!" Chagall shouted, for he already knew that he himself would avoid fighting in a war at any cost. He was Russian, and if Russia didn't want Jews in their schools and his father had to bribe people to get an apartment for his family, then why should he die for Russia in battle? No. And on top of this, he would not have lasted long on a battlefield—too thin, too fanciful.

"France is my home. It matters to me more that I be received here, in Paris, than any other place in the world. I would defend this city with my life gladly. I love you, Marc, but where do *you* call home? What would you be willing to die for?"

Chagall's first impulse was to shout, *Russia is my home, of course!* But he had been desperate to leave Russia. He had outgrown the life of his parents, his ghetto. Yet now that he was here, it was all he thought about. And Bella, his family, would he be willing to die for them?

"Maybe Berlin will be my home," he answered. "I have not been there yet. Maybe my home is a place I have not seen yet."

CHAPTER TWELVE

Phoebe had awoken early, and the minute she opened her eyes, even though she had not moved, the dogs began to wag their tails furiously where they lay on their round beds on the floor, intent, but never lifting their chins from the backs of their paws as they stared at their mistress in anticipation.

"Good morning, beasts," Phoebe said drowsily, and now Mechant and Gamut rose and pushed their snouts into her face and licked her until she squealed and had to blockade herself under a pillow. "Where's your toy, huh? Where's that toy?"

This was a trick she used to make them both leave the room in search of one of their plush toys so she could get dressed in peace. These toys were scattered throughout the house in the form of rhinos, wolves, buffalo—representations of the beleaguered animals for whose salvation she had donated small but annual amounts of money to one environmental group or another. The plush toys were a thank-you for her efforts to help protect the real creatures.

On her way to work, the cell phone rang. It was Molly, breathless and staticky as ever.

"I have some good news," she said. "Remember that dental hygienist I told you about, who always knows about great travel deals? Well, after we spoke last week I saw her and she said she was all signed up to go on this amazing trip to Provence with this active vacation company called Byroads, but now she has a conflict and she'll lose all her money if she cancels. She said you could have her spot for free if you give her a few bottles of your best wine with labels you've designed."

"Why would she do that?" Phoebe asked. "She doesn't even know me."

"I told her how much you need a vacation, and none of her friends can do it, so the whole thing will just be wasted unless you take it. But you'll have to commit by the end of the week, and you'll have to buy the ticket and find a dog sitter and pack and train…"

"Train?" Phoebe asked with concern.

"Well, you're in good enough shape but I think they bike something like thirty miles each day. But she also said it caters to all ages and levels, and there's a van that comes by and picks you up if you're flagging."

"Wow. I'm not sure, Mol—it's coming right up, so not much time to train. Plus, going to France when I can't afford my mortgage? Seems a little hedonistic, don't you think?"

"It's practically free, Phoebe! Don't kick a gift horse in the face."

"Look, Molly, not kick."

"What? Oh wait, a cop, hang on."

Phoebe heard rustling noises, which she assumed came from Molly throwing the cell phone down into her lap until the police passed. Then her friend resumed: "Look, you were just lamenting the fact that you may never get to go back there and you're going through a rough time, and I'm sure some of your friends who have more mad money than I would gladly lend you plane fare. After that, everything's taken care of. You know, Phoebe, things like this happen for a reason. Don't you think it was meant to be?" Molly often described things as being "meant to be."

"It does sound too good to pass up. Just let me sleep on it, Molly," Phoebe said.

"Okay, but I've got the Byroads catalogue right here, so we'll have to rendezvous and look at it tonight. It's like travel pornography. It even made me want to go and I haven't been on a bicycle in over a decade."

"Your friend Molly is a good influence," Chagall said. Phoebe jumped and the car swerved for a split second into the oncoming lane. A driver laid on his horn and Phoebe saw him screaming at her as he passed. Phoebe mouthed "Sorry!" but he couldn't see her.

She turned to Chagall angrily. "You have *got* to give me some kind of warning. I almost killed us…or at least myself!"

"I have no way to announce myself," he said huffily. "I can only arrive. If you were less tense, my visits wouldn't startle you so. You're on edge. Listen to your friend. You need a vacation."

"Maybe later. I've got too much on my plate to just leave the country."

"Why would later make any difference? Now is the time, my dear; now is always the time."

Phoebe liked that. It could be inside a fortune cookie.

"Mr. Chagall…"

"Marc, please," he said, shaking his head and wagging his finger at her.

"Marc. My life is usually more…together, as we say."

"I know together. I was around in the sixties, you know."

"That's right…my God, you lived a long time," she added.

"Two wars I lived through," he said, hitting the dashboard with his hand. "I lived through so much more than that, but the two wars, that's what makes everyone see it as astonishing."

"Well, it is quite a feat. My problems must seem so puny compared to what you lived through."

"No one's life is 'puny,' as you say. Yours is different, but significant in many ways, some you have yet to discover. That is why," he said, reaching across the gearshift and tapping her on the tip of her nose, "that is why France. Destiny. Fate. You must take this trip. That is all I can say."

And again, he was gone. There was something cellophane, transparent but lingering, when his form vanished, like the stained water left in the little jars when she rinsed her brushes, an afterimage. Yet when he appeared, it was all at once, three dimensional, fully there.

Whatever these visitations were—stress, madness, a great gift, and she *was* doing her best to see it as the latter—she was officially going to surrender to them and stop fighting it. She also decided to consider Byroads. Bicycling with strangers. She might enjoy that. She could enjoy anything in Provence, she knew, and certainly, she had not been on a big vacation in years. And at least she wouldn't have to eat alone. Phoebe loathed eating alone. As she pulled into the driveway of her sweet, bright blue home with the mustard trim and the excited hounds waiting to greet her, she decided just like that to let herself say yes. Now is always the time.

CHAPTER THIRTEEN

Bernadette awoke to the sound of bees. A few had gotten into her room, and first came in low, bouncing off of the lamp shades, then sought the high corners above her bed.

She loved the mornings. The evenings always made her a bit lonely, now that Georges was dead and her boys were off living their lives. Many of the guests at her farm lingered and talked with her on the patio by the pool, smoking cigarettes and sipping their wine, but they always pushed their chairs back from the table eventually and headed for their bed together, arms over each other's shoulders. Bernadette stayed until the last guest had retired, watching the bats swoop silently over the water of the pool, catching mosquitoes. Then she blew out the candles and headed for bed. But she had always been excited to start the day. She made long lists of the day's chores, and tackled them with zeal. She reached down onto the floor and shook out her pink slippers, in case a scorpion had ventured in there during the night, then she flung open the windows to greet the day and show the confused bees their escape route.

She wiped off her face with rose water on a cotton ball, just as she had done every morning for the past sixty years. She wore no makeup. As always, she climbed the stepladder to check for pigeon eggs. She found two and hurled them far into the garden. Then, she quietly made her way to her studio. The sweet, high-pitched songs of the resident birds, dunnocks and chiffchaffs, as they flitted about in the branches were wafting through the windows. Bernadette walked the path to her studio, her skirt brushing against a some tarragon and filling the air with its licoricey fragrance.

First, she checked on the hives in the removable trays and saw that there were two of the special queen cells in one of them, noticeably larger than the regular cells, each about the size of a child's thumb. The nurse bees would feed those two larvae the royal jelly, transforming two ordinary larvae that would have grown into mere workers, into queens. The wisdom and industry and group ethic of the bees continually impressed her. How did they choose who got to be the queen? Like people's fate in human life, it seemed random. And then, whichever queen emerged first would simply make a "beeline" over to her rival and sting her dead, right through the walls of the cell. As in most households, here could only be one queen. Next, Bernadette opened the one bee tray that did not hold honeycomb, revealing her precious painting.

The idea to hide it there had come to her in the middle of the night when she first started keeping bees on the farm. Before that, she had hid it under a loose board in her bedroom, but had been worried about dampness or some bug or rodent nibbling on it. She had bought those ingenious glass bee trays, like drawers with handles on top to pull them out for harvest; except in the case of this faux tray, she darkened the glass panels black so that the painting sandwiched within was not visible. Today, as on so many mornings, she slid out her Chagall and gazed at it, lost in reverie. It still looked as beautiful to her as the day she had first seen it.

Suddenly, one of the guests called "bonjour" from the doorframe. The painting clattered to the floor and Bernadette rushed to pick it up and slide it back in its place before the uninvited guest caught a glimpse.

"Oh, I'm sorry I startled you," said the Australian woman. She was now looking at Bernadette curiously, but went on. "I couldn't sleep past light this morning. Isn't it an absolutely gorgeous day? So I stopped fighting it and got up to go on a hike. I found a whole bush of red currants and I thought maybe you could make jam out of them or something. I could even help, if you like. Aren't they beautiful?"

They were moist and translucent. Bernadette regained her composure and popped a few in her mouth.

"Mmm, nice and tart. I like to use them this way. I will make you some *conficture* to put on your baguette tomorrow morning."

"Ta! That would be grand." She started to leave, then turned and said, "Is this your pottery studio? And also your apiary?" She was eying the faux tray that Bernadette had already slipped back in its spot, the painting again safe inside. Bernadette sized up the Aussie and saw that she could be easily distracted. She removed a real tray, which housed a comb oozing with honey and working bees. The woman initially stepped back, then crept forward slowly when she saw that the bees were not stinging Bernadette or dispersing all over the room, but continuing their work, staying right on the hive.

"Ooh, look at them!" said the Aussie. "Look at all that honey! Don't they get mad when they do all that work and you rob the fruits of their labors?"

"The bees and I have an understanding," Bernadette said, touching the tip of her finger to the tray, catching a drip of honey and sucking it off. "I never take too much, just enough to stimulate them to make more but always leaving plenty to feed the hive. And I plant the flowers that they love on the property. We help one another."

The Aussie reached out also to taste the honey, then thought better of it and turned to go. "Can't wait to try the currant jam! You are so lucky to live here. I am already sad about leaving and we have three more days."

"You are welcome back anytime," Bernadette said graciously, her heart still pounding from the intrusion. She had to remember to keep this door locked.

Most of the guests were gone in the middle of the day, so that was when she usually did the cleaning. She snooped as well, but was very discreet about it. Bernadette had named each of the rooms after themes in several of her favorite Chagall paintings. There was the Eiffel Tower room, which had Parisian décor and Eiffel Towers of every shape and size featured throughout, as well as a copy of his painting *The Lovers of the Eiffel Tower:* sideways trees, woman flying with big bouquet and all. There was the Rooster Room, every manner of red or purple rooster prancing across everything from the sheets to the lampshades. There was the Circus Room with a framed rendition of *The Juggler,* grandfather clock boneless and draped over his arm like a towel; every wall here was alive with acrobats, contortionists, tightrope walkers with dainty parasols. The Flying Fish room had a larger copy of one of Bernadette's favorite Chagall's, *Time Is a River without Banks* with its winged fish playing a violin and leaping over a clock. She went all out on this room with everything oceanic and winged or fishy that she could find at flea markets or out of catalogues. The rooms were full and charming, reflecting the theme of their chosen Chagall painting, but never felt cluttered or disjointed. Bernadette hoped that for her guests, as for herself, it would be like stepping into the world of Chagall, always a fantastical place to visit.

"Whose team will you be playing on?" the American asked her jocularly as she was clearing the breakfast dishes.

"Oh," Bernadette said. "I'll probably be too busy with the pistou and also reeking of garlic. Besides," she added, knowing it would throw him for a loop, "I can be pretty brutal when it comes to pétanque. I get quite competitive."

"I want you on our team, then," he said, helping her carry some plates into the kitchen. "Say, I wanted to ask you. Did you know Marc Chagall? You must really be fond of his work, and I know he lived in the south of France for a time. It seems like you may have known him."

Bernadette felt her heartbeat quicken, but answered smoothly, "No, I never had that pleasure. But I feel as if I do know him, from his paintings. They have always spoken to me." This topic always brought out a twinge of guilt.

"Well, your place is like a shrine to the man. I'll bet he would be honored to have such a fan."

Bernadette flushed in spite of herself and looked down at the floor, relieved when the man finally left the room. Only late morning and already a day of close calls.

CHAPTER FOURTEEN

Ray had put in a successful day at Orb Weaver, his small gallery on Minna Street in San Francisco, and locked the doors behind him, eager to meet his son for an early dinner after strolling the neighborhood a bit. It was a tough time for art galleries, but today he had sold a beautiful piece by an artist who had cleverly framed a continuous loop of video showing the undulating and shifting twisters formed by thousands of migrating starlings. Ray turned around and looked at Orb Weaver from the outside. He knew that naming his gallery after a spider was a bit Nature Channel-esque, but he didn't care. If this was his "midlife career move," if he was "redefining himself" or "trying to start fresh," then he could name the gallery whatever he liked. Plus, orb weavers were little artists themselves, scary looking, hefty, mysterious. The incongruous happy face on the female spider's abdomen, as well as the beauty of their webs, filled him with wonder, and since that was what he felt art should also do, the name was apt. But more than anything else: If he was crazy enough to open an art gallery in the middle of a recession, and probably cut even deeper into his savings in the process, he obviously wasn't frothing at the mouth to be commercially viable. And it was appealing that the name was a trifle spooky. After all, Ray, in spite of being a sucker for beauty, fervently believed that art should challenge the viewer, not just look good over the living room sofa.

He loved walking in San Francisco at dusk, before the fog rolled in but after many of the nine-to-fivers were heading home. He avoided Market Street and the Tenderloin, where the homeless camped in doorways or pushed the shopping carts that contained all their worldly possessions, muttering to themselves as they moved. He had once seen a man at a BART station with a five-pound bag of granulated sugar in one hand and a giant spoon in the other. His beard and clothing were dusted with the granules and he shoveled great spoonfuls into his mouth. Ray wondered what it would be like to be in a place where one did not know that eating massive amounts of sugar was harmful for your body, to know only that it tasted good.

Ray avoided such scenes if he could, though he felt guilty for it. Instead, he favored the routes to Orb Weaver that included the secret little alleys of the city that bloomed with French and Italian cafés or chic hair salons or even other art galleries. After work he would meet friends in these cozy alleys, at Café Claude or Tiramisu. Tonight he was meeting his son, but since he was early, he took his time, watching the people coming out of the BART station and looking in the shop windows.

Ray loved that special time of day when the city was slipping into its nighttime persona. Accordion music mingled with stand-up bass at the mouths of many of these hidden streets and he often just stopped and listened for a few moments, pondering the sparkles in the asphalt, his next blind date, or, more often than not, his secret research project, one that had been consuming the bulk of his time and passion for the past four years. For Ray, a man already enamored of film noir, libraries, and art, this obsession suited him to a T.

Ray had been reading the biographies of various artists and was particularly smitten by Chagall's. He knew opinions varied wildly about the man, from angel and genius to self-serving and egotistical. But none of this interested Ray as much as one glaring detail in the man's life: the one hundred missing paintings.

No one could deny that Chagall had been a victim of incredibly poor timing. Just days after he had gotten his artwork set up in Berlin for his first one-man show, he had returned to Russia to marry his Bella, never dreaming that World War I would break out and he would be trapped in Russia for the next eight years.

Every time Ray thought about lost paintings, any works of art that had simply vanished, or had been robbed from their rightful owners, or had been sold and purchased illegally and were now part of someone's secret cache, he felt agitated, fired up. He could well imagine that there were hundreds, maybe thousands more paintings that had gone missing in Paris, left behind in some studio because the artist believed he was leaving only for a very short time—or in Chagall's case, left behind while he dropped off the work for his own show, planning to return after he joined his bride in their village in Russia. Then too, there were all those other lost paintings from the *next* World War. The ones the Nazis had "appropriated" from galleries and right off the walls of Jewish homes. Who knew where those had ended up? Who secretly possessed all these lost paintings? Where had they landed after that war made men disregard the rules of ownership? Surely a few of them were incarcerated in dusty boxes in some European attic, their value, perhaps even their whereabouts, unknown to the people downstairs. Some, plucked before the artists had made a name for themselves, were probably even discarded in ignorance. Such a waste. Ray dreamed of devoting himself to this research and writing a book. *Somebody* should take a closer look at two wars' worth of lost art!

Ray's 6:30 meeting with his son Martin was drawing close, so he quickened his pace. But he kept turning the questions over in his mind. Maybe someone had obtained some of these paintings for a song during that destitute period in Berlin, when theft was rampant and gallery owners were selling masterpieces to pay for food. And then, if approached after the war, these same gallery owners or buyers excused themselves, saying that the old rules did not apply. There was a war on and during a war, you make the rules up as you go. Art sold for nothing or was "lost." Who would know? And since art was probably the last thing on everyone's mind, who would care? But Ray knew that the first thing Chagall did when he was at last free to leave Russia and travel again, was to attempt to track down the paintings he had left behind in Berlin with the gallery owner named Waldin, even taking the matter to court when met with apologies and shrugs.

Ray intended to pursue all of these loose ends further the next time he was in Paris. His best friend had been trying to convince him to join an upcoming bike trip with a company called Byroads that was going to start soon in the south of France. If he decided to go, he could get there a few days early, landing in Paris. He could haunt the same cafés in Montparnasse that Chagall had frequented, ask some questions of the old-timers in his mediocre French—in short, make a fool of himself. For what? Well, maybe for the exquisite privilege of actually laying eyes upon a painting that no one else had seen in almost a century. But he wasn't sure about the biking with strangers for a week part of the equation. He was tired of being The Single Guy in a sea of couples.

"Hi, Dad."

Ray stood up to hug the lanky frame of his boy. How had the little kid he'd pulled around in a red wagon grown to be over six feet tall, with a Ph.D. and a job that paid better than his father's?

"Have a seat," Ray said heartily. "I've got lots of news."

CHAPTER FIFTEEN

"Take Ida with you, my love," Bella called after her husband. She was wearing a loose, pale peach dressing gown made of satin fabric, and it made her look regal, too lofty a goddess for the likes of him. Chagall could never quite believe that they had found one another in this troubled world. Even more improbable was the dismal fact of their current circumstances, married at last but stuck back in Russia due to the War. Chagall couldn't accept that he had come so far only to find himself back in his old village, Vitebsk, experiencing all over again the same insecurities and frustrations that had dogged him as a child. Yet, on occasion, these feelings of futility bumped up against a new sensation: bliss, for Bella was now his wife and their beautiful cherub, Ida, his daughter, had been born in 1916, in Russia, in the middle of a war that showed no signs of ending despite everyone's earlier conviction that it wouldn't last.

Bella was kneading some dough for meat dumplings, though with this damn war, or revolution or whatever they were calling it this month, there most likely would not be money for meat. He came up behind her and felt her breasts through the slippery cloth. She squirmed but pushed back into him and said huskily, "Your daughter is waiting." Chagall turned reluctantly, then brightened as he approached the small girl sitting on a bright orange shawl her mother had lain out, using a paintbrush she had found on the floor as a drumstick and rhythmically thumping the ground.

"Would you like to go to the noisy, smelly market with Papa? Would you like that, my gold? My angel?" he asked her in the singsong voice that made her smile. Ida reached her chubby arms up to him. Even though now she was walking better and better each day, she preferred to be lifted high up onto his shoulders. "Off we go to conquer the market," he said, kissing Bella goodbye and heading out into the brisk day.

The streets were filled with soldiers, and supplies were in high demand. Here he was, making some of his best paintings and yet, for what? Just when his art career was taking off, here came this damn war. What if it went on for ten more years? Chagall would go mad. He was painting up a storm but a virtual prisoner of Mother Russia. How he yearned for the freedom to escape this place, where every aspect of life and art was seen through a military and political lens, as it related to the new Bolshevik rulers. Chagall worked himself up, churning with such thoughts; Ida screeched in protest at how hard his grip on her had become.

As Chagall walked down the stalls of the market, he saw little beyond beets and herring and potatoes, and they were lucky to have those. He shook his head at the sense of humor God must have. *It could have been worse*, he told himself, bouncing his shoulders so that Ida squealed in delight, her fingers tugging his dark curls. *I am not political. I am not a communist. And being a Jew, I would not have been allowed to rise to the position of captain even if I, a slender, bookish man, managed to survive actual battle. Connections*, Chagall thought. *Connections are everything in this life. I am lucky, no? I am alive because Bella's brother was decent enough to find me a desk job in St. Petersburg. And then, with the revolution and the Bolsheviks running the show, I, a painter who paints only street scenes and ordinary village life, am made People's Commissar in Charge of Art. All because of a Russian friend who was in Paris at the same time as I, who now holds the title People's Commissar in Charge of Enlightenment, whatever that may be. I will soon be moving my family to*

Moscow to serve as the voice of culture. Me! One has to laugh sometimes to keep from crying.

"Fresh beets here! Golden beets! Red ones sweet as wine! Come buy my beets!" a woman with a flowered scarf tied under her chin sang out.

"And might there be some sour cream to be had to put on top of these beets?" Chagall asked her, lowering Ida to the ground and taking the child's hand.

"You dream," the woman scoffed. "We are lucky here, we can grow crops, but I have heard in the big cities, if it were not for the railway bringing in food, people would be starving."

"Some beets then," Chagall sighed, wishing for something special— a treat, if only there was any to be had, for Ida.

The woman handed him the beets wrapped in newspaper and smiled down at the little girl. "These will put roses in your cheeks, though that seems taken care of already." Then she reached into her pocket and handed the girl a sugar cube. "The prize," she said. "For being my sweetest customer today."

Chagall thanked the woman and Ida sucked greedily on the delicacy. He needed more money. At least he could teach. Chagall liked best of all to teach the orphans. One girl, Natasha, was his favorite, and showed such promise.

"I dream that I can fly," she had told him once after class. "The most wonderful dreams. I break a branch off a magic tree and hang from it and steer with it and it lifts me up, up over the village, over the cities where my parents went to work in the factories, over the oceans and mountains. I can see it all at once. I wish I could paint something that large." And before Chagall could answer her, her young eyes filled with tears. "I wish I really could just fly. I would fly away from here."

"Where would you go?" Chagall asked.

"I would be able to see a good family, from above, with a fireplace and a horse and a dog and plenty of food. And they would want a girl like me. And they would let me paint and I would have two sisters and two brothers. And a dog."

"Yes, you mentioned the dog."

"Well, he would be mine and I would name him Cake."

Chagall recalled feeling very sad for this girl. For even though she showed talent, she had no one to take her in or stand by her, so she too would probably be sent to some factory job in Moscow or St. Petersburg, and she would work until she was exhausted and eventually lose the will to paint.

"Maybe art can be your family," he had told the girl. "Maybe art can feed you."

"I would like that," she had said sadly, already knowing it was not in her future.

"Papa!" Ida said, bringing Chagall back to the present, the market, his own little girl. "Up! Up!"

Chagall had quite forgotten her, trotting stoically below, trying to keep of and holding onto his hand. "Yes, my pearl, up we go." Once she was seated on his shoulders, holding onto his hair again, he added, "You are a very lucky little girl."

"Lucky," she repeated earnestly, though he was quite sure she did not know the meaning of the word.

CHAPTER SIXTEEN

As they waited for their dinner, Ray described to his son Martin his day with his friend Jack when the whole idea of the Byroads trip to France had come up.

"I need a vacation," Ray had said to Jack as they drove over the Golden Gate Bridge, the wind making the wheels on their bikes spin in the bike rack on the back of Jack's Jeep, as if they were yearning to be set free. "I'm losing the will to appreciate even the little glimpses into the humanity of another person that this dating thing might give me. Frankly, it's all just downright depressing."

"Attitude, my friend," Jack said. "We're all in this together. Keep that in mind and stop feeling sorry for yourself."

"Easy for you to talk about attitude—you're married and nesting and reading sweet stories to cute kids and have a good woman in your bed each night, who, by the way, cooks a mean risotto. I hope I told her that enough last time you guys made dinner for me."

"Relax, Ray, Janice adores you."

"Then why doesn't she have any nice friends she can fix me up with?"

"She's tried, remember? Either they think you're too sarcastic or you think they've been single too long, which, might I add, is a pretty tough criteria, because they're out there trying and you're telling them not to bother, it's too late, like they exude spinsterhood or something. And might I also add that marriage is no walk in the park. No picnic. No bed of roses. No piece of cake. No…"

"Weekend in Havana? Biscuit with gravy? Holiday on ice?" Ray offered.

"The grass is always greener, my friend. Just don't rose-color my world. I'm not complaining, mind you, but life is what you make it."

"We *are* full of platitudes today," Ray joked, but Jack did not laugh.

Outside his window, Ray looked down at Baker Beach, and was sure he saw a nude surfer out in the waves. He must have been freezing, Ray thought, the guys not even wearing a wetsuit. A perfect V of a dozen Mexican Brown Pelicans flew almost parallel to Ray's window, but off about twenty feet from the bridge. He loved these birds. Their grins always reminded him of clowns. They were so earnest, if not perfectly graceful, when they hit the water with a big smack to catch a fish. The Jeep climbed up into the Marin Headlands, the grass still an inviting green. Jack pulled over and they unloaded their bikes and headed out for a ride. They rode single file as they entered the shade and majesty of the redwood forests, cutting in and out, the brightness of the paved road with its downhill thrills and spectacular views of the Golden Gate Bridge, then veering back off-road, into the mossy, obstacle-laden world of the woods. Two hours of this and they were ready for some carbs and refreshment. They started the long, paved downhill spin into Sausalito.

"Why does food always taste so much better when you've worked for it?" Ray asked, wolfing down a warm, cheesy panini in two bites and chasing it with ginger beer.

"Ah, Ray, for a foodie like you, food always tastes good. You experience the world through your taste buds."

"Guilty as charged," Ray said, wiping his lips and leaning back in his chair. Well, if he couldn't have sex, exercise was a close second. He felt great. His muscles were humming from the ride and he felt like a happy, active animal, delighted to get out of his brain for a few minutes and just inhabit his body.

"Listen, Ray," Jack said, polishing off the last of his cappuccino. "You were saying you needed a vacation. I agree. So you ask yourself: what makes me happy? Biking comes to mind, right?"

"Yeah, or hiking. But I don't like to travel by myself, so that limits me in the vacation department. Plus I can't stand eating alone, and when you're a solo voyager, that's part of the deal."

"But listen, I know this organization called Byroads. They take you to amazing places and you meet like-minded people—you just give them a big wad of money up front and they take care of everything so you never have to think about it: tips, lodging, equipment, the works, all covered. And you stay in places you or I could never find on our own, let alone procure a reservation. And the food! Oy, the food!"

"Jesus, Jack, do you work for them or something?"

"No, but before we had Zoey, we used to do these bike trips. To Ireland, and another time, to Costa Rica. They have these really seductive catalogues, and…well, we had a blast, that's all. I think it's right up your alley."

"Yeah, but you were a couple. Would I be the only guy traveling alone?"

"No, they have singles tours. And from what I've heard, there's always way more women than men."

"Not necessarily a great thing."

"C'mon, Ray. It's exactly the answer. Never have to eat alone, great like-minded people, no pressure to hook up, and you're in some fantastic locale."

"Okay, okay. Show me the catalogue."

"No time to reflect, my friend," Jack told him. "With all your fascination with the occupation and art and your love of great food, I've already picked the perfect trip for you. Provence by way of Paris. You could leave a few days before the biking part starts, to have some time in Paris before joining the Byroads group. Just say yes, buddy, and I can fill you in on the details. Trust me on this one."

Ray had nodded noncommittally. He was distracted by the beaming surfer who had pulled up in an old woody that look sandblasted but was probably worth about forty grand. The surfer radiated joy. Ray described wanting to experience that zeal about something again, and wondered if he was too old to take up surfing.

The waiter set a plate of pumpkin gnocci with sage butter down in front of Martin, and a hearty bowl of Cioppino bulging with clams and squid in front of his father.

"Do it, Dad," Martin said. "Since when did you become so hesitant about everything?"

Ray was going to protest, but he knew his son was right.

"Hey, I'm supposed to be giving you advice, not vice versa. And FYI, I already decided. I'm going to go, even though this means taking care of about five hundred details in a matter of days."

"Alright, Dad. Bravo," Martin said, clapping his father on the back. "I'll look forward to hearing about your adventures."

And about forty minutes north of there, Phoebe was already preparing for the same trip, but with far less encouragement from her daughter.

"Mom, this is madness," Audrey said, watching her mother pack. "You can't afford this. Which is more important, keeping the house or some frivolous trip to France?"

"Since when did you get so concerned about my finances?" Phoebe asked. "What are you, my mother?" This last she said in her best Yiddish intonation.

Audrey scrutinized her mother as if she was a creature from another land. She had been a great mom, reading to her each night, playing games with her and speaking in silly voices when called for. When Audrey would get home from school, a platter of delectable slices of fruit would be waiting for her and her friends, arranged in pretty patterns. Her friends always said she was lucky, and their house was known as the "fun one." Still, Audrey could not comprehend her mother's generation's absolute conviction that things would turn out all right. There was a little over twenty years' age difference between them, but Phoebe had come of age in a world of plenty and expected the happy ending, whereas Audrey's generation was one of vanishing species and boomerang kids and global warming and no jobs no matter how many degrees a young person could manage to get. She sighed, a bit envious of her mother's faith in things.

"I'm just sayin'…" Audrey flopped backward onto the part of the bed that didn't have heaps of clothing on it. Once supine, she became distracted by the ends of her own long straight hair, examining them meticulously, ready to pinch off any split end. "I can see how worried you are, and in fact *have been* for almost two years now, and this just seems like one of those things that will feel good for a week but you'll feel worse when you get back."

"Honey, the trip is *free*, F-R-E-E. A person does not say no to a free trip to France, no matter when it comes up," Phoebe said. "Hand me that black dress from the closet, sweetie."

"Which black dress? There are about twenty of them."

"The one that you can squish up in a suitcase and then just shake out and wear to dinner without ironing it."

"Oh, that one!" Audrey said, rolling her eyes and leafing through the hangers. "Mom, seriously, I'm happy to look after the dogs for you and stay here a couple of weeks before school starts up again. This really isn't about me. I just…well, I *know* you and I think this trip will only be a temporary vacation from the inevitable."

"Listen, Audrey. My motto has always been, 'You're never too old to run away.' Before you were born, I ran away numerous times, and by that I mean I surrendered to the great, problem-solving powers of unknown terrains. When you were living at home, I couldn't do that as much. You had friends and school and uprooting is not so great for kids. And I've been pretty good, you must admit—nose to the grindstone, stiff upper lip, what with the divorce and my hours being cut back and this living hell of trying to date again when you're forty…."

"Mom, you're dating?

"Not yet as such but…"

"You promised me you'd try. You look great. Any man would be lucky to be with you. Please don't give up. Dad found someone new and he's happy."

"Honey, your father is a straight man of some means and in good shape living in the Bay Area. Here, that makes him a blue-ribbon prize-winner, a real catch, a god. But do you know how old his new wife is?"

"No, but she's pretty nice…in a wispy way. She tries too hard around me, but she's not so bad, really."

"Right, but the fact that I don't know her age either and he's not saying…well, 'nuff said."

"But you're not going to become one of those eccentric, cranky old ladies that has lots of pets, and gets all bitter and reclusive, are you? With a bumper sticker that says, 'The more I know of people the more I like my dog'?"

"Too late, my sweet," Phoebe said, tucking a lock of Audrey's hair behind her ear. "I am well on my way."

Audrey sat up and gave her mother a rueful smile.

"No, seriously," Phoebe said. "Stop worrying! That's my job. I'm not giving up. I'm always open to the chance Hollywood-caliber romance. But you've got to realize, honey, men my own age want to date women in their twenties. And that would be just fine, except I personally am not attracted to men in their eighties. Call me wacky, but I too would like to be with a man close to my age."

"Okay, I'll shut up. I guess I'm giving you a mixed message here, telling you to put yourself out there but then discouraging you from taking this trip. Oh, go for it, Mom! But I've got to tell you something: you have been acting a bit peculiar lately when I come home to visit. Is there anything you're not telling me? I promise I won't judge you. You seem stressed."

Audrey had moved to the floor now and was playing tug-of-war with both Mechant and Gamut simultaneously, a mountain lion plush toy in one hand and a dolphin in the other.

Phoebe folded some cotton panties that had cowgirls all over them and considered telling her daughter about the ghost, but thought better of it. She felt, overall, that she had done a fine job raising her daughter. Good food, good schools, not too much "screen time." And she knew all the helpful day-to-day tricks a good mother should pass along to her girl: button shirts from the bottom up so they're never buttoned wrong. Leave your spoon in the tea if it's too hot to sip because the metal absorbs the heat. Smash the woody ends of the lilacs outside with a hammer before you put them in the vase so they can drink properly and last longer. And of course, never be so afraid of being hurt that you hold back when you give your heart. Phoebe herself was still learning that one.

"No," Phoebe sighed. "If I'm acting odd, it's just stress…like you said. All the more reason that I *need* to take this trip. Right now. I know there may be repercussions, but I feel it's the right thing. I'm getting really, really excited about it." She zipped some travel-sized lotions and shampoos into a bag with kangaroos all over it, adding: "And besides, you never know—I just might meet the love of my life."

CHAPTER SEVENTEEN

Whenever Bernadette began to feel too guilty about her hidden Chagall, she justified it by telling herself that nobody had recognized its value except her—not the American who found it in the alley, not her brother, and certainly not the worker at the café who had ignorantly put it out with the trash, although granted, with the Germans invading the city he had other things on his mind. But, Bernadette knew that she was not the only one with something to hide. At least her only transgression was this painting. She had known so many people, during the forty years she lived in Paris, who had much to be ashamed of during that period. Some such people had been her neighbors on the little street in the fourteenth *arondissement*, the location of the apartment she had called home for so long before moving to Provence. That Second World War, the war that had so defined her own childhood, had left no Parisian unchanged. When your city is occupied for four years by an enemy, everyone will have their secrets.

There was the young fishmonger with the easy smile and quick wit from whom Bernadette had so often bought her *loup du mer* or *langoustine*—a fine young man who would probably never know, as she knew, that his own father had reported a Jewish grocer for some fabricated offense during the occupation, just to eliminate the competition. There was the old seamstress, who had been quite beautiful in the forties. It was said, when her husband was killed in the war, that she began to receive men at night in the bedroom above her shop—Germans, Russians, it didn't matter—while her children slept in the room next door. Some said she did it to feed those children while others condemned her and said it was because she was unwilling to make any sacrifice, that she could not stand her bread without butter. And surely, although Bernadette did not know their names for certain, there were gallery owners or politicians whose secret was, like her own, a painting of immense value, squirreled away in some dark cache because they did not come by the piece through the correct channels. Not one of them, Bernadette included, asked the correct questions: How did the art get there and to whom did it really belong?

Despite these stories she told herself in hopes of vindication, that old cry of "I am not the only one," her conscience still pecked at her. She fretted, saying to herself, *I am an old woman and I cannot leave this painting to my sons. They would be shocked that their mother kept such a thing secret all this time. What will become of it? It would be a travesty, a crime to let it be lost to the world forever, hidden behind a bee screen. I must make an effort to track down the children of this soldier, to at least try to find the rightful owner. But what could I tell them, after all this time? I could be arrested!* And here she descended into fearful fantasy, scenes of being dragged away in handcuffs, the entire village looking on with sour expressions. No, she decided yet again; she would wait a little longer, until she had a plan.

Bernadette headed out into the fields with two big baskets to gather the ingredients for tonight's pistou. She had made the dish only two nights earlier for the last round of guests, but a new batch was arriving that day and everybody always wanted pistou. That was why, once she had served the guests, Bernadette would have the lamb dish that awaited her in the fridge. She would have turned green by now if she had eaten the dish as frequently as she made it. The worn straw basket was for vegetables and the wire basket for nuts. The basil was glossy and pungent; she carefully pinched off enough leaves to fill one basket almost to the brim. Was there any scent that transported one into the heart of summer as utterly as basil? Well, lavender of course, but for her, on this farm, lavender was a year-round intoxication.

Next, she walked to the walnut grove. It was a little early for her own walnuts, but some had fallen and had nice green hulls, and she gathered those from the ground, expertly weighing each in her palm to avoid the lighter, spoiled ones, before tossing them into the other basket. She carried these over to a cement slab that was stained black from the walnuts' juices. She spilled the basket of her walnuts out onto the surface and began to march all over them, stomping on any that rolled out of her way. It was slippery, vigorous work, and for it, she donned her wooden shoes, which were also stained that glassy black from the walnut hulls. Despite modern technology, which she assumed existed for such a task, she had always found this the most straightforward way to crack the hulls so she could get to the nuts. She had a very old wire brush that the former owner of the farm had left for her, and with this brushed off any remaining hull and skin from the walnuts, ran the wire basket under the pump several times to give them a good rinse, then placed the basket on a hook to dry a few hours in the sun. Lastly, she scanned the garlic bin, and began to dig in the earth with a small spade beneath the brownest and most dried-out-looking of the row of green stalks. She brushed the dirt from five heads of garlic, twisting off the shaggy roots and tossing them over her shoulder. A rooster dashed forward and snatched them up the second they hit the ground. A steady diet of garlic leavings would flavor that rooster well. But her roosters were rarely castrated so their meat was stronger, better for stews. Still, she would have to make *capon au vin* before the summer was over.

Walking back to the kitchen, Bernadette decided to invite the Bion sisters, Jacqueline and Marie-Christine, to join in the inevitable game of pétanque and have some pistou. They were witches, the last of their line, descendants of a druidic tribe that dated back to Roman Gaul. Such inclinations ran strongly in the Bion blood, and even some uncles and a great-grandfather had been practitioners. Both sisters were in their eighties now, still sharp and full of wry wit, if a tad esoteric. The duo were fixtures in the town, and had been on hand for many of the births, as well as, some insisted, responsible for many of the couplings, in the village. The two were hugely respected for their knowledge of healing herbs, and were perhaps the most versed in all of France in the old medicines and ways.

The Bion farm was about a forty-minute walk, and Bernadette called for her dogs to accompany her there, laughing as they barked excitedly and butted their snouts against her legs. "*Allez les chiens,*" she said, putting on her large, yellow straw hat and heading down the drive to the road. "Out you go. Before this day gets too hot."

She was only responsible for feeding the guests breakfast, but often also prepared little aperitifs for them at the end of the day, that adrift time for visitors when it was too soon to eat the evening meal yet too late to start a new adventure. Twilight, or *Entre Chien et Loup,* as it was called, between the dog and the wolf, an expression that was born, no doubt, because it would just be growing too dark to distinguish between the two. At that blurry hour, Bernadette brought outside little bowls painted with sunflowers that she had made herself, filled with olives swimming in her own olive oil laced with *herbes de Provence.* Or, she set down moist scoops of goat cheese, *chevre,* that had been rolled in lavender, and next to that she poured a puddle of walnut oil so that the guests could mop it up with their bread. And to drink, Suze, or Lillet, or if they had somehow acquired a taste for it, the licoricey local favorite pastis, Ricard or Pernod and its ritualistic accouterment, the bottle of water and special glasses required. But now, for a few hours, her time was her own.

The Bion sisters' old stone manor was filled with an amazing collection of metaphysical artifacts that they and their ancestors had been using for centuries. Some of them were simple handmade tools, herb cutters and hand-forged knives of a style one rarely saw in these times. But then there were cauldrons and iron tools hanging from a chain in the hearth that appeared Medieval. Old brass spell arrows lay facing all different directions on an altar. When Bernadette had asked about them once, the sisters told her, "Write your desire on a piece of parchment and tuck it into the back of the arrow and the male force and Eastern winds will carry your wish out into the world and make it so."

Never one to miss an opportunity to make a wish come true, Bernadette wished something simple: that her son would surprise her soon with a visit. When he appeared at her door the next day, she became a believer. The women's working hands were like gnarled roots from a sound old tree, and each wore numerous rings on all fingers, even on their thumbs. Marie-Christine favored owls as the design on her rings, ancient-looking golden ones with ruby eyes or crude silver renditions worn smooth from age, while Jacqueline had all sorts of rings on every finger: a fairy sniffing a Calla lily, the lily a baroque pearl, or a carved jet cat with amber eyes. Bernadette always felt a little woozy around them, though they were perfectly charming, as if she were entering another realm when she stepped through their front door. What she experienced around them wasn't exactly a trance, but everything felt heightened, as if she were watching her own actions from across the room. She had asked them once if they cast spells on everyone they came in contact with.

"*Mais non!*" Jacqueline scoffed. "People have heard so much gossip about us, so many stories over the decades that now they just *expect* to feel funny when we're around."

But the women possessed a keen intelligence, were magnificent cooks, and added immeasurably to any party. Bernadette wanted them at the next pétanque game.

"Bonjour!" Bernadette called out. "*Il y a quelqu'un?*" She filled a cracked bowl with some water from the sisters' pump for her dogs, and after they had drunk, she tied them in the shade of a large chestnut tree, the early sun playing off of its dappled bark. "Be good," she told them as she turned toward the front door. The dogs loved nothing more than chasing cats and this house was home to at least a dozen.

The Bion sisters never locked their doors, so Bernadette called out again, then tentatively pushed open the heavy door with the old Greek ball-and-hand doorknocker, and entered. Even though it was before noon, candles of different hues burned on an altar covered with photos as well as what looked like a child's dolls and toys.

"These belong to little Henri," Jacqueline said, suddenly standing right next to Bernadette and joining her in looking at the altar. "He is ill and his mother asked us to perform a spell for him."

"I hope he gets better!" Bernadette exclaimed, trying to compose herself, startled as always by Jacqueline's sudden materialization at her side. "I brought you some Cavaillon melons." Bernadette held one up for Jacqueline to smell, though the scent was so pungent it filled the space between them. "I think this might be the one thing I have that you don't also grow."

"Ahhh," the woman said, closing her eyes in ecstasy. "Ambrosia." Then she called up the stairs: "Marie-Christine! It's Bernadette. Bearing melons!"

Marie-Christine came down the steps with the aid of a walking stick whose handle was the likeness of a bald eagle's head. "Bonjour!" she said, kissing Bernadette on each cheek, then once again. "Three times," she said, pulling back and studying Bernadette's face. "*Comme il faut.*"

Bernadette was always a bit uncomfortable around Marie-Christine, as if she was naked and exposed. She was certain the woman read minds. Once at a dinner party, her suspicions had been confirmed when, by way of conversation, the old woman had asked her son about "his Tahitian goddess" before he even had the chance to break the news to his own mother that he was seeing her. After that, the boy said he hummed songs when she was near him so she couldn't read his thoughts. As for herself, Bernadette never invited Marie-Christine into her studio, fearing she would hone in instantly on the hidden Chagall, or at least sniff something amiss, even if she couldn't put her finger on it.

"Yes, we do the *bisou* three times in the south of France," Bernadette echoed stridently. "Here, we are not stingy with kisses like those Parisians."

Even though Bernadette was a former Parisian, and had lived there most of her life, she enjoyed joining in the local pastime of Parisian-bashing.

"I am making pistou , *quel suprise,* for the new guests for dinner and I'm sure there will also be a game of pétanque. Would you come join us? Pasqual is coming up for the weekend and he can come and get you."

"Pistou!" cried Jacqueline, as if it were the most novel dish in the world. "Will you promise to use a lot of garlic? I love a good oily, garlicky pistou."

"*Bien sur.* And everything in it, including the olive oil, will be from what I have grown," she said proudly.

"You are sweet to ask us," said Marie-Christine. "We shall come and we shall even try a few shots at the game." Then she studied Bernadette again and asked: "Where is your aviary? I have heard your bees make some of the town's sweetest honey, yet in all this time I have never once seen the combs."

"Oh," Bernadette stammered, failing in her attempt to be offhand. "The trays are here and there on the property. I will show you sometime."

"Yes, and your art," added Marie-Christine, with what Bernadette was certain was a mischievous look in her eyes. "I too have a fondness for Chagall. He seemed to embrace the extraordinary. He was so open to magic."

"Yes, well, you have both already seen how each room is a tribute to certain of his paintings."

"What is your own favorite?" Marie-Christine asked, an eyebrow cocked and a slight smile on her thin lips.

Bernadette had practiced all sorts of ways to respond to such interrogations, so for this she was ready and answered without hesitation:"I like 'Listening to the Rooster,' because he has the pig in the sky and its face is really his own face and a woman's. I like it when he divides faces in half, part horse, part woman, part bull, part man. I like how he merges different creatures so they end up creating a brand new variety."

"Yes, like two sides to every beast. Like Janus, the Greek god who had two faces and so could look forward to the future and backward to the past," Marie-Christine said evenly.

"Ah, but we can do that, too, can't we, Bernadette?" Jacqueline asked heartily.

"Well," Bernadette said, turning to go, "up to a point. But most of us humans are better at seeing the past than predicting the future."

"Perhaps they are inseparable?" asked Marie-Christine, leaning heavily on her eagle walking stick.

"Sister, my goodness!" Jacqueline cried. "Too much philosophy! Let the poor woman go. She has pistou to make."

"See you later today!" Bernadette called back to them, untying her ready dogs. The sister's two forms filled the doorway, and in their flowing clothing from another era, they looked joined at the ribs, Siamese twins. Bernadette practically sprinted toward home with her dogs, eager to be back on her own turf, safe in the anonymity of strangers.

CHAPTER EIGHTEEN

There was an eleven-hour nonstop flight from SFO to Charles de Gaulle, which would put Ray into Paris after dark, around eleven PM, but since his lodging was already arranged and he could just crash when he arrived, he chose that option. Finding his seat, a window, and obliging the others in his row to stand while he squeezed past, Ray settled into his confines, and felt like those old codgers who begin every sentence with, "Why, back in *my* day…" But it was easy to be wistful. Ray recalled with fondness the days when flying was a pleasure, almost luxurious, even in regular class; a time when they used real silverware and drinks were free and one could actually shift in one's seat without knocking over one's neighbor's drink, stretch one's legs without the person in the row in front of you rising up to glare at you over the back of their seat. He had even flown to Australia once on a Pan Am 747 and the plane had *two* levels. He climbed a spiral staircase up to an actual piano bar! Ray somehow thought in a recession that fewer people would be traveling, but maybe Air France had compensated by scheduling fewer flights and packing the bodies in as every singe seat on this flight was full. No matter—he liked to fly well enough to get past all this, and had brought along a slim volume of Chagall's autobiography, *My Life*, in his computer bag. In truth, the book read almost like poetry or theater, replete with exclamation points and a stream-of-consciousness flow of associations.

Eleven hours, three movies, many interchangeable salty or sugary snacks later, with a Charley horse in his thigh, bleary and stiff-necked, Ray shuffled towards the passport check with the other ghouls in the fluorescent light of the Paris airport. He pushed through a door and suddenly stepped into a Mardi Gras of nationalities, languages, and costumes. Massive women in loud patterned fabric and matching headscarves surged forward with their children, intent upon crushing anyone in their path. Haggard, anxious-looking men with black stubble on their cheeks and dirt around the collars of their rumpled "good" shirts muttered nervously and allowed themselves to be pushed forward in this sea of arrivals. Stupefied children with dried snot under their noses were dragged mutely along behind their parents. Ray gave up trying to ally himself with some semblance of a line and just pressed his way forward like the rest of the throbbing horde. So much for one's personal space.

The young man in uniform who stamped his passport was about the same age as his son, and when Ray smiled and said, "Merci," the young man answered, "You are welcome." He had been warned by Lenny, the friend who was letting him stay at his apartment in the Sixth, not to take it personally when they answered in English.

"They are absolutely not giving you attitude when they speak to you in English, like all Americans presume," Lenny had said as he was writing out directions and Metro stops for Ray, including little maps as well to some nearby attractions. "So don't get all huffy. They too want to practice their English and show you that they can speak your language…except for those occasions when they *are* giving you attitude."

Ray took his passport and decided this young customs man was in the former category, the well-meaning English learner. After waiting another forty minutes for his bag, Ray was herded into a bus that took such an exhilarating route from the airport into the city that a hush actually fell over all the passengers, and people pressed against the windows and made those little spontaneous "ahh" sounds one hears after a great poem at a poetry reading. There was the Eiffel Tower, flashing its diamonds in the night, and then all the magnificent statues illuminated along the Champs-Élysées. Ray couldn't wait to get out and walk the streets of this beautiful city, to be a part of it, if only for a few days—to discover what would become "his" café, a spot that he would frequent until it was time to head down to Avignon and meet the rest of the gang on this Byroads trip.

"Gare de Lyon!" boomed the bus driver, coming to an abrupt halt in front of the powerful fortress of a train station. Ray thought of all the embraces and intrigue, tears and elation that these walls had witnessed. So much history here. No wonder they thought of California as the Wild West. America was such a young country.

Stumbling out onto the pavement, Ray breathed in the night air. Paris—that wonderful gumbo of piss and cigarette smoke and cologne and diesel and one other ingredient that he could never quite pinpoint…leaves? The Seine? He squinted against the light as he entered the station, located his Metro line, and headed for Lenny's place. He was suddenly wide awake and ravenous, but wasn't sure if anyone would feed him at this hour, it being past midnight. He stepped out when he saw his stop, Vavin, and dragged his suitcase behind him like a pull toy, along the tiled floors, hoisting it up the steps and out into the Paris night. A large and brightly lit brasserie on the grande Boulevarde Montparnasse definitely showed signs of life. So Ray, feeling conspicuous with his luggage and his corrugated airplane clothing, pushed through its doors, where a Maitre d'Hotel promptly showed him to a seat in the back corner of the room near the kitchen doors. No matter. He was happy to have a half carafe of the house rouge and a basket of sliced baguette placed in front of him. He was content to slurp his briny Bouillabaisse and watch the parade of gorgeous, damp youths ascend the steps from the disco below, laughing and leaning on one another as they headed outside for a smoke. For once, he did not even mind eating by himself, as Paris seemed not to notice. Ray was glad he had come. No, he felt more than glad, mopping up the last of his soup with the fine heel of bread. Ray was grateful, grateful for all of it.

Lenny's directions led him through some dicey alleys, and he felt a bit vulnerable at almost two in the morning, what with the bag that screamed TOURIST and the fact that he was now a little woozy from the *vin rouge* and the jet lag it had conjured. But he eventually stood before the right entrance, typed in the code, pressed a very loud buzzer that allowed him to push open the heavy door, and stepped into a small courtyard he imagined would be lovely in the light of day. Only one light was on in all the apartments facing the courtyard, and from somewhere deeper in the complex a dog barked until a woman's muffled voice shouted, *"Ca suffi, Coco!"* The dog gave one last defiant yap, then all was quiet, except for the abiding noise of the traffic. Ray hoped he wasn't getting off on the wrong foot with his neighbors, coming in so late and so noisily, but he would only be there a few days and he was fairly certain these apartments had seen, and heard, their share of transitory visitors.

He switched the light on in the small, courtyard-level room. Like Lenny himself, it was bohemian, comfy, and a bit frayed, and Ray felt at home right away. Barely able to complete the task of undressing and running a toothbrush over his mittened teeth, he fell into a black sleep and did not stir until that same little dog, Coco, woke him, yapping in the hysterical fashion of lap dogs, right outside his window at eight o'clock the next morning. Ray lingered in a baffled fog until all the cogs in his brain lined up with the necessary information: "Lenny's place," "Paris," "vacation," giving him his bearings. Then he rose, showered, and, not bothering to unpack, hit the streets in search of his café and a strong cup of coffee. Once that was accomplished, maybe he would have the good fortune to meet exactly the right person: a native, someone interested in conversing with him about a certain set of missing paintings.

CHAPTER NINETEEN

The flight to Marseilles was surreal, a melodrama, with Phoebe in the leading role playing the Woman Who Saw Spirits. Chagall was everywhere, then nowhere. She first spotted him *outside* her window and almost screamed, instantly whipping her head around to check if her row-mate had noticed her reaction. Her seat neighbor was an ample woman, who pretended not to notice Phoebe's gasp, or maybe she was just too busy trying to keep her body within the confines of her own seat. She appeared to be engrossed in a dog-eared bodice ripper.

"I guess we'll lose our daylight soon," Phoebe began affably. When the woman merely grunted, she persisted: "Wow, it's so different, seeing the sunset from six thousand feet up in the air."

With her own glance, Phoebe was trying to steer the woman's gaze out the window and into the full clownish antics of Marc Chagall, his long grey curls being blown back from his head, even his jowls being pushed backward from the force of it. He looked like he was enjoying himself. She knew by now that no one could see Chagall but she, still, it wouldn't hurt to make sure. The large woman indulged her, albeit not before emitting a beleaguered sigh, leaning forward and looking out the window before settling back into her middle seat. She smoothed her book open again and stated, as if Phoebe had asked, "A lot of folks mind the middle seat. I don't. Never have asked for a window. I just want to pay my fare, get on the plane and arrive at my destination. I take no pleasure in airplane travel. A means to an end, that's all it is. I have a good book to pass the time. 'Course I've already read this one a half-dozen times."

Had Chagall *not* been doing handstands on the plane's wing and trying to get Phoebe to laugh, this would have been the moment that Phoebe would have asked her dour row-mate why she was going to France, but now she decided to just sit back and enjoy the show. The good news was, this broad, disinterested woman next to her was the opposite of chatty, so if Phoebe indulged Chagall now and again by making a funny face back at him, maybe doing the "wiggly eyebrows" thing that used to delight Audrey, no one was likely to notice. So, to pass the time before the next movie, she turned her back to the woman in the middle seat and went into rubber face mode, playing with the airborne artist.

He truly was entertaining. One minute he was imitating the priggish expression of the woman next to her, the next he was pantomiming that he was about to be blown off the wing and plummet to his death. He bit his nails. He mugged looking down at the earth. He shuddered. But then, just when she was caught up in all this, he stopped the shenanigans and his expression grew serious. He had noticed something inside the plane and he frowned.

Chagall flung himself urgently against her window and began gesticulating, pointing wildly past her to a man with a briefcase, who was making his way down the aisle to the bathroom. Chagall jabbed his finger against her window, them mimed pointing to an imaginary briefcase he held up. *YOU!* He pointed and shook his index finger at her. Then the briefcase. Back and forth: *YOU, THE BRIEFCASE!* Alarmed, she enunciated the word *Bomb?* He shook his head impatiently. She mouthed: *Me? Get the briefcase? Huh?* he nodded vigorously and placed his hand over his heart. *IMPORTANT!* Phoebe shrugged her shoulders up, trying to convey *how? Why? What?* Or more to the point: *No way!* But then the woman next to her cleared her throat and Phoebe saw that even though the lady *appeared* to be reading, one of her brows was cocked, clearly indicating that she had seen Phoebe's strange antics and was not amused.

Phoebe gave her a weak smile, flushed, then hurriedly shut the shade on her window and clamped on the headset to watch a movie— any movie, she didn't care. If Chagall had wanted to, he could have shown up on her meal tray or in her lap, for that matter, so she knew that shutting some little window shade was no guarantee that she was safe from his ridiculous requests. After about a half hour, she relaxed, grateful that he was respecting her wishes not to engage. Curiously, the man with the briefcase was on his way down the aisle again and Phoebe could not help but assess him. Tall. Immaculately dressed. Shined shoes. Blonde, almost towheaded, and coiffed in the carefully tousled manner that broadcasted a one-hundred-dollar haircut.

"Excuse me, sir?" Phoebe called out to him when he was opposite her row. She had not intended to do this. It was as if she was a ventriloquist's dummy at the whims of another, except now that she had started it, no one was supplying her with the words to finish.

The man paused and looked down at her quizzically. The woman in the middle seat looked between Phoebe and the gentleman as if reconsidering her original appraisal. The large woman even batted her eyelashes up at him. The woman in the aisle seat, whom Phoebe had not even registered until that second, stood abruptly, assuming that Phoebe was going to want to exit the row to join the man.

"I?" he answered her, dipping his chin slightly. Ah, German, Phoebe thought upon hearing even that one word.

"Yes, you" Phoebe faltered. "I…I was wondering if there is a line to get into the bathroom? I…I saw you return, from a while ago I mean, and I…well, I was just wondering. I cannot tell from where I am seated so I thought I would ask someone with…first-hand experience."

Looking past the German, across the aisle, she saw Chagall jumping up and down on the other wing, applauding vigorously and giving her the thumbs up.

The man with the briefcase looked at her more closely now, the way one might examine a spider one finds in the bathtub, deciding whether to squash it or go to the trouble to place a glass over it, slide the paper beneath, and set it free outdoors.

"I think there is not so much a line. I think now might be an opportune time." He wore a bemused expression, as if she had been flirting with him. Phoebe thanked him with whatever scrap of dignity she could muster, then started to stand, only to realize the headset was still attached; it pulled her hair, forcing her to sit back down. In the process, she spilled what was left of her neighbor's Snappy Tom juice all over her romance novel.

"Ouch!" Phoebe cried at the same second the big woman barked, "Watch it!" Now she had an audience, and in spite of herself she dug a deeper hole, addressing them all and asking with a nervous chuckle: "Doncha just hate it when you forget these things are on your head? Sheesh." What was this ditzy vaudevillian act that she was lapsing into? "Excuse me," she said, trying to regain her composure and looking directly down at Middle Seat. "I need to get out. I apologize and will replace your book if you leave me your address."

The woman seemed more wary of Phoebe than angry.

"Don't bother," she said, heaving herself up and joining the other woman in the aisle. The German had continued on his way, glancing back once over his left shoulder before entering his row. Phoebe noted that the briefcase he was carrying was made from some sort of stained alligator hide, nubby and a glossy wine color, and that the man was seated in the window seat four rows in front of her. But this was madness, she thought, making her way back to the bathroom. She could somewhat come to terms with the fact that she had been seeing Chagall's ghost for weeks now, and that, were she to believe what he said, she had summoned him herself. She had been trying to heed Molly's advice, pondering what lessons she might need to learn from Chagall's ghost, and why at this juncture in her life he chose to appear. True, he had already inspired her to explore and expand her painting, and had probably, in some mysterious way, even contributed to her decision to take this trip. But now he was showing up willy-nilly and urging her to carry out some sort of theft! And why? She shut the door behind her and closed her eyes. She was dizzy from all of this, but her senses were astonishingly heightened.

Phoebe was confused by the outlandishness of everything that had taken place so far on this flight. She decided not to indulge these visitations. Surely she still had some control over her own imagination, or at least could choose *when* she was willing to see the ghost. She was just going to avoid looking out the window or looking at the German for the rest of the flight. She was simply going to focus on the movies and read and try to sleep. She could do that. There were only five hours to go. But just then, as she was washing her hands, she thought she saw in the mirror a fleeting glimpse of Chagall standing directly behind her, shaking his head in disappointment before vanishing, as if he could tell that she was planning on defying him.

Since her flight was arriving so late and the Byroads trip did not start for two days, Phoebe had booked a room near the Marseilles airport and rented a car so that she could explore The Camargue, that remote, marshy, cowboy and flamingo-filled part of Southern France that tourists rarely put on their itineraries. If she had been hired to design the travel poster, she might have dubbed it The Everglades of France. She wanted to see the white Carmargue horses, taste the pink and grey salt that was harvested from the marshes here, and maybe do some birding at dusk. But primarily, she just wanted to drive from bustling Marseille to this wilder place on little lanes where she might happen upon an artist's studio or a roadside fruit stand. In fact, she wanted happening upon things to be the general rule of this trip, and had promised herself to remain open to it all.

At baggage claim, she tried not to look at the German directly. She practiced casting furtive glances at him without much movement of her head. He was talking briskly in German on his cell phone and looking at his watch, clearly perturbed with how long the bags were taking to materialize on the carousel. She let her own suitcase go around twice, a scuffed chartreuse cloth number that she had chosen thinking it would be distinctive, failing to account for how quickly that color would be soiled and streaked with black marks. Then she saw him reach out for some sort of designer bag with gold initials all over it, hoist it up and onto the floor, snap out the handle, and head off toward the exit. There was not one wasted movement. Phoebe waited one more rotation, then took her own bag and went to catch the shuttle to the hotel.

As she walked to the front desk to check in, she was pleased to see a pool large enough to actually swim laps in without forcing a U-turn every few strokes. At this late hour, there was a wonderful absence of screaming children in the pool. And once Phoebe saw the Lilliputian dimensions of her room—she could touch both walls by standing in the middle with her arms outstretched—she decided on the spot to swim until the light faded. She could grab a bite to eat in the hotel's own restaurant for the sake of ease, then try to get some sleep, determined not to do the traveler's mental calculations as to what time it *really* was back home.

The water was warm and not overly chlorinated, and she gave herself over to being in a tropical place, with its palm trees, bougainvillea, and the local *Goute D'or* fig trees laden with delectable, plump fruits. Hotel guests were dining outside on a patio strewn with hurricane lights that gave it a cheery, holiday feel. She sensed that they were watching her swim back and forth, in her yellow bathing cap and her adequate forty-something body, yet she was not self-conscious in the least. She knew that it was entertaining to watch someone engaged in physical activity, a worker laying bricks, someone mowing a lawn, a neighbor planting a rosebush. She too found it pleasing to watch fellow humans actively involved in some pursuit, especially if she was relaxing with a nice drink. Phoebe could allow for most any human shortcoming except lack of curiosity.

After about twenty minutes it was getting too dark to see, and since no one had turned on the pool lights, the walls on each end sprang up too suddenly before her. She stopped swimming and, breathing rapidly, rose from the water, climbing up the three steps from the shimmering pool. She took her time drying off her hair and arms and legs, breathing in a waft of jasmine, its perfume strengthening as night arrived. Then she wrapped the towel around herself and headed up to her room.

After she had showered and put on one of the many little black dresses she had packed, she stood at the entrance of the restaurant until a waiter showed her to a table by the pool. She chose the chair at her table that would put her back toward the main dining room. While she did not enjoy eating alone, Phoebe sipped her glass of local Rosé, felt the warm evening breeze in her damp hair, and discovered that so far, she was actually enjoying traveling solo. There was time for pondering, for arriving upon ideas for paintings, even opportunities for making new acquaintances. She had found during the years that she traveled with her ex that couples often had a sort of force field around them, cutting them off from everyone outside of their partnered universe. She only met locals and had real adventures after she had separated from him. Being alone made you braver, she decided. The wine, the sawing song of the cicadas, and the smell of warm stones, lulled her into a delicious calm.

Her dinner arrived, an aromatic Bouillabaisse presented in two bowls, one filled with a saffron-colored broth and the other filled with the "treasures," morsels of fresh cod, potatoes, carrots, and a delicate confetti of herbs. Just as she was about to combine the two, she dropped the big spoon, because she noticed the German, being led to a nearby table, toting the burgundy briefcase. Phoebe shifted in her seat, trying to make sure she was fully turned away, and carrying on as if she hadn't noticed him, giving her full attention to the food. What were the chances of this? But inevitably, he had to pass her table to step outside, and their eyes met. She gave him a tepid smile, which he returned as if she were a stranger, though she was fairly certain he could not have forgotten the plane incident so soon. She dabbed at her lips with her napkin and continued to eat.

While she chewed, Phoebe gazed at the waters in the pool and appreciated how the strings of lights played colorfully on the water's gloss. But then she saw a form beneath the surface. Oh God, not here. Not now. But yes, there he was, in some sort of woolen one-piece swimming tog popular in the twenties—Chagall, floating on his back and spurting little fountains of water up from his lips before disappearing into the pool's dark depths. Phoebe saw that though he was swimming with a graceful strength, his movements caused no ripples on the water's surface.

Phoebe no longer bothered to check if others could see the man, here in this new country. She knew it was her own private heaven or hell; the jury was still out on that one. She desperately wanted some distraction, so she dunked a heel of baguette into her Bouillabaisse, bit into it, and promptly began to choke. This was serious choking, not the momentary coughing that a swig of water will cure, but the eyes-watering, bits-of-food-flying-from-the-mouth-struggling-for-oxygen type of choking. Another diner, a tall, very tanned woman with a blue turban, came to her side and began thwacking her on the back, crying: "*Ca-va, Madame? Ca-vas pas?*" Phoebe tried to nod that she would be okay, pointing to her throat as if anyone needed an explanation as to what the problem was.

"You are all right, Madame?" her waiter asked, arriving with another glass of water.

"*Non, Monsieur,*" the bronzed diner said, making a tsk-tsking gesture with her index finger. "*Pain.* Bread. This is best. It pushes the choking down." As Phoebe continued to sputter, she logged that the woman said "poo-chez" in a lovely way. The waiter scoffed and tried to get Phoebe to drink, but the woman stepped in front of him and handed Phoebe a slice of baguette, even though that had been the culprit to begin with, and while it was the last thing she felt like doing in that moment, she bit into it and, through coughs, managed somehow to finally swallow. Culprit and hero, the bread worked, and Phoebe wiped the tears from her cheeks and the food from her chin and said humbly but resoundingly, "*Excusez-moi*" and "*Merci, merci mille fois*" to the woman and the waiter. So much for trying to remain in the background.

The turbaned woman had become possessive of Phoebe now, rubbing her back and asking, "*Ca-va*? You are okay?"

Phoebe stood, reassuring everyone *oui, oui,* and they soon returned to their business. She sat back down, not daring to look at the German. She felt the need to flee, so she signed her room number on the check and headed rapidly for the lobby. As she departed, she saw that the German was no longer at his table and wherever he was, he had *not* taken the briefcase with him. Without thinking, she bent down and, in one fluid motion, picked up the valise as if it were her own and headed up the stairs.

Phoebe was lightheaded and her hands were trembling as she sought the lock with her room key. Luckily, no one had been on the stairs when she was, nor in the hallway leading to her room, though her mind raced with alibis: *Oh this? I don't really know why I picked it up. I felt disoriented after the choking incident and I must have confused it with my own bag. So sorry!* Feeble, but it would have to do.

On the endless journey down the hall to her room, she'd half-expected the German to put two and two together and come bounding up behind her, knocking her down and snatching back the attaché. So she rushed inside and threw it on the bed, praying that the briefcase was not locked. Looking at it, incongruously, an idea for a future painting sprang into her head where the alligator who had given its life for the case was actually *this* color, roaming the Everglades with others of its kind who were bright orange or blue. But no time for such thoughts now.

The case, of course, was locked, and Phoebe was certain now that she heard footsteps in the hall. She fished around in her purse and found a bobby pin, then jabbed, poked and jiggled until the latch popped open. *A thousand-dollar valise with inferior locks,* she thought with immense satisfaction, proceeding to open the latch on the other side with equal ease.

And there it was. Right on top. Protected only by a few blank sheets of printer paper above and below. The small painting was signed clear as day in the left-hand corner with his name, Marc Chagall. Phoebe gasped and reached out to pick it up, gingerly, as if it *were* a bomb. She drew it closer to her face. She touched the rough surface, tracing with her fingertip a small peacock playing a tiny blue violin, a crescent moon with little feet, like a lizard, a flying goat with a half-animal, half-human face, and a floating woman right in the center, looking at the viewer and holding out a voluminous red bouquet. So many elements contained in such a small canvas. Then she stopped and drew in her breath, leaning in closer to study the woman. This floating woman...she looked unmistakably like Phoebe. Not an exact replica, in the realistic way of a snapshot, but something about her reminded Phoebe of her own lines and expressions. Even the breasts were the same, and the short, muscular build.

"You do remind me of her...just a little," Chagall said, suddenly behind her. "Of my Bella. You are brave like her and your shape is the same."

Phoebe had dropped the painting on the floor in her alarm and Chagall bent to retrieve it.

He looked at it long and wistfully before speaking, holding it by the edges.

"I remember painting this one. I was missing Bella terribly, that first time in Paris, and wanted to populate the painting of her with as many of the creatures she loved as I could reasonably fit, so neither of us would be lonely. She loved flowers...and goats. She always said they were so much smarter than sheep."

"They are indeed," Phoebe said softly, respecting the tender way the artist was looking at the piece. She watched him carefully a moment more, then ventured, "Are you able to see Bella? I mean...where you both are now?"

"My God, this one has been missing for almost a full century now, can you believe it?" Chagall said, shaking his head, as if he had not heard her. "I went back after the war to the Beehive, La Rouche, where

I had stayed, but my studio had long since been occupied by someone else. My friends gathered up as many of my paintings as they could, to protect them, as even then, before I was well known, paintings were stolen. It was my earlier work, but still, it is such a violation. My friends, the ones who stayed behind in Paris, kept my rescued canvases here and there, moving them when they moved, but the war made scavengers of us all. I do not blame the other artists for not keeping a closer eye on my work. They were trying to survive, and I was not yet a known painter, and...well, it was inevitable, I suppose."

Phoebe did not repeat her question about Bella.

Chagall peered closer at his painting once more, placed it gently down on the bed, and cocked an ear to the hallway. Then, he put his hands on Phoebe's shoulders and said to her, sadly, "And now you've got to give it back."

"What?" she yelled in disbelief. "After all this? I could go to jail! How can you doubt for one second that this man acquired it in some shady way? Why would he be carrying a Chagall that has been missing for almost a century around in his briefcase, for God's sake? He's a crook!" Phoebe couldn't bite back her incredulity that Chagall was not going to give her instructions that had more moral significance than this, especially after the huge risk she had taken.

"Yes," Chagall said heavily. "You are correct. This man did not come by my painting legally, nor did any of the owners who held it before it landed in this briefcase. But now is not the time. Do as I say and just give it back. All of this will work itself out if it was meant to be. The timing is wrong."

"Marc," Phoebe cried, exasperated enough to shout his name aloud, "you sound like you are resigned to this loss again. Why can't we turn him in or pursue this to its rightful conclusion? We have the proof we need right in our hands. I am more than willing to put up a fight for you, whatever it takes. And beyond all of this: How am I supposed to get it *back* to this person? By now they have surely called the police."

"The same way you obtained it, my dear," said Chagall, starting to shimmer a bit, pre-fade. "Seamlessly."

"But…" Phoebe was now addressing only an empty space in front of her. It was after midnight. She was absolutely crushed and bewildered by the outcome of all this, as she had felt called upon, heroic, and more alive than she'd felt since she was a young woman who took more chances.

And why *should* the German possess something so extraordinary and dazzling when it ought to be accessible to so many eyes? Phoebe hugged it to herself and felt that she might die if she had to part with it now. She pictured it on the wall opposite her bed in her home, the Blue House in Sonoma, waking up to it every day and entering its sumptuous world…such happiness! In a flash, Phoebe considered what such a painting was worth, and how this small rectangle had the power to rescue her from all her financial nightmares. But no, then she would be in league with the German and all the others who had not come forward, war or no war, who had been seduced first by the art and then by the money it would fetch. Phoebe was so spent from her long journey to this hotel and the ensuing bravado that finally, the fight went out of her and she was resigned to her duty. She reverently placed the painting face-down on the paper, laying a few sheets on top of the back of it, but not before noticing another, loose charcoal sketch there on the flip side, in the corner, smudged but clearly a little caricature of a bearded man wearing a jaunty cap. It made her smile. It was a little P.S. from Chagall, a sweet secret only for the owner.

Her room was so narrow that when she opened the closet door it brushed against the corner of the mattress. She groped around until her hand felt the plastic laundry bag most hotels provided. Using her nail scissors, she cut the drawstring from around the top, then used it to tie the briefcase shut, now that its locks no longer functioned.

Phoebe clutched the briefcase to her chest, looking both ways from the doorframe before walking out into the hallway as if stepping into oncoming traffic. She walked quickly but quietly past the elevator and opened the door to the stairs. Also empty. Well, and if they asked her at the front desk how she had come by the briefcase and why it was broken open, she would simply say she had found it this way in the hallway and thought she should bring it down to the front desk. After all, nothing was missing. But, miracle upon miracle, there was no one behind the front desk, everyone apparently having left his or her station briefly to enjoy the live jazz performance that was taking place in the bar.

Phoebe glided past the desk, leaving the briefcase in her wake. She then joined some other guests huddled in the doorway of the bar, who were tapping their feet and swaying at the outskirts of the performance. The man who had earlier been her waiter smiled and cleared a space, inviting her to come inside and sit, but she said, "*Non merci*," and mimed a yawn, making her hands into a pillow onto which she tilted her head. He nodded and wandered back into the thicket of tables.

Once back in her room and too tired to do anything but fall into the narrow bed, Phoebe switched on the petite black-and-white television, hoping to just let the French wash over her and lull her instantly to sleep. The last thing she recalled seeing was the luminous face of a young Candice Bergen, filling the screen. She was tromping through a jungle somewhere, her camera hanging around her neck, her beauty making the French photographer she was working with forget his wedding vows entirely.

CHAPTER TWENTY

During the period when Chagall was trapped in Russia, individualism was an endangered species. Chagall knew his days as teacher were numbered, that he was considered "a disruptive element." What did he care? True, he needed the pittance he was paid, but he was virtually a prisoner now. He knew it was ungracious to be such a malcontent when there were shortages, even famine. At least he had work, thanks to a friend from the Paris days who wound up stuck in Russia, too, but, unlike Chagall, was in a position of some power. Chagall was teaching art to orphans, which was gratifying if often heartbreaking work. Pupils and adults alike addressed one another as "comrade," and Chagall was constantly advised via missives from the Kremlin to incorporate publicism in his teaching, and to make sure that all of Russia's artists were turning out paintings that promoted industry. Chagall found this abhorrent, the idea that a government could predetermine an artist's work, no longer genuine expression but merely the product of some message-mill.

He had been asked to paint a beautiful mural for the theater, and after two years, he had yet to be paid. He longed with every fiber of his being to get his wife and daughter out of this country. It was a bitter winter in Moscow; the preparations for going to bed each night involved brushing the snow off the narrow, hard iron bed. It drifted defiantly into the corners of the small wooden house they had been given when they first arrived to accept his post. A deep disappointment—big title, no big salary. Now, in any case, Chagall was no longer Commissar of Art, just a humble teacher of orphans, and there was no hope in sight, because if he did not paint political paintings, Chagall knew he was unlikely to get a government commission. It was a doomed future any way you looked at it, and each day Chagall grew more despondent.

"You are not as bad off as some," Bella would say to him in their drafty room, the main warmth coming from their two bodies pressed together. "You have friends who are in high positions now who can help us get food, and you are allowed to teach. Plus, you have enough money for paint, and for bread. And best of all, you have never been forced onto a battlefield or thrown in prison."

"I watched your parents stand by as soldiers took everything from them, even the silver and the plates they had just eaten off of!" Chagall said to her. "And I saw how it broke them. Yet still that wasn't enough. They assumed these noble old people must have been hiding more, so they took axes to the walls of your childhood home. Aren't you angry? I can no longer bear what this country has become. It revolts me. I can find no peace until I can take you and Ida away from here."

"Then use your connections, my love," Bella whispered, massaging his shoulders and tucking a wisp of hair behind his ear. How could she not want vengeance? Her family had suffered more at their hands than his had, and yet she was not bitter, just steadily trying to figure out their future. "Try every last one of them, Marco. Anyone who owes you a favor."

"No one owes a lowly artist a favor," Chagall said with disdain. "It is always the other way around. No one even pays the artist for services rendered. No, Bella sweet, they all respond only to bribes. Nothing has changed since the days my mother gave the school money so they would teach a Jew."

"You must keep trying. Your art is becoming better known in the West. Surely there are people in other countries who have heard that you are trapped here and would be willing to help you."

Chagall shrugged. He was weary of it all—the struggle, the bureaucracy, trying to feed his wife and daughter on a teacher's wages. All he wanted to do was paint, and not paintings with slogans or subliminal messages, just whatever came to him naturally. One day he received a letter from a friend in Germany telling him that Berlin in 1922 was like Montparnasse had been in 1914. "There is such a feeling of 'Why not?' here, of anything goes, perhaps because the city seems poised for collapse. If this war ever ends we will need your art more than ever to lift our spirits. By the way, your man Herman Waldin has sold a good many of the paintings you left with him eight years ago in Berlin, some to private collectors, some to his Swedish wife. She has managed to protect them from the ravages of war, but I must warn you: I don't think you'll be seeing much of the money. Yes, the inflation is a valid excuse, but still you need to be compensated. You are well known in Europe. Can't you *somehow* procure a passport? Half of Berlin these days is made up of Muscovites; you would fit right in. May we meet again before too long in the City of Lights!"

When Chagall read that his paintings had been sold but that he might not see his share of the money, he was stunned. If the gallery had been bombed or looted, he could understand Waldin begging helplessness. But if the man had earned money from Chagall's own labor... well, the news made his blood boil. This was the impetus he needed— and surely Bella had reached this point long ago—to drive him to do whatever was necessary to get them out of the country. He racked his brains, trying to think of something he had not yet tried, of anyone anywhere in Russia who owed him a favor or even thought highly enough of him and his family to come to his aid, anyone whom he might beg to secure him and his family an exit visa. He eventually approached the same fellow he always ended up facing—the Commissar of Enlightenment—and pleaded for the papers needed to leave for Berlin.

"My paintings are known outside of this country now, sir. It would cast a good light on Russia, my homeland, if I were allowed to exhibit abroad and come and go as a normal citizen of the world." Chagall tried to keep the quaver out of his voice when putting forth his case.

For some reason, perhaps nostalgic for that time in his own youth spent in the freewheeling city of Paris, the man simply nodded and granted him permission, stamping the documents and sending Chagall on his way. This was so unexpected, such a fantastic turn of events, that Chagall almost did cartwheels all the way back to his apartment to tell Bella. At last, in 1922, Chagall had found a way to leave Russia. The only dark cloud on the days leading up to his departure was that Bella was healing from an injury she had gotten falling off a stage during a performance, and since only one passport was to be granted, all he could do was promise he would send for her, "once I sort out this business with the gallery owner." After a long, tense train trip, during which Chagall's sense of outrage and injustice at not being paid for his work had reached a peak, he arrived solo in the city of Berlin. In his suitcase were nine notebooks, journals of the unimaginable twists and turns his life had taken over the past decade.

Chagall wanted to bide his time to get his bearings and adjust to the new city, but he couldn't rest until he had confronted Herman Waldin. He found him at his gallery, and the man greeted him effusively, not striking Chagall as the least bit sheepish or dishonest. "You are quite famous in the West, my friend," Waldin said heartily, indicating a chair for Chagall to sit down. "They are now saying you are responsible for Expressionism, which is very big in our city at the moment."

While Chagall was secretly pleased that he had not vanished from the art world during his exile in Russia, he scoffed. "Another -ism. But let's get right to the matter at hand. I have come to get paid for all of my work that you have sold since I left."

"Ah, my friend," Walden said, shaking his head ruefully. "I have kept an account for you here and each time I sold a painting, your share went right into that account. But I think you will be dismayed at what that sum is worth now, given the monumental inflation currently in Germany. It is hard to even begin to grasp how little a Deutsche Mark is worth, especially for you, who have been away during the worst of all this."

Chagall's demeanor immediately changed and he took his hat off the table and stood up as if he had been slapped in the face.

"I want a detailed accounting of the whereabouts of every single one of my paintings by the end of the week." Chagall shouted. "And I want to be paid the exact amount we agreed upon, or I will insist that my paintings returned. That is what is fair and there is nothing more to discuss."

"But Marc!" protested the gallery owner. "You cannot be serious! There was a *war*, man. Surely you can see it is not *my* fault our German money is worth considerably less than it was when you had your opening here eight years ago! You must see that. A *war!*"

"And surely *you* can appreciate that it is not *my* fault either, and I have a family to feed and paint to buy. You still have your gallery and you have made money off of me and I want my share."

"My wife had some money for a time and you should know that she bought many of your paintings herself," Waldin retorted hotly. "You should be glad for that, Marc, as they are safe in Sweden. She actually saved them by purchasing them. I can't possibly account for where all the others have ended up. The gallery was shut down for several months during the worst of it. I imagine some soldiers or looters got in and took what they wanted. Exceptional times call for exceptional measures. Surely you have heard this expression. That is the case here. I did what I could to protect your work but you are not the only one who has suffered a loss. The matter is completely out of my hands at this point."

"I am not interested in excuses," Chagall said, stepping so close to the man that they could smell one another's sweat. "I want to be paid and I want my paintings returned, the ones that did not sell. I will speak to the courts on Monday if you haven't lived up to your end of the bargain. Do not think for one minute that I won't. War or no war, what's right is right and I will not be taken advantage of."

With this, Chagall turned and walked out, leaving Waldin standing behind his desk with his jaw hanging open.

Chagall slammed the door on his way out. He was secretly proud of his display of righteous indignation, as it was unquestionably justified, but as events unfolded, it became clear that Waldin must have felt the same way about his own position, for Chagall was forced to hire a lawyer. And even with legal help and all the time and expense, Chagall was still only able to track down a few of his paintings. He did manage in the end to feel some small sense of justice, from the verdict that required Waldin to actually to buy some of the sold paintings back from their private collectors, that, and his wife was forced to return three large oils as part of the reparations to Chagall. Chagall was paid a much smaller sum than he should have been, but that was not what bothered him the most. It was the principle of the matter. The paintings were his insides, his youth, representations of a frozen moment in time when anything was possible. He had lost eight years of his career, and now he had lost many of his paintings as well.

Bella and Ida had joined him by this time. He laid the rescued paintings all in a row on the floor of their apartment and paced up and down, stopping before one in particular, rubbing his chin and smiling at some fond memory he found there.

Eventually, Chagall turned to his wife with tears in his eyes and said, "I am a man without a past."

"Don't be silly, my love," Bella said. "What does that even mean? You are so melodramatic. It is humanly impossible not to have a past. You *are* your past, everyone is."

"I have lost my youth and my past, the part of me contained in those paintings, and I can never retrieve them." Chagall knew he was indulging himself, but he was unable to shake the frustration at how the war had desecrated his life. He would struggle ever after not to be bitter.

"You are lucky—a lucky man who never sees it," Bella said, handing her daughter a glass of water. "You are alive, Marc. You have been able to continue painting. You were allowed to leave Russia. You have a beautiful wife and daughter. When will you appreciate all of this? Sometimes

I wonder if you like being melancholy…maybe a little?" She mussed his hair and smiled at him. Chagall would allow no one but his wife to tease him this way.

Chagall stuck his lower lip out in such a classic expression of pouting stubbornness that Bella had to laugh. He was not going to relinquish his cherished sorrow easily.

"But my paintings…so many of them, lost," he said mournfully.

"So? You will paint more. Starting today. You will paint some more."

She linked her arm through his and spun him around to face the door, saying: "Come, we've wasted enough time. Let's go out into this grey Berlin day and have some fortification. Then, let's figure out a way to get all of us out of this dark city and back to Paris."

CHAPTER TWENTY-ONE

It was difficult for Ray to choose just one café in Montparnasse to call his home away from home, since so many of them, like Hem's favorite La Closerie des Lilas, or Le Verre Volant, had such illustrious pasts, and therefore might hold clues for his prospective book. He ultimately chose Le Verre Volant, that historic temple to bohemia favored by Chagall and his friends so long ago. He chose it because it was one of the cafés that had been known to allow then-unknown artists to exchange a drawing or painting for some food and wine. The affection shown to the artists at these noble brasseries, and the respect for their work, was Ray's favorite discovery during his research.

What had started out as a simple project born from Ray's own curiosity about missing art from both wars, had mushroomed into a full-fledged obsession. Ray never thought he would utter that famous phrase: "I think there's a book in this," but there he was. A new bit of information had fanned the flames as well. Ray had recently read that an auction was to be held in England offering some charcoal nudes of men and other drawings that Adolph Hitler had made for his second failed attempt to get into the Vienna Academy of Art in 1908. Ray went on to discover that many biographers speculated that it was this very rejection from art school, which Hitler blamed on Jewish professors, that forced him to live in a homeless shelter and sell postcards to earn money, a bitter experience that he never got over. And while there were no simple explanations for Hitler's rabid anti-Semitism, Ray could well imagine that in the crazed, paranoid recesses of the young man's mind, this rejection from art school *could* have fueled such hatred; certainly it might have contributed to his later, relentless drive to possess all of the world's great art.

Ray had to admit that much of his willingness to take this bike trip was because it was based in the south of France, allowing him to pass through Paris and ask some questions of locals at various cafés and galleries. He was hoping to get stories from people who had experienced the occupation first hand, and, knowing the Frenchman's propensity for strong opinion, he knew if he could only connect with the right source, the stories would be passionate ones.

At each place he tried, however, the results were the same. Even though he made a point to arrive at off hours, when the staff might have more time to chat, it turned out that there were no off hours, hence no one was interested in speaking with him. These historic cafés, whose former clientele read like a who's who of Lost Generation Paris writers as well as luminaries in the art world, turned out to be immensely popular with locals and tourists alike. Ray quickly discovered that these brass-and-red-velvet grande dames of Paris bistros were no longer the watering holes of the struggling ex-pats and painters. No, these days, a mediocre French beer set Ray back ten euros. Best to stick to the more reliable *vin ordinaire*, which was often quite good and far from ordinary, and to talk to as many people as he could until he found someone both familiar with life during the occupation and also willing to give him five minutes.

Since Ray was due to meet the rest of the Byroads folks in Marseilles in just three days, he didn't have much time. He wanted to see any museum that had a Chagall gracing its walls. He would also allow himself a good chunk of time to view the wonderfully preserved ceiling at the Paris Opera, where Chagall had painted his signature cornucopia of airborne lovers and creatures, all bathed in delicious tones of red. Would there also be time to explore the vast parks, to go to the intriguing and little-known Insect Museum at Jardin des Plantes? Time to watch the little boys pushing their beautiful miniature sailboats with long sticks across the waters in the fountains at Jardin du Luxembourg? And if so, would he still have time to do the requisite sleuthing at his brasseries about those missing paintings? He would certainly try.

His first day, he interrogated as many waiters and patrons at three old establishments, including his own Le Verre Volant, as he could delicately manage without getting tossed out on his ear. In his perfectly decent French, Ray would stop the waiter delivering his coffee with a hurried: "*Excusez-moi, Monsieur?*"

The waiter would do a slight about-face, answering with a drawn-out, nasal, "*Oouuï?*" in an annoyed tone.

Then Ray would dive into the history of "this fine establishment" and explain how he was writing a book and how he wondered if anyone might have information as to the days when artists, specifically Marc Chagall, were habitués here and were known to pay for food and drink with paintings.

Ever the jesters, the waiters in particular would mock: "Oh no, Monsieur. Those days are gone. We do not accept anything today but money." Or: "Your book sounds interesting, Monsieur, and there are many libraries in Paris that can help you, but *hélas*, as you can see, that was before my time and I have many hungry diners to tend to."

Sometimes, Ray was simply ignored, or the waiter would walk away when he was halfway through his prologue, holding up a finger and insisting: "*Ne quitter pas, ne quitter pas,*" the equivalent of *don't go anywhere, be right back*, before they rushed away.

But then, very early on his second day at La Rotonde, he noticed a man staring at him from across the room. He was an older gentleman with a droopy grey moustache and an air of faded glory about him, his long elegant fingers turning the pages of a copy of his *Le Monde* newspaper. When Ray nodded at him, he beckoned him over by pointing to the empty chair beside him.

Without preamble, the Frenchman said, "You want to talk with Benoit, Monsieur. For your book."

"My book? Uh…how did…"

But the man continued as if Ray had not spoken.

"He has been a patron at Le Verre Volant since the occupation, same table, every day, his back to the window—reliable as the ticking of a clock, never varies, always orders the special of the day and two glasses of Bordeaux. Not ever will he go to any other place. You can recognize him also because he always has a short red scarf tied around his neck, in all weathers. He's your man. In fact, he worked at the Louvre during the occupation and has been honored as one of our heroes of the resistance, who hid many of the most priceless masterworks, saving them from plunder."

"Thank you…but how did you know about my book?"

The man laughed and said, "Paris is a large city, Monsieur, but the *cafés* of Paris are very small societies, little villages really. I have seen enough of you these past twenty-four hours to overhear things. And it is not every day that a customer tried to interview a waiter. You see, these are my neighborhood cafés and you are suddenly everywhere."

"Well, again, I appreciate your…"

"My name is Georges," he said without shaking hands. "I myself am a writer and I think your book sounds interesting, which is enough reason for me to try and help you. But Benoit, he will have far more to offer. He *notices* better than I do, has been around longer, and then there is the fact that he loves intrigue and causing trouble."

"Well, I'm afraid my research is hardly rife with espionage," Ray said.

"No? I think missing art is quite the juicy topic, Monsieur. Perhaps you have read of our own recent thefts? Just this year? The Musee D'Orsay evidently neglected to turn on its alarm system and the lone thief simply sawed off a little padlock and voila! One hundred million dollars' worth of paintings, gone. Poof!"

Ray nodded. "Yes, I was appalled. I own a gallery in San Francisco, so on some level I can relate to the enormity of this travesty. But all the same, such well-known art? Surely the thief will have no hope of selling it without being arrested. Talk about conspicuous."

"*Au contraire*, Monsieur Ray. The general consensus is that the robbery took place to fill a special order, as it were. The shopping list of a private and extremely wealthy collector."

Both men were silent, Ray, for his part, contemplating what it must be like to be able to possess whatever one wanted, to not understand the words "unavailable" or "impossible."

"So go find Benoit," Georges said. "Some speculate that he has a long scar across his throat, and that is why he wears the red scarf, to hide it—but then there are many rumors that surround this fellow, so who knows? Perhaps these years of the occupation are later than the time these artists would trade paintings for food, maybe too late for what you are writing about. I do not know. Still, I would guess that starving artists existed during both wars, and continue in their hunger even today. But this man Benoit has seen many, many things in his life, and still remembers them all, down to the last detail, unlike myself, just as old as he but less accurate these days. No matter what, he would be a good resource, first hand experience and all. He is always there sharply at twelve noon, without fail, and while he can be a very big grouch, if you buy him *un verre* he will like the attention and tell you things you will find very…useful. Go today, go now, he will be there shortly."

Ray reached out for the man's hand to thank him and heard a low growl from under his table.

"*Saucisson, ca suffit maintenant!*" the man admonished the loyal Dachshund with the graying muzzle who lay at his feet. "My dog is very fierce and very protective of his master," Georges said with great pride.

"Then you are lucky to have such a fine dog. *Merci*, Monsieur… Georges," said Ray, stepping back and tossing some euros onto the small tray with the torn ticket that the waiter had left. "You have saved the day."

Ray said all this in French, but once out on the street wondered fleetingly if he might have in fact said "you have suffered the day." But Georges had nodded once with great dignity, handed a small piece of buttered baguette to his dog, and continued reading his paper.

As promised, when Ray arrived at noon at Le Verre Volant, Benoit was there, unmistakable in his red scarf, his back to the window. While the waiter tried to sit Ray elsewhere, he pointed insistently at the empty table next to the old man. The waiter argued briefly that all tables were the same. What was wrong with the one in the back, so much "closer to the kitchen, the source of the food?" But the place was crowded and the waiter didn't want to waste any more time fussing with the headstrong American, and so placed the menu down huffily on Ray's chosen table. Benoit continued sipping his red, not acknowledging Ray, just looking around the room noncommittally in between bites of his Cassoulet, no book or newspaper for distraction. Even though it was quite warm outside and this was more of a wintry dish, Ray ordered the daily special also, Cassoulet au Canard, so that he would have some sort of overture for conversation with the man whose creased face and alert eyes indicated that he had seen more than his share of history.

When Benoit finally glanced his way, Ray seized upon the opportunity to engage him.

"Delicious cassoulet!" he exclaimed.

"The duck is dry and the sauce salty. Not one of their better efforts," Benoit replied perfunctorily.

"Yes," Ray back-peddled. "And you should know, being such a loyal regular."

Benoit cocked an eyebrow at Ray. This unearned familiarity had caught his attention.

"Do I know you?" Benoit asked coolly.

"No," Ray answered, sliding his chair a bit closer to the man's table. "But you were recommended to me. From a man at another brasserie down the Boulevard."

"Recommended?"

"Well, I am doing some research, possibly for a book or…something. And with all your years of observations at this very table, you could be a tremendous resource." When the man stiffened, Ray added, "Your wine is almost gone. May I buy you another? Bordeaux, isn't it?"

"I wouldn't say no," Benoit replied, relaxing slightly. "What is your book about?"

"I have heard that many of the painters before the first war, before they became famous, passed through the doors of this establishment and that the owners allowed them to pay with their artwork from time to time."

Benoit was inscrutable, only nodding, taking up his fresh glass and saying: "Yes, that is what is said."

"Well, I know Marc Chagall in particular lost many of his paintings during that time, when he was stuck in Russia and couldn't get back into Paris, and that he frequented Le Verre Volant."

"Yes, but Monsieur, I may look ancient, but that was well before my time, another war entirely."

"I know, but I thought maybe you had seen some of his work somewhere? Here? Over the years? Or maybe knew something about it? Or about this old policy this café had toward the artists had before they became famous? Anything?'

"I try to mind my own business," Benoit said airily, waving a weathered hand. "There have been several owners of the place since I began coming here, so who knows where those old morsels of canvas and painted menus and designs on napkins are now? And today, the place is no longer even in the family."

Benoit seemed to enjoy being evasive. Ray felt the man was testing his chutzpah, so he pushed on.

"But have you ever glimpsed a painting, or one of these morsels, as you say, that looked like it *might* be the real deal? In the back room, say, or by accident, what with all the time you've been coming here?"

"You Americans always imagine yourselves to be Inspector Clouseau," Benoit chuckled. "Who knows what goes on in the back room here? A painting that valuable would definitely not be on display on the walls of a café." He said this dismissively but without malice, so Ray persisted, secretly enjoying the Clouseau reference.

"Yes, I guess this project does bring out the sleuth in me. But you have to ask yourself, where did all these works of art *go*? Somebody surely is not coming forward."

"Well, would you, Monsieur? If you stumbled upon a dusty old scrap of canvas that you thought would be a *vrai* Picasso or a Matisse? Would you surrender it so easily?"

"Well, I would think for the right price, anyone would."

"Ah, now we are onto a different subject: money. If you loved the painting itself, you would keep it, no? Hide it away and have it for your own pleasure? But if you wanted to sell it, something that was not really yours, it might get confiscated and then you would have nothing. What would be the solution?" Ray could tell Benoit was warming to this line of banter as he leaned more forward in his seat and even smacked his lips.

"I don't know…is there a black market?"

"But of course!" Benoit exclaimed, slamming his glass down on the table as if Ray had just given the correct response to a game show question. "There are those who sell to collectors who ask very few questions about how you might have come by such a fine painting. All they care about is that it is for sale. And if you are the outsider who has bought the café from the great-grandson of the café owner, and come across something that a family member would consider of far too much sentimental value to *ever* part with, well, you, not having any attachment whatsoever to such relics, *you* might pass these ancient things along to the right parties and, with a father and grandfather now dead and a great-grandson not interested in running a café, well, there would be no one to stop you. You might sell quite a few of these little canvasses and no one would ever have to know. Mind you, we are just speculating. I know absolutely nothing for certain. I am an old man, and I see things, that is all." Benoit had barely taken a breath during his little speech, and now tossed back the last of his wine as if for emphasis.

"So we are speaking hypothetically, of course," Ray said wryly.

"But of course, Monsieur. So let us theorize further. Let us ask: Why buy a café if you are this outsider and you obviously feel no attachment to the place?"

"Money laundering?" Ray offered.

Benoit shrugged and turned his palms up in resignation. "Ah, that we do not know. And yet…" He paused and gave a sidelong glance at the bar. "Anyone who has been coming here for any length of time can plainly see that these days, it is primarily the staff who cares about this place. It is only they who keep it running smoothly. So let us say your guess is correct, and our once *distingué* café is a front of some sort. And if the new owner suddenly starts dressing better and taking trips to the south of France instead of working behind the bar, people might make assumptions, *non?* People may presume that the new owner may have come into some money, but they would certainly not immediately jump to the conclusion that he deals in black market art or has done anything illegal." Benoit eyed Ray's carafe of wine thirstily.

"But you suspect this, yes?" Ray asked excitedly, half-filling the man's glass with the remainder of the wine. For some reason, he was speaking in a hushed tone even though the volume of the café was deafening at the lunch hour.

When Benoit said nothing, and indeed seemed ready to close the subject, Ray called out breathlessly to the waiter, "*S'il vous plait?*" wanting desperately to extend their conversation by ordering another carafe. If wine was the incentive, then by all means more wine. He saw Benoit glance again at the bar, punctuating the look with his dark brows indicating that Ray follow his glance. Ray saw a short, beefy man behind the bar. He was in his forties, and perspiring an inordinate amount, considering that it was quite pleasant inside the café. His slicked-back hair kept falling across his eyes, resembling a bat wing, and the man furiously shoved it off his face so often it looked like he was smacking himself in the forehead as if he had just remembered something obvious. He looked unaccustomed to being behind the bar, and pulled the levers on the beer taps with distaste, as if he did not want to get his hands wet. He had a permanent look of impatience on his face and Ray knew instantly that this was the "outsider."

"Oh no, Monsieur," said Benoit said, holding his hand up against the proffered third glass of wine. "You are kind, but I have found that two glasses is just right, no more and certainly no less." He thought a moment then pushed his glass forward, saying: "Well, actually two and a half glasses is closer to ideal."

"But let me ask you this," Ray said earnestly. "If the painters willingly gave their work to the café proprietors, then weren't these men the rightful owners of the artworks?"

"Yes, *those* men would be. But what if someone ransacked a studio here and there, way back when, and hid what they found? Or what if certain powerful or wealthy persons ended up with paintings by displaced artists? That is another matter. Or what if it is three decades after the time we have been discussing, and there is a new war, and a group of people happen to have the wrong religion at the wrong time and are forced to sell great paintings from their collections at prices that were no better than having them robbed from them outright, because, after all, you cannot eat art? And what if later these paintings *were* robbed from them outright, because no one was living in these homes to protest? Well, what to do? What to do if you have a madman at the helm and his thugs are running like rats through the streets of your city and wanting all the best things for themselves, including the art? That is a different story, Monsieur, but related, I think you would agree. For another time, then."

He stood to go and Ray tried to physically restrain him, reaching out for his elbow. Benoit looked down at him, amused. He tightened the scarf around his neck and added:

"Many things happen during wars for which no one is ever held accountable. This is lamentable, but surely this is not news to you. In an ideal world, maybe these plundered works would have found their way back into museums, but war always makes a handy scapegoat and when has it ever been an ideal world? I do not point fingers, Monsieur. I and others who were here during the occupation went so far as to hide paintings in laundry baskets, or pass them from safe place to safe place buried under bags of potatoes in the backs of vegetable carts. There are those who believe strongly that great art should be for all to see and an also, that it is worth risking everything for. I cannot speak for that man behind the bar. I can only say that he developed a very sudden interest in art, and in owning this café, once the father and grandfather, the original owners of Le Verre Volant, were both dead. I am very glad that they did not live to see that the grandson sold it out of the family."

Just then, a tall, blond man in a lightweight suit the color of butter passed through the doors, removing his sunglasses and blinking confusedly, as if he had been in bright light for a very long while. When the man behind the bar saw him enter, his face lit up, and he lifted up a plank in the long bar and passed through the gap to approach the blinking blond.

"Claus!" Ray heard the owner of the café greet the man, taking him by the arm. "Welcome, my friend. We have some new wines you might be very interested in. Follow me to the cave."

"Yes, I would like to see them," the German said, cool and erect in spite of the Frenchman's effusiveness.

As the two walked away, the outsider leading Claus by the elbow as if he were a blind man, Benoit sat down again, leaned closer to Ray and muttered, "Wine is not all that fellow has in his cave. I have no proof, of course, but I'd wager you'd find all manner of contraband down there…maybe even some of your 'lost' paintings. I can't be sure, mind you, but I have observed that only a very few are shown the cave, and this German is a repeat visitor."

"Wine lover?" Ray asked facetiously as he watched the two men disappear through a door near the bar.

"Anything is possible," said Benoit, smiling for the first time.

Ray was tapping his foot frenetically on the floor. He gave a low whistle and looked into Benoit's eyes, his heart pounding. It was the most excited he had been about anything in many months, years maybe. Of course there was no time to follow up on any of this, and it would be crazy to try. But if there had been a way, Ray would have given his eyeteeth to poke around in that basement.

"Good luck with your research, Sherlock," Benoit said, standing up again, unsteadily, and saluting him. Then he leaned toward Ray's ear and said in a low voice: "And don't do anything too foolish. One thing I have learned over the years is that when money is involved, people can turn very ugly."

Ray thanked him profusely, then sat back down to scribble some notes in a small pad he had brought along. When he too stood to go, he noticed that Benoit had forgotten to pay his check.

Well, he earned this, Ray thought, leaving some money on the little dish on Benoit's table, weighting it down with a saltshaker. Regarding Benoit's empty chair, Ray marveled at all he had learned. The stories the man must have! Ray could only imagine. And while imagining, he allowed himself to run a little movie in his head, in which he pretended that he was just a dumb tourist, who walked past the bar as if he mistook the door there that led to the cave for the door to the WC. He saw the outsider and Claus grabbing him roughly once he was discovered— a scuffle would ensue, a pistol drawn, and Ray would…but seriously, what *would* Ray do once down there? What could he prove? Everything was mere speculation.

"Anything else, Monsieur?" A different waiter with a menacing look was suddenly by his side. "Have you gotten all you came for today?" He was almost hissing this last question.

Ray was startled out of his little reverie and dropped the coins he was about to place on his own table. The coins scattered noisily far across the floor. Neither man made the first move to pick them up. Ray saw that Claus and the outsider were back, and were having a serious powwow behind the bar, their heads bowed and so close their cheeks were almost touching. The waiter met their eyes significantly for a split second.

"Yes, thanks," Ray answered, taking the ticket from his hand and tearing the check halfway, usurping the waiter's next move. Ray placed some paper bills on the table and stood. "I have *almost* everything I came in for, thanks. But the rest will have to wait."

CHAPTER TWENTY-TWO

The Byroads leaders were waiting on the platform at the train station in Avignon, ready to greet the arrivals who had taken the TGV, the fast train from Paris. The two leaders were wearing hats made from bright yellow and red skinny balloons that had been twisted into the shape of bicycles. With this headdress, they were easy for Phoebe to recognize, and when she stepped off the train, the leaders and the five or six other participants who had arrived before her waved vigorously. Phoebe waved back and walked toward the group of strangers she would be spending the next eight days with. About half of them looked rested and fit, like they had had the good sense to arrive early and get acclimated, while the other half looked dead on their feet, as if all they wanted was a nap. Phoebe felt fairly relaxed for a woman who had been consorting with ghosts and stealing strange men's briefcases. Her drive through the Camarge was a perfect anecdote to her art adventures at the Marseilles hotel. In the all-encompassing solace that only nature could fully provide for her; she had not once seen Chagall. What she had seen, pulling her car over whenever she felt like it, was majestic white horses, pink flamingoes, and vast, salty expanses of untouristed land. She had purchased a salt grinder made from the lovely striated wood of an olive tree, and two jars of the rock salt that the region was famous for, which had a rosy blush to it, like quartz. Parked in her rental car by an impossibly green field, she had taken to grating salt on things she had bought from local markets: melons, peaches, cheese, foods that she normally would not have salted. She wanted the full pink-salt experience, and while enjoyable, she ended up consuming a whole lot of water afterward.

"Are you Phoebe?" a young blonde leader asked affably, her ponytail pulled out through the opening in the back of her cap and bobbing as she approached

There was a male and a female leader, and they both had the most muscular thighs Phoebe had ever seen on someone who was not in a dance troupe. They reached out for her hand, both of them bursting with energy, youth, and good will.

"None other," Phoebe joked, releasing her scuffed chartreuse wheelie bag to shake hands.

"Well, I'm Jane and this is Michael, and no, we don't always wear balloons on our heads. But it worked, right?" She said this nodding animatedly at everyone gathered around her. "You all found us."

Michael looked at a clipboard briefly, then stepped forward and stood in the middle of the circle. There were about twelve people besides the leaders gathered there now, and Phoebe did a quick assessment, concluding that about half were in their early thirties and half were her age or older. Then she saw Ray Fitch. Unbelievable. The guy from the restaurant in San Francisco and, later, coming down the steps at Glorieta's. Immediately she felt her ears grow hot and knew she was blushing furiously. The man looked at her with the bland cordiality of a total stranger, obviously not recognizing her. This both irked and relieved her, allowing some of the blood in her face to drain back down into the rest of her.

There were more women than men, as was typically the case, Phoebe had found, in these types of group ventures. Language classes, wine appreciation classes, book groups—always about a three-to-one female-to-male ratio. Phoebe's friends had said taking classes would be the best way to meet someone, but the numbers never cooperated.

"Okay—welcome, everyone. I think we're all officially here, so what we like to do now is…can anyone guess?" Michael had such white teeth that when he smiled, Phoebe imagines little sparkles dancing off them as in a cartoon. Phoebe was sure all the women in the group, regardless of age, appreciated how handsome he was.

"Introduce ourselves?" ventured one of the younger guests, a tall freckled woman who was already dressed in her biking spandex.

"Bingo!" Jane shouted. "I can see this is going to be an especially sharp group." Everyone laughed, and Michael suggested they start going around the circle, telling where they were from, what they did, and why they were excited about this trip.

"Would you like to start?" he asked the freckled woman.

"Okay…my name is Laura and I am incredibly excited to be here since I have never been to the south of France. I am looking forward to just biking down country lanes and stopping to smell the lavender, as they say. I am a photographer and have recently had a show called 'Poor Isn't Pretty' at a major gallery in Indianapolis. My photographs were of homeless or struggling people in doorways of downtown businesses, usually taken at night."

The group nodded their greeting at her. Another artist, Phoebe thought, wondering how in this economy any artist could afford a four-star adventure vacation. The individuals continued their stories. As Phoebe listened to the introductions, a podiatrist from Philadelphia here, an IRS employee there, she found it poignant which aspects of themselves humans chose when trying to sum up their lives and make a good first impression. Some focused on their job or their pets or the fact that they were parents, or how many miles they biked daily back home. A few mentioned that they were a little nervous about what it meant to be on a "singles trip," letting everyone know that they certainly weren't in the habit of needing help to meet people.

"Hello. I'm Ray Fitch and I own a small gallery in Minna Alley in San Francisco called Orb Weaver. Yes, it's a funny name and no, I don't sell much art, but I was in the dot-com industry for long enough that I find this work extremely appealing."

"Are you an artist yourself?" Phoebe blurted out, and some turned to look at her curiously. She had not had her own turn yet, so everyone was probably trying to figure out what her asking this said about the type of person she might be.

"Art appreciator," Ray said with a slight smile. He was studying her now and Phoebe could see the cogs of recognition clicking in his head.

"Okay, Phoebe? It's your turn," said Jane.

Phoebe tried to give a confident smile. "I am an artist, mainly watercolors, but to pay the bills—or a few of them, anyway—I design wine labels and do whatever other jobs I can at Ravenswing Winery in Sonoma, California. I live in a blue house with two dogs and trees full of birds that I spend a ridiculous amount of time and money luring into my backyard so I can watch them." Everyone smiled but she wasn't quite finished. "Oh, and I am more of a hiker than a biker, so if I don't roll in by dinner time, someone come and find me." Phoebe had always had a propensity toward hamminess if given an appreciative audience.

"Great. Well, I'm Michael and this is my fifteenth Byroads trip." Here he paused for applause, prompting people to clap. "I usually lead the Tuscany trips but this year they did a big shake-up and I got the unlucky job of biking through Southern France in peak lavender season and eating gourmet food and hanging out with great people all week. Bummer!"

"Poor Mikey," said Jane, rolling her eyes at the group. "And I'm Jane and this is my tenth time leading a Byroads trip, mostly in Puget Sound, so I am happy to be in France! Michael and I are literally here for *you*, completely at your service. If you need a Band-Aid or a fresh water bottle or even, depending on how long you've been in the hot sun and how often you wash your socks, a foot massage, please, please don't hesitate to ask. I mean it, we hope that every one of you will ask us for anything you need this whole week."

"And guys," Michael said, "no shame in getting bumped ahead to the next portion of the ride. You're on vacation. It's not a marathon or a competition. We want you all to enjoy yourselves."

"Today," Jane went on, "we're just going to have a leisurely French lunch and then shuttle you to your home for the next four nights, a beautiful working lavender farm near Lourmarin, which is not one of the famous perched, hilltop villages, and I know those of you who enjoy vertical biking up mountainsides will be deeply disappointed."

Phoebe laughed when the woman who worked for Christies Great Estates snapped her fingers in mock disappointment.

"But it's a magnificent setting amongst fields of lavender and sun-flowers and vineyards and olive groves and centuries-old walnut trees… in other words, paradise. We're starting the ride at eight tomorrow— that means on the road by eight, and parts of the ride are challenging, so you'll want to get a good night's rest. And I think the patroness at our lodging, Bernadette, the wonderful octogenarian, has something pretty special planned for our pre-dining pleasure tomorrow after the ride. I won't spoil the surprise, but it involves garlic and pêtanque, if you've all still got the energy. She always likes to offer this as a special treat at least one evening of her guests' stay."

Phoebe relived that innocent excitement she used to feel at the start of summer camp—new friendships, new experiences, new skills, new places all ahead of her, even down to the leaders, willing to teach her new things and make sure she had a great time. Her only job was simply to remain open to everything. Phoebe gathered up her belongings and headed toward the van, beginning to relax for the first time in months. She hadn't realized how the foreclosure worries and the loneliness had been gnawing steadily away at her all this time, but now she breathed in the warm air and felt her shoulders drop and a sense of ease and be-longing wash over her.

She was just about to step into the van when she looked up and saw Chagall, lying on his side on top of the van, a sprig of lavender between his lips. She stopped in her tracks, almost causing the woman behind her to step on her heels; then he winked at her, and was gone. The fact that he eventually turned up everywhere she happened to be was actually starting to feel comforting to Phoebe. As long as he didn't ask her to steal any more suitcases, she would just try to think of him as her own personal guardian angel.

CHAPTER TWENTY-THREE

Bernadette sat in the kitchen sipping her milky coffee from a bowl she had made that was decorated with cheery wedges of watermelon. She let the early morning light gently warm her as she went over the guest list before she had to start the day's chores. It was Sunday, the day that old visitors typically left and new ones took their place. The group from Byroads was due to arrive that afternoon. She liked having them as guests. Byroads was a well-organized company and they were a sporty bunch, so they were gone most of the day exploring. As well, all that exercise made them hearty eaters and they were usually helpful and enthusiastic.

"*Ici*, Madame?" Her young helper, the daughter of the head field worker, entered the kitchen with a full pail of goat milk.

"*Oui*, Sophie. By the counter is fine."

The surface of the milk was foamy and had a wonderful, grassy aroma. Bernadette admired goats' intelligence almost as much as she was impressed by their digestive systems. It wasn't true that they ate anything. They were actually quite fussy and would turn their noses up at food that was less than clean or fresh. And the sad thing about this "iron stomach" myth was that farmers often left the poor goats to their own devices, believing them tougher than they were. So they got their reputation as creatures who would eat tin cans and clothing form

the clothesline, simply because they were starving and, being inquisi-
tive creatures, tasted this and that to see if it *might* be suitable for filling
their bellies…not unlike Bernadette and her family during the years
of the Occupation. A California guest had told her once that there was
a man in Berkeley who hired out his goats to devour hillsides covered
with poison oak, a bane for hikers. She smiled recalling this. Ah, the
great, serviceable goat.

"She is generous this morning," Bernadette said, looking admiringly at the full pail. "It is Gigi's milk, yes? You must be feeding her
flowers or giving her lots of caresses."

"She is my favorite, such a good mama!" Sophie said, wiping her
hands on her skirt and kissing Bernadette on each cheek before heading
back out into the fields. Bernadette watched her go. She enjoyed being
around young people. They were so full of life, so fresh. She missed her
sons just then, or more accurately, her own youth.

The pêtanque game and pistou dinner wasn't until tomorrow evening, but Bernadette already felt that acceleration inside herself that
always signaled a long list of things she needed to accomplish before
the end of the day. She distractedly read down the list, noting the
guests' ages and where they were from. She had only been to one place
in America, New York, and that so long ago. But from her years as the
sole host here, from the long parade of guests she had encountered, she
developed certain ideas about the different regions in the United States.
Maybe they were vast generalizations, but it was her belief that stereo-
types had their roots in certain truths, and her own observations often
confirmed this view.

Southerners were polite, dressed up for dinner, and loved to eat and
drink well into the night. Easterners were often on their cell phones and
seemed reluctant or incapable of distancing themselves from their jobs
while on vacation. People from the Midwest seemed less chatty, slower to
try new things. And the Californians gushed about everything they did
or saw, were moved by it all and seemed in possession of more physical
energy than puppies. And they all seemed very radical in their politics.

Bernadette tossed back the rest of her coffee, then glanced down the list one more time. Suddenly her stomach plunged and she dropped her bowl. Phoebe Rosen. Rosen. Right there on the list. How many times had she read that signature on the back of her hidden painting? "For my dear wife Ruthie Rosen...Yours forever, Ben Rosen." But no, it couldn't be. *Calm down,* Bernadette told herself, bending down to pick up the larger pieces of her broken bowl and to blot the blood on her ankle with a cloth. Certainly Rosen was a common enough name. What would be the chances of anyone related to the same Rosen who'd fought with her brother showing up all these years later at the farm? *Merde,* she admonished herself. I've gone and overreacted and lost one of my favorite morning bowls. Highly unlikely that this Phoebe was in any way related. She picked up the sheet again and searched for where this Phoebe was from. Aha, California, not Oklahoma, where her brother had told her his buddy hailed from. Bernadette tried to relax. The guilt had been inside her for all these years, dormant but alive, and for some reason, while she had always been able to justify her reticence to track down the rightful owner of the Chagall, seeing that name on the list made the worry and guilt spring to life, like a roused nest of hornets. Chores. She needed to throw her energy into something.

Bernadette pushed on the heads of garlic with the heel of her hand to loosen the cloves. While she was not big on gadgets, she did allow for an ingenious rubbery tube that saved time getting the papery skin off so many cloves. But she still held strongly to the conviction that the mortar and pestle made for the best pistou, precisely for the coarseness of the paste. No food processor for her, and she dared say, she was still a strong enough and an adroit enough chef to mash the basil, walnuts, and garlic needed to feed dozens, no small feat given the small batches the mortar and pestle accommodated. She threw herself into the long work and tried not to think about that name on her guest list.

Sophie had changed the sheets in all the rooms and put fresh flowers in the vases. She put a teaspoon of sugar in each vase, believing that it made the flowers last longer. The only guests who were remaining a second week while the Byroads group took over the place were the German, who always booked ahead for their fortnight in August, the high season. They had been coming for years and stayed long enough that Bernadette agreed to charge them the off-season rate. They were used to the ever-changing guests around the pool at breakfast, the husband probably not even noticing, likely lumping all tourists together. The wife was more personable, and would certainly strike up a conversation with any who approached. And the game of pêtanque was a fine icebreaker and a way for the guests to mingle with locals, which Bernadette knew was a vital part of any traveler's experience.

After about an hour of mashing the ingredients and turning out the pungent green paste, making sure to fold in the parmesan and walnut oil at the end, Bernadette felt satisfied that she had enough to feed at least twenty people. She transferred the whole batch into a large, shallow earthenware bowl decorated with crows, a piece she had made the year before, then took a smooth piece of stainless steel shaped like an egg out of her cutlery drawer and rubbed it vigorously along each finger and under her nails. The steel removed the smell of garlic or onions, though she was fairly certain she still smelled of one or the other much of the time.

She walked toward the hives behind her atelier under the pretext of gathering some honey, but since she had not even brought along her headgear or the smoker, she knew her true desire was to check on her painting. Bernadette *never* took it out of its hiding place except very early in the morning, before the guests or workers were about, but here it was late afternoon and she had to touch it, check on it, as she was still jittery from seeing that name.

When she got to the tray, she immediately noticed that someone had been there. They had tampered with it. Bernadette's heart raced and she was both angry and frightened. Then it hit her—that Australian woman. Nosy and persistent, she had snuck back in when Bernadette was busy and satisfied her curiosity. Bernadette rushed over to the hastily replaced tray, its crookedness the tattletale, and lifted it carefully out of its groove. She exhaled heavily when she saw her painting—still there, if not absolutely undisturbed anymore. She could panic, but the Australian was long gone and there had been no confrontation, so Bernadette allowed herself to enter its beautiful world again, let herself be lifted up into that bright sky where she joined the lovers and mythical creatures, where all was well.

"They are here, Madame," Sophie said, appearing in the doorway. "The group of Americans." When Sophie saw how startled Bernadette was, how she had whipped her head around as if ready for battle, she added, "I knocked quite a few times but you did not hear me. I am sorry I surprised you."

"Oh, Sophie," said Bernadette, surreptitiously sliding the Chagall back into the empty tray. "I was just checking on my bees. I think my hearing isn't as good as it used to be. Thank you. I'll come right up."

"*Oui*, Madame," Sophie said, looking at her curiously before turning to go back up to the house.

Bernadette was angry with herself for breaking her own rule, taking such a risk after being careful for so long. *Your hearing isn't all that's not what it used to be*, she chastised herself. Before she locked the door behind her, she wondered briefly if her secret had been compromised somehow and if she should find a new hiding place. But no—the Aussie had left it there, hadn't she? She probably thought it was another reproduction if it was treated as a bee tray liner instead of hung on a wall, and she was certain Sophie hadn't seen anything. All this worry for nothing. *You're a silly old woman*, the angel on one shoulder told her, as she walked up to the main house. But the devil on her other shoulder added *who deserves to be found out…*

CHAPTER TWENTY-FOUR

The wine that the group had been served at lunch, coupled with the excitement, the heat, and the jet lag, made for a raucous trip to the Place of Happy Bees, the Lavender Beehive, or whatever the name of their lodgings for the next four nights was.

"So we're going to be roomies," Laura, the Poor-Isn't-Pretty photographer said, kneeling on her seat and facing backward so she could peer over at Phoebe. "Do you snore?"

Phoebe laughed, assuming she was kidding, but Laura went on: "Well, just FYI, I am an early riser and I like white noise to help me sleep, so I have a little machine that plays the ocean, waterfall, crickets, that type of thing. I hope that doesn't bother you."

"As long as you don't set it to 'city' I think I'll be fine. I get up pretty early, too, and on this trip, I think we don't have another option."

It was about a two-hour drive from the restaurant, and those who had flown directly were nodding off against the window or on the shoulder nearest them. Fitch was seated in the row in front of Phoebe, his black curls bobbing slightly as he spoke. Fitch. Phoebe had a strong desire to touch the top of his head and feel the curls under her palm. Instead, she summoned up her courage and tapped him on the shoulder. He turned to look at her.

"Economic Darwinism," she said triumphantly.

"Excuse me?" Ray said, looking at Phoebe with a new curiosity.

"I'm from the Bay Area, too, and I believe we were in the same restaurant a while back, a chi-chi place called Absinthe. Your, ahem, *charming* friend was sort of putting forth the proposition that all the mom-and-pop businesses that are dropping like flies in the current economy is actually a *good* thing, because it weeds out the weak. I almost dumped my water glass over his head but then I heard your retort and I felt you had taken care of it for me…if only verbally."

"Oh yeah," Ray said, thinking back. "You were there? Wow, and now here? Yes, well, that's Chaz. Charles. He's sort of a blowhard but has a few good qualities that make it possible to be his friend. I also think he overstates things just to get a rise out of me. What is your name again? I'm terrible with names. Maybe we should all be wearing those sticky nametags they give you at conferences."

"I'm the same way. I remember everything about the person—the stories they tell, like your gallery named after those amazing spiders and all—but I never recall the person's name. I'm Phoebe. Phoebe Rosen."

"Like the bird," Ray said.

"Excuse me?"

"Say's Phoebe. It's a beautiful flycatcher with a yellowy, buff underbelly. It hovers like a hawk to catch insects and has a lovely *pidireep* call. It's a wonderful bird."

What am I, Ray thought as soon as the words had left his lips, *a science teacher? I sound like a bird geek*. He assessed Phoebe. Easy to talk to. Slim and sturdy looking. Big green eyes. Ready smile. Her round face nicely framed with thick red curls.

Wow, thought Phoebe, *a fellow birder. And such expressive hands*. She wanted to talk more with him.

"Well thank you," Phoebe said heartily. "Actually, I bird, too, and when I first heard your name I thought it was 'finch.' In truth, though, I'm in more of the 'Look! A little brown bird!' school of identification."

Ray chuckled and the others in their row looked at them, sniffing intrigue.

Leader Jane twisted around from the front of the van and said: "Oh good, we've got some birders here. On the weekend, there's an amazing flea market in Les Baux de Provence and when we bike there, I can show anyone who's interested a church where we have a really good chance of seeing a lovely little crimson-winged Wallcreeper or two. They're my faves around here and we don't have them in the States. Oh, and also there is a great chance of seeing a kingfisher."

"I *love* kingfishers," Phoebe whooped, which was true. She had paintings all around her home featuring kingfishers prominently.

"What if we get separated from the group?" the Florida consignment woman asked in a shrill voice from the back of the van. What a fearful woman, Phoebe reflected. She had been warming to the discussion of local birds and resented the interruption.

"That won't happen," Michael, ever calm, addressed her from the driver's seat, looking back in the rearview mirror. "I will be sweeping the route all day in the van, Jane on her bike"

"And if it should happen, there are worse places to be lost!" Jane added gaily. But when Michael shot her a look, she added, "No seriously, even if you take your sweet time and have a meandering sense of direction like myself, we will always find you in time for supper."

Everyone chatted as they bounced along past old stone farms and mountains that looked familiar already from their depictions in Impressionist paintings. The van grew quiet as they passed mile upon mile of lavender fields, interspersed with fields thick with huge sunflowers lifting their faces to the afternoon rays. Eventually, they turned off the main road and drove down a long lane lined with Plane trees. They came to a halt in front of a lovely old farmhouse, its terrace lush with potted plants and the pleasing gurgle of a working fountain, a lion's head that produced water from purring lips, right in the middle of the circular drive. Phoebe was taken by a striking older woman standing in the doorframe, wearing a modest cotton dress that looked hand sewn from local fabrics. Her chin-length grey hair was thick and luxuriant, drawn off her face with a large clip. She held her chin up at a slightly defiant angle and her legs still looked like they could carry her wherever she needed to go. She looked anxiously at the van, then put a smile on her face when Michael shut off the engine and stepped out.

"*Bonjour*, Michael!" she said, approaching and giving him a kiss on each cheek, then one extra, repeating the process when Jane stepped out. "*Bonjour*, Jane."

"*Bonjour*, Bernadette!" said Michael, seeming genuinely pleased to see her. Phoebe thought about the lives of these guides, meeting people and making strong connections, then moving on wherever their boss sent them. It must be hard to have a relationship back in the States when you were on the move so much of the year. She wondered if this might be a job for her daughter Audrey, who loved travel and adventure and was certainly a skilled enough cyclist. She imagined the interview process was rigorous, but nonetheless, she would mention it to Audrey when she returned. She missed her daughter at that moment, and wished they were on this trip together.

"*Nous voila*," Jane said, gesturing to the guests spilling out of the van.

"Welcome," Bernadette said with a lilting accent. "Your rooms are ready and you can have aperitifs by the pool in one hour if you like, before you head off for dinner. I'm sure Michael has something delicious planned for your first night." She smiled up at him coquettishly. Phoebe liked her already.

The leaders were true to their word about all the pampering in store for the group, insisting upon carrying all their luggage up the many smooth stone steps and placing the bags outside the doors. Phoebe noticed that Poor-Isn't-Pretty (uh-oh, *what* was her real name?) had a massive amount of luggage for such a brief stay in Provence. Phoebe allowed her to lay claim to the bed she preferred, by the door, which worked out fine since Phoebe had a bladder the size of a buckeye and her bed was closer to the bathroom. But what struck Phoebe more than anything she had yet seen on the farm was the weirdly synchronistic discovery that her room was entirely fashioned after her own favorite

Chagall painting, *Time Is A River Without Banks.* Her jaw dropped the minute she set foot in the room. Bernadette had not overlooked a single detail. The soap dish by the sink was a jolly-eyed flounder, a fish already born in the Cubist style without any alteration needed. The quilt on her bed looked hand stitched, a colorful patchwork of flying fish leaping across its surface. Even the ceiling had a mural spotlighting all things nautical, mermaids and sailors playing blue violins and serene-looking women with kelp tresses holding shells to their ears, and all the ripples of water outlined in a rosy crescent moon glow. Phoebe stepped back and brought her hand to her mouth.

"Are you okay?" her roommate asked.

"It's Chagall! This whole room! It's…amazing!" Phoebe was still dazzled. Seeing the other woman looking around with only mild interest, added, "He's my favorite artist."

"He is pretty great…but I'm more into photography."

Phoebe decided this woman was okay for a roommate, but she would definitely spend her days and evening with others…perhaps even Ray.

"Are you staying longer in France, after this trip?" Phoebe asked as her roommate unpacked stacks of folded skirts and shirts and arranged many pairs of shoes in the bottom of the shared closet. Phoebe was trying to see something with Poor-Isn't-Pretty's name on it, to jog her memory.

The woman continued hogging the closet. "No, back to Indianapolis and then work two days later. You?"

"No, I had my little adventure a bit farther south before I arrived here. And do you have a nickname or anything at work? A title?"

"Nope, just Laura," she said, an endless flow of dresses and skirts pouring forth from her suitcase. Bingo.

Will there be any hangers left or room in the shared drawers when this woman is finished? Phoebe decided to explore the grounds and let her roommate claim as much space as she needed. It seemed to matter to her. "I think I'll head out for a while before aperitifs and get the lay of the land."

"Don't you want to unpack? I don't feel like I've actually arrived until I have my shoes lined up underneath my clothes in the closet. But okay, to each her own. I'll leave some space for your things."

"Thanks!" Phoebe said, pulling the door shut behind her.

Phoebe stretched and stood on the terrace, taking deep gulps of the perfumed air and scanning the bounty and vastness of the property with deep appreciation. Even the farming tools were beautiful. She had noticed en route that the French hay bales were round and loosely woven, not the rigid cubes with sharp edges that she was used to in the States. That alone seemed like a significant cultural difference. Also, the cows here seemed more apt to be lying down, and same with the horses, relaxing in the shade with their legs folded neatly beneath them.

"Beautiful, isn't it?" a voice said from behind her. It was Ray. The late afternoon sun made some of the strands in his beard glint copper.

"Amazing. I don't think I realized until about five minutes ago just how much I needed this vacation."

"Too much work?"

"Too much recession. I guess I have been spoiled, in that I've grown too used to things being a certain way, but the past two years have been one struggle after the next…and not just financially." Then Phoebe felt like she was complaining too much, so added hurriedly, "Is your room also done up in an homage to some great painter?"

"Chagall," he said soundly. "My favorite. Red roosters and a whole zoo of wondrous centaur creatures! And not just minotaurs and centaurs, but all manner of hybrids, many of them playing a red violin. I was reluctant to leave my room, but my roommate wanted to rest…you know, before the grueling tasks of aperitifs and dinner."

"Chagall! So maybe they are all in his honor. My room is as well…" She almost said: "You'll have to come see it sometime!" but that was too Mae West for their first real conversation. "My roommate will be unpacking for the next few days. I will be lucky if I can even push the door open to get inside. No, I'm sorry, she's fine, really…this is bad, making disparaging remarks about our roomies."

"Yes, it is," Ray said, unapologetically. "We are terrible. So, were you heading out for a walk? Mind if I tag along?"

"Not at all."

"It's funny," Ray said after they had been walking for a while, gradually climbing up into a terraced vineyard. "There seems to be a lot of Chagall in my life lately. It's like that saying: 'There are no coincidences.' I know that sounds like California therapy-speak, but it feels especially true right now."

Phoebe looked at him intently. *A lot of Chagall in your life? You have no idea*, she thought.

"You took the words right out of my mouth, Ray." She felt emboldened saying his name. "I mean, he *is* my favorite artist and all, so maybe I am more prone than the average person to seeing the Chagall in things. But he keeps showing up in my life…I mean, in some form or another, influencing my paintings—and now here, too." She was stammering, trying not to say the word "ghost." She definitely didn't want to let slip the fact that in her case, Chagall made personal appearances. She wondered if somehow he had a hand in getting her to this place? As Ray had pointed out, things happened for a reason.

There was much more to be said on this subject, but something about the light and their glorious vantage on the land stretching out below urged them to walk quietly for a while. The bees were so profuse on the lavender, even this late in the day, that their steady hum was a constant accompaniment to the faint crunch of their footsteps.

"I forgot my watch," Phoebe said. "Do you think it's time for Dubonnet?"

"I forgot mine, too," Ray said, grinning. "On purpose. But these shadows are getting longer, so lacking a sundial, I would say we'd better head on down. I'm still full from that lunch, though. What an introduction to local food!"

"Don't worry," Phoebe said, and she was in such good spirits and felt so comfortable with this stranger that she almost linked arms with him, as if he were an old friend. "I think they don't eat dinner in these here parts until after nine!"

"Ah…so the aperitif is a pre-dinner appetite-whetter?"

"You got it."

As they wound their way back down the terraced vineyard, Phoebe caught sight of Chagall, feeding handfuls of green grass to a fine flaxen horse. She was tempted to wave, but instead focused on the strong profile and broad shoulders of the man standing right beside her.

CHAPTER TWENTY-FIVE

Claus had noticed that the same old guy man with the red neck kerchief who seemed to be a fixture at Le Verre Volant, but this time an American had joined his table. He registered the way the two were sizing him up, but he was in a hurry to meet with the owner, Paul, and tell him once and for all that, despite the fact that the delivery had gone smoothly in Marseilles, this would absolutely be his last job. Claus was resolute about telling him, today, no further discussion, but when Paul motioned for Claus to step behind the bar and follow him down into the cave, Claus trotted behind his boss like a trained monkey. He had driven straight to Paris from Marseilles and had not had time to fix the alligator briefcase that now was held shut only thanks to some twine the man at the front desk had offered, "just to get you wherever you are going." It offended Claus's sensibilities on every level to be seen carrying a designer briefcase, now stuffed with cash, webbed haphazardly with a long, shredding length of cheap jute. As he passed through the café, Claus was forced to clutch the bandaged thing to himself to keep the contents, millions of euros, from spilling to the floor. There was such a ridiculous amount of cash in the valise that on the drive back from Marseilles, Claus was assailed by fits of arbitrary tittering whenever he considered it.

As he followed Paul down the stairs, he thought again about those two at the table. He had never liked that old man, always there in the same seat, with his knowing smirk and that silly red foulard. Claus knew plenty of old people like him, impotent in their day-to-day lives, but feeling some sort of power by sticking their noses into everybody's business, as if they could actually *do* anything with whatever wild stories they fabricated. Still, the whole scene, as well as the encounter with that odd woman from the plane at the hotel yesterday, had unnerved him, and made it hard for him to be in the right frame of mind to conduct any sort of business, let alone to tell Paul he was quitting. Could one actually "quit" an illegal job?

Once they were in the cool, dim light of the wine cellar, Paul asked him, "So, did he buy?"

"Of course he bought," Claus said tersely.

"Full price?"

Claus had always felt a slight repugnance toward Paul, from that very first day when the sweaty little fellow had entered Claus's gallery in Grenoble. There was something oleaginous about him, greasy forelock flopping into his face, his clothes sticking to him no matter what the weather. A wave of wistfulness washed over Claus for those early days in his gallery, when he had been a legitimate gallery owner, before Paul had asked in his graveled voice, "How'd you like to sell some *real* art?"

Claus stepped back a bit from Paul and went on: "He argued that the larger Chagalls are going at auction for twelve million euros, and…"

Paul snorted, interrupting, "Yeah, but this ain't Sotheby's. These things are hot. Maybe remind him next time…"

"And *since*," Claus went on, clenching his jaw, "since this is a smaller one, he thought we had a lot of nerve asking for five. Or as he put it: Who else could you trust to buy your offerings? Who else can you be *sure* will not make trouble for you? Who else would keep such beauty hidden away from prying eyes?'"

"Fuck that," Paul said, reddening violently from neck to ears. "I hope you…"

"In the end, though," Claus said lightly, again cutting him off, "he paid the five million."

Paul stiffened, considering momentarily the fact that Claus might actually enjoy jerking him around, but then let it go, slapping his delivery boy on the back. He took out a cigar, passed it lovingly under his nostrils, then went through the great show of lighting it puffing out his cheeks like a blowfish.

"Attaboy, Clause. Makin' it faster than we can spend it, eh?"

Claus thought how strange this business was, for he did think of the procuring and selling of the black market art as a business. So odd for himself, and certainly even more so for Paul and the others, who made the real money—even for the collectors, to have all this wealth, to obtain these masterpieces, but to have to keep it all under wraps, to never have the freedom to flaunt any of it. He had asked himself more and more frequently lately what then was the point of owning art, if you could not openly display it?

"By the way," Claus continued, shaking his head at the offered smoke, a cigar of dirigible proportions. "He says if you ever come across a Modigliani, or a Max Jacob, he wants it, no questions asked."

"Hm. I think we've liquidated all of the treasures from my little collection. The ones that came with the place, anyway," Paul said, making air quotes around the word liquidated.

"Came with the place unbeknownst to the original owners, you mean?"

Paul snickered. "Finders keepers."

"Lucky the cave was part of the sale. Ridiculously lucky, too, that the guy's great-grandson never moved any of the wine bottles around."

"Yeah. I mean I *know* why the guys hid the stuff behind the racks— the war and all. But shit, all that dampness and the spiders and rats… it's a miracle that whole trunk survived."

"Well, it *was* a good hiding place. You wouldn't have discovered the stash either if you hadn't had a hankering for a 1918 Château Mouton Rothschild."

"Yeah, Claus, but I *did*," Paul said triumphantly. "And the Germans *didn't.* But hey, never fear, there's more where these came from. Our resources are not dry, my friend. I'm gonna lecture you a minute here, son." Claus winced when Paul called him that, even for reasons beyond the fact that Paul was only about ten years older than him.

Paul's voice took on a professorial tone, and he sucked on his cigar thoughtfully.

"Art may endure, but so do thieves. I have certain acquaintances, men who, shall we say, fell upon some art during the last war, when people had other things on their minds. Back then, the locals were inclined to look the other way if certain paintings, especially the ones hanging on Jewish walls, happened to go missing. Acquaintances whom you might call lucky men—men who pounced upon good art, recognized it when they saw it, and squirreled it away for a rainy day. These paintings have passed through many hands over the past century. I'm just one more link in the big chain. These thieves, or let's call them procurers, and all the ones who were at the right place at the right time who came before them, they were all very *patient.* So who knows? Tell the guy in Marseilles I might just turn up a Modigliani yet. In this business, ya just never know."

Paul was in full form, gloating, his lips fairly smacking at the five million euros, or eighty percent of them anyway, after he paid Claus. That would buy him a lot of time in Monte Carlo.

"You should know…there was an incident," Claus added, trying to make his tone light.

"Incident?" Paul snapped, his voice bouncing off the dusty bottles and hoary walls, the accusing echoes having the effect of repeated blows on Claus's aplomb.

"In Marseilles. I hadn't let go of the valise for one second during the entire journey, I swear, but I left it by my table at dinner for no more than two minutes to use the toilet, and when I returned it was gone."

"What the fuck?" Paul sputtered, throwing the soggy half-cigar down onto the floor. Claus jumped pack involuntarily, as if the skittering sparks had been aimed at him. "What kind of *moron* lets a painting worth millions of euros out of his sight? Even for a nanosecond! Jesus fucking Christ, Claus, are you nuts?"

Sweat rings the size of dinner plates were showing in the underarms of Paul's shirt. Claus viewed the rampant sweat as a sign of weakness, and it calmed him. He speculated, since the man sweat like a pig, why he insisted upon wearing these pompous, resort-wear colors. Pink, powder blue, Kelly green? Not a good look with stains spreading across the back. Claus wondered sometimes if Paul would ever hurt him. No, he decided, looking at his florid face. But he might have someone *else* do it for him.

"Relax," Claus urged. "The story has a happy ending, right? And I delivered the goods, right? I handled it, Paul, I always handle it. I didn't want the police involved, but I did mention the missing case to the front desk, saying something offhand like, 'I'm very tired so I probably just misplaced it, but if it *does* happen to turn up…' I can tell you, inside, I was frantic, but nobody would have been able to read that. And right when I was about to leave my room and do a bit of reconnoitering myself, I got a call from the front desk saying someone had turned it in but it looked like it had been 'tampered with.' Sure I was freaked, but when I got the case back up to my room, the painting was in still there. All's well that ends well, right?"

"This is very bad, very bad," Paul muttered, beginning to pace.

"What are you talking about? No one stole the painting and I sold it for five million euros! What's so bad about that?"

"Well why *didn't* they steal it, eh? It's a trap, you idiot. They want to catch us, don't you see? For all we know, that broken briefcase of yours has a microphone in it and they are hearing all of this."

"You've been watching too much television," Claus dismissed him, sounding less concerned than he actually felt. "More likely, the thief wanted money, or jewelry, something they could sell quick. When they didn't find that in the case, only some small, flea-market painting, they just split. They've probably never even heard of Chagall."

Paul stood before Claus bug-eyed and a full head shorter. He jutted his chin out pugnaciously, clenching and unclenching the fists at his side.

"I hope you're right, Clausie, I really hope you're right. I've been very much enjoying our little partnership and I'd hate for either of us to go to jail and spoil the party."

"Yes, that would be…unfortunate," Claus said. He was asking himself, given the inopportune timing of this distressing drama, if now was maybe not the ideal moment to tell Paul this would be his last job. Claus kicked himself for even having mentioned the incident.

Paul walked across the stone floor of the cave and ground the still-smoldering cigar under the heel of the puce driving moccasins that he always wore with no socks. Instinctively, Claus stooped down and picked up the butt with a napkin, to dispose of upstairs.

Paul shook his head in disbelief, clearly amused.

"What?" asked Claus defensively.

"You Germans. You're so fucking fastidious…sometimes."

Claus got the jab and, timing be damned, shouted, "Listen, I've been running these paintings for years now without a break. My parents are vacationing in the Luberon, same place they go to every year, and they've asked me to join them for a few days. I said yes, okay? Contrary to what you may think, I do not have nerves made completely of steel. This is taxing work." He hadn't realized how angry he was until he spoke, though the way his voice had raised on octave in the heat of the moment probably wasn't helping his case.

"That's fine," Paul said, still maintaining that stupid smirk, patronizing him. "Take a week, Clausie, take two. Oh and, happy coincidence, there is an interested buyer who happens to be right down there in the lovely Luberon. Perhaps one last deal and then enjoy your vacation."

Claus bit the inside of his lower lip in annoyance. "I do not really care to mix this business with my vacation. If the two are too close in proximity, meaning my real life and this business, I worry."

"Hey, I'm not asking you here," Paul said, looking Claus dead in the eye. "Besides, when are you gonna just accept that this *is* your real life, huh? Listen, this is an easy one, I promise. The man is in Rousillon, away up behind those red rocks that the tourists can't get enough of. I doubt anyone wherever your parents are staying will have the faintest idea what you're doing. You're there and back in less than three hours and then you can enjoy your little break."

Claus looked down at the ground, knowing that he would not tell Paul, *I don't want this to be a break. I want to stop doing this!* He sighed in defeat and asked: "Is it small?"

"Yes, another one that could fit right into your briefcase…*after* you replace this probably bugged, broken piece of shit, of course, with a new one that you will never, *never* let out of your sight."

With this Paul untied the twine on the case and transferred the money into his own waiting briefcase without counting it. Snapping it shut, he said, "Wait here," and turned down one of the many rows of bottles, which suddenly looked to Claus like rows of telescopes, surrounding the two men, spying on their exchange.

Far at the other end of the cellar, Claus watched Paul squat and stick his arm under the narrow space between the bottom row of bottles and the floor. He withdrew a small parcel wrapped in some muslin cloth and tied with string. He stood, dusting off the knees of his pants, then returned and handed it to Claus, saying, "A real beauty, this one. Go on, open it. And do not take less than eight for this. You'll be delivering it to one collector who will not quibble. A pro."

Claus nodded. Left to his own devices, he would not have taken the cloth off to see what the painting was like. This would make the twentieth black market transaction he had done in two years and he was no longer even curious—but Paul was practically drooling in anticipation, eager to show him what was worth so much.

Claus followed Paul back to an area of the cave where there was more light, and as he slid the little framed canvas out of its wrapping, caught his breath. So small, so bright, it drew him in. It seemed too alive for the dark space, possessed of its own spirit, as if it might slip free of their hands and take flight like a bird. The painting depicted all manner of entwined creatures; women with wings embracing birds, mermaids hugging bearded men, fish riding on the backs of goats. All were in the midst of a dance, or in flight, as if they had all drunk from the same potion and were filled with rapture. Claus took in all this in an instant, and felt a moment's hesitation, a pang of guilt at delivering such an exquisite painting to yet another obsessed collector who would hide it in the shadows. This was a first for him; it made him more certain than ever that he had to get out of this business, and fast. He vowed that this would be his last transaction, but knew better than to tell that to Paul right then.

"A beauty, *non*?" Paul asked, nodding incessantly as if the spring holding his head to his neck was loose.

"Yes," Claus said somberly. "Another Chagall. And where did you come by this one, might I ask?"

"Oh, someone long ago who knew someone who knew someone else who happened to know which studio was Chagall's in La Ruche and happened to know also that the painter was indisposed to travel, and so thought to look after some of his paintings. You know how it goes. Hey, Claus," Paul added, gripping his arm with surprising strength. "This gentleman you will see in the south…he is a big cheese. Part of our network. He has a magnificent…er, you could say *extremely private* collection of Impressionist, Fauvist and Cubist art, all done by the great masters. He has a special room in his house with false walls and bookshelves that open into this secret gallery. It is quite the experience, a real film noir deal."

"I shall look forward to it," Claus said grimly. "But wait…when the artists were at La Ruche and Chagall was in Russia, that was, if my memory serves me, World War I? That was almost a century ago! How…"

"If something wants to remain hidden," Paul said, handing Claus the parcel, "it will remain hidden. Like all the ones we found tucked away down here."

Claus resented his use of "we," but reached out and took the package. *Admit it*, he said to himself, *you're as mired in this as everyone else, up to your eyeballs in it. If you're so morally outraged, why spend the money you make doing this so freely?* Resigned, Claus flipped the painting over and expertly peeled off the ancient brown paper on its back, the old rabbit-skin glue already disintegrating. Next, he pulled out a slim silver knife and began to carefully bend back the numerous small nails to release the stretched canvas from its frame. Then he saw a faint title written on the back: "Midsummer Escapade." At the last minute, he decided to leave the oil in its gilded frame for extra protection. It was small enough to fit, frame and all, into his broken valise, with the additional padding of his hefty take of euros from the last job. Claus headed up the stairs without saying goodbye to his boss.

Yes, he mused to himself, considering Paul's last words, *perhaps it's true that if something wants to remain hidden…but suppose that is not really what it wants at all?*

CHAPTER TWENTY-SIX

Chagall lay propped up on one elbow in a lavender field, hidden deep in the fragrant wands, waiting for Phoebe to return from her day's cycling. Not that he was worried that anyone else could see him...well, he wasn't certain yet about those two sisters, the witches who would be at the pêtanque game that evening. *I have never been good at being invisible,* he reflected. Dying was easy compared to going unnoticed. Dying was peace at the end of a long battle, the surrender to the light, the moment the fear was replaced by absolute innocence, another birth. No, death was out of his hands, and in the end, he was ready, as much as any human being could ever *truly* be ready, to let go of life. But after that passage, the segregation from his former life, so full of flesh and color and appetites and dimensions—losing all of that was the real challenge. There were other compensations, of course, but now that he was back, earthbound and surrounded by the living, he seemed to have contracted amnesia about the afterlife. There was only the here and the now.

Chagall could not feel the whiskery tickle of the bees' feet, laden with balls of pollen, as they crossed his cheek or landed on his forehead, but he could hear them. Why sight and hearing, yet not taste or smell or sensation? Death was such a curious state. *I should be grateful for two senses,* Chagall chastised himself for the one-thousandth time. He knew that once he had done his job, Phoebe would have no more need of him and that made him sad, as he had grown quite fond of her game way of plowing through life, her willingness to be moved, and the way she had not hardened after the recent difficulties. Ah, hurdles! He had known his share, he mused, rolling onto his back to look at the sky.

Ach, I am a sentimental man, he chuffed, making a bridge with his hand so that a bee could walk across it to the next blossom. He knew he would indulge himself in reminiscing now, as he had often done since he had died—a heart attack at the age of ninety-seven! He'd almost made it to a full century. He gave a short, rueful laugh. As the decades marched on, his longevity had surprised him. He thought of the strong will of his father Zakhar and his mother Ida, in Vitebsk, his formative years of struggle, the impact and friendships of Paris, going back to Russia for his love, Bella, the birth of their daughter, his Ida. Birth/Death/Birth/Death—ultimately, it all came down to that infinite march. And, he would add to that, Beauty. Fleeing the Nazis and arriving by boat in New York City, June 23rd, 1941. The day after the Nazis invaded Russia! The irony! And that dark year, after Bella died, when for the first time he was unable to pick up a brush and paint, such a clobbering, immobilizing grief. His seven-year romance with Virginia who gave him his son David. Then, the final years, cloistered back in the south of France with his possessive Vava, jealous, yes, but who accepted who he truly was: an artist first, a partner second. If anyone had foretold that he would see so much in his lifetime, that his work would endure, and live on immortal, he would have laughed out loud. No, today he would allow himself to lie in this field and reflect upon the moments of peace in his life, what he had loved, what had brought him joy. It only made him wistful, now that he was not able to dwell amongst the others there, but every once in a while, he had to let the entire grand, mad parade of his earthly existence play in his head. Hadn't he himself said on many occasions: *I am a dreamer who never woke up.*

He had a strange and vivid memory then, lying in that field. It was just a flash of a scene he had been allowed to witness from the beyond, long before he was sent back to this world to help Phoebe. It had disturbed him then, and the memory of it disturbed him now. At the time, he had felt like a voyeur, as if he were in the same room as the man he was observing. But Chagall knew he was being shown the covert spectacle for a reason, so continued to watch, invisible to The Thief. He took away from this experience that The Thief was in all places, in all eras. He had always been, and would always continue to be. He was an interchangeable creature. When one Thief died, another would step up to replace him. They were pros, the ones who always managed to procure the best pieces, the special "lost" paintings that collectors would find irresistible. Chagall had witnessed a youngish man with an expressionless face in a sterile, modern room on the eighteenth floor of a hastily constructed building in a very crowded city. Cairo? Shanghai? The man was impeccably dressed and entered the room noiselessly as a cat, tiptoeing across the plush carpeting, even though clearly it was his own room. He locked the door behind himself, drew the shades, and undressed. His actions were practiced, ritualistic, and careful as a surgeon's. He bent at the waist and removed a blue peasant's blouse made from some sort of course fabric, from beneath his regular clothes that were folded in the bottom drawer. It was an article of clothing such as Vincent may have worn when he painted, evocative of that era. He pulled it on over his head.

The full-length mirror on The Thief's bathroom door detached to reveal a niche, where he had hidden an easel, an unopened tube of paint, and an unused paintbrush. These were his props. Next, he knelt, folding back a portion of the carpeting under his bed, extracting a medium-sized painting in a dark frame. Chagall gasped to see what was clearly a Van Gogh, depicting a lone man wearing a blue hat, his face revealed only in profile, staring out a window at a tumultuous sea. The paint on this tour de force was thick as paste, as if Vincent could not bear to diminish the color in any way. It was spectacular, a painting Chagall had never seen in any book or museum while he was alive. He stared, fascinated, as The Thief placed the Van Gogh on his easel and mimed painting with his barren brush, the failed artist, like so many thieves before him, forced to make do with vicarious mastery. It was heartbreaking really, the depth of the coveting, the futility behind the charade. Then, after only a few pretend strokes of the paintless brush, in that rarified air only an inch from Vincent's creation, The Thief stopped abruptly, shed his costume, robotically replacing all of the cryptic props in their respective hiding places. He strode over to the bedside table, opened the drawer, and took out his little black book, reaching for the telephone, knowing exactly whom to call.

The distressing memory disappeared as quickly as it had arrived. Chagall rolled over onto his stomach to study a lovely bug, iridescent and emerald. *At least I got a few of the paintings back,* Chagall thought, allowing himself that rare sense of accomplishment. He recalled the days in Paris, in the thirties, the pride he felt straightening the retrieved painting with the red angels, no devil but red *angels,* that was now safely back on his wall in Paris. My lost children, he called these paintings, holding Bella against him in the ornate iron bed that took up almost the entire bedroom in their place on the Ile St Louis. "Our pirate ship," Bella called it. He would step back and look at the paintings that he had managed to rescue, and felt at last that he could stop torturing himself so. It troubled Chagall that he had been forced to take Waldin to court, for he did not hate the man, but Chagall was convinced he was in the right and his sense of justice would not allow him to let it go. Gratifyingly, the court agreed with him, and the gallery owner had been obliged to go and buy back as many paintings that had been purchased before and during that first war as he could track down. So Chagall had made it back to Paris and painting with enough esteem in the art world to have some money in his pocket and all that allowed him to finally make a good life for Bella and his sweet daughter Ida.

But peace was a flighty creature. Chagall sighed. He let the emerald bug climb up his finger and admired its active antennae as it moved forward. "I wonder if you can see me, little friend, or maybe my finger is just some rise in your path as you make your way along, unquestioningly. I have never mastered that: acceptance, unquestioning. Bella always told me that I worried too much," he said to the bug, "that I related every hurdle to my being Jewish. 'No one gives it a thought but you!' she told me—never cross, just in her firm way, trying to show me my own folly. But she was wrong, about that, so wrong. How long had we been in Paris, thinking ourselves safe, when the hatred again reared its head? Bug, be grateful for your ignorance of such things! Why was I forced *again* to flee? Always staying one step ahead of these wars and revolutions and persecution. Syria, Egypt, Palestine, Jerusalem. I have illustrated the Bible, Bug! Such an honor! Holland, Spain…my God, I saw the world." The beautiful bug continued to crawl up and down the hills and valleys of Chagall's fingers with a frantic energy.

"Time is a river. I could drown in the memories. Italy, Mexico, New York." Chagall wondered if tears were falling from the corners of his eyes. He brought his fingertips up instinctually, but of course there was no sensation. The clouds overhead looked like a long row of…what? Can-can dancers? Soldiers? So many things, good and evil, blurred in all this indulgent recollecting. "At least when I died and Vava put me in that Catholic cemetery—the cross still sits above my casket, if you can believe it!—at least my daughter stormed The Fortress of Vava and made sure the Kaddish was read at my funeral. A wonderful girl, my Ida.

"But I was happy, little bug. I tried it all: poetry, sculpture, glass, set designs, fables—I was open to it all. To remain open, that is everything. The *soul*, that is what matters. I must somehow impart this to Phoebe. Life has a way of grinding us down, sure, but to continue to create, to stay true to one's passions, that is what saves us. I loved many places and made them home, all of them. Yes, you can make a place home, even for a short while." Chagall lowered his finger to ground level again and the scarab hurried away.

I tell you that, too, Phoebe: Seize it all while you can, dive into it and swim. Versatility, that is the key. Chagall stood, and even though his body could not feel the old stiffness, he stretched and rolled his head around as if loosening kinks. Well, there was that in death's favor. No aches and pains, of the physical variety anyway. The line of clouds had separated now, and he saw thin trails extending from several of them, like arms outstretched, trying to reconnect. *Phoebe, tonight may you see what you need. Maybe I can help, or maybe you won't need me. I want you to see.* He looked up again at the active clouds, and like a smoky genie, was soon a part of them.

CHAPTER TWENTY-SEVEN

Even though the rest of the world was well into the twenty-first century, the Bion sisters did not own an automobile. This was yet more fodder for the village rumor mill, and locals never tired of embellishing when talk turned to "our two resident witches." Along with numerous cats and pets of all sorts, including a rather imposing and ancient iguana named Darwin who always wore a jeweled collar, the sisters kept a team of four sturdy Percheron draft horses, which they strapped to a plow occasionally and, more often, to an old buggy. This was still their preferred means of transport, whether directly, on horseback, or as passengers in the carriage. Darwin the iguana was the official greeter of the house. When he sensed a visitor, he ambled over to the front door, sitting up on his hind legs like a dog and freezing, narrowing his eyes and swishing his tail excitedly. He had been given to the sisters by a visiting gentleman from Mexico City in the early 1960s, a gentleman whom many in the village claimed had enjoyed a steamy ménage-a-trois with Marie-Christine and Jacqueline that lasted many years. In fact there were some who insisted that Darwin *was* the Mexican fellow, transformed and now captive amusement for the sisters. After all, the man had disappeared the same year as Darwin arrived, and while the gentleman had never returned, the iguana lived on.

Their friend Bernadette had confessed to them that the woman who sold her meats at the Wednesday market in Gordes always inquired after the pets of the Bion sisters, as if Bernadette, only a neighbor to the sisters, could possibly know. She would beckon Bernadette closer and hiss: "Familiars, *heh?* Each and every one of those beasts. They never grow old and my husband and others always spot these pets miles from their farm, trotting along like they are on some sort of mission." Then she would cross herself, arrange her face back into its cordial, pre-gossip expression, and sing out, "*Ensuite?*" handing Bernadette the fragrant *poulet roti.* The Bion sisters reveled in their notoriety.

Today, Marie-Christine was harnessing two of their Percherons: Buffalo, a massive stallion with a mane so copious she often wondered how he could see, and a tail so long it almost swept the ground, and his love, Indigo, a roan mare with a gorgeous blue-grey coat and long chin whiskers and eyelashes.

"You like the carriage, yes? A little freedom to clop-clop?" Marie-Christine asked Buffalo in the doting tone she saved for her beasts. She brushed some burrs off his backside with an ancient wire brush, and he snorted and shimmied the skin on his rump. "Yes, you are *beau*, yes you are, such a proud fellow," she cooed, looking into his sage eyes. He seemed satisfied with this praise and lowered his head to continue grazing.

"*Et ma belle*," she said, turning to Indigo, "it will be after dark when we return, so no hijinks on the road, promise?" Indigo gazed intently at her mistress and Marie-Christine gave the star on her forehead a little scratch. The horse pushed her head harder into her hand and whinnied.

"You are not guaranteeing a thing, eh?" Marie-Christine chuckled. She often thought that if given the choice between the company of animals with four legs or those with only two, she would choose the quadrupeds every time.

The sisters had made several tarts from the wild blueberries that grew profusely on their land. Many things were unique to their property: a variety of quince that had no thorns, nor grittiness in its fruit, and whose flowers were white instead of coral colored. A fig tree that bore figs the size of apples, which were almost black and tasted faintly

of port. They had even cultivated a banana tree with dangling pink
flowers that looked like the heads of the flamingoes farther south. No
one could understand why these tropical trees didn't freeze and die with
the fierce Mistral winds of winter.

"Jealousy fans the coals of gossip," Jacqueline would say haughtily
when they went to market and certain villagers teased them or pulled
their children away to give the duo a wide berth. "All fear is ignorance."

The horses' nostrils quivered, either from the intoxicating aroma of
the pies, or from their excitement at pulling the carriage and being on
the road.

"Guard the house, Dee-Dee," Jacqueline said when the iguana scut-
tled up behind her as if he too wanted to come. She tossed him a morsel
of quail pate leftover form lunch, knowing his fondness for charcuterie.

Marie-Christine was in the driver's seat. She snapped the reigns
gently and the horses lurched forward, starting into a pleasing clip. The
women tried to take the longest route possible. The horses enjoyed it,
and as the sisters got older, they had fewer and fewer such invitations,
so they wanted to stretch out the diversion. They were dressed in spotless white linen layers, lightly starched and festooned with a treasure
chest of pearls and brooches. It was a fashion perhaps more suited for
a high tea from the flapper era, but it was their style, and the costumes
were loose enough to allow them to play pétanque. They were not often
invited to Bernadette's pétanque games, though she hosted them often
enough. As the carriage jostled through the narrow paths of the road
and entered a small forest, they passed a group of cyclists, who waved
enthusiastically and pulled their bikes farther to the side so as not to
spook the horses. The Bion sisters nodded back in a more dignified
salute as the riders streamed past them. And then, despite their blinders
and good training, Buffalo and Indigo were tossing their heads, trying
to look up, twisting their necks wildly against the harnesses. It took
considerable effort for Marie-Christine to pull them to a halt in the
middle of the road, as the beasts seemed so agitated.

"Whoa, whoa…what is it? What do you see?" She looked around, but then heard her sister say, "Over there, who is he?"

Her gaze followed the finger that was pointing up, and she saw him, Marc Chagall, sitting in a high branch directly in front of them.

"He is Marc Chagall," Marie-Christine told Jacqueline, a note of pleasure in her voice. "I met him once at an art opening in Paris."

Hearing his name, the painter tipped a nonexistent chapeau and alighted on the ground next to their carriage. Just as he suspected, they *could* see him.

"*Mesdames*," he said in a playful voice, bowing chivalrously. He was delighted to be able to interact with yet two more people, especially ones so interesting. "Might you offer a poor painter a ride?"

"Why ride when you can fly?" asked Jacqueline huffily. She and her sister behaved as if seeing departed painters was a daily occurrence.

"And miss out on such divine company?" While Chagall was very much enjoying not being invisible, he worried that it might affect the outcome of his mission with Phoebe somehow, so he added: "Only one other at this party is able to see me. So perhaps you should be discreet."

"One other?" asked Jacqueline, cocking a brow. "That is one more than is usually the case with ghosts. Is she a witch?"

"No, no," Chagall said quickly. "Just a living woman who needed some help."

"From a dead painter?" asked Marie-Christine, looking him up and down. Sometimes these spirits were so informal.

"It is too long a story for now," Chagall said. "But may I *please* have the pleasure of joining you, or must I transport myself?"

"*Allez*," said Jacqueline, softening. He was a very good-looking man, dead or alive, and she loved to flirt. "Climb aboard."

The horses had calmed down a bit, and Chagall took in the whole picture: the muscular legs and necks of these fine equestrian beasts, these two wonderful characters, the witches, in their flapper garb, even the carriage itself, which looked like it had been fabricated from cinders and brocade. All of it filled him with that longing he had felt so many times at such moments as these, when he was so engaged in his adventure that he forgot that he was only back here for a short stay. The strongest pull was the craving to paint—to take up his brushes, enter the cosmos of creativity, and just capture it all. But now was not the time to be wistful. He was en route to a party, a lively gathering, and the possibilities for fun, and naturally some mischief, seemed boundless.

CHAPTER TWENTY-EIGHT

At breakfast that first full day of the Byroads trip, Phoebe had approached Jane and Michael after the route talk, after everyone had scooped spoonfuls of dried fruits and nuts out into little baggies, adjusted their helmets, made sure they had plenty of water, and double-checked their maps. Everyone but Phoebe put their toes into the toe-clips on their pedals and shoved off.

"Ready, Phoebe?" Michael asked, preparing to ride with her since she was the last one out.

"You are sweet, Michael, but I have to warn you, I actually am more of a meanderer on my vacation. I sort of like exploring and taking my time, so I don't want to hold you up!"

"We encourage that!" he said cheerily. "And don't worry, I won't be your shadow the entire ride. I just have to make sure no one has fallen off a cliff or gotten drunk at a café en route. I am just the sweep person whose task it is to get us all back here by four for the pêtanque and pistou extravaganza."

"Thanks, I appreciate that. I just didn't want to feel like I had to keep up with everyone. I'm sort of an ambler. The French actually have a perfect work for it: *flaneur*. That's me."

"Hey," he said over his shoulder, pushing off. "I hear ya. So don't worry. I also do some of my best thinking when I'm peddling solo. *A bientot!*" With that, he took off down the drive.

The early morning coolness was perfect for cycling, and Phoebe rode happily mile after mile. While the route occasionally sent her into small villages, the roads she pedaled down were mostly little untraveled byways, living up to the company's moniker. Too late she realized that she should have referred more often to her route map. All the roads seemed to be named D571 or D111 and then, without warning, she saw that she was on D5, and then not even D anything, but suddenly E202, which troubled her briefly. Still, she consoled herself, how lost could one get in two hours?

Phoebe rolled past grazing horses and those lovely round bales of hay she had first seen from the van. Everything seemed soft and dozy in the summer light, and Phoebe grasped why so many artists before her had been seduced by this region. After a long slog up a steep grade, she arrived in a little village with a charming square that beckoned her to stop and have a cool drink. As luck would have it, it was also market day, and the far side of the plaza was buzzing with commerce. She checked her watch: 1:00 PM. Plenty of time. She tugged off her helmet and ran her hand through her damp curls, then chose a table with a direct view of the main street. The waiter was friendly to her and told her that she spoke French very well. He couldn't resist making a joke, asking if she was training with Lance Armstrong for the next Tour de France, and she laughed and replied that yes, he was giving her some pointers. When the waiter left, she sipped her Orangina through two yellow straws and took out her sketchbook. She began to draw a man in a stall not far from her table, who was selling fabrics and who had the most wonder-fully shaped nose, which curved down and off to one side at the tip, like a tapir's.

"Quite a sniffer on that fellow, eh?" Chagall said, looking over her shoulder. "But you've made the crookedness too extreme. Look again and you'll see it's more subtle than that."

Phoebe had actually grown accustomed by now to Chagall's sud-den appearances and had trained herself not to talk aloud to him in an obvious way, nor to jump, two disciplines she hoped would help her maintain some air of normalcy.

"A nose like that must be sensitive as a hound's!" Chagall continued admiringly. "How I miss the talents of the nose. Mine was no slouch either, as you can see." Here he sat down and turned his profile to her.

Phoebe smiled and said, "You're in a happy mood." But then, glancing around at the populated café, thought better of speaking to him. Instead, she flipped to a blank page in her sketchbook and wrote NOT HERE! in bold letters, then turned the book to face him in a clandestine manner, looking elsewhere.

"Okay, okay," Chagall said grudgingly. "But I think you should get back on your bike and stop being such a *flaneur*! A leisurely pace is one thing, but you have lost the entire group and will miss the gathering, at this rate."

She gazed around at her surroundings then scribbled surreptitiously: WHAT ARE YOU, MY FATHER? Aiming it at him and smiling out past his head.

"No, no…but tonight is important…and this first day, everyone is bonding and you are missing out and," he smiled wickedly, "Ray is looking for you."

Phoebe perked up at this, Chagall saw. She wrote: I KNOW. JUST WANTED TO GET MY BEARINGS. AM ENJOYING BIKING LIKE THIS. DON'T WORRY. TONIGHT: MISS CONGENIALITY. BUT TODAY: FLANEUR!

Chagall sighed, standing up heavily and walking around to look at her drawing again. "Your downward curve is still a bit too exaggerated. His is not such a hook. But besides that, not bad." And with that he was gone.

Phoebe paid, and, leaving her bike locked, walked stiffly over to take a quick tour of the market. The steel-soled biking shoes made a clopping noise on the cobblestones and she felt conspicuous in all her emblazoned spandex. That morning when the group was preparing to go, Ray had looked her up and down and said:

"Okay, fuchsia biking shorts, orange jersey with red seahorses all over it, socks decorated with mermaids and an acid green helmet? You are definitely going to be visible to passing traffic. I'm wondering, is there a theme here?"

She had blushed and, trying to sound enigmatic, said only: "Life's too short for beige."

But the people here in the South seemed more good-natured, less formal than the natives of Paris. A French friend of hers in Sonoma, a Parisian, had once told her, "In France, life takes place more on the streets than in America. People do not stay inside as much in front of one screen or another. When you step outside for the day, it is like stepping onto a stage. You think about how you look, as you will be onstage for most of the day."

Here, though, Phoebe appreciated the less urbane approach. All of the venders were cordial to her and had a spark of merriment in their eyes when she asked them questions in French and they teased her a bit, each playing their part in the witty repartee of commerce in France. France was definitely not a place for one to be too thin-skinned. Life here was all about that back-and-forth, that spry banter, and foremost, *interaction*. Phoebe perused delicious soaps molded into the shape of bees or goats or "cigales," which were the omnipresent cicadas that began their chorus in the heat of the day and were thought to be good luck and a symbol of Provence. She caressed the fine table linens which portrayed landscapes of olive groves or poppy fields or laden fig trees, running them between her fingers. With a proud flourish, the vender with the tapir nose unfolded tablecloth after tablecloth before her, like a magician with his scarves, each one more remarkable than the last. Soon she held up her hand for him to stop, shaking her head ruefully and explaining that she was on a bicycle. Without missing a beat, the man insisted that he could easily roll the one she had admired the longest into a "*petite paquet*" and give her the best price. Phoebe surrendered. By the time she hit the road again, her little red handlebar pack was so heavy with local treasures that she wobbled a bit as she started back down the hill.

Phoebe checked her watch and saw with alarm that it was after two-thirty. She had to admit now that she was hopelessly lost, and she felt bad that she would be late for the event and cause extra work for Michael, who had respected her wishes to roam but now would be required to search for her. It was quite hot and Phoebe kept squeezing her eyes tightly shut as she rode, trying to avoid the salty sting of her sweat. When she finally pulled over and leaned her bike against a massive chestnut tree to tie a bandana around her forehead under the helmet, Chagall was there, tapping his foot impatiently, his arms crossed in front of him.

"You have crossed the border from happy wanderer to lost soul, I see?" He tsk-tsked her.

"I am going to miss the whole thing. I am such a poor judge of time," Phoebe said dejectedly.

"And direction, my friend. And direction." Then he softened and said with the long-suffering patience of a parent indulging a child. "Follow me. I know a shortcut."

Phoebe brightened at this, but as he hovered in the air in front of her, far enough away that she had to pedal furiously just to keep sight of him, she noticed that he was taking her through forests and over rocky terrain that was clearly not meant for any form of wheeled travel. It made no sense. This was no trail at all, just a rocky quasi-clearing in a dense forest. She was about to call out to her guide that she was worried about a flat tire and didn't want to be stranded out here, when it hit her. She was biking almost straight up the side of a mountain, over massive and sharp slabs of rock, but she felt no more strain or jarring than if she had been biking on a paved country lane! She grinned, giddy from the magic of it all, and just followed this spirit who had, for some blessed reason, taken her under his wing. It was almost as if she too were flying, though her legs continued to pump and her heart was racing.

After what felt like no more than a few minutes, they came around a bend and she was suddenly at the crossroads of a busy main thoroughfare, paved and distinctly back in civilization. She had gained so much momentum that here she was forced to squeeze with all her might at the brakes on her handlebars to avoid careening into oncoming traffic. She looked around to see if Chagall was getting a kick out of all this, but he was no longer in sight. She unsnapped her feet from their lock in the pedals so she could back up a bit and look at her day's ride map, the same one she had *not* referred to since the route talk at breakfast, except to confirm that she had gotten lost. Miraculously, when Phoebe squinted to read the markers for this particular busy road, she saw the number D2, and noted with delight how that corresponded to what was written as the last entry of the day on her route map alongside the description: "A nice two-mile downhill to home!"

"*Merci*, Marc," she said aloud, exhilarated from the "shortcut." This, and experiencing him painting through her in her backyard that day, had been the most spectacular parts of having a ghost as a companion. She looked both ways hurriedly, then pushed off into a brief opening in the traffic, crossing and heading directly onto a quieter road, back to the farm to join the others and see what other new adventures the evening held.

When she rode up the long drive to the terrace, everyone was already showered, sipping aperitifs and wearing their pretty, non-spandex attire.

"Phoebe!" her roommate Laura cried. "We lost you! Everyone was worried."

"There she is," said leader Jane, coming over and relieving Phoebe of her bike, then locking it with the others for the night. She flipped open her cell and called Michael, letting him know that the last one had shown up. Then she looked Phoebe up and down and said, smiling, "Did some off-road cycling, did we?"

Jim the podiatrist reached out to pull a leaf out of her hair, adding: "Looks more like she did some actual bushwhacking."

"I know, I know," Phoebe said, moved by the easy camaraderie of the group. "I promise tomorrow I will not be the lone wolf. Today I... sort of lost track of time."

"Well, Michael's traced every path or stretch of land anywhere near the route three times today!" said Jane. "And he never saw one trace of you on any road. How'd you find your way back here? He's definitely going to want to hear about your mystery route. If it was a pretty one, maybe we can include parts of it in next year's trip."

"I have a guardian angel," said Phoebe, enjoying being enigmatic. "A native. He showed me the way."

She looked over at Ray, who appeared sun-kissed, healthy, and happy, and she suddenly felt self-conscious, sweaty and bedraggled.

"Now if you will all excuse me," Phoebe said, bowing deeply at the waist, "I'm going to rinse off the day's adventures and join you all for a fast Lillet. Do I have time?"

"Just hurry," Jane said, shooing her away. "Your drink and olives and salty lemon walnuts will be awaiting you upon your return."

Once in the room, Phoebe looked at herself in the mirror and gasped. She had black grease marks from the bicycle chain all over her calves. They looked like those Polynesian island tattoos if they had been made by a tattoo artist with the hiccups. Her face was streaked with dust where the sweat and sunscreen had acted as a magnet. There were leaves in her hair and stuck to her jersey, and a dead moth on the left lens of her sunglasses. But she looked incredibly happy.

Once scoured and scented with the lavender lotion she had bought at the market, she joined the others. The leader, Michael, was already back, showered and ready to get some answers from her. But maybe Jane had filled him in, since he did not subject her to *too* heavy an inquisition.

Ray watched her cross the patio and could scarcely believe the transformation. She had traded the kaleidoscopic biking attire for an extremely flattering black dress, and his eyes took in her shape, charmed by the fact that even all dressed up, the woman had a sock tan.

"There she is," he said when she sat down in front of the promised Lillet. "The problem child."

Everyone, including Phoebe, laughed at this. Just then, the gathering turned in unison to watch as an otherworldly black carriage pulled up in front of the main house. It was drawn by two massive draft horses, their flanks lathered with sweat from the trip with all its intentional detours. Perched in the driver's seat was an elderly woman with hair almost as long as her horse's tail, and next to her, a slightly younger, plumper woman with curly grey finger waves. Then Phoebe saw Chagall perched on top of the carriage, looking down and assessing the Byroads riders. When he winked at her, pointing to the two older flappers and giving her the thumbs up, she gasped and took a large gulp of her aperitif. Bernadette came out of the kitchen, wiping her hands on her apron, and greeted the two women in the carriage as if she had not seen them in ages. "*Bonjour, bonjour!*"

An older farmhand helped the ladies down, then unharnessed the two steeds and led them away to the stables to brush them out and feed and water them. As they passed, their massive hooves stirring up little clouds of dust, Phoebe got a delicious whiff of some sort of lemony herb mingled with barn smell. She had never smelled anything like it before, and certainly not emanating from a horse.

"Byroads group," Bernadette said, tapping a glass to introduce the two new arrivals. "These are two very distinguished guests from our village, Marie-Christine and Jacqueline Bion. They are, *evidemment*, sisters, and also, ah, very knowledgeable in the Old Ways. They can answer any questions you may have about local history or customs. But don't be fooled by their sweetness," she cautioned, raising a finger melodramatically. "They play a mean game of boules."

Ray, who had already had an aperitif or two, raised his hand immediately and asked, "Just what ways are the Old Ways?"

The sisters spoke enough English not to need constant translation, and Bernadette shot a quick look at Marie-Christine to see how she would react to this question, hoping her tendency toward feistiness wouldn't rear its head quite so early in the evening. Seeing a flash of light come into the woman's eyes, she knew this hope was a vain one.

"Witches, my dear," Marie-Christine answered frankly. "My sister and I adhere to the Old Ways, which means herbs and planting by the phases of the moon and spells and the like, because we are practicing witches."

Ray was from the Bay Area, a part of California known for experimentation and openness, so Marie-Christine was perhaps a bit disappointed that her response hadn't caused more of a reaction in him. Instead he joked:

"Well, now I *really* want you on our team!"

The group drew cards to divide into teams, odd numbers sent to one side of the lawn, and evens to the other. Phoebe had admired Bernadette since first meeting her, impressed that any woman Bernadette's age could run such a plentiful and large establishment. She insisted that her hostess play also, resorting to pulling the woman by the arm until she gave in. Phoebe was intrigued by Bernadette, and hoped to get to know her better during her brief stay at the farm.

Michael had the Byroads group gather round, along with a German couple, the sisters, Bernadette, and two older gentlemen from the village who were clearly pros at the game and were amused by the green Americans.

"Okay, basically," Michael said, holding up a bright green wooden ball, "this smaller ball is the Jack or *cochonnet*. The goal is to try and get these balls," here he held up a larger silver ball, "as close to the Jack as you can. You stand with your feet together like so. And even though technically we're supposed to have no more than four players on each of our teams, we're going to bend the rules so that we can all get a chance to hurl these suckers."

The locals shook their heads in mock disdain.

"So a good strategy would be to have your pointers *and* your shooters on each team. Pointers actually try to skillfully lob the ball as close to the Jack as possible, while the shooters take a more offensive approach and just try to knock the Jack out of the circle. Whichever team gets to thirteen points first—and since we are so numerous we're going to play best of two out of three so we really earn our pistou—wins a fabulous prize, handpicked by Jane and myself. We will flip a coin to see which side goes first and who sets the Jack."

Phoebe and Ray were on opposite teams, and as the afternoon wore on and everyone grew more confident with the rules, the two started to razz one another.

"Hey, good shot! That one was *almost* within the lines."

"Say, you must have forgotten to wear your glasses this afternoon."

Jacqueline Bion, as well as the wife of the German and of course the two men from the village, were the most serious and skilled at the game, and since they were all on one team by the luck of the draw—Ray's team—they handily trounced Phoebe's team. This despite the fact Chagall used his powers to help Phoebe make some amazing shots, though not consistently, as that might have aroused suspicion.

Jane and Michael made a big ceremony out of presenting each member of the winning team with a large plastic medal that read Numero Uno tied onto a blue ribbon, and they slipped these decorously over each bowed head. The two village men, Marcel and Hervé, accompanied the awards ceremony with dual accordions, their tireless musicality fueled by copious amounts of pastis.

"A table!" Bernadette called out from the kitchen, clapping authoritatively from the doorway, and with the help of Sophie and the Bion sisters an endless stream of platters were placed before the guests all up and down the long table set up on the lawn.

Phoebe was touched by the effort that went into this meal in their honor, and she tapped a glass and stood after the last dish was set down to make a toast.

"To Bernadette, lavender queen and most gracious hostess. *Merci mille fois!"*

"Hear, hear!" said Jane, raising her glass toward Bernadette.

The table burst into applause and Bernadette waved her hand for them to stop.

"Eat your food," she said, blushing, and heading back to the kitchen. She returned with another beautiful platter she had made herself, decorated with yellow and purple iris. It was mounted high with steaming morsels of chicken breast, as well as potatoes, carrots, little eggplants, turnips, and any fresh vegetable that could be first roasted then dunked into the green paste.

"We dunk!" she said, setting it down first in front of the older German man, handing him some tongs and instructing: "If these get too cool the pistou won't melt on them. *Allez, mangons!*"

Phoebe was sitting next to Ray, and the chairs were set so close together that when she reached for some food her thigh pressed against his. Neither felt the need to move away.

CHAPTER TWENTY-NINE

As he made the drive from Paris to Menerbe, home of the Lavender Beehive and the vacation spot his parents had been frequenting for the past decade, Claus grew more and more resentful of his employer. After he had purchased a new briefcase, this time a blue alligator model, he had again dared to look at the radiant little Chagall. Claus, much like his father, was not a man given to excessive displays of emotion, but this was a painting so beautiful, so *hopeful* in its exuberance, that it brought tears to his eyes. *Sheisse,* he said, banging his hands against the steering wheel. He'd been driving a few hours now and since it was August, and a weekend, all the roads heading south were jammed, the French drivers honking at one another and making suicidal maneuvers in their lust to start their vacations. He downshifted and swerved the BMW, black and shiny as a roach, into the fast lane, tearing out with a great roar just ahead of a rapidly approaching Renault that honked at him but quickly fell behind. In his rearview mirror he saw the man gesticulating in anger, and smirked triumphantly.

This one really is my last deal, Claus thought, clenching his jaw. What a shitty way to make money. He'd been raised with all the advantages, exposed to all things cultural from the minute he could crawl, and, once he saw that his passion lay in the world of paint, was even able to open his own gallery with assistance from his parents. God, if they ever found out what he had become. So here he was, contributing to keeping great work *out* of the public eye. The irony floored him. And how was Paul risking a damn thing? No, *Paul* simply had to pick up the phone and Claus would come running, a well-trained flunky. The black-market art dealers were well known to Paul and vice versa. They always seemed to find one another, which was why Claus could never quite convince himself that the authorities couldn't find them just as easily. Business was brisk, as someone was always available to supply contraband, if the buyer could afford the asking price. The phone would ring, bringing the news that "a colleague" had "come by" certain paintings, and was "willing to part with them" for a proper sum. These were the paintings that had been scooped up during wartime, hidden for decades, then delivered in secret, never progressing through the normal channels of commerce, never gracing the walls of any gallery. And when the owners of this nefarious art wanted to convert it into cash before he died, it was Claus who did the dirty work. If Claus was caught, he would go to jail and Paul would just pay some lawyer thousands of euros to say he had never known the German.

Claus also felt rotten when he thought about the history of Le Verre Volant, all the struggling artists who had been supported by the old owners, who truly appreciated art. With the last of this line of noble proprietors barely cold in the ground, and the latest generation apparently not having inherited any aesthetic genes, the time was ripe for the plague of this new breed of "art aficionados" in the form of Paul. Here was this total outsider who slapped all that history in the face and blithely started selling off little pieces of history that had been tucked away behind some dusty bottles of wine, treasures he did not deserve or earn. And worse, he could always augment his windfalls from these with pieces of stolen art. *This* he could somehow have rationalized, but the Nazi-era "acquisitions"—these were clearly thefts from Jews. Sellers, collectors, middlemen—everybody knew it. Even certain museums and galleries that had come by such pieces made no attempt to reunite them with the families of the rightful owners.

"*Ach mensch*," Claus said to himself in disgust, zipping around a car packed to the gills with children. "A little late to be developing a conscious, *nicht?*"

"Ownership," Paul had lectured one day down in the cave, as he cooed over a new painting…a Fauvist? An Impressionist? There had been so many of these runs that Claus couldn't keep them straight anymore. "Ownership is such a difficult thing to actually *prove.*" Gloating, the man was. And Claus wanted badly to wipe that self-satisfied smugness right off his face.

Claus was hot and tired now and it had taken him twice as long to get from Paris to Menerbe as it should have. Plus, he had been gradually working himself into a dither. It was almost dark. He had hoped to do this last transaction before he joined his mother and father on their annual Provencal getaway, to have it behind him. But the day and the wretched traffic had ruined that possibility.

Suddenly, an idea came to Claus that lifted his spirits immediately. What if *he* kept that little masterpiece tucked away in the new briefcase in the backseat? It was brilliant—a well-deserved parting gift! Paul couldn't make a public fuss over it going missing and risk getting himself caught, and neither could the collector. Claus would have a transcendent piece of artistic grandeur and be done with the whole sordid business. Claus was giddy with the wildness of his plan. But just as fast, the impossibility of such a scheme was glaringly apparent, and his shoulders slumped in defeat. Claus knew that Paul had many other employees besides Claus, including a pack of large, devoted thugs who would merrily carry out any orders involving retribution. Claus was still a young man and did not want to spend the rest of his life looking over his shoulder.

He switched on the radio, hoping for some heavy metal that would match his feelings of futility and rage. Instead, every station emitted insipid French pop. He drove past the entrance to the Lavender Beehive twice before finally seeing the faint outlines of an unlit sign telling him he had arrived. He drove the BMW up the long drive and saw a lively gathering of people of all ages, seated at a long table on the lawn illuminated by blazing Tiki torches. He pulled into a parking spot and walked toward the group, feeling timid, like a new boy entering a classroom on the first day of the school year.

"Clausie!" His mother hailed him in a delighted squeal, standing and weaving her way toward him, arms outstretched for a hug.

"*Mütter*," he said in a low, formal voice, reaching down to embrace her.

Those with their backs to him at the long table now turned in their seats to have a look, and there, en route to join his mother and father, he saw her, the woman from the plane and the hotel in Marseilles. She looked absolutely stricken when she recognized him, her jaw hanging open and her eyes wide. This expression was far beyond normal surprise at such a coincidence, and it puzzled Claus, yet at the same time set his mind churning. What were the chances of three such encounters? But she couldn't be following him, as it was he who chose at the last minute to make a spontaneous visit to see his parents. So he nodded curtly to her, then registered briefly the man seated next to her, also familiar. He couldn't place him, however, and knew the familiarity would bother him all night. No time now, though, so he turned to join his parents.

"Is everything okay?" Ray asked Phoebe, his eyes following her shocked expression to take in the well-dressed new arrival. He put his hand on her bare back protectively and felt her shiver. Ray instantly remembered him as the man at Le Verre Volant. What was he doing here? He decided, for now, to chalk it up to a small world and refocused on Phoebe. "You look like you've seen a ghost."

The irony of this inquiry from Ray, coming at a time when she *hadn't*, for once, seen a ghost, almost made Phoebe laugh. She tried to compose herself and sound offhand.

"Oh no, it's nothing. I just…I somehow keep bumping into that fellow. He was on my flight and also at the same hotel in Marseilles."

"Maybe he's stalking you," Ray joked, then added, "and who could blame him?"

Phoebe had not been flirted with so brazenly in a few years and it felt wonderful, though she felt herself turn red from her chest up to her scalp. She was out of practice. Maybe tonight she could work on that.

The tapping of a glass interrupted their little tête-à-tête. It was Jane who rose from her seat.

"I'd like to toast a great group and an even better first day. And also, a question: Is there any *garlic* in this pesto?" When everyone laughed appreciatively, she called out, *"Santé!"*

"Santé!" they all chimed in chorus.

Jacqueline was on the other side of Phoebe and she had been regaling her with fascinating stories about the Bion lineage.

"We are the last of our line, *cheri.*" Jacqueline sighed wistfully. "And a long and powerful druidic history it had, too. My uncle was sought out time after time, from as far away as Spain, to perform rituals with the brass spell arrows that call upon the masculine forces to cause change, to get things moving that are frozen. Love, business, health—that arrow was so powerful we kept it in a velvet box facing south to get the sun's full strength and only brought it out to the altar when it was needed. And you needn't doubt for one second that this arrow brought results!"

Jacqueline was a very physical talker, touching Phoebe's arm and leaning in close to heighten the drama of her tales. She was flushed with her passion for the subject and her skin looked almost dewy in the candlelight. She smelled like apricots one minute and sage the next.

"I thought witchcraft was all about feminine energy," Phoebe said.

"It takes both, *n'est-ce pas?*" said a male voice from behind Jacqueline.

Phoebe recognized that voice as Chagall, so was going to try not to respond by turning, but then Jacqueline turned to him and said: "Oh, of course it takes both, Monsieur. You are right. Balance. All the great spiritual practices are about balance."

She had answered him as if he was just another guest at the table, just as naturally as you please, and Phoebe felt vindicated, delighted to be able to share the vision with someone, albeit a witch. Jacqueline was oblivious to any drama, or maybe she just didn't care that others might wonder whom she was talking to, and she turned happily back to her food, dipping a piece of zucchini into the pungent green sauce and then popping it into her mouth with unadulterated gusto.

"Never too much garlic, I say," Jacqueline announced, washing it down with some Bordeaux. "Bernadette makes the best pistou for miles."

"Whom is she talking to?" Ray asked from behind his hand, *sotto voce*. Phoebe was still trying to come to grips with the fact that she wasn't the only one who saw the ghost.

Jacqueline overheard and answered for herself. "Why, Chagall of course!" she said, leaning forward to address Ray. "Can't you see? His spirit is everywhere in this place."

"Mmm, yes, it sure is," Ray said to her, then whispered to Phoebe, "She's certainly enjoyed some wine."

"I can hear you, you know, Monsieur," Jacqueline retorted curtly. "I have ears like a bat. And it's not the wine, though certainly I have enjoyed my share. Bernadette's place is a true homage to Marc Chagall. Don't you also feel his presence? He is surely here with us."

Ray was abashed that the eccentric old woman had heard, so, chastened, he quickly concurred. "Yes. I *do* feel him everywhere here. And since I have always been a huge admirer of his work, I am happy about that."

"Good man," Chagall said, giving Phoebe's shoulder a squeeze. "I approve."

Then Marie-Christine looked back at the ghost mid-bite and chided, "Oh, don't be such an egoist, Marc."

Chagall gave a *mea culpa* shrug, smiling at Phoebe, but there were too many surprises coming at her at once for her liking. Claus, witches, the discombobulating feeling of Ray's palm against her skin, the wine— it was almost too much. The rest of the table, happily, was distracted by good food and conversation, and the sisters talking into thin air could be chalked up to senility. But Ray was looking at her funny and Phoebe needed to regroup. She gathered up a few of the empty plates and said in a higher-pitched voice than usual, "Will you excuse me? I'm going to see if I can help in the kitchen for a little bit."

Bernadette looked abashed when Phoebe entered her kitchen, to the point where she dropped one of her exquisite plates and it shattered into a dozen pieces on the stone floor. Phoebe hastily set her dirty dishes onto the counter and knelt down to help pick up the shards.

"Oh, I'm so sorry, Bernadette," Phoebe said earnestly. "I didn't mean to startle you. I too am very territorial about my kitchen, but I just wanted to help, and to talk with you a bit. I admire so many things about the place and you are certainly the driving force behind it." The words tumbled out in a rush.

"Oh, thank you…but you shouldn't be in here," Bernadette said shakily. "I just was in my own world. Now *allez*—it is your vacation! I am getting paid for this. You go back out now, I am fine."

"It's no problem at all. While you make coffee, I can dry dishes. That way I can talk with you a bit."

"About what?" Bernadette asked, her eyes darting around the room like a cornered mouse.

"Oh, Chagall, first of all. He is absolutely my favorite painter and this entire place is like a shrine to him. I would love to talk with you about Chagall and how you came to be smitten with him."

Bernadette studied Phoebe as she scooped some fragrant coffee grounds into a half-dozen French presses. Outside, the cigales were chanting at the approaching darkness and the electric static of their cries wove in and out of the guests' laughter and talk. To Bernadette, they sounded chiding, reproachful. Yet when she met Phoebe's eyes, she could see that the American was guileless in her question. There was no trace of accusation or interrogation in her manner, so she told herself to try and calm down.

"My name is Phoebe, by the way," Phoebe said, extending her hand. "Phoebe Rosen. I have a…special relationship with this painter, and I see in you a kindred spirit. I am not trying to be nosy."

"Can you pour some coffee into the six cups I have on that counter over there? Only six want coffee. You Americans always worry that you will be unable to sleep."

"I am one of those Americans. I don't suppose you have mint tea with honey?"

"Yes, I've already started a large batch of *tisane* for the more prudent. When you have poured the coffee, I can carry it out and you can pour the infusions in the other cups on that counter."

"Infusions?"

"Herbal tea," Bernadette said, lifting up the round tray and heading outside.

As she approached the table, her brain was a hive of activity. How could she evade this woman's questions about Chagall for the remainder of their stay? Impossible. She would seem even more suspect if she tried.

"Café?" Bernadette sang out with false gaiety, and those who had wanted one raised their hands. It was a beautiful evening and she noticed that two of the guests were swimming, the man with curly dark hair, and a tall blond woman with very pale skin. The woman seemed more than a little tipsy. Bernadette always worried about these spontaneous after-dinner swims that the guests often took. Her mother had always insisted that she and her siblings wait an hour after eating before entering any body of water, and not to swim at all if there had been any alcohol involved. She had been a little more progressive with her own children, making them wait only twenty minutes, scaring them with the old adage: "You don't want to get cramps and drown."

What if one of these guests sued her? Americans loved to sue people, even when they had made the mistake themselves. They were a culture of blamers, and if there was one thing she had little tolerance for, it was people who did not take responsibility for their own faults and shortcomings. But she did her best to control her worries. If one couldn't swim late in the evening, in a beautiful tiled pool filled with water the temperature of a delicious bath while on vacation in Provence, then what was the vacation for?

The Bacchus-looking man, whom she had previously been thinking was keen on that Phoebe Rosen, saw her bringing the coffee and emerged from the water, standing up where it was waist deep and heading for the steps. The moonlight flickered off the beads of water on his back, and the young woman still in the pool, knelt behind him, whimpering like a puppy and tugging at his leg, trying to pull him back in. He looked anxiously toward the kitchen, then grabbed the railing, pulling himself up out of the water and free of her grasp, scolding, "Now, Laura, gotta get my coffee. You be good."

He pulled a towel over his shoulders—it was finally cooling off a bit—and stood near the leaders, blowing on the tiny cup so he could drink the foamy brew right away.

"I think we greenhorns all played pretty well today," said Michael, sipping his own coffee. "Especially after biking thirty miles. Say, this *is* decaf, right?"

"Thirty miles?" cried Marie-Christine incredulously. "You come on vacation to kill yourselves?"

"Why not? It's fun!" Laura slurred from the pool. She was lean and muscular, with an absolutely unlined forehead that you could bounce a penny off of. Too thin. An afghan. Marie-Christine took an instant dislike to her, as she had already noticed the spark between the woman who could see Chagall and the dripping wet Mediterranean-looking fellow.

"To each his own, said the old lady as she kissed the cow," Marie-Christine replied airily, repeating some esoteric maxim that she was sure none of the guests had ever heard before.

Phoebe was coming out of the kitchen with her cup of tea, Bernadette a few steps behind her with the whole tray.

Phoebe slowed her step so they could walk alongside one another.

"This honey is so good," Phoebe told her, taking little sips as she walked. "I would love to see your bees sometime. I have always wanted to raise bees, but I worried that my dogs would get stung."

"If they're smart, they will only get stung *once*," Bernadette assured her, passing her to set down the tray. "*Tisane*, anyone? It will give you good dreams." She picked up a cup and saucer and extended it to the gentleman opposite her. She smiled tightly at Phoebe. How could she shake this woman? So eager to be her best friend. Why couldn't she just interact with the others on the trip?

"We've got a forty-mile day tomorrow, people," Michael said amiably once everyone had their drinks. "I know this is a group of party animals," this was greeted by raucous laughter, "but we'd better start thinking about winding it down soon. The light can trick you, here in paradise. It's actually after eleven and I'll bet some of you are still fighting jet lag."

The group exclaimed at the hour and many tossed back their tea or coffee and stood to go, excusing themselves.

"Route talk here on the terrace at 7:30 tomorrow. We should be on the road again by 8:00, so come have some of Bernadette's amazing homemade croissants and wild berry jams and walnut bread—oh my! I think I'm hungry again! Unbelievable!" Michael declared. Jane rolled her eyes at the others and ballooned out her cheeks, mocking him.

Michael puffed his cheeks out as well, then continued, "Where was I? Oh yes, then we'll go over the route. It's a hilly one. We're going to try to catch market day in the spectacular perched village of Rouisillan. Although *one* of us has already been to a local market."

He was teasing Phoebe and she curtsied to the remaining bikers and said, "Just call me Problem Child." She checked to see if Ray was watching and was inordinately pleased to see him smiling at her, damp curls and all. And there was her roommate, Laura, also damp and listing slightly so she was practically leaning against Ray, who was allowing it. Phoebe felt a surge of jealousy, but gulped her tea and tried to join in the banter. It was no use; she had lost her desire to linger.

"I think I'd better hit the hay," she said and turned to go. "See you all tomorrow." She *almost* added: "Laura? Aren't you coming also?" But she had her pride.

Heading back to her room, she passed the infamous German having a cigarette with his parents on the far side of the terrace. She nodded perfunctorily at the three of them as she walked by and noticed that they stopped talking as she approached. And then there was Chagall, sitting opposite the young German, pointing heatedly and lamenting, "Phoebe! He's got another one! Another of my paintings! Go see for yourself! I'll show you his room." Phoebe had never seen Marc so worked up.

Phoebe almost responded but stopped herself at the last second, keeping her eyes forward and putting one foot in front of the other. Chagall followed her, persisting.

"Phoebe, this fellow is a bad egg. You've got to do something! I would take care of it myself, and I can help you, but I need you to physically lift the painting. This time I know exactly to whom this particular painting belonged. They were friends of ours in Berlin when we were there in 1914—a wonderful and cultured Jewish family, and they stayed there all those years, until the next war, but this second war, they could not survive. I have not one doubt in my mind or heart that this painting was stolen from them. I gave it to them as a gift and I know they cherished it. You've got to intercept it before he profits again from my work, without a thought for the rightful owners."

Phoebe pushed open the door to her room. There was too much Chagall in her life. The walls were covered with it. The witches joining in, making it a *folie a trois*. Bernadette, who had been unexpectedly cagey about sharing her own thoughts on the man's work and how she came to revere him so. Ray, witnessing those two witches as they talked quite openly to his ghost, and then swimming with her dreadful roommate—though that wasn't truly related. And unbelievably, another run-in with the German. She needed a breather from the whole thing. If she had indeed, as Chagall informed her, called out to him for help, she could no longer guess the reasons for that subconscious cry. What could the ghost of a painter, or of anyone, for that matter, possibly do to help her keep her home?

She supposed she had to be grateful to Chagall for opening up her own work, and in a roundabout way for making this trip seem like a great idea. But what good was this trip if she was managing stolen art

and ghosts and was not even able to be a part of the group or ride or…
okay, she'd admit it, pursue something with Ray? Right now her roommate was probably canoodling with the man, while she was talking to
an apparition. The only positive thing Phoebe could extract from all
this was the validation that she wasn't absolutely crazy, as the sisters
had seen him, too. She shut the door behind her, neither responding to
Chagall's urgency nor inviting him in.

As it turned out, an invitation was not necessary. When she turned
around to enter the room he was already sitting on the floor.

"Marc!" she cried, stamping her foot. "I am a bit saturated with all
this art espionage and drama. I need a break."

"My dear woman, I never took you for a quitter," Chagall said,
and the lines in his face deepened, making him look a thousand years
old. "This is serious. We have come this far and it wounds me that you
would abandon the whole enterprise so easily."

"That's just it," Phoebe shouted, forgetting that her roommate
could walk in any second. "I am not clear on exactly what the enterprise
is! I have some vague inkling that it pertains to stolen art, but when I
got the last painting—at considerable risk, I might add—you told me to
put it back. Frankly, this is all starting to seem like the larks of a bored
phantom."

Chagall was no stranger to a woman's ways and he knew that once
they were all worked up about something, it was best to just let them
erupt. He sat on the edge of her bed, watching her calmly, yet still looking sad-eyed and hangdog. His silence infuriated her.

"Don't I even deserve some sort of explanation about the mission?
The big plan? My role? Anything?"

"*You* are the mission, Phoebe," Chagall said somberly, standing and
pulling a crushed felt hat out of his rear pocket. "Ultimately, you…I've
told you that from the beginning. All this espionage, as you call it, it's all
connected. Just for now, it's more about the art, the fact that art is meant
for everyone. Even if someone buys it, it should be aired out on occasion, shared with other eyes as often as possible. And it should certainly

not be stolen, and profit should certainly not be made off of vandalism and theft, and don't even get me *started* on the topic of forgery. If the person who had enough appreciation and respect for the art to buy it in the first place dies or is killed, and can no longer decide where this art should go, then someone has to step in on behalf of these wronged people. On behalf also of the paintings! Surely his children, the next generation after these terrible wars, if they managed to survive—shouldn't they see some of what is rightfully theirs? Art is valuable, but beyond the money, it is invaluable in a world that needs as much beauty as possible." In the passion of delivering his speech Chagall knew that some tears had escaped from his eyes, and for one brief second was certain that he had felt the moisture on his cheeks.

"But people buy art for their own walls all the time," Phoebe argued. "People will always want to possess beauty, have it right in front of them when they wake up. If that's wrong or selfish, then how could you ever justify selling a single painting to your collectors?"

"No, no—if the artist benefits, if the person has acquired the work through the right channels, then I take no offense at that. It is when art is stolen, then sold, when the art lover is a victim of thieves who no more care about art than the man in the moon. And so it goes; the person handling the smarmy transaction is often not even an art appreciator, unmoved by the very work that is making them millions of dollars. That is what I cannot abide. Let those who love the work and sacrifice to have it near them, let them or their children benefit! That is only what is right."

Phoebe sat on the bed wearily. Maybe she wasn't up to the responsibility that came with having art and life lessons given to her directly from one of the great masters.

"Well, you seem to know things I cannot, to *see* things I cannot. For example, that piece Claus has in his new briefcase. You possess these powers, not me, so I am baffled as to why you even need me to perform these dangerous missions. You are invisible to most and could whisk the piece out of his room before he even knew it was gone. Why make me do it and put me in harm's way?"

"It's complicated, Phoebe," Chagall sighed, sitting beside her. "But suffice it to say, lifting the three-dimensional things from this world presents a great challenge for me. Even light objects, like this hat, take concentration and something more like will than strength for me to even get something to budge. I don't know if I could open the briefcase, but even if I could, I don't know if these hands could physically lift the small painting and carry it out."

Phoebe considered this new information, then said, "But you held a paintbrush and painted. I watched you, in my backyard…seems so long ago now."

"Ah, but you were there and, since it was you who called me, some of your strength goes to me. It was you holding that brush, after all. And besides, a paintbrush is quite a different matter than a briefcase."

He saw he was making no headway with Phoebe, so he stood to go.

"I told you it was complicated. But if you really want to help me, and not only me but your ancestors, the art world, and the world in general, you will figure out a way to get that painting back. And the other, too. Especially the other."

"My ancestors? Who do you mean? And what other? You said there's more than one?"

But just then, the door opened and Laura, her utterly inebriated roommate, walked in, toppling like a felled oak onto her bed and passing out. Chagall was gone and Phoebe watched the dead sleep of her roommate with envy. Well, she thought, switching off the light, tomorrow's would certainly be an interesting ride.

CHAPTER THIRTY

Claus showered and strode naked over to the briefcase, tenderly extracting the Chagall painting from in between the fine, handkerchief-weight Egyptian cotton pajamas that had been protecting it. He stood by the single bed, looking down at the priceless thing, the midnight breeze scrumptious in his damp hair. His love of the painting was always followed by a crushing sadness, remorse, then impatience with himself for letting sentimentality impair his judgment. *This is a job*, Claus told himself. *Which would you rather have, idiot, a colorful little piece of canvas or many many thousands of euros?* It came as a surprise to him that he even had to consider this question. Claus turned his back on the painting in a huff, as if it were a woman he was having a spat with. Then he stepped into the pajama bottoms and cinched them tightly around his waist. This is no time to be self-indulgent, he reasoned, swishing minty mouthwash around in his mouth and spitting it into the basin with vexation. Years of taking the risks and this, if he played it right, had the potential to be his last job. Why behave stupidly now?

Yet the painting stirred something deep inside Claus. Righteous indignation? A yearning to reinvent himself? This particular painting, coming to him at this exact point in time, felt like a personal challenge. Like many embattled cultures, the Germans had thousands of years of blemished history to contend with. His countrymen were always cast as the villains. How to put something as enormous as the Nazis behind you? Then there was the angst. The arrogance. That Teutonic ice. Cautionary fairy tales that were meant to instruct rather than transport, the authors' names as scary as the morals they weighted their tales with: The Brothers Grimm. And of course, the general darkness of his culture. Christ, even the bread was dark. In cinema and literature, one never heard the words "jolly" and "German" in the same breath. Never had he read a reference to "that Germanic sensuality." And why not, Claus wondered, offended. Wasn't he as capable of warmth and spontaneity as the next man? The image of himself stooping down to pick up Paul's cigar butt flashed tauntingly in his mind. So what if disorder offended his sensibilities? Did that make him a monster? Efficiency was no crime! He couldn't undo the history of an entire nation, but maybe he would have the chance to rewrite his own.

Claus returned to the bed and held the painting at arm's length, fearful of its power over him. In spite of his resolve, it brought tears to eyes, and somehow that mist in his vision was the ticket away, from everything. Deeper and deeper he went, into the underwater world of the painting. It was as if he were being hypnotized. He could hear the Klezmer strains of a violin, passionate yet melancholic, a crying violin, off in the distance, punctuated by tambourine. Claus felt disoriented but could not look away. There was that smiling pearly fish, large now, and he could actually *smell* it, kelpy and full of the sea. And the fish was riding the goat, the bright green goat. But where were they? And him now, too? Were they all underwater, or was all this surrounding blue the sky?

Claus was confused. He felt his present, physical body disappear, and some other version of himself emerge from it like sparks from a log, released. He found himself *inside* the painting, swimming with red mermaids and flying dizzily with bird-headed women, in a school with them, in their flock, until swimming/flying became one action, one verb that resulted in an ascending tumult of contact. The bare breasts of these sea and sky nymphs rubbed against his own naked chest and he let them all pull at him, a circle of creatures pressed against him, aloft and soaring. And he belonged there; he was a part of it all.

But then Claus looked down and saw himself, far below, as if the room had no walls or roof—and that was him also, a lonely, middle-aged man standing by a single bed looking at a painting and wearing slightly droopy designer pajama bottoms. That earthbound version of himself looked so small and limited, and from this new world, Claus felt drenched with pity for this man. And while he might have been frightened by the swirling and tugging, the speed at which all his senses blurred and peaked, for some reason, he was not. He was open to it, trusting as a child. Shockingly, he was not even resistant to being so out of control. Claus looked away from that powerless creature below, wanting to separate himself from that tethered man, and let himself be caught up in it all, drenched in a world of colors. None of the beasts, human or otherwise, made sounds that could pass as language, yet even the blood rushing in his own ears was a sort of speech, or music, and all in the circle seemed to be communicating, with lips or sound or scale or flesh.

Claus resisted looking down for as long as he could, but that other self, a husk really, niggled in an otherwise perfect domain. He shuddered, not wanting to lay these new eyes upon that former Claus—but when he finally gave in to his curiosity, he watched mesmerized as a man with wild grey curls approached the pathetic doppelganger standing by the bed. This man was wearing some sort of smock, polka-dotted with flecks of paint. The older man smiled at the Claus below and reached out for the painting. Claus below turned robotically, returning the smile, and, nodding, with tears streaming down his face, relinquished the painting. The man in the smock appraised it with the close attention of a parent, then handed it back to the Claus below and motioned for him to follow, putting his index finger to his lips as a warning to tiptoe. Then the Claus below was following the paint-speckled man out the door, compliantly, the painting tucked under his arm. That was all Claus witnessed before being propelled in yet another direction, higher into the sky, deeper into the water, dancing opposite a bearded man playing hide-and-seek behind an oversized clock. And while Claus felt on some faint level, in some feeble blip in his wiring that he *should* be concerned, that he *should* return down there and fix things, he was enjoying himself too much in this place, wherever it was. He was quite happy there. Perhaps happier than he had ever been in his life.

CHAPTER THIRTY-ONE

Phoebe awoke to the sounds of her roommate retching pitifully in the bathroom. The light of the new day spilled in with a brilliance that made Phoebe's heart go out to the woman, now that she would not be a part of it.

Phoebe saw that she had time for a short walk amongst the bees and rows of lavender before joining the rest of the Byroads gang for the route talk, and she slipped her feet into the Birkenstocks she left beside the bed, splashed some water on her face using a second basin that was luckily in the bedroom, and was just about to head off down the hall in search of a toilet so Laura could have some privacy, when she noticed a flash of color from the corner of her eye. She walked over to her open suitcase and there, lying on top, was another Chagall. In an instant she knew it was the one the painter himself had asked her to procure.

"I did this much for you," Chagall said, appearing behind the valise stand. "It was no easy feat for me, physically or logistically. I had to work *through* the thief himself, so I am sincerely hoping you can take care of the rest."

"Shhh!" Phoebe commanded, looking at the bathroom door. "My roommate is here. God, what am I going to do with this?" Phoebe looked around the room wildly as if she were looking for a window to escape through.

"She'll be in there a while more, I think. One should *never* mix wine with pastis," Chagall said, shaking his head. Then he did a new trick. As he held his stomach and head, acting out a hangover, the skin on his face turned green. *The man could not resist being playful,* Phoebe thought. *Even in the middle of a crisis.*

Chagall saw how she was looking at him, cleared his throat and continued: "And as to what to do with it…I think you should, for now, give it to Marie-Christine. She and her sister are the local witches. She is a clever woman and the painting will be safe with her. I have brought her up to speed a bit."

"And me? How about bringing me up to speed? And what about after she has it? What then?" Phoebe whispered, an edge to her voice. "And how will I even find her?"

"She is in Bernadette's atelier. If you run right now, you can catch her."

Phoebe heard Laura moaning and pushing open the door. In one swift motion Phoebe swooped down and shoved the painting up under her nightgown, hugging her arms around herself as if she was chilly, to keep it from falling to the floor.

But clearly Laura had not noticed anything. She collapsed into bed and began to cry.

"Oh God, I still have the spins! I am so mad at myself," she said miserably. "I always overdo it when I'm traveling and having fun, and now I'm going to miss the whole ride today and everyone will become close and I'll be left behind. I am such an idiot!" With this she began to wail harder, turning her face into the pillow.

Normally, Phoebe would have immediately gone to her and hugged her, put a cool washcloth on her forehead. But there was no time for this. Instead, she tried to soothe her from across the room.

"Don't be mad at yourself; we all go too far from time to time. I'll tell everyone you have a touch of the flu but that I think you'll be fine by dinner. I will go find you some honeycomb to chew on. Bernadette keeps bees. It will make you feel better."

"Ugh, I'm too nauseous. Just aspirin. Aspirin and water."

"I'll be back in a minute."

Phoebe walked down the hall still hugging the painting, the canvas scratchy against her skin. She scanned the walls frantically, looking for a place to hide it until she could dress and take it to Marie-Christine.

She shut the bathroom door behind her, locked it, then examined the painting closely for the first time. She caught her breath and traced the entwined figures reverently with the tip of her finger. Flying fish, mermaids, roosters, a violin. Even a green goat made an appearance in this one. It was spectacular. Scanning the bathroom, she saw some towels stacked high up on a silver rack. She stood on the toilet seat and slid the painting under some folded towels on the uppermost rack, careful to hide any glimpses of its edge.

Telling herself to calm down, she returned to the room and handed Laura a glass of water, but the poisoned woman could only manage a sip or two before falling back onto the bed, muttering, "Idiot, idiot" and hitting her own forehead weakly with the heel of her hand.

Phoebe hurriedly tugged on her biking clothes, gathered everything she would need for the day, and dashed back down the hall to the bathroom, but when she tried the door, it was locked.

"Moment," a German voice called out, and Phoebe's heart bucked. Claus. How had Chagall managed to distract him? How had a ghost orchestrated lifting the painting out of the room and into her suitcase? And this one, unlike the one she had seen in Marseilles, was framed! Hadn't he said he couldn't move physical objects without human help? And most of all, how had he gotten the painting into her room without anyone waking up and noticing? He said he had been forced to work "through" Claus, as he had painted through Phoebe. So flesh and blood characters were his conduits?

A toilet flushed and Phoebe tried to pretend that she had been thinking of walking away to find another bathroom instead of hovering outside the door, but when Claus stepped out he smiled, going so far as to hold the door open for her. He was looking well rested, relaxed even, though a little dazed. Obviously he hadn't yet noticed that his painting was missing. She nodded at him curtly, though her true impulse was to study him, to try and read what had so changed about him. Was he actually whistling as he headed back to his room? She locked the door behind her and again stood on the toilet seat and stretched her hand up, groping for the painting. For one sinking second, she felt nothing but the soft give of the towels. Then she recalled it was one shelf up, and when her hand found the corner of the frame, she almost yelped with joy. She decided if she put it up the back of her tight jersey it would be less noticeable as she walked to the atelier, with the added advantage that she wouldn't have to hug herself as she moved. If anyone saw, maybe they would just think she had broad shoulders...or extremely good posture. Maybe she could, if the situation demanded it, walk backward for a bit. She flushed the toilet so as not to arouse suspicion, and practically sprinted down the hill to the atelier, the buzzing of the bees echoing her own zigzagging emotions.

CHAPTER THIRTY-TWO

Marie-Christine had planned to awaken early to gather herbs at dawn, when the dew was still beaded on the leaves and they were at their most potent. But now, thanks to the information Chagall had given her, she had something far more serious to tend to. She left the wicker basket there with a not for Jacqueline and made her way down to Bernadette's atelier, the layers of her gauzy white linen dress holding the scent of the lavender she waded through. Bees seemed drawn to the soft haystack of her white hair and encircled it, forming a golden, living crown, and the woman hummed in chorus, encouraging them.

Marie-Christine knew that some friction persisted between herself and Bernadette, and she thought it probably stemmed from her own natural inquisitiveness—or as Bernadette might perceive it, nosiness. But Marie-Christine felt justified in this probing, because she *knew* that her friend was weighed down with a heavy secret. Years ago, to clear the air, she had asked Bernadette if there was anything she wanted to disclose to her, for even though Marie-Christine possessed pronounced powers of prescience, it did not require much clairvoyance to see that her neighbor was hiding something. Bernadette had muttered something about "needing a vacation" and they left it at that.

Marie-Christine looked about on the landing of the small stone studio. Her halo of bees dissolved as they dispersed toward the back wall, where they entered their hives. Marie-Christine shielded her eyes and looked up at the sun.

Neither of the sisters had many physical characteristics, apart from their unorthodox choices in apparel, that would alert outsiders to the fact that they were witches. Yet the keen observer might notice that even in the bright sun, their pupils barely contracted, giving their eyes a piercing intensity, an avid attentiveness that had made more than one person shift uncomfortably during conversation.

Of course, if an outsider was invited into their home, there could be no doubt as to *some* sort of proclivity in that direction, given the massive collections of skulls and wings, brass arrows and pelts, Zuni fetishes from the American Southwest and voodoo dolls from New Orleans. There were rows of ancient jars holding tinctures and tisanes in the enormous kitchen. Bunches of drying herbs stirred from the beams when a breeze blew through. Cats of every stripe, strangely silent, wove between the legs of humans and chairs, their eyes golden and watchful. A plentitude of talismans lay upon every flat surface from basement to attic. And then there was Darwin the iguana.

But the amplitude did not stop inside the walls of their home. On the grounds, an inexplicable fecundity, which was the source of much envy in town, made the branches of their fruit trees sag, but never snap, from the weight of hefty pears or apples. Every trellis and every fence was garlanded with cascading wisteria or intoxicating honeysuckle or lavish walls of climbing roses, each rose as big as a teacup. Creatures, too, seemed drawn to the place, from lizard to deer to an impossible number of exotic birds. One wag in the village had sworn that she had found a nest on the road leading into their property that contained monkey fur and gold leaf. Yes, *real* gold leaf. At the center of this maelstrom of rumor, Marie-Christine and Jacqueline sat back and enjoyed the notoriety. Some might even say they fueled the rumor mill in their village with their eccentric manners. But the sisters believed in the Old Ways, practiced living their life by those creeds, and never felt that they had anything to hide. More than that, they did not suffer fools gladly.

No one was up yet at the bed and breakfast, but Marie-Christine knew she had to be swift. She turned the knob, a beautiful old glass thing that looked like a chunk of amethyst, to enter Bernadette's atelier and was not surprised to find the door locked. She tsked under her breath at her neighbor's furtiveness. Then she simply removed one silver hairpin from the many nesting in her long white tresses and used it to gain entry. When the lock clicked open, she stuck the silver pin back in her hair and stepped inside, her eyes taking a moment to adjust to that dimmer, cooler space. The place smelled like wax and clay. She stood facing the wall of honey trays that contained the hives, studying their handles, which lined up in a neat row, ready to be pulled out whenever the beekeeper wished to harvest the amber sweetness. Then, decisively, Marie-Christine marched toward the darkest handle in the row—darkened from the oils of the beekeeper's hands, and the one worn smoother than the others from frequent touch.

"Bingo," Chagall said, appearing by her side. "Good detective work, Madame."

"Marc, I am fond of Bernadette," Marie-Christine said with regret, her hand hovering over the handle, her brow furrowed. She was reluctant to pull open this drawer and reveal what she knew would not be just another tray containing a hive. "I feel we should let her explain herself."

"As you wish," Chagall shrugged. "But there is another who has been affected by all of this. Phoebe. She will be here any moment. We need to count on you to hide these paintings until we can figure out what to do."

"I can do that," Marie-Christine promised solemnly. Then she asked: "These? But there is another?"

"It's a long story," Chagall sighed. "This place certainly has no dearth of my work, but suffice it two say that there are now two of my paintings on the premises that are originals. So please, just let me know we can count on you until we figure out the best course of action."

Marie-Christine slowly lifted out the drawer by this most-worn knob, and there, sure enough, instead of a hive filled with honey, she saw the back of a painting. There was smudged writing on the back; she lifted it out and read aloud: "For my dear wife Ruthie Rosen. Paris, Liberation, August 28th, 1944. May our world together always have such magic. Yours forever, Ben Rosen."

Marie-Christine let out her breath and looked at Chagall, shaking her head in disbelief.

"I always knew she was hiding something," Marie-Christine said, mostly to herself, stomping one white-booted foot emphatically. "I could see, when I looked inside her, something shrouded like a black cloak draped over her heart."

"What, may I ask, are you doing in my studio, Marie-Christine?" Bernadette demanded, suddenly in the doorway, her voice shrill and furious. She rushed at her neighbor as if preparing to tackle her.

Without turning, Marie-Christine replied evenly, "I am looking at something that does not belong to you but that you have kept hidden away in spite of that fact. Clearly it is something that has been in your possession for many, many years. I am wondering how I could have ever called you a friend, knowing that you have lied about such a stolen treasure…the lie of omission."

Bernadette had practiced her explanations so many times over the years, just in case she was ever found out—yet now, when that time arrived, all of her clever retorts fell away and she blew up, assailing her accuser.

"How do you know this is stolen? I do not steal! And what business is it of yours, in any case? You have broken into my studio and are a nosy old bat! And one who talks to herself *en plus!*"

Just then, Phoebe pushed through the door, breathless and wary. She froze when she saw the two women, and looked over at Chagall in the corner, who encouraged her to enter.

"Oh," she stammered. "I'm sorry…I was told to meet Marie-Christine here. I…"

"What is your last name, child?" Marie-Christine asked her, regarding her steadily and holding up a painting, slightly larger than the one currently pushing against Phoebe's own spine but minus its frame. Phoebe had not been called "child" in so many years she looked over her shoulder to see if the woman was addressing someone else.

"Rosen," she answered. "Phoebe Rosen."

"And what were the names of your paternal father and mother? No, make that your grandfather and grandmother."

Phoebe looked at Marie-Christine and made the decision simply to answer rather than quibble about why she was being interrogated. But she couldn't help noticing that Bernadette was shifting her weight from one foot to another, her eyes darting toward the door like a trapped animal.

"My grandfather was named Benjamin and my grandmother, Ruth."

"Then I believe this belongs to you, my dear," Marie-Christine said, passing Phoebe the painting triumphantly.

Phoebe reached out for it, unsure, and as she did so, Bernadette charged past her toward the door. A nanosecond before she got there, however, it slammed shut, Marie-Christine pointing at it from across the room with her long, ring-laden index finger.

"You will stay!" Marie-Christine commanded in a low, booming voice that seemed to belong to a much larger being. Bernadette froze, then, and, giving up, she crumpled to the floor, saying over and over, "*Mais non…non…*" Her shoulders heaved with sobs and she repeated, "*Ce n'était pas de ma faute. It was my fault.*"

Phoebe held the small painting in her outstretched arms, the way she used to hold Audrey as a newborn baby, afraid of any sudden movements, afraid of dropping something so precious. When she read the inscription on the back, tears began to course down her cheeks.

"I don't understand," she said, addressing Chagall but also beseeching the room at large.

"Bernadette will explain," Marie-Christine said, pulling Bernadette brusquely to her feet. "I'm sure she has some answers for you, do you not, Bernadette?"

After a moment where it seemed she might try to bolt again, Bernadette exhaled in a long, ragged stream. "What are the chances?" Bernadette asked, her voice tiny and constricted, almost as if she were talking to herself. "What are the chances of you showing up here, so many years later—*you*, from so far away?"

"Maybe it wasn't chance," Marie-Christine said, touching her friend's shoulder, giving her a slight push in Phoebe's direction.

Phoebe waited for Bernadette to speak, but then she remembered the other painting digging into her back and reached for it. She stretched open the bottom of her biking jersey and tugged it free.

"Chagall said you would know what to do with this," Phoebe said, handing it to Marie-Christine with her free hand.

"Chagall?" Bernadette asked, looking around the room, baffled and afraid.

Marie-Christine studied the second painting solemnly, then proclaimed, "The only way to find the rightful owner of this one would be a séance. I am willing, but I'm sure they are long dead, and no doubt dead in the horrible circumstances of that last world war. *En plus*, names can be iffy when I'm under. I mostly see scenes and imagery. So, no séance. Instead we can put out announcements in the newsletters of some of these worldwide organizations that reunite families with art stolen during wartime. Again, people will come forward who are not the rightful owners, but the truth will cast them off. We will report this painting to such venues—but in the meantime, we will donate this one. To the Cezanne museum in Aix-en-Provence or another one. Surely any art lover alive or dead could wish nothing more for such a fine painting."

Chagall grunted out the name Cezanne, his old painterly rivalry surfacing.

Marie-Christine ignored him and continued: "I'm sure any museum would be most grateful, and such great work should be seen by many eyes; it should be shared." On that note she shot Bernadette a look and crossed her arms over the painting.

Phoebe looked at Bernadette, who looked down when their eyes met, her lower lip trembling. Everything about her disposition was that of a young child.

"Did…did you know my grandfather?" Phoebe asked her incredulously. "He often mentioned this painting, though I'm sure he had no idea who Chagall was or that the painting he found was an original. His brief time in Paris—the people he met, the intensity of that time and place, that was a life-altering experience for him. He was just a farm boy, you know."

"I never met him. My brother knew him," Bernadette said, looking at the floor.

"Ah, so it must have been your brother he gave it to. When Grandfather Ben spoke of the painting, he only said that it was a lovely thing, and that it had been lost in the mail. Not one of us ever knew it had been a Chagall."

"No. Nor my brother, either. No one knew, but *I* knew. Even so young. I recognized this as something extraordinary," Bernadette said pridefully. "My brother fought alongside your grandfather during the liberation. The American, your grandfather, must have thought that somehow the painting would be safer if mailed back to him. But your grandfather, he had no sense of the value, the worth of such a piece. No one knew. And besides, he had found it—can you imagine? To *find* such a treasure discarded in an alleyway!" Bernadette let the incredulity of this fact wash over the room, hoping for some sympathy.

Marie-Christine was having none of that. "If this painting was in an alley, the owner of it, of the café next door I'd imagine, was not the one who put it there. It's hard to decide what is of value and what should be left behind when soldiers are swarming in your streets. Someone was cleaning out the place and just thought it was a trivial little nothing."

"Still," Chagall harrumphed. "This person must not have seen many paintings."

"You cannot understand what it was like," Bernadette continued hoarsely. "I was a confused young girl. There was chaos in the streets. First the Nazis, for so long…then all at once, Americans! And my brother, whom I had not seen in over a year, we did not even know if he was dead or alive, suddenly there in front of me! But for only a day, about to be sent somewhere else to tidy up this long war. I wanted....I felt I *deserved*...something special. I had not seen anything of beauty, of such pure loveliness in four years. I did not think anyone would mind, in the long run. No one knew but *me*, you understand. I thought the American would have plenty of other pretty things there to distract him and would not miss it so much. And by then, by the time I laid my eyes upon it and my brother had entrusted it to me, then vanished—well, by then it was too late. I had already fallen in love. In my defense, it was never my intention to profit from it."

Phoebe did not say anything. She herself was an artist. She knew firsthand what it was to tumble into the world of a painting, to be transported and transformed by it. She had lived over four decades never knowing what it was like to have a war fought on her country's soil. And since she had grown up without ever seeing the painting, how could she miss what she never knew? No, she could relate to Bernadette's wrong, if not entirely forgive it yet.

She looked back to the painting and allowed herself to drink in the world of flying creatures with her eyes. She imagined the small canvas on the wall opposite her bed, the glory of waking up to such a jewel every morning. But wake up where? Her house would surely be foreclosed on, and then what good would a pretty painting do her? She tried to picture her grandfather in his uniform in the streets of Paris, thinking ahead to his reunion with her grandmother, the stories he undoubtedly regaled her with, both so young and hopeful. She couldn't quite believe how he had come by the painting, because she could not fathom anyone ever throwing it away.

As if reading her thoughts, Bernadette continued: "I rationalized it all, telling myself that this American had not lived through hunger or the occupation like I had. *He* had not known deprivation and fear as I had under the Germans—such ugliness fear brings out in people! No, this painting just fell into his lap, and so briefly! How could he possibly miss such a transitory thing? My brother said your grandfather believed it would be safer in America. Can you imagine?" Bernadette was working herself up into a froth. "What if it *had* been lost in the mail? Would that really have been better? Absolutely not. It was *I*," she said, hitting her chest for emphasis, "*I* who wanted to protect it. I see you are thinking no, that is too self-righteous. You are right. I also wanted it close by me always. *C'est ça.* But Phoebe, you must believe me that not a day has gone by that I haven't felt remorse that your grandmother never saw it, that I kept it from your family. I was bewitched by it. That is all can I offer you. It is no excuse for my behavior, but there it is."

Chagall watched Bernadette from across the room. He was conflicted. On the one hand, he was puffed up, proud that his paintings inspired such emotions in people. Yet he was also slightly appalled that his work was so exorbitantly valuable that it reduced people to theft and lies—though in Bernadette's case, the motivation had not been money.

"Oh, good. I see you have found my painting," Claus called out genially from the doorway before he stepped into the room. While his voice sounded upbeat, nonchalant even, there was no denying the threat underneath. Phoebe saw that he shut the door behind himself and locked it with a certain finality.

"I see this Auberge has problems with theft." He directed this comment at Phoebe, then continued addressing the room at large. "Yet my parents are fond of the place, so what can a good son do?" His voice dripped with a sort of put-upon sarcasm. He reached out then for her painting, confusing it with the one he was to deliver...the one he had already made his mind up to keep for himself, no matter the consequences. His demeanor, the way he extended his hand, did not allow for the possibility of refusal.

"This is not yours," Phoebe said, whipping the painting out of his reach. She'd be damned if she was going to lose it a second time.

"Well, I certainly doubt that it is *yours*," he smirked. Then the false lightness of his banter stopped abruptly and he pulled a small and

somehow mesmerizing little handgun out of his breast pocket, pointing it at her and saying tersely, "Actually, I was not asking." He relished
repeating the phrase Paul had used on him at the start of this dismal
assignment. Claus snapped his fingers twice.

"Young man, put that weapon *down*," Marie-Christine demanded,
in a tone that showed she was used to being obeyed. The next sound
they all heard was that of Jacqueline outside, humming the can-can
song to herself as she passed close to the atelier. Phoebe checked her
watch and knew that Michael and everyone would be wondering why
she wasn't present for the route talk, why, yet again, she wasn't riding
with them. How she *wanted* to be riding with them, longed to be anywhere but here.

"I do not have time for this," Claus said, ignoring Marie-Christine
and taking a step toward Phoebe.

"What exactly is your line of work, Monsieur?" Marie-Christine
asked him archly. "What is it that you do to be able to afford a painting
by one of the great masters?"

Claus turned to face her and the gun turned with him. His eyes
flitted between Phoebe and this annoying old woman in her outdated
clothing.

"I am an errand boy," Claus said scornfully. "The pay is not as bad
as one might imagine."

"Oh, indeed not," Marie-Christine said. "I'd imagine you are paid
quite well. Dirty work is always at the top of the pay scale."

As this tense back-and-forth transpired in the center of the room,
everyone had forgotten about Bernadette, on the periphery, who had
lowered herself to the floor and was now inching her way toward the
painting that Phoebe, registering Bernadette's plan in an instant, had
set down at her heels. Chagall wished he could have knocked the gun
from the German's hand once he too read the situation, and he cursed
his own ghostly impotence.

"Enough," Claus barked, shaking his head impatiently as if he had
been momentarily bamboozled by the old woman. He turned back to

Phoebe and said again with icy menace, "I believe you have something that belongs to me."

"Is this what you are missing?" Marie-Christine asked, producing the other painting from the depths of her shawl.

In the moment that Claus turned his attention to Marie-Christine, Bernadette managed to cover Phoebe's painting with her body, hiding it beneath her and laying very still. Claus noticed her prostrate there, then turned back to Phoebe, uncertain. The gun was a wild bird in his hand, capable of anything. Everyone held their breath and Jacqueline's can-can song boomed incongruously into the room. Finally, he snatched from Marie-Christine the painting for which he would risk everything—the painting he knew, the one he loved, the one he had, no doubt in his mind, actually *occupied*. It was the painting that would change the course of his life, and it was rightfully his, for all he had endured. Claus vowed in that instant that he would not think about consequences—about his parents, what they would do once they got an earful of today's proceedings, nor about Paul. He would think only of himself for a change. He would be the jolly German, the rouge, the wild one. He was going to lay low, if that's what it would take to get out of the trap his life had become. He hugged the painting to himself like a life preserver and backed toward the door.

"Oh, you're all here!" Jacqueline sang out from the doorframe, the room filling with the scent of the tarragon and lavender in her basket. "Everyone was looking for the American woman. *Especially…*" She paused, oblivious, and batted her eyes at Claus. "The Monsieur Ray. But they could wait no more and have gone now on their ride."

Claus spun around to see Jacqueline entering the room as blithely as if she was arriving at a tea party.

"What is…?" Jacqueline stammered when she saw the gun.

Claus whirled to face the others, turning his head back and forth wildly, from the door to the gathering, then back again, waving the gun like a dowsing rod all the while. Phoebe stood straight and tried to erase all expression from her face. Claus shoved the stupefied Jacqueline out of the way and bolted out the open door with his painting clenched under his arm.

CHAPTER THIRTY-THREE

"**C**lausie?" Claus's mother surprised him in his room when he burst through the door. She was folding his clothes neatly into his suitcase. Claus had no time to hide the painting he was carrying, but luckily, he had thought to slip the gun back into his jacket pocket.

"*Vas ist das?*" his mother asked, frowning at the Chagall.

"*Mütter!*" Claus cried, exasperated. "Why are you in my room?"

Claus was poised for her recriminations, then reminded himself that it was too soon for her to know anything about what had just happened in the atelier. With some luck, he could make his escape and put miles between himself and his parents before they began connecting the dots and learned about his other life.

"Don't be cross. I was only trying to help." She extended her lower lip in a mock pout. "I know you are always on a tight schedule, but we had such a short time together and I thought maybe if I had you all packed we could relax and even go on a walk before you go?"

"There isn't time…" His voice was gruff, and when he saw the hurt on her face, he tried to keep focused on his exit without being deterred. "I mean I do not have time for that, dear *Mütter*. I am so sorry. But we got in a little visit, no? Dinner at least—and next time, you have my word, more time. I will have more free time soon."

She searched his face, then crossed her arms and said bluntly, "What is going on, Claus?"

His mind raced. She always knew when he was lying. He decided that the truth was so farfetched, so extremely the opposite direction from all of their hopes for him, their belief that he simply owned a successful gallery and was an art dealer, that she just might buy it.

Claus adopted a deadpan expression, put his arm around his mother's shoulders and whispered in a low, conspiratorial voice: "I am scheduled to meet someone to deliver a stolen painting. It is an original by Marc Chagall. I have to leave here *tout-suite* because if I am late for this meeting, there is a man in Paris who will most likely have me hunted down and shot."

His mother looked at him dumbfounded for a nanosecond, then burst out laughing and gave him a little shove.

"Well, I always knew you were the master of excuses when it came to getting out of time with your parents, but I must say, you are certainly getting more colorful."

Claus walked over to the valise, casually tossing the painting on top. Lest she comment on it further, he waltzed her over to the door, and, kissing her on the forehead like a child, promised that he would come visit them in Germany "just as soon as I tidy up these affairs." She chuckled and waved goodbye to him, adding, in that same cloak-and-dagger voice: "Be sure to stay out of trouble, Clausie. Your father and I would not like to see you shot over a painting... even a Chagall."

Five minutes later, he was doing ninety, heading in the direction of the drop-off but still not committed to actually parting with the piece. He was hoping that somewhere along the way he would come upon some kind of a sign, so that he could finally decide the fate of the damn painting—and by extension, his own.

Claus couldn't see his stowaway. Chagall was crouched in the impossibly small back seat of the sports car, hugging the valise that held the painting. The painter watched the scenery rush past him and thought about some of the missing paintings that had never reappeared, some of his favorites. "Woman with Four Pigs." "Bird's Eye." "Above St. Petersburg." "Nocturne with Lamb." "The Red Violin." Each painting Chagall created was like one of his children, each loved for its own reasons, and he ached with the knowledge that the world would never see these lost works. But this little one he was now holding, "On the Banks of the Sky," would have a different fate, Chagall vowed. He wracked his brains for some solution as to how to get that painting safely into the public eye, wondering if Claus was really en route to make the delivery, or whether he might consider a life on the lam a fair exchange for a work of art.

If only Chagall could get the German back inside the painting, but there was no time now for the necessary prompting and induction. He knew the power of persuasion the art possessed. It might be enough to make the man remember his higher self, encourage him to do the right thing. For that brief moment, Chagall had seen Claus's humanity and knew it was accessible, if currently repressed.

Just then, Claus took a hairpin turn at too high a speed, the velocity sending the valise, with Chagall still holding on to it, flying out the open roof of the convertible. They landed, thanks to the supreme efforts of the painter, with little damage to the ejected valise, on a bluff hundreds of feet below this winding road on the cliffs above the Mediterranean Sea. Chagall sat up, the suitcase touching his hip and, for the moment, out of harm's way. He had landed in a patch of wild fennel and broke off a few sprigs of its feathery wisps, chewing on them thoughtfully. What was this? He could have sworn there was the faint taste of anise from the herb in his mouth. He stood and inhaled greedily at the sea air, testing to see if his sense of smell was returning also. Could be...faintly. *Merveilleux,* Chagall said, deeply gratified. He stood and surveyed the coastline, guessing he had been pitched out somewhere above Monaco. He looked out at the vast blue and wondered how long it would take the German to notice his loss. Then he sat back down on top of the case, and tried to come up with a plan.

CHAPTER THIRTY-FOUR

"**W**ell, my friend," Michael said to Ray, clicking the toe of his biking shoes into the locking pedals, "I think we're just going to have to admit defeat and hit the road. It's almost nine o'clock, and if Phoebe were joining us, she would have been here long ago. C'mon, cheer up. It's going to be an awesome ride today. Hilltop villages, wild strawberries, picnic lunch with fare from the local *marchées…*"

Man, this guy was upbeat. Ray nodded and looked one last time toward Phoebe's room, then pushed off, following Michael down the long shady lane and onto the first leg of their route. It was a superb day, still early enough for them to be able to enjoy the back roads before the traffic picked up. But Ray couldn't help feeling uneasy. He already liked Phoebe, and knew that they had forged some connection, something he hadn't felt in far too long. He was certain that it wasn't one-sided. And hadn't she said yesterday at dinner that she was looking forward to riding with group today, promising not to become separated again? He'd sensed she was upset last night because her roomie was a bit loosey-goosey with him in that pool. But Phoebe had been the one to check out, rising abruptly from the table and chasing Bernadette into the kitchen. If she really liked him, why had she given up so easily?

Michael and Ray were biking in good pace with one another. As if noticing his preoccupation, Michael said, "Don't worry, man. She's probably out picking cherries or checking out artists' studios in Men-erbe. There's lots to explore here and some guests would rather march to their own drummer than do the group thing. Phoebe strikes me as that type of gal."

"Yeah, I'm just surprised we didn't even see her at breakfast. She said she was sorry she got lost yesterday, so I thought for sure she'd be right with us today."

"Hey," Michael said in his best surfer-dude imitation, nodding his head like a dashboard figurine. "Getting lost is cool. Getting lost is what vacation's all about."

Ray smiled and tried not to worry, but he was surprised at how strong his disappointment was. It was the first time since his divorce that he had felt that potential, that curiosity, the excitement that this one really might work. After all the fizzled dates, all the effort it took to "put himself out there," he just wanted straightforward chemistry, to click with a woman on that level that was subterranean, that went beyond common ground, but was simple and subtle, a precious mystery. He liked that Phoebe was a birder, even that she had the name of one of his favorite birds. Plus, she was an artist, a mother, she loved wine and bik-ing. And she had red hair! He pedaled morosely and thought, *Well, this must be one-sided if she not only didn't want to bike with the group but also couldn't be bothered to tell me.* Yet he was certain he had *felt* that spark, and that never happened to him if it was one-sided. He took a deep breath and focused on his cycling, his legs pumping hard for the next hour, until he had caught up with the rest of the group, gathered under a plane tree, sharing their snacks and trading tales of the ride so far.

Phoebe, in the aftermath of her crazy morning, also had her mind on Ray and the group, but there was no time for regret. She had to deal with the more pressing matters at hand. Before she even made a move to leave the atelier, reunited with an actual Chagall that was rightfully her very own, this incredible, long-lost gift from Grandfather Ben, she had to figure out some semblance of a plan. Her brain was on overload. Chagall was nowhere in sight.

Phoebe had made sure that Claus got a good ten-minute head start to set into motion whatever the hell his next move might be. She had had to physically restrain the witch sisters from chasing the armed German, while Bernadette wept inconsolably from the floorboards and begged for Phoebe's forgiveness.

"All of you, just *stop!*" she had finally screamed. "Please get up off the floor, Bernadette."

"Are you going to call the police?" Bernadette asked meekly, standing slowly and sniffing.

"No. I just have to…I have to think. I am more concerned with getting back the multimillion-dollar painting that just walked out of this room than I am with punishing you. Now just…everybody, *try* to go about your day, as if none of this had ever happened."

The Bion sisters protested and Phoebe held up her hand.

"In truth," Phoebe said, "we can't do anything right at this moment. We have to accept that. Claus has to carry out the delivery if we want the authorities to be able to get a foothold in this operation. Our hands are tied for now. We can be more effectual if we can just be patient, say, till supper. I'm asking that we all hold tight until then."

And with this, a little amazed that the three women had obeyed, she rushed back up to her room, hid her own reconciled painting on the high rack under the towels in the hall bathroom, then called leader Jane's cell phone and asked her to come back in the van and bump her ahead to join the group on the route. Maybe Phoebe shouldn't have been thinking about Ray and the ride when more important matters needed her attention, but it was, after all, the first vacation she had had in years and she'd be damned if she was going to miss out on it. Her hopes were that by giving Claus a few hours time, he would somehow implicate himself and the matter would be out of her hands. If they had gotten the police involved so soon, it might have botched everything, no catching the bad guys involved in the black market ring, no proof, and most likely, no rescued painting. Also, Phoebe had a sense that if she was patient, Chagall would certainly tell her what was expected of her.

It was market day in Isle Sur La Sorgue, but in that village, this meant *Marché aux Puce,* featuring antiques, not just the local produce and crafts that Phoebe had experienced the day before. The streets were teeming with shoppers wearing straw hats to protect them from the sun and carrying brightly colored net bags erupting with fresh greens. Phoebe thanked Jane for the lift, and, happy not to have to find a parking space like those in automobiles, she rode off on her bike. In almost no time, she spotted Ray chatting with a man selling artfully displayed baskets of little peaches, two leaves still attached to the stems of many of them like small wings. She watched him for a moment as he said something to the rosy older farmer that made him laugh. She observed as he bit zealously into a peach, and wiped the juice off his chin, nodding appreciatively and pointing to one of the baskets.

With no deliberation, she walked straight up to Ray, threw her arms around his neck, and kissed him wholly on his lips, tasting sweat and peach juice. If he was surprised, his response didn't betray it, and he kissed her back, holding her close. The farmer smiled at them when they pulled apart, placing two extra peaches in the bag and shooing them away saying: "*Allez, allez les amoruese.*" Ray took her hand and they roamed the stalls, not saying much, but leaning into one another giddily. Phoebe never envisioned that she could feel this way again, this heightened state induced by the power of another's proximity, and she was stunned by it all.

Ray bought her a lovely old faded pink café au lait bowl with a gilded rim that the vender insisted, when she asked about its age, was from "*les jours de Napoleon.*" She rolled her eyes at him and offered him a little more than half of the first price he mentioned, knowing that offering exactly half would probably offend.

"*Ah non, ca, non! C'est un tresor!*" he protested hotly, snatching back the bowl as if she was being punished for not appreciating the thing.

But after this *de rigeur* exchange, they settled on a price and Ray paid the man. Phoebe slipped "the treasure" into her bag.

"I collect these bowls, you know," she told him. "Amongst many other things."

"Such as?"

"Old things. Things with stories. Old pitchers. Snow globes. Handbags. Charm bracelets."

"A minimalist, eh?" he said, giving her hand a squeeze. "I would like to see your home when we get back."

"Mm," Phoebe responded ambiguously. She wasn't ready to elaborate on that particular part of her life just yet.

She bought Ray a bar of citrusy Vervain soap that had been molded into an octagon with a raised goat insignia. Then, the sides of their bodies pressed together and moving in tandem, they drifted over to a shady spot on the banks of the river.

After they had settled, Ray said, "I was ready to be mad at you, you know. I thought you had your own itinerary planned for this whole week and none of us were a part of it."

He tucked a tendril of damp hair behind one of her ears and continued: "I'm glad you did what you did back there. I was hoping I would have the chance…tonight maybe, in the safety of the dark, but you beat me to it. Also I wasn't even sure…"

Phoebe put her finger up to his lips to quiet him, then began haltingly, "Ray, there is a lot I should be telling you about why I'm on this trip, my life…a lot of…complicated things, but for now, I just need to be really and truly on vacation. Even if it's only for an hour or so before all the madness starts up again."

"Madness? Should I be worried about you?" Ray asked, peeling off his shoes and socks and wiggling his toes. He scooted closer to the edge of the bank and dangled his feet in the river.

"Probably…God, it's such a long story. Really long," Phoebe added, a frown on her face. "And most of it entirely unbelievable."

"The best kind of story," Ray said, handing Phoebe a peach.

"Hey, you two!" a voice called out from behind them. It was Michael. He looked down and saw how close together they were sitting and winked at Ray. "Phoebe: either you're as fast as Lance Armstrong or you hitched a ride."

"Definitely the latter," she said, standing and brushing off the seat of her shorts.

"Well, I hate to break up your little *tête-à-tête,* but I'm here to gather everyone together in one spot. We're meeting under those umbrellas at the head of this road for lunch. It's only noon and I've already lost about half the group. You are *such* an unruly bunch!" he said in mock exasperation.

After they had all found one another and wolfed down (what was it about eating outdoors after exercising that made food taste so good?) a quick *sandwich au jambon,* with butter *and* cheese on the baguette, the leaders loaded their bikes on top of the van and Jane drove them toward the Côte d'Azur while Michael pointed out places of interest, kneeling on the passenger seat in the front of the van so he could address them all.

"I will now go into full tour-guide mode. Ready? The post-war years saw the influx of many, many artists to this area. Picasso, Matisse, and Chagall all called the Côte d'Azur home. In fact, Chagall is buried in St. Paul de Vence, not so far from Nice, where there is a great museum with many of these artists' work. I would suggest we include a ride up to see the man's grave, given how fond our hostess is of Chagall, but the cemetery is located in one of those perched villages and that means a *very* steep ride. If this is a priority for anyone, just let us know before the trip's over and we'll come back. But this afternoon, you'll have time to explore Nice. We've got dinner reservations at 8 o'clock at a wonderful outdoor seafood restaurant in Antibes, with a patio overlooking the Mediterranean,"

Phoebe was very quiet as he spoke of the artists who had lived in this region for so many years. She gazed out the window and thought of all the great works that had been painted in this part of the world. She shut her eyes and pictured Matisse, almost blind, cutting out the bright, perfect suns and birds of his later collages, his hands instinctively knowing the way to form their shape. She thought of the rivalry between Picasso and Chagall, how all great artists were both inspired by one another and fiercely competitive. She itched to paint.

Phoebe had not allowed herself to think of the inconceivable drama that had just taken place that morning, nor of her own little Chagall. *Her* Chagall. It overwhelmed her to even consider the value of such a thing. It would surely save her home from foreclosure, give her enough money to live off of the rest of her days. When she opened her eyes again and looked out the window, she caught her breath. The van was snaking its way around hairpin curves with views that dropped straight down to the rocky cliffs and blue waters below. How many car chase scenes in movies featuring Monte Carlo must have been filmed on this very stretch? Some in the group had lurched over to the seaside windows of the van to ogle the dizzying view.

"Careful, gang," Jane joked from the driver's seat. "If we get too much weight on one side of the van we may just topple over the edge."

The Florida Consignment Shop woman remained on the far side of the van, her eyes squeezed tightly shut and her lips moving quietly as if in prayer.

Phoebe and Ray were garnering curious stares from the rest of the group, who sniffed romance. When Phoebe leaned forward in her seat to get a better look at the sea, she caught her breath, spying a man a long way down from the road. He was holding a familiar valise, his grey curls being tousled by the wild ocean winds.

"Oh no," she said aloud.

"What?" Ray asked, following her gaze down the hill.

She didn't answer but craned her neck to try and get a better look at Chagall. He looked up at her—imploringly, she thought—before the van turned around another curve and he was lost from view.

CHAPTER THIRTY-FIVE

By the time Claus had arrived at his drop-off destination, he was reconciled with his decision to part with the painting. There was no other alternative. He was not a hero, nor was he the type of man who would enjoy a future that required constant aliases and relocating. On this anxious drive, during which he continually felt someone breathing down his neck, he had looked at his situation from every angle. He had asked himself whether he really wanted to risk his life and lose hundreds of thousands of dollars for a little square of canvas and ultimately, had answered no. He had not been himself since arriving here. He had mistakenly believed that the sea air and seeing his parents, plus his determination that this would be his last job, would all have a calming effect on him. Certainly that pinnacle experience with the painting, that waking dream *inside* it…how could he not see that as some sort of message? But then that woman, all those women—they had messed everything up, forced his hand.

The more agitated Claus became about his decision, grasping the full extent of what was lost, the faster he drove, taking treacherous curves at lethal speeds, unaware of the ghostly stowaway bouncing around in his back seat like a pinball. Claus clenched his jaw as he shifted the gears, biting the inside of his cheek so hard he tasted blood, indignant and wanting only to put the whole day, in fact the last week, behind him. He raced the car up the seaside cliff until at last he found the address Paul had given him; he pulled into the long driveway with a screech and shut off the engine, the acrid smell of burning brakes lingering in the air. Then, crushingly, he felt his own insignificance, all pomp and bluff sucked out of him. This monumental mansion perched so ostentatiously on its bluff, looking down on all below was having the intended effect on Claus.

He lingered in the car and worried about his current predicament. Before this particular saga, Claus had always prided himself on his efficiency, his aptitude for getting the job done seamlessly and drawing little attention during any leg of the journey. Not this time. How much did those women at the inn know about him? It would be easy enough for them to track him down simply by asking his parents for his whereabouts. His parents would give them his gallery address—but he would not be there. And in truth, he reasoned, a part of him still not quite ready to relinquish the painting, if he *didn't* make the delivery, what could they arrest him for? Stealing back a painting that had been stolen from him? But the police would ask him so many questions—where he got the painting, why he had the gun, who had the painting now, how he had come by it. No, he would definitely have to disappear for a while, let the inquisition go to the bottom of some overworked *policier's* list. Best to just finish the job and jump off this merry-go-round. Make a decision and stick to it.

"Welcome, my friend," said a low voice, addressing Claus still seated behind the wheel. An older man in an opulent brocaded bathrobe with a golden rope belt and tassels tied loosely around his generous belly filled the doorframe. "We have been expecting you."

Claus gave his client a thin smile. The man was corpulent and un-callused, a fleshy baby in a giant's body, with the rubbery lips and intimidating underbite of a grouper. Claus stepped out of the convertible, and then reached into the back seat for the valise. But there was no valise there. He gasped and looked nervously at the large man, who was studying him intently.

"But what? Where? I…I cannot understand this. I had your painting in the valise right there," Claus stammered, pointing to the unoccupied spot on the back seat. "I came straight here and have not stopped once…but it's gone! You can see for yourself that…"

The man eyed him coolly. "Yes, I can see that there is nothing there. Yet as to the first part of your story, that is unproven. Valises are not known to possess the gift of flight. And paintings inside valises, paintings that are promised to someone else, should not simply disappear. No, certainly not."

His voice was educational, as if he were explaining the basics of physics to a classroom of fifth graders. The man waited, then asked brightly, as if giving Claus a second chance to do better, "Now, what is another possible explanation?"

The breeze was cool upon Claus's temples and upper lip where he was sweating. "You cannot possibly think I…" Claus saw the glaring irony in what was unfolding and it offended him all the more. "Why would I drive all the way here empty-handed? Can you tell me that? I honestly do not have a clue where that painting is. I tell you it was right on the back seat only two hours ago. I swear to you!"

The man sighed. "This is very, very bad. I don't need to tell you, my friend, that we are meticulous about discretion. We do absolutely nothing to draw attention to my collection. Did you encounter anyone who might have seen the painting? Who might have stolen it?"

As if someone had pressed the "play" button inside Claus, he poured out the entire saga, starting all the way back with the man watching him at Le Verre Volant in Paris, the woman on the plane to Marseilles, then her showing up at the same hotel. He even related the altercation at the Lavender Beehive that morning. Words were spilling out of him like candy from a busted piñata but he couldn't seem to stop himself. The more he went on, the deeper he dug his grave. Too much had happened and Claus thought it best not to keep anything hidden, for he knew that this man, like Paul, would dispose of him in an instant if he suspected that his secrets had been compromised.

Desperate to minimalize the damage, Claus found himself finishing, "But despite how all of this might sound, since I left that place I have been guarding this painting every second. It's simply not possible. No one could have taken it."

The man regarded Claus in silence for a full minute, incredulous at the glaring contradictions in his tale, then clucked wearily. "I have come to observe over the years, my friend, that indeed *anything* is possible. You'd better come inside and we'll try to go over this again until we come up with a more acceptable explanation."

But Claus did not want to follow the man inside. He wanted to flee. He did not know what awaited him inside this isolated fortress, but it was probably not going to be good. He turned and strode the few steps back to the car, reaching for the door handle, wondering if he could mange to simply drive away. But before he could open it, he saw that from the deep pockets of his dressing gown, his host had casually produced his own gun, the weapon dwarfed within his hammy mitt.

"Come, sir, I insist. We must at least try."

He motioned with the gun for Claus to step inside, and Claus, bewildered, numb with fear, and maddened by the injustice of it all, bowed his head and shuffled into his den of doom.

CHAPTER THIRTY-SIX

There was no way Chagall could lift the valise by himself. Even if he could manage to somehow open it and liberate the painting, what then? He couldn't fly to Phoebe carrying a solid object, and even though he knew she had seen him down there in the brambles, how could he tear her away from her vacation again? How could he describe where the case was? And finally, how could she make it down a cliff without attracting attention from the rest of the group? No, he needed the help of the sisters, creatures of the earth but with special powers, too. It was an immense comfort to know that these women could also see him.

It took him over an hour of fierce concentration and will, but Chagall took the probably unnecessary precaution of burying the valise with some lightweight brush. Once this was accomplished, he took off for the Lavender Beehive.

When he arrived, he observed the scene in the kitchen for a while before enlisting the Bion sisters. Bernadette was clearly shaken but trying to calm herself by going through her daily routines. Routine, Chagall remembered, was the greatest balm. She was rolling out dough for tomorrow's croissants, her hands shaking even after sprinkling the lavender sugar on top. She was muttering to herself, Chagall observed, but what he could not see was the courtroom drama unfolding in her own mind, where she was trying on the roles of both prosecutor and defendant. Bernadette looked older to Chagall, deflated, like one who was grieving. Though he knew she could not see him or feel his sympathy, Chagall placed a hand on her shoulder. She paused, looked around the room, then bowed her head to the task at hand.

On the patio, the German couple was having an aperitif, while at the next table Jacqueline sat organizing her herbs into little wands and bundles, stopping to bring some chamomile flowers up to her nose for a sniff. Marie-Christine meanwhile had aimed her focus so intently in the direction of Claus's mother, staring at her so persistently that the woman finally looked up and ventured, "*Bonjour*?"

Seizing the entrée, Marie-Christine approached their table and sat in the empty chair next to the wife. Her husband nodded at her perfunctorily then went back to his paper.

"Do I know you?" the wife, who had introduced herself as Mindy, asked, cordially enough.

"No, not before last night at dinner, Madame. I am a local woman. We, my sister and I, have known Bernadette many, many years. She is our neighbor. But I *have* had the pleasure of meeting your son…Claus, is it?"

She beamed proudly. "Yes, Claus. How did you…?"

"Let us just say we are both great lovers of art…fine art."

"Ah, so you have been to his gallery, in Grenoble?"

"No, we do not leave the village much. But tell me, what type of art does he have there?"

"Oh, mostly modern things from local artists—unknowns, but some of them quite talented. Clausie is a champion of those artists whose careers he sees as poised to take off. Many of his clients are wealthy collectors and they want to buy work *before* the artists become known. They like to think that they discovered these painters themselves."

"Ah, these collectors are gamblers, then," Marie-Christine said, raising a tiny glass of amber liquid to her rouged lips.

Mindy laughed. "Well yes, I supposed you could say that. And you are…?"

"Marie-Christine Bion. *Enchanté*," she said, extending her bejeweled hand. Out of the corner of her eye she noticed Chagall waving his arms at her from the plank diving board of the pool. Marie-Christine abruptly retracted her hand and stood, saying, "I must visit Grenoble someday. Your son strikes me as a very…ambitious fellow."

Mindy looked quizzically at this odd woman, wishing that her husband would put down the damned newspaper and join in the conversation somehow. But without so much as a nice-to-meet-you, Marie-Christine simply returned to her own table, tapped her sister on the shoulder and motioned with her chin for her to follow. They met Chagall in the pool house, the scent of chlorine mixing with wet pavement and the marjoram oil that Jacqueline wore to ward off evil spirits.

"What is going on?" Jacqueline demanded of Chagall and her sister. "I have been one step behind all day."

Chagall grasped the hands of both women and said fervently, "I've got the painting. I mean, not *with* me, but I can show you where it is. I want to give it to the museum in Nice. Phoebe is going there this afternoon, and if we work together, we could just leave it somewhere where the curators will find it and hopefully see it as authentic straightaway. I cannot lift things of the physical world without help."

"Where is it?" Marie-Christine asked excitedly.

"What painting are you talking about?" Jacqueline asked, stamping her foot in exasperation.

They finally recapped the entire saga for her, since she had been shuttled out of the atelier immediately, and had not the slightest clue as to why Bernadette was weeping on the floor, why some German fellow had flashed a gun, and why these two paintings were causing such a fuss. When Marie-Christine had finished the tale, Jacqueline nodded, saying:

"Bernadette must be so relieved to have this burden lifted after all these years."

"Perhaps," Marie-Christine answered wryly. "But maybe not so happy to be unburdened of her Chagall. Unfortunately, there was no

way Bernadette could have both peace of mind and the Chagall. Now
go, ask her to give us a ride. We have to get to the spot where Chagall left
the painting, and we only have the horses."

Jacqueline, who loved a good caper as much as her sister, scurried
off.

Bernadette asked few questions once the sisters told her that she
had to help them retrieve a stolen Chagall.

"The one I…? My little *Contorsioniste?*"

"No, the other one," they said in unison. "The story is too *compli-
qué;* we'll tell you en route; the timing is important. We must recover
the one Claus took. It's got a title inscribed right on the back: *Midsummer Escapade.*"

She didn't persist, eagerly agreeing to drive them, like some
naughty child trying to make amends with her angry parents. And even
though Bernadette could not see Chagall, she sensed throughout the
entire drive that Marie-Christine was getting her directions from some
unseen source.

As Bernadette's old *deux-chevaux* rounded a particularly tight
switchback Jacqueline shouted, "Stop! Here it is!"

Bernadette swerved onto the narrow shoulder, the car that had
been nosing her bumper for the past ten kilometers honking and making a rude gesture as he passed.

"Where?" Bernadette asked, looking up and down the road.

"Down there," Marie-Christine said, indicating the free fall of the
sheer cliff.

"I can't climb down there," Bernadette protested. "I'm too old and
it's far too steep. And we're drawing attention to ourselves already,
pulled over on this torturous road."

That part was true. Cars full of families headed for the beach ogled
the trio as they slowed to pass by, some even honking and shaking their
fists.

"You are younger than we are," Marie-Christine said, holding her
gaze. "And you must. It is a way of making everything right. It is your…

recompense."

Bernadette started to protest again, but then yielded. She knew that her friend was right, and in truth, she been desperate for some way to redeem herself.

"How will I find it down there?" Bernadette asked, waiting for another car to go by before opening her door then walking around the car to look down the hill.

Marie-Christine paused, listening to Chagall's instructions, then described the location of the valise as best she could, her directions limited to "past the rock that looks like a teepee" or "a little beyond that branch shaped like a Y." Bernadette began picking her way down the steep trail, overgrown with roots and things that jabbed her in the calves. Her shoes were wrong for this, espadrilles, and three, four, five times she slipped and, there being no branches the right height for her to grab onto to slow herself down, she slid, skinning her knee and left palm in the process. Still, the difficulty of the task made it feel all the more like her penance, and she got back on her feet each time without complaining. Finally, she spotted the corner of the valise peeking out from under some leaves and loose dirt. She raised it triumphantly above her head to the women standing on the cliff above. Making it back up with one hand bleeding and the other holding the case was even trickier, but at last she managed.

"Bravo," Jacqueline said, hugging her once she stood again by her car. Bernadette felt vindicated, the great beast of guilt pushing off her shoulders to take flight. In her mind, it was like a moral balance sheet: two paintings returned erased one long hidden.

"We've got to hurry," Jacqueline reminded them. "The group is meeting at the museum in Nice at 3:30."

Chagall, meanwhile, had been watching Bernadette's struggles on the steep hillside. She reminded him of a model he'd had before the first war, when he was so young, that first time in Paris. In spite of everything, he felt a great affection for her in this moment, even, or perhaps *especially,* for her secrets and failings. She was all that he missed of this earthly place, all the inconsistencies and contradictions that made a creature human. She was a very lovely woman, and Chagall wished he could paint her another small painting, a replacement, offer it to her alone, since she appreciated his work so strongly. Maybe he would ask Phoebe to help him accomplish this. In that moment, sitting in the back of the *deux chevaux*, an avalanche of profound sadness encompassed Chagall. It hit him for the first time everything that would be lost to him, all over again, when he left this place.

When they arrived at the parking lot of the museum, dusty and discombobulated from the hair-raising drive, the Byroads van was already parked. Chagall snapped himself out of his gloom and advised Marie-Christine to have Bernadette hide the painting under her blouse somehow, for surely the guards would insist that she check the valise if she tried to bring it in.

"Her blouse?" Marie-Christine asked dubiously, turning around to look at the ghost in the back seat. Bernadette looked, too, but knew she would see nothing. When she had asked the sisters whom they had been talking to all this time, Marie-Christine said: "The spirit of a deceased art lover" at the exact same moment that Jacqueline had answered: "Marc Chagall."

Experience had taught her that blind trust was the best course of action when in the company of the Bion sisters. But today, for the first time, instead of just assuming that they were slightly off their rockers, Bernadette actually found herself wishing that she too *could* see this phantom, especially if there was even the slightest chance that it was Marc Chagall.

"*Mon Dieu,* the painting is framed. Now how on earth will she manage that?" Marie-Christine asked the heavens, but explained Chagall's instructions to Bernadette anyway.

"Then, if you make it this far, you are to find Phoebe, *tout suite,* and insist that she meet you in the bathroom. Transfer the painting to Phoebe there, then walk calmly back out to the car."

Bernadette swallowed hard, but she nodded.

The scratchy canvas against Bernadette's skin matched her prickly nerves. They had tried several angles before arriving upon her *derriere*, held in place by her underwear, as the best place to conceal the work of art. The corners of the frame could maybe, if she was lucky, be perceived as the broad seat favored in the days of bustles. She was disheveled and sweating, but summoned the inner composure that had served her on so many occasions over the years. She thought to herself, as she held her chin high and nodded a greeting to the bored woman taking tickets, how funny it was to be sneaking a painting *into* a museum.

Bernadette spotted Phoebe, and winnowed her away from the group under the pretext of needing assistance in the ladies' room, ignoring the delighted salutations of her guests. Phoebe, though alarmed, knew enough by now not to resist, and promptly followed her to the WC and into a stall. They waited until a toilet flushed and they were alone.

"Marie-Christine said you are to leave this painting here...not *here* in the toilettes, but somewhere," Bernadette whispered urgently. It was cramped with the two of them inside one stall, and Bernadette jabbed Phoebe in the ribs with her elbow as she unbuttoned her skirt and produced the Chagall from behind her back.

"You decide where to leave it," she continued, her eyes boring into Phoebe's. "But it must be a place where the right person who can recognize such things will know that it is a real Chagall. You and I have both seen what can happen when people don't recognize the true value of a painting."

"But how can I..."

"You *must*," Bernadette demanded. "The Bion sisters, who have explained to me that the great master has been appearing to them and to you, said that you of all people should know how much it means to Chagall to see the stolen painting back where it belongs, where it can be enjoyed by many. I'd better go now. We have confidence in you." Impulsively, Bernadette kissed Phoebe on each cheek. She turned before she left the bathroom and said again, "Phoebe, I'm so sorry."

Phoebe heard the bathroom door close, but remained in the stall, wondering what to do. She couldn't stay in there forever so set to work adjusting the painting against her spine as best she could and stepping out of the stall to look in the mirror, praying that it was not too obvious,

"This clothing you wear," Chagall said with disapproval, now sitting on the edge of the basin. "It leaves nothing to the imagination. It is so tight the frame of the painting makes you look like a scarecrow. Can't you lean back or something so it's not so square?"

"What can I do?" she pleaded, sweat forming on her upper lip. "It's what I happen to be wearing."

"If we could get it into an office somehow. Not the cloakroom or on a chance table, but the office of one of the higher-ups; that would be ideal. I will explore. Stay here."

"Hurry," she shouted after him, a woman coming in at that moment lowering her eyes in discretion, thinking she had caught this American in the bright spandex costume talking to herself. Phoebe cleared her throat and made sure to keep her back, with its ungainly passenger, turned away from the intruder.

Chagall glided past groups of schoolchildren and the tourists enjoying the air conditioning and the view of the Riviera out the second story window as much as the art. He passed sincere docents lecturing about the "wild beasts," *Les Fauves,* so called for their bold use of color, Matisse being king of that movement. He saw the Byroads group looking reverentially at Matisse's easel and jack-knifed tubes of paint. But it was on the third floor that he found what he was after and dashed back down to Phoebe, still in the powder room.

Chagall motioned for Phoebe to follow him up a back staircase that led to the top floor where all the offices were. She sprinted up the steps to keep up with him, opening the door inside as quietly as possible. A guard was leaning over a drinking fountain but straightened and looked at Phoebe suspiciously.

"May I help you?" he asked, facing her. People never really meant that, in situations like these, Phoebe thought. They didn't really want to help you at all.

Thinking fast, she said, her breathlessness assisting the act, "In the bathroom on the second *étage!* There is a woman lying on the floor of one of the stalls! I did not want to touch her and I could not find another guard, so I ran up here. Please hurry!"

The bored look in the museum guard's eyes was replaced by a delighted, purposeful expression and he pushed through the doors like a man with a mission and disappeared down the stairwell. For some unfathomable reason, when she most needed him, Chagall was no longer by her side and she cursed him under her breath. As hurriedly as possible, she tried the knobs on all the office doors, each one locked. Her heart was pounding and she almost screamed in frustration, but then she turned the knob on the very last door in the hall and it swung open, beautifully silent on its hinges. She glanced down at the nameplate on the desk inside, which read: *Jean Marie DuFort.* Then underneath, a single, sublime word: *Acquisitions.*

CHAPTER THIRTY-SEVEN

Elated that at least one of his lost paintings was now safely back in a museum, Chagall flew off to find Claus. He had very mixed feelings about the young man. For although Chagall didn't have anything against private collectors per se, and indeed had done quite well by some of them in his lifetime, he could never fully abandon his socialist roots, which dictated that art should be available for all to see. He liked the idea of "roaming" art—the owners could have a piece for a while, of course, but then they would be obliged to send it out into the world, on loan to various museums. Shared custody. But the one thing he could not stomach was the collector who had come by stolen art, a losing proposition for the artist and the public.

Chagall didn't really have a concrete plan for rescuing Claus, and by rights owed the lackey no sympathy. Yet Chagall, during his lifetime and certainly now, in this current state, had an uncanny ability to read emotions, and he could plainly see that ever since Claus had been inside the *Midsummer Escapade* painting, had experienced that feeling of wonder and vivacity first hand, the man was undergoing a terrible crisis of conscious, or at the very least an internal struggle about the life he had chosen. Maybe he was still making stupid choices, but that had been a moment of epiphany for him, forcing him to wrestle with it all, and that was a start. Besides, Chagall knew that Claus was but a small fish in the big pond of black market art. And in this instance, maybe he could be used as bait.

Constantly amazed at his navigational agility, Chagall found that he had no trouble finding The Collector's residence from the address Claus had left on the back seat of his car. He quickly located the study in The Collector's sprawling manor, which was now serving as a cage for the unfortunate Claus. Chagall roamed about the room, taking in the distraught delivery boy, and then chuckling at the "bookshelves," which even he could tell were a false wall straight out of an old horror movie. Despite the gravity of Claus's predicament, Chagall's inner sleuth was on fire. He was thoroughly enjoying himself. All of these new friends, the intrigue, excitement, the sense of purpose—well, it could almost give a spirit the feeling of being alive. Chagall's post-death state was wispy and insubstantial, accompanied by a pervasive melancholy. It was as if his fate in the great beyond, perhaps the fate of all who died, was to eternally mourn the loss of their own life.

He perched on a ledge, above which hung a small Bonnard showing a winsome young woman kneeling by a pool, reaching out for a floating water lily. Chagall had always appreciated the tenderness of Bonnard's work, and traced the outline of the floating flower with his finger. Claus's angst was distressing him, so he moved on to another room, this one painted in the bright, almost Moroccan colors of a Matisse. French doors were flung open onto a balcony with a vibrant red table, the Mediterranean billowing like an unfurling bolt of azure silk in the distance. He spotted a vase made by Picasso, never questioning its authenticity, since Chagall himself recalled the day he had watched the artist working on a similar one. He stroked a bronze by Giacometti, the figures stretched long like taffy. Then he asked himself with no small amount of disgust: *I wonder whom all of these really belong to?* But no, these works were all on display, out in the open, so perhaps The Collector had come by these legitimately, at a real, if absurdly overpriced, art auction. These were probably the decoys, there to lend a whiff of credibility.

Chagall returned to the library and watched Claus pace The Collector's room, trying the door again and swearing in German. At least he wasn't bound and gagged, but things at the present did not look good for the man.

Outside the makeshift cell, The Collector was on the phone with Paul in Paris. Chagall took an instant dislike to the big lush. He had the narrow eyes and capacious nostrils of a rattlesnake.

"*Oui, oui,* my friend," the hulking man, still in the regal bathrobe, said dismissively into the phone. He turned his head away from the receiver and tossed a fig down his gullet with fingers plump as plantains. "I know you say we can trust this fellow, and yet that does not solve my problem, which is now *your* problem as well: where is my painting? I would hate it if you were forced to return that very large sum of money I gave you as a deposit, only half of what you stand to make here. And even more, I would hate to draw unwanted attention to our sweet partnership after all these many years. But, *hélas…*" He trailed off, pausing to gobble a wedge of Morbier cheese, the line of the ash it was cured in running down the center like a dark scar. "Your German insists that the painting must have just vanished into thin air. You would surely agree that this is a flimsy excuse, and one which gives us no answers."

The Collector picked a piece of fig skin from one of his back teeth, studied it on the end of his finger, then licked it off and swallowed it.

"Be reasonable, Jean-Claude," Paul said, on the other end of the line. In the background Jean-Claude could hear the clattering of plates and glasses, orders being shouted and delivered, and he thought noncommittally that perhaps *he* would enjoy owning a café someday, the hubbub and aromas, the contacts, the status of being *le chef du patron.*

"Why, after all these years, would Claus jeopardize his own bread and butter? He's not a fool, Jean-Claude. A little headstrong, maybe, but what if he is telling the truth? What if the piece *was* stolen from his car?"

And yet even as Paul was trying to persuade The Collector of Claus's innocence, his mind was ticking in fury. How could one just *lose* a multimillion-dollar piece of art? If he had never left the briefcase unwatched in his car, how could it be gone? Clearly the German was lying and must have let it out of his sight. Well, Paul allowed, everyone fucked up once in a while. But when they did, there was a price to pay.

"That is not my concern," Jean-Claude thundered. "All that matters to me is that there is currently no Chagall, that this man was the last to have it in his possession, that a contract has been broken leaving me the loser, and that I am out millions of euros. Hence, we have only two choices: I make this man tell me what he really knows about the whereabouts of my painting, or you return my money. Which is it?"

Paul considered. Jean-Claude was a big bull of a man, and his smooth demeanor belied a temper so fierce that Paul had once seen him hurl a stray cat from a cliffside restaurant when its meowing under a neighboring table got on his nerves. After the incident, the group at that table had watched open-mouthed as Jean-Claude daintily dabbed at his lips with a linen napkin and continued his story exactly where he had left off, as if he had done nothing graver than shoo away a fly.

Paul sighed. Millions of euros were at stake. Maybe Claus could be persuaded to come up with some answers. That was the thing with stolen goods—they were worth a fortune, but only a select few knew of their existence. So if a man involved in such a venture were to vanish, no one would ever suspect the cause. Paul looked around his café and thought of the generations of former owners of Le Verre Volant, when it had been a family business, all of them genuinely fond of the artists who frequented the place. In that moment, Paul wished he felt something as old-fashioned and sentimental as these other men must have in the presence of great art; wished he felt any impulse to do the right thing in the eyes of his forbearers. It would have made his life so much easier. But that was not the case. Paul knew that he was, and always would be, nothing more than a businessman, a modern man—some might say a man prone to excesses, but this he did not question. This was surely no time to waver.

Paul sucked wetly on his cigar and swallowed the smoke, relishing the burn, then he shouted gruffly over his shoulder to a waiter: "*Oui, j'arrive,*" before telling The Collector: "Well I guess we have no other alternative then. Do what you must. Just let me know what you find out before the day's end so I know where we stand. I have to go."

"As you wish," said Jean-Claude offhandedly, replacing the ornate receiver back into its cradle, wolfing two more figs, then turning toward his study, licking the tips of his fingers.

Chagall recognized that Claus had finally given up on the idea of escape when he kicked the door, then sat down heavily upon the sofa and lowered his head into his hands. He was not necessarily an evil man, Chagall speculated. Greedy, yes. A bit chilly perhaps, and removed from the throb and juice of others of his kind. That not altogether rare species of man who was quite capable of separating business from conscience. Therefore, a dangerous man. But not so much so as Paul, the boss.

Chagall had made a concerted effort not to despise Germans on principle, even when he had seen what they were capable of during the Second World War. If he hated everyone in all the places he had lived during his long life, any French or German or Italian or Russian or American who harbored a secret anti-Semitic streak, then surely he would have had nowhere to call home. And when Chagall had allowed the young German to enter into the actual world of his painting, had Claus not been moved? A part of himself awakened and touched? The tragedy was that this opening and delight, and more, what he had learned from it, had been so short lived. Even the man's resolve to keep the painting, come what may, Chagall would have respected more than talking himself out of it and just delivering the goods. Always be more than you think you are, Chagall had learned from his long stint in the world. And now Chagall knew Claus might pay for the painting with his life, when in truth he was just the messenger, not the mastermind like Paul, nor even in the same league as all the clandestine collectors. He hoped Claus was clever enough to save his own skin, because in truth, there was little Chagall could do to come to his rescue, except perhaps create a diversion at an opportune moment, and even that was iffy.

The door opened and Jean-Claude strode in, looking put-upon and deadly serious. Dangling the gun carelessly from his index finger, he sat his large bulk down on the couch, so close to Claus that their thighs touched. It was all the prisoner could do not to move away, his boundaries having been so violated. Up close, he saw for the first time the beauty of the fatal weapon, it too a work of art. Its handle was an elongated skull, carved from ivory, with ebony inlay for the mouth, eye sockets, and nostrils. The skull appeared to be grinning in manic delight.

"I must be honest with you, my friend," Jean-Claude said crisply. "Things do not look so good for you at present. You say my Chagall has disappeared, yet it was your responsibility and you were the last to have seen it. You have been in this business a few years. Maybe the price this one would fetch was too great a temptation for you. Yes? A possibility? You are only human. I do not hold that against you. But if you were I and had spent such a sum on this piece and trusted in its delivery boy, would you not be irate at its loss? Would *you* not want some answers as to its true whereabouts?"

"But I have *told* you," Claus cried, bringing his hands up toward his captor beseechingly. "I do not know what…"

With astonishing speed and force, Jean-Claude brought the butt end of the gun down on Claus's left kneecap. Like a child taking a second to register the full depth of the pain before letting loose with wails and tears, Claus froze for an instant, then bellowed a howl of agony, doubling over to clutch at his damaged knee.

Jean-Claude stood and looked down at him placidly, then checked his watch and repeated:

"I am not inclined to believe in things just vanishing, my friend. Please, I implore you, show us both some respect and tell me the truth so that you can at least limp back to your car and get to a hospital. You can be assured that I will let you go once I have my painting. I am an art lover, not, in general, a murderer. So, I ask you again: where is my Chagall?"

Chagall was horrified that a work of art, his own art, could be worth so much as to make killers out of men such as Jean-Claude, Paul, Claus—how many others? What was this impulse? It baffled the painter. Power by proximity to greatness? The feeling of omnipotence that comes with being able to buy anything in the world that you desire? Chagall had never thought of artwork as a status symbol akin to a jeweled necklace or a fine racehorse. Art was supposed to *move* the viewer, to excite and engage. Art was meant to go beyond existing merely as an object of value. At least that was what art had been about in his lifetime.

The pain in Claus's knee felt like someone had ignited a small stick of dynamite in the joint, set it off, then filled any open spaces with sulfuric acid. The contusion there was rising so rapidly that he could feel it push against his clamped fingers like a beast trying to burst out of a pen. He knew the kneecap was broken, in pieces small enough that it would be a struggle for even the best bone doctor to reassemble it. Claus wept bitterly, something his mother used to say rising up in his mind: a glued vase will never line up to its original beauty. He was terrified now, and his mind scrambled for some story, *any* story, that might spare him from such pain ever again.

"All right, all right, yes, I will tell you…just please, don't hurt me," Claus pleaded, rocking back and forth bent over his leg.

Chagall applauded from his corner of the room. He had been waiting for the German to snap to, to do whatever it took to save his neck. Claus was making it up as he went along, unsure if whatever came out of his mouth would work to his advantage or simply dig a larger hole, but no matter, at this point, he forged ahead. Anything held more promise than that gun and the lunatic it belonged to.

"The truth is," Claus stammered, considering what he would say next. "The truth is, that for the first time, I really *looked* at the art I was carrying and was, quite simply, smitten. I know it sounds crazy, but I wanted this one, badly, enough to risk my entire future, even my life."

Chagall watched this scene in fascination. Having lived through two wars and almost one hundred years, he had learned that any man is an actor when the situation demands it. Would the fat fellow fall for this tale, which also happened to be the truth, or would he reject it— that was what remained to be seen. Chagall was also rooting for Claus because so much depended upon the merit of his fabrication. Chagall, Phoebe. the Bion sisters, no one would be truly safe until Chagall could report to them what The Collector's next move was.

Claus continued breathlessly, "And so I hid it. I...I was visiting my mother and father at a place they stay in Menerbe and I hid it there, hoping to come back for it. This is the truth; I swear it." Claus was panting like a dog after a chase, woozy from the pain and the ongoing danger.

Jean-Claude considered. Then he put his hands on his mammoth thigh and pushed himself up off the couch with a grunt. He twirled the gun around his index finger, and walked over to straighten a painting depicting some sort of smeared mask, ever so slightly crooked on the opposite wall.

"This does not make any sense, my friend," he said finally, delivering his verdict. "Why would you come all the way here empty handed if you knew you had nothing for me? No, this makes no sense at all."

"I...I thought that, if it came to that, I could maybe convince you that the painting had been stolen, that I let it out of my sight and that you would maybe believe me."

"But you insisted you had never let it out of your sight! And besides, had you done that, your goose would really have been cooked, as *someone* would have had to pay for this sloppy failure. And you must have known that someone would still have been you. No, that story would have gotten you into even more trouble, as then we would have no chance of retrieving my painting and that would, as you now see, be unacceptable. As it stands..."

"But I had to *try*," Claus said, interrupting him excitedly. "I couldn't just disappear with your painting, as I am not so stupid as to believe that Paul would not find me. So I came here in hopes that you might believe that the painting was stolen and take it up with Paul. I wasn't thinking straight. Look at my spotless record; you can see I have never done anything like this before."

"But this is absurd! You would still have been made to pay somehow."

"I had not thought ahead that far. I somehow hoped that if it was out of my hands, that you and Paul might pursue the theft and let me go. I know that all you really want is the painting. I can show you where I hid it. I was hoping to get away with it, but now I see that is impossible. I apologize. I'm an idiot! I swear I never thought the whole thing through; it was just stupid, stupid. Please, I'll show you where your painting is. You can come with me in my car and I will drive us there. It is only an hour and a half from here. Or…or you can follow me and…" He was blathering nonsense, he knew, but his desperate line of thought was that if enough words fell from his lips, The Collector might eventually believe him.

"Oh, I think not on that one, the 'following you.'" Jean-Claude grinned at this and Claus saw incisors so tiny in the cavernous mouth that they looked like rodent's teeth, as if he had taken a file to them. "I am not the trusting sort. No you, no painting. But how will you drive after your…accident?"

"It is the left knee that is…compromised. I can drive with the right one. I would most appreciate a painkiller before the journey." Was he going to agree to this? And then what, when they got there and there was still no painting? Claus didn't care. He knew he was doomed if he didn't get out of this house.

Jean-Claude chuckled as if Claus were making a joke. He regarded him with narrowed eyes, then shook his head and sat next to him again, this time clamping a large paw affectionately across his shoulders. Claus didn't know whether to tense or relax under the weight of it.

"Ah, my friend, you have fallen under the spell of a great painting. Who can blame you? They say art is business, to be bought and sold, profit and loss. But they all forget those among us who want to *possess*. These paintings," he said, sweeping the hand still holding the gun across the space in front of them, "and these sculptures, all of this—things of beauty. The great pride yet also the great secret of my life. A collector can never get enough. It is an obsession, like a tapeworm in the gut of a glutton. He will eat and eat and never know what it is to feel satisfied. Maybe you felt a bit of this fever all collectors catch?"

Claus nodded vigorously in agreement, then hung his head to let The Collector know of his shame. The two men sat in silence, Jean-Claude considering his own grandiose words, and Claus trying to keep his face calm, frantically plotting the next step of this plan he was making up as he went along.

"Come," Jean-Claude said genially, helping Claus up as if he weighed no more than a paper airplane. "Let us retrieve my Chagall."

It was all Claus could do not to faint from the pain that accompanied any movement of his damaged knee, but he leaned heavily on Jean-Claude, hopping on his good leg, and the two of them lurched forward, toward the car.

CHAPTER THIRTY-EIGHT

S econds after Phoebe had accomplished placing *Midsummer Escapade* into the acquisitions office, of the Matisse Museum, she had one goal and one goal only: getting out of the museum without the accompaniment of sirens or the gendarmes' whistles. Once safely outside, she felt triumphant, that she had actually played a role in making sure that the painting would have a proper home at last, and Chagall had assured her that the Matisse folks would pass it along to the museum that was dedicated to *his* works, the nearby Chagall Museum that housed his storied stained glass and large biblical canvases. This part of France sure knew how to honor its local painters.

"Where did you go this time?" Ray asked once Phoebe had emerged from the museum flushed and wild-eyed.

"I was returning a stolen painting." Phoebe decided to answer with the truth. "Yes, I was smuggling art *into* the museum."

Ray shook his head at her. "And refresh me, just *when* are you going to tell me about all that stuff you said was making your life so complicated?"

"It won't be long," Phoebe answered. "I promise."

An hour later, she and Ray were sipping Campari and soda, underdressed in their sweaty bike clothes at a lovely little café in Antibes on the Côte d'Azur a few miles from where they were to join the others later for dinner. The two of them had ridden in silence for a time, Ray dropping back a bit to tail Phoebe so he wouldn't lose her again. Every time he thought they had gotten some momentum going together, she would vanish. He told himself to be patient, not to be demanding of her. Right as he'd decided that, Phoebe looked back over her shoulder and smiled at him. The fragrant air had cooled their skin as they rode, the winding country lanes so much less crowded than the chaos of Nice.

"That was a great museum, wasn't it?" Ray said, once they were seated. He reached for a few salted nuts from the small bowl festooned with sunflowers that the waiter had set before them. He loved how the cafés here always gave them little bits of food, olives, pretzels, almonds, to go with a drink. It made the visit more substantial somehow, inviting one to linger. It also allowed one to have some pre-dinner spirits without becoming shnockered.

"So much color under one roof," Phoebe agreed, the Campari making a low whistle as it descended back down the empty straw, her tongue creating just the right amount of suction at the top to produce this sound. She had been playing with the straws of her beverages like this, ever since she was a small girl, and did it almost unconsciously now. "It's no wonder Chagall's museum ended up in Nice too, the two of them begin such great colorists. Hasn't it just been a stellar day?"

Ray looked at her curiously. Phoebe had the jitters, still feeling the charge from the successful caper in the museum. She thought she sounded manic, overly enthused, behavior she tended toward to cover up when she felt shy. But *why* was she shy? They had already fallen for one another, managed to kiss and share little bits of their life stories—in between flirtatious roommates, art theft, ghosts, and witches, that is. She knew that Ray was aware to some extent of these behind-the-scenes dramas, but to explain all that had been going on to him would have taken more that she could muster right now. No, she just wanted to savor the ease and spark, that rare combination they shared. She took a deep breath and told herself to calm down, but how she wished she could somehow share the exploits of what she had just done with *someone.*

"What do you know about investing in art?" Ray asked her out of the blue.

Any topic surrounding art these days made her heart gallop, but she said: "Absolutely *rien*."

"Okay, I'm going to confess something here, and I know when you're ready, you'll be doing some confessing of your own," Ray said, as if reading her thoughts.

They let that sit in the air between them for a moment before Ray continued.

"I was doing a little research about our Monsieur Chagall during my stay in Paris before joining the Byroads group…"

"Research?" Phoebe asked, lifting her brows.

"Yes…well, I don't know if it will amount to anything beyond satisfying my own curiosity, but yes, I have been researching the one hundred paintings by Chagall that went missing from Paris and Berlin while he was stranded in Russia during the First World War."

"Yes, I've read about those. Such a loss. And…?"

"Well, I arrived a few days early, planning to visit the same cafés that Chagall used to haunt, when he was an unknown, young and homesick for Russia yet also in the thrall of Paris. It was an art mecca for such a roster of greats back then, it was unbelievable."

"I know," Phoebe said, warming to the topic. "I used to fantasize about being a part of that scene. Just think what life must have been like in Paris back then."

"Pretty dazzling, I imagine—and I *do* imagine it. Constantly. Anyway, I met a fascinating fellow named Benoit at an old brasserie in Montmartre—that famous one, Le Verre Volant. He wasn't old enough to have been alive during World War One, of course, but he *was* around in the years after, when many of the exiled artists returned. Incredibly, the man was also there when they left yet again because of the next war, during the occupation and everything. He was a wealth of information, this guy, and has never missed a day at Le Verre Volant for sixty years. So many artists and writers frequented the place over the years, and I felt remarkably lucky to be talking with this man who had actually been a part of that great parade. I had to control myself so I didn't just bombard him with questions."

The waiter whisked away their empty glasses, and, as if by magic, another round appeared.

"After a few glasses of wine, Benoit confided in me that there was often a back room in many of these old cafés that housed miscellaneous art—pieces the artists might have traded for a meal way back when. Some of the artists never did become famous, of course, but *some* of these traded drawings or paintings were the early offerings of the artists we now consider to be the great masters and they are priceless. They were rendered on everything from pieces of floorboard to napkins to handkerchiefs, and occasionally on actual canvas. The old guard had more reverence for the work, donating some of it to museums or even choosing to display it right there in the café, a bit of living history for all to enjoy. But Benoit told me that in many cases, the most recent generation of owners, often family members who inherited these dusty paintings, just don't appreciate the work in the same way that their elders did. Many of them have made a fortune selling off every piece they could get their hands on."

"That's so sad," Phoebe said, looking down into the melting ice of her drink. "Their first impulse was to make a quick buck, not to share some of these treasures with the world—to donate them to museums, or even better, to keep them in these cafés on display somehow."

"Some did, I'm sure, but that's not the only issue here," Ray said, leaning in excitedly. "There are over twenty *thousand* missing works from around the world from the *second* war, and this is the more serious situation, as a lot of these paintings were filched by the Nazis from the homes of Jewish collectors. The paintings Chagall traded for a cheese sandwich a century ago, one could argue, for better or worse, belonged to the descendants of the old café owners, to do with as they pleased. But these *other* paintings were stolen outright, and apparently there is a thriving black market for them. Collectors who acquire them ask no questions and certainly aren't about to step forward and donate them to the families of the original owners, let alone to a museum."

"Certainly the police must know? And aren't there networks, like the Lost Art Database and such, that try to reunite descendants with artwork like this? I keep hearing about cases where Gustav Klimt paintings are being reluctantly turned over to Jewish heirs from various Austrian cities."

"All true. There is one type of private collection, where this or that painting travels the world's museums and the plaque reads, 'On Generous Loan from the Private Collection of Mr. and Mrs. So-and-So.' But then there are the more clandestine private collections, which very few have ever laid eyes upon besides of course, the black market dealer and the collector."

Phoebe let out her breath in a whoosh of amazement. She thought of Claus. He was just the go-between, surely. He had that hunted look about him, a gangly man with a gun she hoped he would never use. A man who had lost his way somehow. She wished for Chagall's sake—no, for everyone's sake—that she could find out whom he worked for, the real king pin. Aloud, she said, "This is all very Hitchcockian."

"Oh, there are more layers to this than even Hitchcock could have dreamed up!" Ray was on a roll now and reached out to grasp Phoebe's arm. "Did you know that today, some down-at-the-heels royalty or strapped-for-cash gentry may hire an agent, a type of go-between, to sell *shares* of a painting—not even the actual painting—that has maybe hung on the walls of the family mansion for generations, or perhaps was purchased when the family coffers were spilling over. Suddenly the coffers are not so full, and the owner may not want to part with the actual painting, so this is a way for him to have some ready cash. When or if he does decide to really put the painting up for auction, it is like stock for the investor. If the market is up, everyone makes a killing—owners, investors, even the agent."

"Fascinating," Phoebe said. "I know I would buy your book, especially if you are able to track down these paintings and it has a happy ending."

She loved the way Ray's cheeks colored and his eyes flashed when he was so engaged in a subject. She traced his jaw line with her finger, letting her hand linger there against his cheek. The warmth in her veins from the Campari and the intoxicating conversation were getting the better of her. It was hard to stay focused. She shook her head regretfully and added, "What ever happened to good old art appreciation? Before a painting became some sort of business commodity?"

But even as the words were leaving her lips, reality struck her. She was now in league with these collectors, or at least in possession of one true Chagall. What would *she* do, sitting on such a potential fortune? She could save her house! The years of worry and mortification, all of that stress surrounding the impending foreclosure, that feeling of being at the bank's mercy, of being an uninformed pawn in their cunning maneuvers—it could all be erased with the sale of that one little painting, *her* Chagall. No need to justify; it was rightfully her own, wasn't it? Something her grandfather had come by fair and square, and had intended for his wife. One man's trash is another's treasure, she had heard him say more than once during his lifetime. Call it a family heirloom, then. Plenty of people had precious items that had been handed down. And certainly Chagall's own children had sold some of his work for income. No sin there. This was a topic for debate: investment fodder? Mere merchandise? Or a thing of beauty that would enrich a person every time she encountered it? Phoebe collected many things herself for that pure pleasure—old things, glorious oddities—but her art collection was comprised of her own work, plus posters, reproductions, and the occasional piece bought off of some café wall for no other reason than it pleased her. Yet this was different. There was no denying that she could, in fact, be set for life if the little beauty fetched a good price.

God, owning such a valuable masterpiece was already corrupting her convictions.

"Here, here!" Ray said, raising his glass and downing the last of the aperitif. "To art appreciation and me solving mysteries and living to write about it!"

Then he picked up his chair and stepped over to place it next to hers and kissed her, his lips warm and sticky from the drink. He looked at her with an expression of wonder, his damp forehead still pressed against her own, and said: "Phoebe, I am so…*happy* we found each other. Should I not be saying things like that so soon?"

"Say them early and say them often, Ray," she murmured, burrowing into his neck and kissing him again until they were both panting a little. When they pulled apart, she told him, "You can be assured that I am feeling the same way. I still can't really believe it."

"Whoa, the time!" Ray said suddenly. He tossed some bills and coins onto the little Ricard tray that held their bill. "We'd better ride like the wind or we'll be late for that seaside dinner with the group. And we still have to change."

"Ah, so many obligations," said Phoebe, pretending to grumble. taking his hand and letting herself be pulled to her feet. "I could get used to this life very quickly."

Chagall had positioned himself on a branch in the same tree where they had locked their bicycles. He tried to give Phoebe some encouragement, a smile, a thumbs up, after the little *tête-à-tête* he had witnessed there, but for once, she was too spellbound to even notice.

CHAPTER THIRTY-NINE

Claus drove back down the torturous roads as slowly as possible, wincing every time his thigh moved, all the while frantically considering his options. He could crash the car into a tree and hope that he survived and that Jean-Claude was impaired enough that Claus could make his getaway. But no, even if he managed to limp away, Paul and his lackeys would surely find him. He knew all about the vast reach and risks of this world. While he couldn't say exactly how, he knew that he had brought this upon himself, some sort of punishment for even considering keeping the painting. Then a new plan popped into his head: what if he drove the car right into a police station and took his chances with jail time? No, Jean-Claude would shoot him in the ribs the minute they got to the gates. No matter what, someone would hurt him, either today or somewhere down the road, for the double-cross, and of course the wealthy Frenchman, and probably Paul as well, would go unpunished.

The sad thing was, Claus truly *didn't* know what had become of his valise and the beautiful painting, and this killed him. Instinctually, his eyes began scanning the shoulder of the road as he retraced that fateful route.

Meanwhile, Chagall had caught up with Jacqueline and Marie-Christine and explained that any time now, Claus and a very large, dangerous man would be arriving at the lavender farm and that they had to head the men off somehow.

"How do you know he'll come back here?" Jacqueline asked. "Why would he?"

"I don't know for certain," Chagall told her. "It's a hunch. But let's just say the fellow has very few options, and I think eventually, he will land on our doorstep out of desperation. Right now, he is basically just stalling for time."

Bernadette was in the kitchen, still worried that despite her heroics on the cliff she might still somehow be held accountable for her deception. As she whisked some lemon juice into the grassy olive oil she had pressed last summer, making a vinaigrette for a salad to serve the sisters after dinner, she wondered what reparations Phoebe Rosen would ultimately demand. And then that man with the gun! As her grandson would say, what was up with that?

Suddenly, Jacqueline burst into the kitchen and said: "Bernadette, come! We must use your car again. It is a matter of life and death!"

Marie-Christine rolled her eyes at Bernadette and amended, "What my sister means is this. The son of that German couple who stays here with you every year? Well, he is the one from this morning—yes, the one with the pistol. He is in very bad trouble."

"Why should we care if he is in trouble? Why don't we just call the police?" Bernadette asked, her voice rising in alarm. "I think all of this cops and robbers stuff is too much for us, for all of us. It's time to defer to the ones who do this for a living."

Marie-Christine cocked an eyebrow at her, then retorted archly: "Well, *cherie,* if you *really* want the police involved, here, in our small village with its wagging tongues, all of them asking a lot of very thorough questions about stolen art—all kinds of inquiries about various paintings directed at *everyone*—then yes, we should definitely call the authorities." She made a move toward the telephone.

Bernadette saw where Marie-Christine was going with this and cried: "No, wait!" In her panic, she dropped the whisk, the dressing splattering all over the hem of her skirt. "You are right…that is maybe not such a good idea. But honestly, what else can we three old birds possibly do to change anything?"

"You're more resourceful than you allow," said Marie-Christine. "You managed to save Phoebe's Chagall this morning by covering it with your body, and let's just hope she had the good sense to hide it somewhere safe. But the little framed one, *Midsummer Escapade*, walked right out the door with that German."

Jacqueline rejoined in a low voice, her eyes darting around the room. She was clearly loving all of this. "That one was stolen during the war from a Jewish family with quite a large art collection—in France, no less. Such things in our own country! The shame!"

"This surprises you?" Bernadette asked her incredulously. "All of us were there during that abominable war. Surely you were not unaware of the fate of certain of our more outspoken citizens, not only the Jews, but also poets, gypsies, and our more flamboyant entertainers. It wasn't just art that got spirited away. For such old crones, sometimes you two act surprisingly naïve."

Marie-Christine was about to take offense to that, but Jacqueline was eager to go on with her story. "Chagall has informed us that there is a man in Paris who bought a revered old café, which has now become a front for money laundering, money made from art sold off the record. No one can prove anything, but this man has a reputation in certain circles as someone who will pay for such, um, *appropriated* artwork. He pays a tenth of what the stolen piece is worth, knowing that the party delivering it to him will gladly accept the low amount—after all, what can they do about it? The art is pirated, so they can't complain, or ever put it on the market themselves without getting into trouble, losing it completely, and probably serving time in jail. So they sell and the front man in Paris takes care of the rest."

Marie-Christine jumped in. "That young German man was the third link in the long chain of stolen artwork. He was hired to deliver that Chagall, to make sure that the *Midsummer Escapade* arrived into the waiting hands of some collector who doesn't care how the art was procured, as long as he can own it. He was en route to one of these black-market collectors who must live somewhere near here, in the Luberon. But on the way there, the painting fell out of his car."

"Aha!" Bernadette said, catching on. "The valise on the hillside! But the painting is safe now, in the museum in Nice, *non?*"

"*He* doesn't know that! All the German knows is that he left here the morning with that painting in his briefcase, after taking it at gunpoint. The problem is, when it landed on the hillside, this collector does not know where the painting is and neither does Claus, who was hired to deliver it! Everybody is out the money and the goods." Jacqueline was almost shouting in her excitement. "This collector thinks the young German stole his painting and is this close to closing his umbrella for him." The old woman held two fingers close together to make a gun, right in Bernadette's face to show her just how much trouble Claus was in. "They are on their way here now. So *that's* why we need your car again."

"Why would they come back here?" Bernadette exclaimed. "How do you know all this?"

The sisters just pointed to the counter across the room where Chagall sat, swinging his legs over the edge. *All the man needs is a lollipop and a cap with a ribbon in the back and he's a ten-year-old boy,* Marie-Christine thought, looking at the old goat. Bernadette looked, saw nothing, but knew that it was useless to protest. Besides, she was pretty much game for anything at this point.

"Okay," Bernadette said, ripping off her apron and grabbing her purse. "I still don't know what the three of us can possibly do if these men are armed, but I give up. Let's go."

"Create a big distraction, that's what!" Jacqueline cried breathlessly, running down the drive after the other two women.

Marie-Christine hopped into the front seat of the car and clapped her hands at her sister. "Hurry."

"Distraction? *Divertissement?*" Bernadette asked, revving the old engine, throwing the car into reverse and backing up too fast, so that she narrowly dodged the trees.

"We're going to create a road block with this car," Marie-Christine said. "It was Chagall's idea. Trust us, it's brilliant. And then we also have this!" With great flourish, Marie-Christine produced an amethyst bottle from her bodice filled with red liquid that looked chillingly like blood.

"Poison?" Bernadette asked. She was so alarmed she accelerated by accident and an oncoming car laid heavily on its horn.

"No," Marie-Christine drawled. "Not poison—blood. Fake blood. We're going to splash it all over the 'accident victim.' It's mostly red wine for color, with some other herbs to hide the scent and give the liquid the right viscosity. Just a little mixture I came up with that will buy us some time and maybe see justice served in the process."

Bernadette wondered anxiously if she was included in that sentence about justice being served, but she did as she was told, parking her *deux chevaux* horizontally across the road about a mile from the farm.

"Okay now," Jacqueline said to Bernadette. "Out you go. Just lie down in the road in front of the car so they see you first thing."

"Me?" Bernadette shrieked. "But why me? You two are far better actresses than I. I'm not even sure what the plan is."

"It is exactly for that reason," Marie-Christine said, hurrying her out of the driver's seat, "that we two will do the acting. You will simply play dead…or at least injured. Now hurry up."

Bernadette tried to keep her clothing from getting too dirty as she lay down on the road, but that was for naught since Jacqueline began dousing her with the viscous red liquid, merrily splashing it all over her skin and clothes, as if it were holy water. The sisters were titillated by all of this hullabaloo and play-acting, but Bernadette felt a deep fear inside, and only hoped that Claus and whoever was by his side, would, in fact, be the first to happen upon this staged accident. And what if they simply didn't stop? What if they just passed right by them, or worse, crashed into her car and ran her over? She tried to calm her breathing and to get into her role by moaning softly.

Chagall had climbed to the top of a nearby tree and could just make out the sports car, winding down the road at a good clip, headed directly for them. Chagall rocked back and forth as the car came closer and closer, timing his jump. When the convertible was directly under his tree, he sprang off the branch and dropped neatly into the back seat.

Claus noticed the sisters and their car facing the wrong way before Jean-Claude did, and it was almost enough to make him believe in angels. He still had not come up with a plan for the time when they would arrive at the farm and there would still be no Chagall. But the good news was, some sort of shock had set in, so that his yowling knee was less noticeable. He didn't even know why he was taking The Collector to the lavender farm, possibly endangering his parents and certainly destroying once and for all any pretense that he was their good, hardworking son, with a legitimate gallery in Grenoble. Jean-Cluade would tear the place apart until he got what he came for. And for what? Claus was still trying out stratagems in his head. Maybe he could introduce this man who wanted to kill him to his parents? Offer him a tour of the various Chagall-themed rooms to stall for time? But eventually, he would have to produce the painting. Still, anything that put off the inevitable, that bought him more time, was fine by him. And this magnificent accident blocking the road certainly fell into that category,

"Uh oh," Claus said with what he prayed was a gravity that betrayed none of the hope he felt. He slowed way down, informing his captor: "Accident ahead. Looks like a bad one."

Jean-Claude strained to get a look, then said, "Go around it."

"But…"

"I said go around it," Jean-Claude repeated, motioning gruffly with the gun. "Someone else will stop."

Before Claus could protest again, the sisters were running toward the men, the layers of their white dresses fluttering behind them like plumage, forcing Claus to apply the brakes. After that, Jean-Claude couldn't insist that Claus give the car gas and go around, because the women had literally thrown themselves onto the hood, alternately weeping and waving their arms.

"*Messieurs! Messieurs!* Oh thank God you have happened by," wailed Jacqueline, wringing her hands and looking heavenward. "Our friend, our neighbor, like a sister to us, she was—Bernadette, known through-out the village as the kindest, most generous woman, a true creature of the land, a beekeeper and baker, why there was nothing she could not do, *would* not do for any one of us—and now *she...*" Here she gestured despairingly toward the bloodstained body crumpled in the road. "This gentlest of women was giving us a ride home and swerved to avoid a rooster—a rooster! Can you believe it? This woman, a saint, risking her own safety for any fellow beings, no matter how small! Oh why, *why*? It should have been us!"

Marie-Christine picked up the tale, her delivery more grave than that of the impassioned Jacqueline, but no less urgent. "The force of the sudden turn, as you gentlemen can see, made her door fly open and she was thrown from the car. We do not drive, neither my sister nor I, but, after a terrible moment, the car came to a screeching stop, sideways, with us, *incroyblement,* unharmed. But *she*," Marie-Christine cried, in-dicating with her chin the moaning Bernadette, "she is hurt very badly, Messieurs. Very badly indeed. Quickly, we must get help."

Jean-Claude pursed his lips, coloring in irritation and clearly un-moved. He slyly let the gun drop to the floor and kicked it under his seat with his heel, then reached into his jacket pocket for his cell phone, when suddenly Jacqueline was on him, weeping and thrashing, causing him to drop the phone, whereupon Chagall, summoning some store of strength he did not think he still possessed, managed to use Claus as his muscle, impelling him to secretly lift the device and fling it out his window into the woods. Claus looked in astonishment at his own hand, watching as it seemed to act independently of his brain.

Jean-Claude batted at Jacqueline in irritation, but she clung to him like a lamprey. In the confusion, Marie-Christine was climbing into the back seat, saying in an unstoppable tsunami of words:

"Claus! Your mother and father will be so grateful for your helping us!" How did this woman know his name? And wasn't she the one from the atelier, where all this madness had begun?

She continued: "They speak so often and so highly of you. Or so Bernadette tells us. They are very fond of Bernadette, as you know. Or maybe you don't know that, but I assure you it is the truth. Of course, how could you know it, as you are off somewhere doing whatever grown children do, and your parents can only hope, pray even, that you are making good choices and living a respectable life. Parenthood, eh? We do our best but then all we can do is send them off with a hope and a prayer. Now come, drive us to our house, it's just there, down the road, and we will bring help. Hurry."

Buoyed by his ability to will Claus to move the light cellular phone, Chagall tried to use him again to get rid of the gun, but he was too distracted by the mayhem of the Bion sisters, so only nudged the thing a few inches. Now it lay dangerously in plain view on the floor behind the passenger seat.

"Stop this! " Jean-Claude commanded. "We are not going anywhere. We have very urgent business that needs attending to immediately and have no time for this." Here he flung the persistent Jacqueline roughly against the passenger door, shouting: "Get off of me, woman! I'm sure someone will be along shortly. Claus and I are not doctors and have to be going. Get out of our car immediately."

"It is true that we are not doctors," said Claus, philosophically. He was picking up the refrain, but taking it where *he* needed it to go. "But we must do what we can."

Claus knew this was his only chance. He just might be saved by joining in the fray. He felt giddy and put the car back into gear while Jean-Claude groped around his feet for the gun. But Marie-Christine had spotted it, and while Jacqueline rebounded for another round of flailing in the big man's face, Marie-Christine feigned collapse, elongating as much of herself into the sporty back seat as it would accommodate, nimbly squirreling the pistol into a pocket deep in the fold of her skirts.

"Tell me the way!" Claus commanded in some matinee idol's heroic voice. He was operating on sheer adrenaline and hope now. He reached across both Jean-Claude and the fitful Jacqueline, who was draped across The Collector's lap weeping into his fat stomach, and pulled shut the passenger door. Marie-Christine was trying to sit up as the sports car lurched around the still-immobile Bernadette and her catawampus Citroen. Chagall was hitting Jean-Claude on the top of his head with all his might with one of his wooden shoes, but it was hard to tell if the man felt much, as he was still desperately trying to extricate himself from Jacqueline. The woman was like an octopus, Chagall observed admiringly. Each time he pried off an arm she wailed anew, talking incoherently about man's duty to his fellow man and the village problem of the wild roosters. She was unstoppable, and by now they were moving down the road—the sisters' plan was in action. There was no turning back. Chagall just hoped that the grouper would not lose his last shred of patience any second and simply fling Jacqueline out the open roof. Were his paintings really able to cause such behavior in people? A curse and a blessing, Chagall decided.

"Slow! Turn here!" Marie-Christine commanded once Claus was at the long driveway that led up to their house. "This is it."

Claus turned the wheel sharply toward the gothic majesty that was the sisters' home. He had never been so grateful for disruptions and detours in his life.

"*Mesdames!*" Jean-Claude thundered, fed up to the gills now with Jacqueline's theatrics. "Enough! We simply do not have time for this. You are home now and we will leave you to your work so that we may continue with ours. We cannot spare one more second. *Ca suffit!*" he shouted again, twisting away from Jacqueline and feeling around more seriously under the seat for the weapon.

"Time?" Marie-Christine roared imperiously. "*Time?* What type of man are you, sir, that would speak to us of time in a moment such as this, when a dear friend, a sister and fellow human being, lies dying not five kilometers from here? It could be you or any one of us. Shame on you, sir. *Shame.* Someday, in dire need such as she is now, you should only hope others would not treat you with such callous disregard!" She spat out these last words and fixed him with a damning glower that made even a man such as Jean-Claude fall silent.

"Now come," Marie-Christine commanded, snapping her fingers, the entire car under her spell. "We will go inside and we will get blankets and bandages, and as we wait for help we will go back and tend to this poor woman."

As if on cue, Jacqueline instantly stopped her histrionics and peeled away from Jean-Claude. Before he had time to attack, she took his hand, the same hand that had thrown a cat off a balcony, the same hand that was now extremely close to slapping this nuisance of a woman so hard her teeth would rattle and she would be forced to get out of his way. But once their hands made contact, he stopped fighting. As she stepped lightly out of the car, she beckoned the men soothingly: "Come, follow us." For some reason, The Collector found himself unable to do otherwise.

Jean-Claude glared at Claus, but Claus was miles away, watching himself as if from above, as he had done the night he explored the world of the painting. He saw a tiny, insignificant creature again, this time being led like a child into the front hall of this great house. He felt liberated, vulnerable, and humbled by this momentary reprieve from punishment and retribution, even death. In that moment, Claus was so overwhelmed by gratitude that he vowed to help these women in any way he could.

Once inside, The Collector was distracted from the pressing matter of his investment by the vast collection of taxidermy stampeding from the walls. The eyes of the wild boar seemed to follow him and he could have sworn its tusks were glistening with fresh saliva. A giant anteater looked like a jazz musician, frozen for posterity on its hind legs, its paws positioned playfully as if its own hefty snout was a saxophone. He blinked hard but immediately after was certain that an aardvark had wiggled its donkey ears at him in salutation.

He was on their turf now, and maddeningly incapable of doing any-thing but watching as Jacqueline took a massive iron key from a cord tied around her waist and used it to unlock an ancient-looking trunk, its wood rough and bleached, as if it had washed ashore after months at sea. On top, there was a raised image of the Pagan goddess Brigit, goddess of, amongst other things, new beginnings. Her image had been worn smooth by time, except for her right arm, which was holding a scepter outlined with flames. Jacqueline, with the same authority as a surgeon readying herself for an operation, produced a pair of elbow-length black leather gloves and worked her hands into them, pushing down in between each finger to attain a snug fit, regarding Jean-Claude with an expression of what he could only call menace. The hinges of the hope chest groaned when she opened it, and from its depths took out the two folded blankets that she had doctored earlier in the day. If one knew what to look for, one might have been able to discern a faint dusting of greenish powder on each coverlet.

She wrapped the yellow one maternally around Claus, and, know-ing that Jean-Claude might not allow himself to be cocooned in his cur-rent state, thrust the folded red blanket into his arms instead. She was wondering why the man had not protested with more physical force, why he had suddenly grown so docile, and made a mental note to ask her sister if she had had something to do with that. Marie-Christine was in the kitchen gathering bandages and tinctures, placing everything into a black wicker basket with all the command of a Red Cross war nurse. From the next room, the others heard her on the telephone, giv-ing the police the location of the accident and explaining the situation.

"Back to Bernadette. Our friend in need!" Marie-Christine pro-claimed as she burst out of the kitchen and began marching out to the sports car. Jacqueline was right behind her, purposeful and erect, as if she were on a real rescue mission. But as they moved toward the car, the men began to teeter, their feet leaden and uncooperative. Moving forward demanded colossal effort, as if they were making their way through a thick sap.

Jean-Claude's jowls were trembling from the strain of attempting speech, and spittle collected at the corners of his mouth. He managed to protest thickly only in monosyllables: "No! Not! Go! Now! Bad!"

Jacqueline tapped her foot in mock impatience, winking at her sister and saying, "Well? What's keeping you gentlemen?"

The sisters were relieved to see that the treated blankets were taking effect so swiftly. Chagall was imitating the men behind their backs, staggering, Chaplan-esque. And before they had even made it to the car, each man toppled like a chess piece, Claus face first and Jean-Claude flat on his back, the latter causing a puff of dust to rise from the ground like a soft burp.

The sisters stopped and turned, walking a few steps back to where the men had fallen, and stood peering down at them.

"Sleeping or dead?" Marie-Christine asked her sister matter-of-factly, nudging Jean-Claude's padded ribs with the toe of her boot.

"Well," Jacqueline said, raising Claus's hand high above his head then letting it crash to the ground. "This one, sleeping. I used valerian and some other sedatives on his blanket. The big one, also sleeping, but I used passion flower, the truth serum herb, with some other stronger ingredients that I'm afraid might have more serious side effects once he awakens."

"Amnesia?" she asked, eagerly, studying the great balloon of Jean-Claude's stomach as it rose and fell with each heavy breath. "Well, maybe it won't last too long. Do you think you got the proportions right?"

"Are you doubting me?" Jacqueline asked indignantly.

"Well, no, but that time with the blacksmith's daughter, you *were* a bit heavy-handed with the coltsfoot."

"I was only doing what she asked me to do," Jacqueline cried. "She demanded a love potion, a *strong* love potion and I complied."

Marie-Christine waved her off. Then, looking down at the unconscious body of The Collector, she said: "Well, at least he won't remember it once he loosens his tongue and starts sharing things with the police."

"In my defense," Jacqueline replied haughtily, "I did try to get the proportions exactly right with this task, but all I can say with certitude is that the trance of the big fellow's will fall somewhere between a drunk's blackout and Alzheimer's."

"That's a pretty wide field," Marie-Christine said, gingerly lifting the yellow blanket from Claus's shoulders with the end of one of the many walking sticks she kept leaning against the side of the house. Jacqueline, still wearing her protective gloves, pulled the red blanket from Jean-Claude's body, holding it far from herself as if it contained a particularly foul stench.

"Is it okay to burn them?" Marie-Christine asked as they made their way to the backyard.

"Yes. It's a skin contact potion, not airborne."

The Bion sisters stood and gazed at the small fire, each lost in her own thoughts. Marie-Christine was thinking how good it felt to still be able to have an effect on the world, to work her magic successfully. *The older one gets,* she mused, *the more one feels unnecessary.* Much of the time, the spells and consultations with locals in need required only a bit of common sense and conviction on all sides. They primarily just used the sisters as therapists or confessors. But this caper had reinvigorated her. At her side, keenly aware that Chagall too must have been gratified by this feeling of usefulness, of being necessary, Jacqueline was wondering if the dead ever really *knew* that they were dead; did the spirits experience some sense of continuity in line with their former selves, or was it more like standing outside the world and looking back in? That would be a lonely place to spend eternity, Jacqueline decided. The last patch of fabric had turned to ash, with Chagall weaving in and out of the wisps of smoke, eyes closed in some private rapture, as one partner in the throes of a tango. At that exact moment, they all turned, the jarring sirens announcing that the police had arrived.

CHAPTER FORTY

"**W**ere these men involved in the accident?" the younger of the two policeman asked, standing by the snoring bodies and producing a writing tablet from his back pocket, which he flipped open with so much vigor that a sheet inside tore in half.

"No. In fact—well, I couldn't really say it in front of them, but these two…" and here Marie-Christine winked at the policeman and mimed tossing her head back and chugging greedily from a bottle.

"The younger one is the son of one of Bernadette's guests, at her inn. So when she recognized him, having narrowly survived their impaired driving, she insisted that we drive them back to our house to get them off the road and sober." Marie-Christine gave the officer her sweetest smile.

The policeman sighed, nodding his head with a knowing smile. "Oh, I see. Well, they're going to wish maybe they *had* been in a car accident when they wake up tomorrow feeling the way they're going to feel… and in jail." He scribbled something on the paper, then looked up again. "Okay, but the woman by the car, that is the more pressing situation. Let's have one of you show me right away where the accident occurred."

"Oh, she's gone back home by now," Jacqueline said, as if that was obvious.

"What do you mean, 'gone?' She can walk?" the policeman asked. "I thought you reported that she was thrown from the car."

"Well, not really *thrown*," Marie-Christine explained easily. "She just seemed a little shaken. I think maybe I was more upset than she was—when I made the call, I mean. But she's a willful one and she did manage to tell us before we left her that our job was to deal with these stupefied fellows. She said she wasn't going to just wait there for help forever by the side of the road. Very independent, as we told you. Knowing her, even if she was a bit bruised, she probably mustered up the energy to drive back to her inn."

The older officer approached then, tipping his cap to the sisters. He had a lantern-jawed face that lent him a sort of military crispness that the sisters both found fetching. He told the younger man that the snoozing duo should be "either hoisted or dragged" into the police car.

"I don't think you'll wake them," he added, giving Jacqueline a flirtatious nudge with his elbow.

"No chance of that," Marie-Christine muttered under her breath.

Bernadette, as she had been instructed, was already back in her kitchen, hair washed, a fresh dress on, putting together a late lunch. Her car was unscathed, which looked a bit suspicious, and she too looked none the worse for wear, except for the fresh bandage stretching almost the entire length of her forehead, which the sisters had devised for her for credibility's sake. The strange red dye they had brewed was still seeping through the gauze. It smelled like pomegranate juice mixed with turpentine. She hoped it didn't look too over-the-top. She sprinkled coarse salt on the *salade* before turning the lettuces gently over and over with olivewood tongs, until each leaf glistened from the vinaigrette. She made the best vinaigrette of anyone she knew, and it gave her a little more courage, knowing she would be serving this superior *salade* to the policemen and the Bion sisters. A good meal, she had found over the years, could solve many problems. Even the most unlikely guests were united at the table. Her help and a carefully prepared lunch—that was what she could offer today. What would be required of her in the future remained to be seen.

CHAPTER FORTY-ONE

The Byroads group was seated at a large round table on a terrace over-looking the Mediterranean. Everyone was beaming with sun-kissed energy. They made short work of a platter of local Cavaillon melon slices festooned with mint leaves and the generous dishes of *Olives Niçoises.*

Phoebe's eyes were shut in rapture and her chin was shiny with melon juice.

"So," Michael asked the group. "We could get used to this, eh?"

"I'll say," Laura raved. She was fully recovered from her earlier de-bauch in the pool and had switched her attentions to the podiatrist. "We met this man at the marina who said that Keith Richards from the Rolling Stones had a house near here in the seventies and would race his motor boat across the bay at all hours and in varying stages of inebria-tion. The Stones' bassist, Bill Wyman, lived around here too, and, ap-parently hit it off with his neighbor, Marc Chagall, if you can believe it!"

Phoebe looked around surreptitiously for Chagall for confirma-tion, but he was not at the restaurant. She realized she had not seen him for hours and actually missed him.

"Must have been quite a scene around here," Ray said admiringly. "So it looks like Picasso got the museum in Antibes, while Chagall and Matisse share Nice. What a tribute, to have an entire museum dedicated to one artist's work."

"Well," Jane said, "we'll still use Bernadette's place as our home base, but we're moving a little farther afield in the coming days to Aix, Arles, and Avignon—the three A's. But don't worry, Ray. If you didn't get your fill today, there are plenty of museums to spare in all those towns."

"I have a feeling this week is going to race by," sighed the nervous woman whom Phoebe now knew to be named Shanti, and whose face had already softened in the few days since they had all embarked on this trip. "We'd better appreciate every moment."

Phoebe almost clapped her hands with delight when the waiters whisked away the melon and replaced it with boat-shaped baskets lined with paper doilies, piled high with calamari, the olive oil they were fried in forming little petticoats of grease. Flecks *of Herbes de Provence* and lemon peel had been included in the frying, so each bite delivered a blast of savory and citrus. Phoebe took in the wide expanse of blue below, and the painterly array of boats rocking in the harbor, christened with charming names like *The Saucy Siren* or *Frog's Folly*. On the towering granite cliffs in the distance, she could make out some terraced vineyards and felt a fleeting pang of nostalgia for Sonoma. This was followed by a short-lived cloud of dread, a twinge of the problems that would still be there when she got back to the real world. As humiliating as it was for her to admit to the bad choices that had led to her current, suspended state, she knew she could no longer put off telling Ray about the whole mortgage mess if they were going to pursue this romance, which she desperately hoped they would. *Right*, Phoebe thought sorely, *foreclosure and ghosts. That will definitely make me seem like an alluring choice as a partner.*

But now that she owned an authentic Chagall, was she really saved? Within seconds of looking at it, Phoebe had grown attached to the piece, its circus voluptuousness. A world to escape into, where anything was possible. She even loved the title, *La Contorsioniste*, and read a direct message there, that life required constant flexibility, and much creative contorting of her own. Of course she didn't want to sell it, but she wasn't sure what other choice she had.

She panicked then, fearing that her painting, her ticket back to her former life as a citizen in good standing, might have been discovered in the stack of towels—history repeating itself when a cleaning girl might think it some cheap flea-market find and toss it away for the second time in its life! She shouldn't be worrying about what to do with the painting yet, she told herself; she still had to get it home. To the group, she said,

"Hey. Did anyone ever dream in a million years we'd be sipping an earthy Roussanne with nutty undertones on a terrace on the French Riviera after surviving a forty-mile bike ride? *Sante!*"

"*Sante!*" they cried in unison, joining in the toast.

CHAPTER FORTY-TWO

The first thing Claus saw when he woke up was his mother's face peering down at him. Mindy was not pleased. He shut his eyes again. His tongue felt like a damp rodent and there was a hyperactive child banging drums inside his temples. Reality was the pack of wolves at the gate—thus, for now, all he wanted was to go back into his dream, where he was in a polo match with an old man with grey curls, but they were both underwater and their steeds were seahorses.

"Clausie," his mother said, shaking him hard, her eyebrows merging above the bridge of her nose in a dark V. "You are too old for this."

"*Nrrrr*," Claus protested, turning away from the source of irritation. She shook him again. When he tried to sit up, there was pain like a mallet blow to the back of his head. The clout of this was surpassed only by the molten bowling ball that had replaced his left kneecap.

"*Ach*." He groaned and fell back down.

"Such intoxication!" Mindy went on, mercilessly blaring and scornful. "We did not raise you to be this way. You could not even stand! I was so embarrassed that when that policeman asked me if I knew you, I wanted to say no. A jail cell, for shame!"

Claus tried to open his eyes again. They were dry as sawdust, and in his mouth, the foul taste of something putrefying. Police? Slowly the previous day came back in jagged fragments, and despite violent pain everywhere from his knee to his face, euphoria washed over him. He was safe—or at least, alive!

"And who was that big fellow with you? The poor officers could barely lift him out of his cell. Then he shouted at them, making no sense. It was "I will have satisfaction! I will have satisfaction! Over and over, *Ach mein Gott*. He was going on about my gun this and my money that, and some oil painting, on and on. He didn't even want to tell them where he lived, so for all I know, they have simply left him in the same jail cell I bailed you out of. That's where I would have left him, until he started to show some remorse. He smelled like he had been sleeping in a hamper of dirty socks for a month. Why do you associate with such people?"

"I...I only met him yesterday, *Mutter*. He is no friend." Claus sat up gingerly and his mother handed him a cold glass of water, bending the plastic straw for him so he could drink more easily. He sipped and looked around, realizing he was in his parents' room at the lavender farm. "He is only..."

Only what? The man who would make sure he was hunted down and punished for failing to deliver? Only his worst nightmare? Claus did not know how to finish that sentence. For now he would just try to savor the fact that he was still alive. But what *had* become of that Chagall?

"And what on earth happened to your knee? You should be in the hospital, and as soon as your father gets here, *if* he can rearrange some of his plans, that's exactly where we're taking you."

Claus saw that she was on the verge of tears. Her face was set, equal parts hurt and angry.

"And Bernadette...?" he asked worriedly.

"She is fine—a cut on the head is all. Honestly, if it was between me and a wild rooster, I'll tell you right now who would go, and it wouldn't be me! Those strange sisters told me all about what happened. Bernadette came in to check up on you this morning, do you remember?"

Claus slurped greedily at the water and shook his head no, absurdly grateful to the point of tears for normal bodily functions—swallowing, propping himself up, even the pain—for it all meant that he was amongst the living.

"She took one look at you, then said, 'You'd better keep an eye on this one,' and I turned as red as a beet, I was so ashamed of you, Claus. How could you? Tell me this heavy drinking is not something you are making a habit of. See where it lands you!"

"No, no, little mother. I am sorry. Yesterday was...not a normal day. It was like a day lived by some other man, not me. In fact the past few years have felt that way..."

Mindy would not press him to explain right then, but instead went into her comfort zone: efficiency. She set upon one of the pillows, plumping it ferociously.

"I am glad to hear that. Even though we don't see you that often, your father and I think you have been acting strangely for quite some time now—irritable, secretive. You're a grown man now, so we did not want to interfere. We just hoped you would sort it out, but then this..."

"I have...made some unfortunate choices, Mother. Stupid ones. That is all I can tell you for now. Except that I have learned from this and hope to be allowed to...to be able to..." Claus felt the pull of slumber and only wanted to lie back down and succumb, drift back into oblivion until all his troubles disappeared.

"I am sorry you cannot tell me more," Mindy said, sniffing. "I always thought us friends, you and I, as well as mother and son. But your father and I just assumed that you must be overworked, or stressed about something. If it is a money issue..."

Claus shut his eyes and shook his head. What could he do to fix this? Even if the police detained The Collector for long enough that Claus could make his getaway, Paul would find him. Just as he despaired of ever being able to start fresh, to live his life differently, the answer came to him as if whispered directly into his ear by an angel. The solution was so obvious now. Snitch. The French had a word for it: "*vendre la meche*." Squeal. Rat. Sing. Tattle. He let these various words for informant dance about in his head and felt for the first time in many years—since he had met Paul, really—a sense of his own power. He had names, of both dealers and collectors, information to trade for his freedom. Maybe not the whereabouts of the suppliers, but under pressure he knew Paul would supply that information. Surely the police would offer him protection in exchange for the chance to break up one of the largest black market art rings in France? Claus sat up, forgetting his pain entirely.

Mindy started. "What? What's going on?"

"Mother, the hospital can wait. I need you to drive me back to the police."

"Come, Clausie, you're exhausted. Look at your knee! Your father will—"

"*Now,*" Claus commanded. He had never spoken like this to Mindy, and she saw that it must be urgent.

"I'll go find someone to help get you into the car. Are you ever going to tell me what all this is about?"

"Someday, Mother, but right now you just have to trust me."

As Mindy dashed out of the room, Chagall paced around Claus's bed, beaming with approval. He was privy to the plan Claus had come up with—well, come up with via a little help from himself, planting the idea into his dreams. Certainly, fear for one's life enforced a certain breed of loyalty, as well as, in the case of the lesser cogs, paralysis. Yet Claus was finally going to save Claus. He would be implicated as well, but better to pay some fine than take a bullet to the head at some point down the road the minute he let his guard down. But these crooked art collectors were not solely thugs and criminals, were they? Didn't their appreciation of beauty somehow elevate them beyond the common gangster? Evidently not, Chagall admitted. When a painting became valuable enough, certain people saw only the dollar signs. They didn't deserve to own these paintings, Chagall decided huffily.

He took off for The Collector's house, suspecting that was where the next drama would unfold. He lingered a moment, as Claus's father pushed through the door, wearing an expression of extreme irritation. Mindy bagan to walk in step behind him, jabbering to bring him up to speed as they hoisted their son to his feet, Claus yowling from the pain this inflicted. Supporting him between the two of them, they got him out of that room and into the car, none of them knowing just what Claus was up to, least of all, as the weight of what he was about to do fully hit him, Claus himself.

CHAPTER FORTY-THREE

Jean-Claude was having extreme difficulty re-entering the here and now. There was an unrelenting fog that had filled his brain ever since he'd encountered those damn sisters. Sometimes the fog had color, apple green or flamingo pink. Other times it was a heavy black shroud that knocked him out before he even had time to dread its arrival. The fog robbed him of his ability to function, dragged him down into a fuzzy realm where all edges were smudged, where his own past, even his sense of who he was, vanished in the mist. He lusted for particulars. Just when he would think that the fog was lifting, and would try to communicate urgent names and phone numbers to his captors, it would descend upon him again, a beast taking its time in consuming the prey. In the fleeting moments of relative lucidity, he had no sense of how much time had passed, and could only recall bits and pieces of his original mission. There was a German man who had lost or stolen a painting that he had wanted very badly and had already paid something for. Oh, and it was a Chagall, that painter who did all the colorful, fantastical stuff. The German was going to show him where he had stashed the Chagall, *his* Chagall.

Jean-Claude was not a man familiar with the feeling of helplessness, similar to being sucked out to sea in an undertow. Underneath this despicable condition in which he currently found himself, he nursed a simmering outrage that he wanted desperately to hold onto, for without it he was nothing more than a gibbering idiot, and who knew what he might say, or had said already. His tongue had its own agenda and Jean-Claude, the aesthete, the savant, the almighty, the keeper of secrets, was now powerless to stop the tongue. Strangely, he kept recalling a very clear memory of a cartoon he had seen as a boy, where a ferocious alligator came charging toward a sailor, ready to attack. The sailor casually flipped the raging reptile onto its back and began to rub its belly, which rendered the seething beast impotent, a trifling plaything. Jean-Claude recalled feeling immense pity for the alligator, even back then, as it was robbed of the will to fight.

He was certain about very few things, uppermost being that he had spent at least one night in jail, or rather a makeshift jail, some sort of "holding tank" no doubt reserved for town drunks at this rural outpost. He had only transitory memories of how he had gotten there, but waking up with his cheek on a stone floor that smelled of piss was all the confirmation he required. The police had somehow attained his address, and had informed him that when he "sobered up" they would escort him back home. He willed himself not to utter a word, as his tongue had done enough damage already.

Gradually, the periods when the fog receded grew longer and longer. Jean-Claude tried to regain some modicum of his dignity and status, despite a flagrant and pungent stain of unknown origin that ran down the front of his formerly white, starched shirt. The fact that he was wearing only one shoe and that his hair seemed to have been coiffed with glue was not helping his matters.

"Sirs!" he called out from behind the locked doors in what he prayed was authoritative voice. "I demand my right to phone my lawyer!"

The two officers ignored him for a good half hour. He watched them through a small window, shuffling papers and leaving the building for a smoke. He recognized them as the same ones who had brought him and the German here in the police car, while the two useless detainees flopped against one another in the back seat. In between bouts if unconsciousness, Jean-Claude recalled them going over the report they had taken from "those charming Bion sisters," and extolling the delightful meal that the accident victim had prepared for them at her inn.

Jean-Claude beat at the glass of his cell, becoming increasingly annoyed. The officers shot each other a look.

"Ah, the tiger has awoken from his nap," quipped the one with the moustache, neither of them making a move to see what he wanted. At least someone had claimed the German; but they had had their fill of this other fellow, his pompous, nonsensical yammering and incoherent confessions. It had been a long two days, so while they would be more than happy to be rid of him and oblige with the phone call, they doubted that this time, his fifth attempt, he might actually retrieve the number from the disarray inside his brain.

Finally, they walked over to his cell and asked him through the window, "Do you think you might really have his number this time? Or possibly his name?"

Jean-Claude had only one set of numbers at the forefront of his brain, and he was not sure to whom it belonged, but demanded the telephone anyway. A familiar voice picked up, irritated and brusque.

"*Oui?*"

"Who is this?"

"Who is this," the voice retorted. "You called me."

"Jean-Claude," he answered tentatively.

"Jean-Claude!" the voice hollered. "What the hell is going on?"

"I seem to be in a jail somewhere in the south of France."

"Apt!" the gendarmes offered, eavesdropping merrily.

Apt. Jean-Claude had a vague notion that this was not too far from his own house. He felt anxious that the fog would ambush him at any moment, so asked again: "And your name is?"

"It's Paul. At the café. What is happening? I have heard nothing in forty-eight hours and now you are in jail. Where is Claus? Did he deliver?"

"Can you call my lawyer?" Jean-Claude asked, feeling the ground beneath him turning swampy again. "I seem to have misplaced my phone."

"*Merde,* Jean-Claude, you're not making any sense!" Paul shouted. "What is this lawyer's name, at least? And tell me what landed you there. Are they onto us? Wait, you're not there right now are you?"

"I seem to have misplaced my phone as well. It contains the lawyer's and many other names. These men are going to escort me home soon. I will call again…Paul."

Paul heard Jean-Claude pronounce his name carefully, as you would the name of someone you were newly introduced to at a party. This was bad, very bad. He wanted to keep The Collector on the phone, to get more information. Were the cops in the room with him?

"Wait, Jean-Claude! Don't say anyth…" But Paul heard only the abrupt baying of the dial tone.

The police decided that, despite his lingering befuddlement, their prisoner was sober enough to leave captivity. They wanted to have him out of their hair so they could settle into a good long lunch. They would make sure that the fines and repercussions he suffered for this bender would stretch far into his future, but for now, they had no real reason or desire to keep him.

When they opened the door to his cell to lead him out, Jean-Claude felt not liberation but fear. His mind was so clouded he did not know how to proceed. Maybe the sight of his house would jog his memory, bring it all back to him. He ground his sharp teeth and saw everything around him as a nemesis. The police had somehow procured his address and he wanted desperately to ask to look at whatever identifying morsels of documentation they had come across, but he would not give them that satisfaction. He tried to hold his head erect and walk nobly to the waiting police car. His cell phone was gone. His gun was gone. His power and pride trampled beyond recognition. And the minute he tried to reconstruct the events of the past week, or day, or even the past fifteen minutes, they would scatter like startled gulls, leaving him standing on the shore. He could not complete one damn thought. Perhaps he had had a small stroke? The doctor had been telling him to lose weight for years now. What was that doctor's name? And wasn't there something pressing he should take care of—an investment?

"I need a doctor," Jean-Claude said thickly from the back seat. "I have had a stroke."

"You have had too much to drink," the older policeman corrected. "I suggest some *soupe a l'oignon* and a long nap."

Jean-Claude nodded and dosed as they chauffeured him along the winding road toward the alien and mysterious destination of his own home. He tried to keep alert for clues along the route, but everything whooshed by, blurred and unfathomable, as if he were stuck on some strange carousel, no one manning the controls to let him off.

CHAPTER FORTY-FOUR

Chagall passed back and forth between the library, where The Collector had held Claus captive thirty-six hours earlier, and the quite remarkable hidden room that existed on the other side of the false wall. This antechamber was like the hull of a great pirate ship after a conquest, filled to the rafters with treasures of inestimable worth. A Gustav Kilmt depicting a gilded swan in the arms of a swooning woman leaned haphazardly against a large bronze of an owl by Picasso. There were paintings by Bruegel and Velazquez rubbing elbows with Rubens and Wassily Kandinsky. Cubists, Expressionists, Fauvists, Dadaists, Surrealists—they had all ended up here, out of sight, in this repository of loot. There seemed to be neither rhyme nor reason to the collection beyond the fact that all were painted or sculpted by the great masters. The sheer worth and magnitude of the contents of this vault made Chagall reel with—what? Disbelief? Outrage? Awe?

Yet the way these purloined masterpieces were displayed was so willy-nilly, with a randomness that was tantamount to disrespect, that Chagall would hardly call The Collector a great lover of art. The pieces were dusty and neglected. And yet the pieces on display on the other side of the wall were clearly a source of pride and prestige for the man. Was it simply a question of legitimately bought art versus those from the black market? What was his relationship to this cornucopia of canvas? Baffling. One thing was certain: He could hardly be so bold as to actually display these works, given their questionable journey to this room. Surely they were listed as missing in some record *somewhere?* Chagall strongly hoped that a person existed who had bothered with such records.

Chagall had known another hoarder once with such an appetite, during his brief stay in New York City in the 1940s. The man was quite well off and collected military paraphernalia—Civil War, French Revolution, it didn't matter, as long as it was related to battle. So obsessed was this man that his collection grew to the point where he could not house it all. He spent thousands of dollars each year renting warehouse spaces in which to store his ever-burgeoning goods. Chagall had asked him once, "How is it satisfying to stockpile these objects if they are not in front of you to be enjoyed? If you cannot even display them or look at them? Are they not removed from your life?"

The man had looked at him as if he were a simpleton and replied, "But they *are* in my life. I know where they are and that they are mine. I own each and every one. The pleasure for me is in the hunt…and of course, the catch. Each one is a trophy."

Chagall moved about Jean-Claude's hidden room reverently, pausing in front of one masterpiece after another—well, at least the ones on top or facing out, as indeed many were stacked so that he could only imagine what the layers of each pile contained. It begged the question: What *was* art when there was no one to look at it? Art without a witness? Wasn't it the viewer that made the painting come to life? What were these framed stories without anyone to be moved by them? It grieved him on so many levels to see these *chef d'oeuvres* treated in such a cavalier manner, and he wished the stiffest possible sentence upon this philistine. All the money in the world could not change the grouper's basic boorish nature.

Chagall hovered above a charming rendition of a monkey by Henri Rousseau that had been placed on a table, its saucer eyes staring plaintively up at the ceiling. He had no doubt that some of his own missing paintings were buried in this miscellany. Indeed, one had been en route to this shrine of greed before providence bounced it out of a sports car. It pained him not only as a fellow artist, but also as a Jew, knowing that many of these treasures were no doubt ripped from the walls of Jewish homes with no recompense whatsoever, as if a Jew was not deserving of anything beautiful or fine. Clearly Jean-Claude, not to mention whoever procured the pieces for him, had no interest in the history of such work, and no conscience either.

Chagall shook his head ruefully and passed back into the library. He knew the time was fast approaching when he would need to focus on tying up all the loose ends of this earthly adventure. That was his job now, not to lament the past. But for the life of him, he could not figure out the trick to opening the false wall between the two rooms. That absolutely had to happen in front of the police if Jean-Claude was going to be punished and this black market ring brought down. He scrutinized the numerous volumes on Jean-Claude's bookshelves. The majority of the books were antiquated, gold-leafed, leather-bound affairs with tissue-weight parchment pages that Jean-Claude had probably inherited from someone and had never bothered to read. The books seem to be arranged not alphabetically or by subject, but more by shape and size, as if they were notable not for their contents, but for their appeal as objects.

This Jean-Claude is an odd duck, Chagall thought, as he took in each row, the short, fat volumes all on one shelf, the skinny, tall books on another. And then, right at eye level, he spotted something curious. While all of the books were in French and the majority of them were the great classics, here was some sort of coffee table book with a torn jacket, sticking out like a chicken in a flock of peacocks. It was entitled, in English, *Wonders from the Louvre,* and was the type of thing one might find on the remainders table in the bookstalls along the banks of the Seine. Chagall had a memory of those old Vincent Price movies, where there is a mad laboratory or someone is trapped or there is a dungeon behind just such a false wall as this. In these films, a certain book is removed and the bookcase slides open. Could it be? Chagall recognized at once that this book was the key to opening the divide between the antechamber and the library. It probably blocked a sensor of some kind or pulled a lever, allowing the false wall slip open.

Chagall did a little jig of delight, but then stopped abruptly, cursing his inability to move things, to be more physically effectual, especially now when he wanted to test his theory about this book. Then he remembered how he had worked *through* others—Phoebe with the paintbrush, Claus in the car. The same way he had allowed the man to be inside his painting. It was beyond the power of suggestion, more like hypnosis from the inside. But each time he had achieved this, it surprised him a little. He wasn't sure just what the method had been, so he couldn't just access this skill on demand. How had he managed to get someone to move the gun *for* him? He knew it was some version of *inhabiting* the individual, of finding an entryway into their psyches.

Just when he was beginning to get an inkling of the mechanics of that power, he heard the front door opening and saw Jean-Claude, flanked by the two officers, staring fuzzily around his own house with an unmistakable look of misgiving. Since Claus was off in Apt spilling the beans to any cop who could write fast enough to keep up with his confession, Jean-Claude's demise was only a matter of time. Still, Chagall would have some fun with the grouper, help him fall on his own sword.

"Well, thank you, officers. Here we are," Jean-Claude said, shifting nervously between his unevenly shod feet. "I appreciate the lift. Now if you'll excuse me, I am desperate for a shower."

While Jean-Claude still did not fully have his bearings, there was something about having the police in his library that he knew instinctually was a bad idea.

"Quite a collection," said the older officer, leisurely stroking the little belly of a bronze Degas ballerina. "You didn't tell us you were an art lover." The younger officer sniggered and Jean-Claude smiled feebly.

"Yes, well, every man has his passion and mine is art. Now if you don't mind…"

"And a book lover, too," the younger offer remarked, ignoring him. "I see you have some unique system going here, in the way you arrange them." He reached out for a weathered copy of Shakespeare's *The Tempest*, leafed through it rapidly as if trying to find a dollar bill sandwiched in its pages.

Suddenly Jean-Claude felt queasy. He could not stop looking at a large volume near the top shelf. He knew this book was significant but he did not know why. His heart pounded in his chest. *Stop staring at it, imbecile*, he chastised himself. But it was like picking a scab. He could not stop himself.

The officers noticed him standing there, gulping and blinking, and followed his gaze to the book. And just like a marionette dancing on its strings, Jean-Claude stepped forward, reached up, and extracted *Wonders from the Louvre* from its row. A great groaning noise of gears accompanied the sliding of the bookshelf wall.

As he and the officers stared dumbfounded at the impossible mountains of art now revealed in that secret chamber, Jean-Claude's memory returned to him in full.

CHAPTER FORTY-FIVE

The sting operation at Le Verre Volant, despite the poor timing of taking place during the peak of lunch hour, was swift and deftly executed. The police had tried to cordon off the entrance with yellow tape, but while they were occupied inside, many of the patrons simply ducked under the tape and proceeded to their regular tables. While the diners enjoyed a good scandal as much as anyone, lunch was sacrosanct and trumped all else. Besides, what better way to gawk than with a warm *Croque Monsieur,* some crisp cornichons made from tiny gherkin cucumbers, mustard so hot it made the eyes water, and a carafe of flowery rosé before you? Paul, in all his bantam fury and panic, had been stupid enough, when the police first burst through the doors, to reach under the register for his gun. Within seconds he was tackled by several officers and his hands cuffed behind his back.

"But what have I done?" Paul cried from beneath the two strapping policemen who sat on top of him. "I have my rights!"

The larger of the two jerked Paul roughly up to his feet and hissed: "*Ta gueule, Monsieur. Vous etes en train de nager dans la merde.*"

Benoit loosened the faded red kerchief from around his neck and scratched at the scar underneath. He chuckled at the business unfolding in the middle of his beloved café. One had to appreciate the precision of the French language; Paul was being told by that officer to shut up because he was currently swimming in shit. Benoit knew that the original owners, some of them his friends, had been spinning in their graves all the while this lout used their brasserie as a front for some sort of illicit operation.

Understanding that the serving and eating of food took priority over all things, the officers worked around the waiters and staff as they methodically combed the bar area for any evidence of the art ring that Paul was said to be a part of. Benoit, as if he had been waiting for this moment his entire life, rose from his table and approached the bar, only too happy to oblige in pointing the police toward the cave, downstairs and through the low door. Benoit did not know exactly what was kept down there besides wine, but he had witnessed Paul and that German and various other louche types go down there often enough that he knew it must be something crooked.

Down in the cave, with Paul in tow to answer any questions they might have, the police unearthed painting after painting that had been hidden behind bottles of wine.

"These came with the café!" Paul protested. "That was half the reason I bought the place. I am an art lover and knew of Le Verre Volant's illustrious history, its famous clientele. Surely that is no crime!"

"Why then are these paintings hidden down here, Monsieur? If you are so fond of art and such a history buff, why not display them upstairs, if indeed they are the work of artists who once patronized this place? That is what most people who love art do, is it not? Hang it on the walls to enjoy?"

"They are too valuable," Paul answered indignantly. The collar of his lime polo shirt had darkened to pine green from the steam of his fear. "There is no law against me doing whatever I want with my own collection. You cannot prove that these paintings were not the ones left behind in this café ages ago."

"No, Monsieur, you are correct," said the officer in charge, motioning for his men to continue removing wine bottles and gathering up the paintings behind them. "*We* cannot prove that. It is for that reason that we employ experts, who can tell from one tiny fleck of paint when a piece was created, who painted it, and if it is authentic. These people can also tell us if the piece was, indeed, stolen."

Paul clenched his jaw. Who had ratted on him? Claus, certainly, after he had made off with the Chagall—but Jean-Claude? Wouldn't he too be implicated in all this? It made no sense. If he ever got out of this mess, he would personally see to it that Claus never blabbed to anyone ever again.

As the officers brought more and more contraband art out into the light, a cataclysmic vision flashed in front of Paul. He saw a long line of procurers, his "business associates," taking the fall from Paris to Salzburg to Corsica. And still, even Paul himself would not be able to provide the police with the name of the biggest cheese, for no one, from the lowliest delivery boy to the richest collector, knew that man's identity. How he envied that one at this moment! The biggest fish never got caught. These thieves were the lynchpins in enterprises such as this. They had the product. Whenever someone possessed something rare and desirable, there would always be a buyer.

As they were climbing the stairs, Paul made one last attempt at bravado: "This is an outrage! My lawyer will make certain that I am compensated for this injustice!"

The café was silent as everyone watched the slow procession. Hearing the ridiculousness of his own shout, Paul bowed his head and allowed himself to be led outside to the waiting van.

Inside Le Verre Volant, the volume quadrupled as the siren wailed down the street, leaving behind a cloud of mystery. People were raucous in their speculation, reluctant to return to work, gossiping and trying to top one another with their guesses about Paul's crime. Seamlessly and without dissent, Benoit, a man who had lived in Paris for more than eight decades and had frequented this café for almost that entire time—and, lest anyone doubt it, a man who remembered every moment of it all—stepped behind the bar, slipped a clean black apron over his head, and tied it around his waist. The headwaiter, harried and poised for argument, paused in front of him for only a nanosecond, then shouted out his order for two beers, turning on his heels and returning to the fray. Benoit nodded and pulled the old brass tap handle, the one Jaun Gris had fashioned for the owner so long ago in the form of a mask, comedy/tragedy, tilting the glass expertly to ensure the perfect head of foam.

CHAPTER FORTY-SIX

The same day the Byroads trip ended, the Provencal newspapers were filled with rabid headlines: Largest Black Market Art Ring in History Apprehended! Hundreds of Missing Masterpieces Recovered! Jewish Progeny Step Forward to Reclaim Their Due! Priceless Pieces "A Windfall for the World" Says Curator for Louvre, Tate, Others! Kingpin Breaks Down in Court! Collector Sells Memoirs for Record Sum, but Will Be Writing in Jail! Mysterious Menerbe Sisters Deemed Heroes! Chagall Museum in Nice Calls Gift "Mystifying Miracle"!

"I haven't see this many exclamation points and so many headlines in twenty-point bold type since we impeached Nixon," Ray quipped as the guests traded contact information and wheeled their bags out front for the leaders to load into the van.

Phoebe had packed the night before and was down by the atelier watching Bernadette harvest her honey from the oozing trays. There was so much she wanted to say to her, but the hum of the bees provided the only dialogue. Finally Bernadette, not meeting Phoebe's eye, asked, "What will you do with it?"

Phoebe stepped closer and helped her by holding the honeycomb tray while Bernadette gently guided the bees off the comb and back into their hive. She never used smoke or protective clothing, and, perhaps due to more assistance from the Bion sisters, her bees never turned defensive, knowing this beekeeper would always leave enough to feed the hive. The two women worked in silence for a good while before Phoebe answered:

"I haven't decided yet," Phoebe told her. "I don't really have the luxury of keeping it, I'm afraid. My life is sort of…up in the air right now and that painting, or rather the selling of it, could solve a lot of problems."

Bernadette searched her face. "Money isn't everything," she said pointedly.

"Bernadette," Phoebe said. "I want you to know I don't blame you at all. You're only human, and you were so young when it happened. I can see the power Chagall's work has over true appreciators like you… and like me. I wish my grandfather had found *two* Chagalls, so that we could both have one."

For some reason, Phoebe burst into tears. She always cried at the end of things—movies, relationships, trips, concerts, books. But this felt larger, all tangled up with Ray and her house and, most of all, her worry about what would become of Chagall himself, now that many of the paintings were reunited with their rightful keepers. It had been such a privilege to have him in her life, an impossible share of magic.

Bernadette set the jars of honey down on her pottery wheel and took Phoebe into her arms. Even though she too was weeping, she tilted Phoebe's face up and used her thumbs to smooth away the tears. Bernadette smelled of lavender, clay, and beeswax, and Phoebe felt safe there in the cool sanctuary of her studio. She did not want to go home, to reality, to those more ordinary demons. Her life had been so heightened since Chagall appeared. Despite her initial fears, she had found that she liked such intensity; she had felt so alive in the tumult of all their adventures. Plus, she had confessed everything to Ray last night after numerous glasses of wine at the farewell dinner. Ghosts, foreclosure, divorce, stolen art—she had not held back. Ray had listened to her, his face unreadable, then squeezed her hand, kissed her on the cheek, and said goodnight, that they would "revisit this" the next day. It had not been a chilly leave-taking, but definitely not the torrid culmination of desires she had hoped for on their last night together in France. But what did she expect? At this stage in her life she wasn't exactly a good prospect.

"*Merci*," Bernadette said softly, linking arms with Phoebe and heading back up the hill. "You will stay in touch with me and let me know the fate of our little masterpiece?"

"Yes," Phoebe said. "I promise you'll be the first to know."

Phoebe had not seen Chagall in two whole days and she missed him. She wondered if that was how it would be—if he would just disappear from her life without a goodbye. He had always insisted that he was only there because she had needed him. Didn't she need him still?

Phoebe sat behind Ray in the van. While he was not indifferent to her, she could tell something had cooled. She was bewildered by this; it had taken courage for her to disclose everything, and Phoebe believed that courage should always be rewarded. She was also a great proponent of keeping no secrets. Ray was leaving for California from Paris and Phoebe from Marseilles, but at least they would be on the same train from Avignon for a short while.

As they boarded the train, he helped her up the steps with her bag, saying: "We don't want to lose sight of *this* piece of luggage, now do we?"

She studied his face for some trace of sarcasm, but saw only the short ginger beard, the bemused lips that she badly wanted to kiss, and his kind eyes.

"Shh," she joked, looking left and right in exaggerated paranoia.

Ray had switched seats with another passenger, who smiled at the two of them, moving so that they could sit next to one another. Once they were settled, he started, "Listen, about last night…"

Phoebe cut him off. "Hey, I don't blame you for backing off. I wouldn't want to get involved with me right now either. I must seem…"

Now it was Ray's turn to interrupt. "A bit wacky?"

Phoebe flushed. He was mocking her.

"Hey, Phoebe," he said, putting his arm around her. "I like a bit wacky. A bit wacky is good. A bit wacky is exciting. I just don't…"

"Want to rush into anything," Phoebe said. "I understand."

"Could one of us maybe finish a sentence here?" Ray asked. "What I was *going* to say is that I just don't want us to plunge into what I hope will be a long and happy relationship until we're both on sturdier ground. It's not just you, Phoebe. My gallery is barely making a profit. And yes, I'll admit that the ghost stuff was a little much for me, but you seem like an intelligent and—dare I say it—bewitching woman, so I'm willing to allow for your, er, sightings. And you know, maybe I can actually help you with your foreclosure woes. Remember that guy you first saw me with?"

"Ugh, not the Economic Darwinism guy?"

"I know, I know—but even though he can sound like a jerk, he's actually a damn good lawyer. And while he may not play for your team on this one, he told me an associate of his has started gathering information for a massive lawsuit against your bank for all the bundling and swapping and wheeling and dealing these banks did before it all came back to bite them. This lawyer thinks the homeowners have an excellent case, and with his help, people like you might be able to keep their homes. Listen, I know if you get your home and work issues resolved you'll have much more room for…well, me."

Phoebe had been experiencing that queasy, dangling feeling that often followed a bout of candor, but now hopefulness flooded her, and she threw her head back against the seat and yelled: "Yes!"

"Yes?" Ray asked, startled by this sudden zeal. "Yes to the lawyer?"

"Yes to everything!" Phoebe said, profoundly relieved that she had not lost Ray. "Yes to lawyers! Yes to Chagall! And mostly, yes to you!"

"How do you know I'm not just after your Chagall?" he asked her, leaning close.

"How do *you* know I haven't already sold it?" she returned.

They spent the rest of the train ride talking about Ray's book, and ideas Phoebe had for a large encaustic oil painting that would be some sort of circus scene showing through honeycomb. Bernadette had actually given her a sheet of beeswax and she was eager to incorporate that into the painting. Phoebe got off the train in Marseilles and began to run alongside it, following Ray, who was waving ardently from behind his window. There was something about a train station that brought out the romantic in everyone. They had agreed to meet for dinner in San Francisco one week from that day. It was something to look forward to.

Once Phoebe had settled into her seat on the plane, this time having scored the whole row to herself, she found that she was actively looking for Chagall—curled up in the luggage rack, out on a wing, she didn't care where, she just wanted to see him. She sincerely wanted to thank him for everything. For Ray, which she was certain he had something he had a hand in, the old Cupid; for pointing her toward her grandfather's gift; for the whole wonderful whirlwind of the past weeks—but more than any of that, she wanted to thank Chagall for reigniting her own passion for making art.

Phoebe had been operating on sheer adrenaline for what felt like months and she suddenly crashed. After a failed attempt to focus on some abysmally bad airplane movie, she started to nod off. It was then that Chagall appeared in the seat next to her.

"Marc!" Phoebe cried. She didn't care who saw or heard her conversing with the ghost. "I'm so happy to see you! I was afraid…"

"I know. I was afraid, too," he agreed.

"You go first. What were you afraid of?"

"That all of this—my worldly furlough, helping you, the thrill of resolving these big dilemmas, being around great art once again—that it would be snatched from me without warning. I feel the clock ticking, Phoebe. Being back here has been…such a gift."

For the first time since she'd seen Chagall at her surprise party, she felt empathy welling up in her. He looked so melancholy. What a tease, to have been yanked from this world at the end of one's life, then to be allowed only a fleeting taste of it all again.

"I could not visit you right away," he said. "This business with the German and his boss and The Collector. I'll admit it: I have thoroughly enjoyed being in the thick of such cloaks and daggers. I feel like I played a part in seeing justice done, and that is immensely gratifying. But just when I start to feel satisfied that we've put an end to something heinous, that we've actually gotten art back into the world and out of the dens of these wicked ones, I realize that even though we've broken up *this* ring, there is no doubt another one waiting in the wings to profit, to steal. I find the slipperiness of the main thieves, the long line of them, very disheartening."

"You have done so much, Marc. My God, the quantity of art you rescued is huge. And you had a giant effect on my life, and the Bions, Bernadette, Claus—the whole circle, good and bad."

"Do you think so?" he asked, and it hit Phoebe that even an icon like Marc Chagall needed reassurance and to feel some sense of accomplishment. "And I helped you in some way, too, I hope?"

"Of course," she said, squeezing his arm, though what she felt there was not solid, as if she was clutching at smoke. "In a thousand ways. But Marc?"

"Yes? Wait—I know what you're going to ask, and the answer is, I honestly don't know. I have no idea what to expect. I'm afraid that I won't have any warning and in an instant, it will all just...be over. One day, poof! I simply won't be here anymore."

"Oh, Marc," Phoebe lamented. "I'm not sure I can bear having you gone. So let me just thank you now, for everything."

He waved her away and she saw his eyes fill.

"Maybe if I can create some new crisis, you can stay and help me?" she asked, sniffling.

"I doubt that it works that way, my dear," he said sadly. "But who knows? This is all new to me, and the assignment arrived out of the blue, so we cannot rule that out completely. Still, we accomplished a lot, *toi et moi*. You should feel proud."

"Miss? Beverage?"

Phoebe looked up and saw the flight attendant regarding her queerly.

"Oh yes," she said forcefully. "Red wine, please. Or, make that two.

One for my friend."

The woman scribbled the order and moved on as fast as she could, as if Phoebe's peculiarity might be contagious. Phoebe turned to give Chagall a conspiratorial nudge. But he was gone. She felt like she had been socked in the stomach, and she brought her hand up to her throat as if she might cry out. This time, she was not at all sure if he would return.

CHAPTER FORTY-SEVEN

Blessedly, when his stint amongst the living was truly over, Chagall returned to that place he had come from unburdened by longing or nostalgia. One second he was on Earth, the next, not. Memories were different in the afterlife, because time was such a nebulous thing. Events from birth to death all seemed to have occurred on the same plane, simultaneously. Chagall thought of that old mantra of the sixties: "Be here now." In this place he had landed after his death, the present was all you had. He wished he could explain it to Phoebe or Bernadette, the Bions, all the people he had grown fond of, that once he departed from that terrestrial, striving place, everything just *was*. But that was not his job, and indeed, he did not have words to adequately make them understand what awaited them. He did wonder if he would ever be needed back there again, but acceptance was the only choice available to him now and he was not one for pining.

Every once in a while, incredibly, unexpectedly, Chagall was allowed a glimpse of Phoebe's life—this time from beyond, not amongst the living as before. He saw a long table, in that backyard behind her blue house where he had, with her help, painted again. It was summer, but he did not know which summer after the Byroads trip in France. Certainly, the faces he had come to know had not aged so much. He hovered near Phoebe like a bee, testing to see if she could see him. He discerned, with a tug at his heart, that she could not. Many were seated around a table that was laden with platters, ones that looked like the handiwork of Bernadette, holding figs from Phoebe's prized tree, halved with a dollop of mascarpone, and tomatoes from her vines, sporting a chapeau of fresh basil. There were a dozen people gathered around, drinking wine from mismatched glasses, and Ray was there, right next to Phoebe, his hand on her thigh. The expression on both of their faces could only be described as beaming.

Another time, again with no warning, he was able to see them quite clearly, lying together in Phoebe's four-poster bed, peaceful in slumber. He thought maybe Mechant and Gamut had looked up at him from their mats on the floor, but he could not be sure. Maybe he was just wishful. He watched Phoebe and Ray for some time and decided that they did look somewhat older now, though just as connected. He thought how much they resembled the lovers in many of his paintings, two halves of one creature. Again he felt that profound yearning to be able to paint again. But he did not dwell on what, for now anyway, was impossible.

Then he saw it, there on the wall opposite the bed. Somehow, she had held onto the small painting that they had gone to such lengths to retrieve: *La Contorsioniste*, with the inscription from Phoebe's grandfather written on the back. "May our world together always have such magic." She had hung it right there, where it would be the first thing besides one another that they laid their eyes upon, each and every morning. Chagall rejoiced and in the next instant, was gone. But when Phoebe opened her eyes that morning, she noticed immediately that something was different about her painting. The fanciful creatures, the flying fish and acrobats were all in their places. But the contortionist had changed. The feet were still arched over the head like a rainbow, but the face that now looked out at her was unmistakable. She would recognize that smile and those wild grey curls anywhere.

ACKNOWLEDGMENTS

There were numerous people who had a hand in helping this novel escape from the confines of my laptop and out into the world, and my appreciation knows no bounds.

First and foremost, in the red corner, middleweight champion of all things literary, possessing a noble and determined love of actual books, Agent Extraordinaire, Mr. Andy Ross, who believed in this book so strongly from the very first round, that in no time, I was believing in it too. A million Madeleines for you.

Many readers slogged through the early incarnations of Phoebe and the Ghost of Chagall. For their generous patience and feedback, I bow to Beverly Crawford and Christine Schoeffer, and also to Albert Kutchins, for connecting the dots.

To The Santa Fe Four for celebrating with me every time I made it past some hurdle, and to Lori Holt, for all things witchy. And of course, to C.C.: Life coach, Lifebuoy, and partner in crime.

For Daniel Bruce Huntsinger, an exceptional artist in his own right, who listened to me read aloud on many occasions, asking: "Is this working?" And for her edits par excellence, Michelle Dotter.

For my father, who gave me my first thesaurus and my first electric typewriter, who always encouraged my writing, but was known to insert: "Why not write some songs? That's where the money is!" And my mother, who could recite Wordsworth and Keats from memory and introduced me to the writing of Hemingway.

And finally, to David Poindexter, editor and genie, who read my book and on January 9th, 2012, said the most important word in the dictionary: YES. I hoist my glass to all of you.